noirotica 3: Stolen Kisses

edited by
Thomas S. Roche

Black Books
San Francisco

Cover Design © 2001 by Terrence Boyce (izone@home.com)
Back Cover Photo by Phyllis Christopher (pc3711@yahoo.com)
Typesetting and Graphic Design by Bill Brent (BB@blackbooks.com)

First Printing, November 2000

ISBN 1-892723-03-4   9 8 7 6 5 4 3 2 1

Manufactured in the United States of America

Library of Congress Cataloging-In-Publication Data

Noirotica 3: stolen kisses / edited by Thomas S. Roche. - 1st Black Books ed.
  p. cm.
 ISBN 1892723-03-4
 1. Erotic stories, American. 2. Detective and mystery stories, American.
I. Roche, Thomas S. II. Title.
 PS648.E7 N65 2000
 813'.0872083538—dc21   00-010245

Alternative Cataloging-In-Publication Data

Roche, Thomas S., editor.
Noirotica 3: stolen kisses.
San Francisco, CA: Black Books, 2000.

24 short stories.

1. Erotic Fiction 2. Noir fiction. 3. Short stories.

813.54--dc21

Published by Black Books • PO Box 31155 • San Francisco CA 94131-0155
     (415) 431-0171 •   (415) 431-0172 fax • www.blackbooks.com

For sales to individuals, specialty stores, and mail-order catalogs, please contact Black Books.

For information on distribution to the book trade, please call (800) 818-8823.

Copyright Information

Books by Thomas S. Roche

Collections:
Fragrant Sorrows
Dark Matter

Editor:
Noirotica
Noirotica 2: Pulp Friction
Noirotica 3: Stolen Kisses

Editor, with Michael Rowe:
Sons of Darkness
Brothers of the Night

Editor, with Nancy Kilpatrick:
In the Shadow of the Gargoyle
Graven Images (forthcoming)

Dedication

To Cathie

. . . . however far away . . . .

Table of Contents

The Godfather of Sodom: An Invitation

by Thomas S. Roche

When I started reading stories for the first *Noirotica* anthology, I had no idea what a force in my life "noir" was going to become. That was four years ago, and since then I've read a few hundred submissions to the series, and seen a wide variety of interpretations of that four-letter word. Some of them were pretty far from what I thought noir was. Others were right on the money. Still others (and these are really my favorites) were very different from my concept of noir, but somehow seemed to fit perfectly into the anthology by exploring some aspect of the theme which its editor (me) hadn't even thought about. These stories did me the greatest service a writer can do a reader — they made me think differently, perceive things differently — and in doing so, like all great writing, they made me *be* different.

The question I get asked the most when people hear of the concept for these anthologies is "why sex and crime?" The glib answer, and the one I give at cocktail parties or in cafés, is "These are a few of my favorite things." But it was also true in 1995 that erotic crime stories "*hadn't been done yet*." Circlet Press had been publishing anthologies of erotic science fiction and fantasy for a few years, and erotic horror (which, some years before, had been the new kid on the genre block) was quickly becoming overdone. Horror writer Nancy Kilpatrick suggested that I do a book of erotic mystery stories, but that idea didn't quite click.

Then it occurred to me that erotic noir had never been done in an anthology — at least, not explicitly so. At that time, noir was a catchphrase for any horror or erotica writer trying to justify either (1) extreme violence or (2) an obsession with serial killers. The other place the word got used was in the service of science fiction: Any futuristic novel with a criminal or police protagonist was perceived as being influenced by William Gibson, John Shirley and *Blade Runner* and therefore labeled "noir." More often than not, they were labeled noir by the writer (who no doubt smelled film options). Nobody seemed to remember that noir was a genre of *crime and mystery fiction.* That it was a kind of fiction that was considered trash until about twenty years ago. Mysteries (like erotica) were considered trash by everybody — but especially by those who read them. Which was just about *everybody.*

Any label affixed to a writer's forehead can be poison to her or his creativity. But far more often it is poison to the way that writer is perceived in the marketplace. Maybe that's why people who create books about bug-eyed aliens are fond of saying "I am not a science fiction writer" and authors whose novels are titled *Love's Torrid Whirlwind* claim they do not write romances.

Fine, then. This is not a noir anthology, I am not a noir writer, and noir doesn't exist, never existed, or if it did exist it died of gunshot wounds in a Kansas City motel room in 1954 after being fucked bowlegged and cross-eyed by a blonde in a skintight red dress with a tattoo on her ass that says "Don't Hate Me Because I'm Beautiful."

But these are fucking well noir stories.

And they're about sex.

And therefore, any way you slice it, they're about crime.

Crime and sexuality are made to go together, because they're two forces, maybe the *only* two forces, which make their own rules and exist on their own terms in any society, no matter how restrictive that society may attempt to be. There will always be laws — as if they existed to be broken. And there will always be sexual repression. Which means that those who rebel against such repression — they have to *fuck harder.*

I've often heard the observation that the villains in any movie or book always get to have the best sex. Oh, but there's more to it than that.

Sex is the first crime, the prime force of human nature, the one transgression that cannot be prevented by cops or priests or teachers. From the destruction of Sodom on down, the forces of law and order and holiness have fought a supposedly noble battle against perversion, and sometimes it looks like they're winning. But Sodom, like every metropolis, has a Godfather. And like most crime bosses he's one mean son of a bitch.

And the vengeance of Sodom's Godfather is that sex will dominate all attempts to contain it, because it is what we, as human beings, live and breathe and eat and shit and dream. Even those of us who choose to remain celibate, which is as valid a sexual choice as any, cannot possibly deny (though we might try) that the need, the desire, the hunger bubbles somewhere inside us, that the potential of sex and eroticism still slumbers in our bodies. This potential might be labeled sin. But even the holiest among us rarely claim that they are wholly without sin — that the potential for such sin does not exist within them. When they do claim such things, their claims ring hollow, false, insipid. They don't even convince the speaker.

We all think of sex now and then. It's what humans do. And is that sin? I don't know the answer to that one, because the face of God still eludes me like the shadows cast on my apartment windows by the red and blue lights of the passing cop cars. I see it, but I'm not sure it's there.

But I do know one thing — it's a crime, and one that you, reader, will commit again and again and again, no matter who you are or where you live.

Because Sodom will have her vengeance, and the vengeance of Sodom is that *sex sells*. And, like most of us, it's pretty goddamn cheap.

So look into the shadows, Officer. Step into the shadows, Lieutenant, Father, Brother, Mother Superior, Captain, Private, Friend of Ours, Friend of Mine, Mayor, Godfather, Wiseguy, Don, Chief, Mr. President, Madame Ambassador, Your Honor, Your Highness, Your Eminence — Your Holiness.

Step into the shadows, motherfuckers, because you're the criminals, too. And you all know as well as I do that sex, like crime, *does* pay.

So it's your turn, reader. Enter the urban shadowlands, step into the darkened alley where desire breaks all boundaries and renders all social structures irrelevant. Where human laws are made null and void, because the law of the jungle prevails.

But don't be surprised if it looks a little familiar — this darkened land is where you and your hungers live. It's where we all go when the doors are closed, the lights are out, when the boss isn't looking and the neighbors can't hear. This dark alley is a stage for the 24/7 morality play that stars you and me and God and the Devil and everybody. It is a dangerous world, and a violent one, but it's a world where the chance for redemption lies at the bottom of every sin. Where the human soul still shines under the layers of grime and soot and motor oil. This is the city where need and want and kindness and sacrifice can still occasionally mean something, the street where honesty walks hand in hand with deception. It is a place where you may dare to tell the truth. It's where you left your soul so many years ago, but perhaps that soul still nestles amid the slumbering homeless and the discarded candy wrappers, calling to you: sleeping, dreaming, wanting, waiting, hoping. This city is your home. And it's a place where you might have to get your hands dirty.

So bring a pair of gloves — preferably black leather. And don't leave the light on.

Thomas S. Roche
San Francisco, Summer 2000

"My name is Sherlock Holmes.

It is my business to know what other people don't know."

— Sir Arthur Conan Doyle, *The Blue Carbuncle*

"That man is the richest whose pleasures are the cheapest."

— Henry David Thoreau

"Justice is incidental to law and order."

— J. Edgar Hoover

Syndromes

by Brian Hodge

For the first hour he doesn't say much of anything. Lying there with his face pressed down on the leather cushion. Cracked old brown thing. The cushion, not the face. Hands cuffed behind his back, and ankles to the table. Ass tipped up in the air like that, smooth as a peach — good god, what's he do, shave his own ass? Embarrassing, Tweeter thinks, just look at him like that.

"Okay, smart guy. Mister Big Brain. You set this thing up." Janelle, down the hall from this strange playroom, bitching to Woofer. "So where *is* everybody?"

"That's what I'd like to know, they should be here by now," Woofer is telling her. "Something must be going on. Something is going very much on."

"Everywhere except inside your head, maybe."

Woofer stomping around out there in the living room. Tweeter hears his approach and it's not a calm one, Woofer in the doorway to the playroom, looking sharp in that Italian suit, you know, but his face. All red, blotchy; veins ticking away at either side of his sweaty forehead.

"You! Bun Boy!" Yelling at the guy on the table. "*I* didn't have any problems finding this place, so why can't anybody else?"

The guy lifts his head, tilted in Woofer's direction, homing on his voice. Stuart, that's the guy's name. Stuart. With the shaved ass. And the leather blindfold, like a Lone Ranger mask without eyes. Voice nervous as he says he can't really answer that, how can he, he doesn't even know what's happening here.

"Christ, is it too much to expect people to get a little pro-active about keeping their commitments?" Woofer's raving to no one in particular. "Am I the only one around with any business sense?"

"Woofer, listen," says Tweeter, "maybe you should take a time out and do your breathing. Your forehead's looking really China Syndrome, you know?"

"Hey! Hey! Fuck my forehead!" Woofer all wound up tight, gun in his hand but it's not like he knows it's still there — the way accidents happen. Tweeter persists and finally he gives in, "Yeah, maybe you're right." Looking around, uneasy. "Only not in here. This room gives me the heebies."

Woofer's down the hall before Stuart raises his head again. "Do his breathing, you said. Does he have respiratory problems?"

"Huh-uh. Last time he was in jail for misdemeanor assault, the judge decided one of the conditions of his release was taking a stress management class. They taught him how to breathe better, how to hold, like, pictures in his head to calm him down."

Stuart nods. "Creative visualization."

"That's it. He goes inside his head, visits his happy place. Keeps him from, you know, going postal." Tweeter flicking the safety of his pistol on and off. Something to do, at least. "Woofer said it wasn't wasted time, he got a lot out of it."

"You care a lot about his well-being."

"He *is* my brother."

"Deep down...? You're the nurturing type, I can tell."

"I suppose that's a good thing," says Tweeter, "but it still sounds fruitcakey to me."

Stuart shaking his head. "Sensitivity to someone's needs is nothing to be ashamed of. Which is why I'm *begging* you to keep him from going postal on *me*. That's my need right now. And...her too."

"Janelle? Yours and mine both." Tweeter looks the room over. Nurturing. Caring. Sensitivity. Guess that explains the whips and paddles hanging on Stuart's walls. "Woofer's stress management class? That's where he met Janelle. She kicked the teacher in the shins. I don't think she ever did find her happy place."

Stuart groaning, a little whimper — can't help but feel sorry for him. Puts his very first ad in one of the sex newspapers and look what he gets. Tweeter tells him not to worry, they only need his house for a couple hours and that'll be that.

Woofer's finished his breathing. Got his tie knotted again and all his veins back in place. When he's stressing Woofer looks like a drill sergeant, close-shaved and bug-eyed, a volcano with skin. But after he mellows you wouldn't know him from Wall Street. Cuff links, even.

"All right. *Mister* Bun Boy," he says now. "I've given you time to prioritize your thought agenda. Can you provide any illumination on why my customers haven't found your front door?"

Tweeter about to say come on, lay off, the guy's not psychic.

"Forty-seven-fifteen Algonquin," Woofer says. "That's the address, right? That's exactly what I told them."

"Wait a minute," Stuart says. "When you gave it to them, did you say Algonquin Terrace, or Algonquin Street?"

Woofer frowns. "I think I just said Algonquin."

"Well — this is Algonquin *Terrace*."

Woofer starts to go pale. "Meaning..."

"Meaning they probably assumed *Street*," Janelle says from behind them, the doorway. "Meaning you sent them to the wrong address, genius."

And look. Just look. There go the veins again. Woofer getting his color back, the red glow creeping up from his collar. He tells Janelle to shut her mouth and leans over the padded leather table. Even though Stuart can't see him he knows Woofer's there, starts to shrink in on himself, like the slugs they used to pour salt on when they were kids.

"You're in real estate, you told me?" Woofer asks. "So you know what's where. How far away is Algonquin *Street*?"

Stuart tells him maybe forty-five minutes, this time of day. Too scared to spout the usual laziness to the average L.A. traffic question, everything twenty minutes from everything else.

"Meaning," Janelle calculates, "*you* sent them to the opposite side of the fucking *city*!"

And from there it's just more collateral damage. Tweeter's heard them argue about everything from TV channel to condom color. Hammer and tongs, it's the way they go at everything, from fights to make-up sex. Give them thermonuclear capabilities and the world would be seven continents of gray ash in a hot salt bath.

You wouldn't think a thing like this should be so difficult. At least not before the buyers even show up. Need a place to do some undisturbed business for a couple of hours, then vacate, clean, no connection? It was Janelle's idea, keep them from wasting one or two hundred dollars on a hotel room. Plus it's more impressive, an entire house — paintings, vases, good furniture.

Get one of the newspapers with the sex ads, she said; find some queer advertising for discreet encounters, wants to entertain at home. Then just make an appointment, then set up shop. Odds are, if he wants discretion in Los Angeles, he's so far in the closet he'll never find his way out. He won't even report the incident — too much to explain.

It's an education, seeing how other people live. Stuart and his big house and kinky playroom and shaved ass. Men pop boners over each other every day — fact of life. But never once has it entered Tweeter's mind that antique proctologist tables would have anything to do with it. Straight, gay, whatever — roll out the medical equipment and any normal guy will shrivel right up; three Adam's apples and an empty nutsack.

Look at the thing. Just look at it. Horrifying. Standing on its ancient iron framework, like it's ready to start galloping. The tabletop is thin, covered with that padded leather, cracked and brown as an old bomber jacket. A little pillow for your humiliated face, then move halfway down from the head, and the table splits and spreads, one side for each leg, with an open V in the middle for the doctor to roll his chair right up close and personal. Even worse, it bends in the middle, tilts the ass up in the air several degrees. It's adjustable, too, levers and cranks and big-toothed gears down there in the framework, thick with grease.

Tweeter can hardly take his eyes off the thing. Stuart cuffed on top of it, *to* it, still wearing a shirt but his pants hung from a peg. With his black leather blindfold and shaved ass.

Woofer and Janelle are still fighting out in the hall when the trill of Woofer's cellular phone cuts in. The only thing at this point that can shut them up.

Woofer smoothtalking them. Tweeter listening. No question the situation's fucked — just waiting to see how deeply. Woofer trying to explain to whichever potential buyer is on the other end that it's not his fault; not getting very far by the sound of things. Tweeter steps into the hallway just in time to see Woofer, calm as death, fold the cellular and slide it back into his pocket.

"Well," he says. "Isn't *that* just the king's piss-pot."

"Who's out?" Janelle asks.

"Quintero for sure. Probably the Player Dog posse. Quintero passed them on the other Algonquin, looking for the same address. That crew, we'll never even hear back from them." Woofer trying to look hopeful. "That still leaves Sloane. We're still in the game."

"It's not a game when the players can't even find the table." Janelle and her vicious rendition of the obvious. "It's not an auction when you've got one bidder."

She looks great today, nothing new there. Short black dress, long black hair, pointy black fuck-me-and-you-both shoes. Janelle pumps iron. But a soul like a cinder. She's, what, twenty-four? A full decade younger than Woofer, but Tweeter figures he needed the extra ten years just to prepare for her, she probably cannibalized all the guys her own age. In her late teens she was a Nazi skinhead. Woofer says if you root around in her hair and look close enough, you can see the swastika tattooed on the side of her head. Tweeter thinking 666 is more like it.

"Christ almighty," she sighs. "Know what? The Mayan calendar says the world ends in 2012, and all I want to know right now is, what's the fucking hold-up, if I have to wait with you."

Have to feel a little sorry for Woofer. Big brother standing there, everybody knowing whose fault this is. Can't blame the fag. Poor Stuart, just being the best fag he knew how to be.

When Woofer's cellular rings again, it's Sloane and second chances. Good to see Woofer back on the situation again. He snaps the phone closed an inch from the tip of Janelle's nose.

Tweeter, back in the playroom. Stuart hasn't moved, but where can he go? A dull job, guarding this guy. Like there's a need? He gets noisy, all you do is gag him — plenty of those around, too.

"It won't be long now," Tweeter tells him. "The buyer's on his way. Soon as he gets here it should take another fifteen, twenty minutes, tops, then we're gone."

"Drugs? Is that what you're selling?"

Tweeter laughs. "That'll be the day. Janelle'd take 'em all. No, it's just cell phones. You know — clones. Clone phones."

"Tweeter? Could you take this blindfold off me? So I can look at you when I talk to you?"

Tweeter isn't sure about this. Woofer's pretty adamant about the blindfold. Plus, Tweeter can stand against this wall, let his gaze meander over to Stuart's shaved ass, check it out without Stuart knowing. Nothing behind it, doesn't mean he's turning gay or anything. Just curiosity is all.

Because it's not a bad ass. Smooth. Hairless. Pink with just a buttery blush of gold. Appears pretty toned, down there in the muscle. If you narrow your vision, make a point of not looking at who it's attached to, it might just as easily be a woman's ass. You know, just because it's Stuart's doesn't make it a bad ass. A nice ass is a nice ass.

"Tweeter? Are you still there?"

"I'm thinking, I'm thinking."

"I've seen your brother already. I've heard your names. How many Woofers, Tweeters, and Janelles can there be? So what's to gain from keeping me from seeing your face? You picked the right guy, okay? I'm not–" Voice breaking, then he finds it again. "I can't do anything about this. So the least you could do is treat me like a human being while you're doing this to me. That's not a lot to ask for."

All this over a blindfold that belongs to Stuart to begin with. Like everything else, Tweeter supposes, there's a time and a place. He moves over to the table and takes hold of the mask with his fingertips. Pulling it off Stuart's head, slowly, so the thick elastic band doesn't snap. Back of his hand brushing Stuart's sandy hair, longish on top, moussed, flattened around the sides from its ninety-minute cinch. Stuart blinking at the light, pale blue eyes like an uncertain sky. Staring up at him.

"That's better. Thanks." Gaze lowering. "So you've got a gun too. I didn't know that. Is it absolutely necessary?"

"Today? Probably not." Tweeter pulling his shirt out around the waist to drape it over the gun. Out of sight, out of mind. No, probably it won't work that way, but it's the best he can do.

"Clone phones, you were saying? I don't think I follow."

Fill him in, or not? Tweeter's never had a hostage before but this isn't the way he imagined it, like talking to somebody in a bar. Saying *How 'bout those Lakers?*, and next thing you know you're checking out somebody's ass. Admiring the muscles down the backs of their thighs, the hamstrings. Their definition.

"You a runner?" Tweeter asks.

"Five miles, every other day. I cross-train."

"Weights too, then."

"Oh, religiously."

Tweeter wanders over to the doorway, glancing down the hall. Listening. From around a few corners he can hear Woofer lugging boxes in from the garage. Janelle no help, unless nagging boosts adrenaline. Okay, give Stuart the crash course, no harm done.

"If you're in real estate, you use a cell phone, am I right?" Stuart saying sure. "They're like computers. Hardware's basically all the same, it's the program-ming that makes it yours and nobody else's. They're installed with codes to link with their particular carrier. Satellite codes. Codes to tell the carrier that it's you instead of, say, your boss. So pretend you get a batch of uncoded phones. Then you find a bunch of codes. And then you program the phones yourself. That way, whoever buys a phone can make unlimited calls for a few days before the carrier mainframe spits out an alert, something looks funny about the call patterns, so the company has to call the guy who has the codes for real. Check with him, if he really does know somebody in Singapore or wherever."

Stuart, following it all. "Where do you 'find' these codes?"

"Sometimes you can buy them from snitches at the company, but that's no good if they get caught, to save their own asses they'll sell you out in a minute to the D.A. What we do is, we got a frequency scanner. When it locks in on a close signal it reads the codes, stores them in memory."

"Just how many of these phones did you bring with you?"

"Ninety-four."

"You're joking."

"One day's work at the airport. Plus it was Janelle's idea to monitor the calls, figure out who'd be across the country, or *out* of the country, for two, three weeks. So we got almost forty phones that'll be good for that whole time, because the legitimate owners aren't even around to tell the company, no, I *don't* know anyone in Singapore. What Woofer was hoping to do was get bids on those."

And look. Just look how into this Stuart is. Can't fake that. Never would've guessed. But then, Stuart shaves his ass and likes paddles. It's always the quiet ones that surprise you most. Stuart asking who buys clone phones in bulk. Tweeter telling him anyone with a highly mobile business who doesn't want to risk discussing it on a traceable land-line. Drug crews, prostitution rings. Or, like the guy on his way — he and his crews move illegals up from Mexico, stash them with sweatshop operators all over the state.

"It sounds dangerous, some of these people," Stuart says.

"Not really. We just provide a service." Besides, Sloane, what he really wants to do is produce movies, maybe direct. "Look, *you're* the one with dangerous habits, letting strangers into your house like this."

"Touché."

Tweeter's been trying to figure him out. Something not quite squaring here. "You can't just admit you're queer to your office. This day and age, out here, and you still can't do that?"

"It's a very conservative agency. They wouldn't take it well, I don't think, and my commissions are too good there for it not to matter."

"But you still advertise for some stranger to come in and slide whatever he wants up your ass."

"Within reason." Stuart shuts his eyes. "Can you help what excites *you*? I don't think so, Tweeter."

Tweeter not wanting to get into that, not now. Starting to rethink some things and it's not a good time for that, either.

"That's not the point," he tells Stuart. "When you start advertising it, bringing strangers in that way, it's not just a good time. It's, you know, you *want* to get outed. Can't open the closet yourself, so you're hoping maybe something'll happen and just kick the door in for you."

Stuart's shaking his head and frowning, trying to argue his way out of this one when there's movement behind him, and Tweeter turns, sees Woofer in the doorway. Woofer gaping like a fish.

"Hey! Tweeter? Hey! What's he doing without his blindfold? Did I not distinctly advise you to keep that blindfold on him?"

Tweeter tells him to mellow, nobody's reporting anything to anybody. Woofer's not having it, then there's Janelle backing him up, and Stuart trying to shrink down again, melt into the leather.

"It's not an I.D. I'm worried about!" Woofer shouts. "The Stockholm Syndrome, remember? Just in case? Now you've blown it."

Worries about everything, and when nothing's there Woofer finds it anyway. The Stockholm Syndrome. Like this is some hostage standoff, fifteen bank tellers and loan officers tied up and it's time to pick the first one to kill. You go shoot one, Tweeter, get that helicopter here faster. Woofer sure loves his drama.

Janelle and her heels go clicking across the floor to a rack of kink toys on the wall. Moving the way she does when she's got some point to prove. Grabbing a black riding crop.

The Stockholm Syndrome, Woofer's studied up on it. Say you're holding somebody prisoner. The longer it goes on, the more you get to talking, the more you see each other as human beings. Opposite sides of the same gun but you're both still hoping the other makes it through. Every hour, getting harder and harder to shoot your new hostage buddy if that's what it takes....

Unless you've kept his eyes covered the whole time.

Janelle stalking back across the playroom. Stuart knows it's coming, and how bad. She brings the riding crop down as hard as she can. It slices air and cracks Stuart across the ass. Tweeter flinching at the sound of it and Janelle watching him do it. She keeps hitting, eight, nine times, whole shoulder and arm into it. Tweeter trying not to flinch any more, but goddamn. There's pain and there's pain, play and the real thing, and if any of them know how far apart the two are it's Stuart. Stuart with the shaved ass covered in thick red welts and the tears in his eyes.

"See?" she says to Tweeter. "*That's* why the blindfold."

Right here. This is it. Why he's never liked her — tolerated her for Woofer's sake, but never liked her. Maybe hating her now. It's things like this. No reason to do them other than meanness, prove how she's got no real stake in living, in feeling.

"Are you finished?" Woofer asks her. No. She isn't. Tweeter watches her drop the riding crop and go for her purse in the hall, Woofer looking at him, like daring him to do something about it, but admitting neither of them can. It's Janelle. What can you do?

Lipstick. Only her lipstick is all. She gives it a twist and the shaft rises out of the tube, like her own little dark cock.

"You like this shade?" she asks Stuart.

"Yes," he whispers.

She draws a thick blotch on his cheek, deep violet with a blue sheen. One on the other cheek, a couple on his forehead.

"It's called 'Plague.' Just so you know." Janelle puts her lipstick away. Looking at Woofer. "God, I hate fags."

"Does this mean you're ready to sell some phones now?"

"Not so fast. What was going on in here between the two of you, first thing? You couldn't just cuff him and that's it? You have to let him strip naked for you before you make your move?"

"Hey. Hey. Watch that kind of discourse." Woofer shaking his head, can't believe what he's hearing. "I'm here all of sixty seconds, I turn around, next thing I know he's got his pants off. What am I supposed to do, put 'em back on him?"

Janelle smiling now, coy. Sweet as honey. "For god's sake, baby. You don't have to take it so personally."

They leave him alone with Stuart. Stuart and his welts and his bubonic blotches. Stuart looking him in the eye until Tweeter has to turn away. That didn't go so well. Janelle going postal and he stands there letting it happen.

What was the worst they were doing in here, anyway? Sharing some conversation. Stuart showing an interest in what he had to say. Tell me about the clone phones, Tweeter. Happy to. It was a nice feeling. Like he could look at Stuart's ass now and then and maybe Stuart knows and it's *still* no big deal.

"I could maybe, you know, try wiping that off your face."

Stuart shakes his head. "She'll just put it back. Or worse."

Now when he looks at Stuart's ass it bothers him, those welts as thick as Janelle's little finger. Tweeter can't take the sight so he heads down the hallway to the kitchen, the fridge, grabs a bottle of tea to take back. Downs a few swigs, then asks Stuart if he's thirsty. A grateful nod. Holds the bottle down to him, tips it. Watching what Stuart's mouth does around the wide rim of the bottle. Never paid attention to a thing like that before.

Taking turns, they finish the bottle.

"How'd you get a nickname like Tweeter, anyway?"

"Just the sort of thing that happens when you got an older brother called Woofer." Stuart watching him like he's not really answered the question. "When he was fourteen or so, and I'd've been eight, he started boosting stereos. The name just stuck."

"You don't look like a Tweeter. Maybe then. But not now."

"Could be worse. If we'd had one more kid brother, they probably would've called me Midrange."

It makes Stuart laugh, first laugh all afternoon, grinning down at the leather pillow. Tweeter glad he said it, like he's gone above and beyond for Stuart, brightened his day. Tweeter seeing what a smile does for his face. A smile never hurts.

"Where she hit you. How's ... how's it feel?"

"It burns. A lot."

Tweeter's still holding the empty bottle in his hand. Sweaty. The bottle. Not his hand. Not his hand. *Not* his hand.

"This glass. It's kind of cool, still."

Stuart looking at him. At the bottle. No expression, just a nod. Tweeter takes a few steps, and there he is, so close to those welts. Looking at the door. Listening to them out there, waiting for Sloane.

Tweeter rolls the bottle across one ass cheek, then the other. Slow as he dares. Watching how the curve of skin and muscle flattens, reshapes itself after the bottle's pass. Wondering how this would look without these horrible stripes. He rolls it again, notices the muscles flex along the backs of the tan legs, Stuart starting to grind himself down against the padded tabletop. Rolls the bottle until the glass warms in his hand. He steps away.

Stuart's breathing harder. "You don't belong with them out there. I don't care if he *is* your brother. Do you plan on doing what he tells you the rest of your life? Don't you have any goals of your own?"

Thinking about this one. Drawing blanks, mostly. "I — I'd like to own a Jet Ski."

Stuart going bug-eyed. "I'll *buy* you a Jet Ski. Get me out of this and I'll buy you a Jet Ski for every ocean."

It's just turning into the strangest day. Not the day you expect when you wake up. Pacific, Atlantic, Indian ... how many jet skis are they talking about, anyway? Seems a little overkill.

Then it's the doorbell, so Tweeter has to leave him alone for a while, raising a finger to his lips before closing the kinkroom door. Woofer checks the peephole before he opens up, lets in Sloane and another guy, some squat Mexican in a muscle shirt and prison tattoos. Sloane, the wetback's friend and fat as Marlon Brando.

Tweeter hangs back, away from talk but in plain sight the way Woofer likes. The Mexican guy staring at him, maybe he gets paid by the glare. Tweeter returning it, this dead-eyed glaze that Woofer's always pestering him to practice, no humanity left, only a general boredom with watching people die.

Woofer's in sales mode, opens up the boxes of clone phones, hands one over. Curious about the time and temperature in Guam? Here you go, on some other asshole's dime. Janelle jumping in on it, Sloane getting an eyeful as she praises the near-forty special phones, why they'll cost extra.

"...since the owners of the originals aren't even in the area right now. Do you see the beauty of this? They can't be consulted for a security check in the first place."

Sloane just blinks. "That's it? So what?"

"I don't think you understand," she says. Woofer glancing at her, like, you know, be nice. "These phones can stay active four or five times longer than usual."

Sloane, nodding. "So when the cell company decides to do a security check-up for some guy, they can't raise him. So they try an alternate number, maybe call his office — let's say there's more than just him in the office — then they're all in on this with you. *Nobody's* gonna mention, 'Oh, Joe? He's in Paris, he won't be back for three weeks.' They'll all just sit on this information. Because it's you. This is what you're telling me."

Janelle and Woofer stare at each other, how'd we overlook this? Tweeter wants to grin but doesn't. Wondering if he should've told them right off at the airport. No, better this way. Mostly he just wanted to see this look on Janelle's face. Priceless.

"I'll still take the phones, but premium markups this time, you're out of your fucking minds," Sloane says. "Let me tell you what I *do* understand. Between the address thing and now this, I've seen eight-year-old Mexican kids, don't even speak the language, whose brains would've functioned better."

And after it's over, Tweeter's still wondering how something can escalate so wrong, so fast. No reason it should happen, it just does. Some hothead bitch in her plague-colored lipstick not liking the way some guy talks to her. Grabs her boyfriend's gun from under his jacket and starts blasting away. Not especially good at it, but the guy's so fat, you know, he's harder to miss, and his buddy's probably mean as shit with a knife but he's confused too, because who starts shooting over telephones? So the bubonic bitch, what she lacks in aim she makes up for in surprise.

Their ears are ringing and the air stinks and Woofer's having a fit, screaming at Janelle, how could you, how could you do this to me? Ballsy guy, though — snatches the pistol away from her and steps back out of her reach.

But Janelle's kicking Sloane between his flabby dead legs. Yelling, "As long as they brought the money, what's the problem? And we can still sell the phones. You're always talking about maximizing our efficiency vector, well, this is the way to do it."

Woofer starts walking in circles, moaning, falls into a plump chair. "Oh Christ, I gotta do my breathing." Shutting his eyes. "I gotta visit my happy place...."

Janelle's kneeling on the floor, groping around in Sloane's pockets. "Would you get hold of yourself? Let me find the money, we'll do the fag, and we'll get out of here." Looking up at Tweeter from the dead men. "*You* were a big help."

Heart tightening in his chest, Tweeter fades back to the kinkroom, see how Stuart's doing. Not good. But what's he expect? Don't you worry about that mess, Tweeter, I'll clean it all up.

Over and over: "What happened out there? What *happened*?"

"It went bad. Guess who."

Stuart stares at him like he's afraid if he blinks he'll miss something important. "Tweeter?" Shaking his head. "Don't let her...please don't let her...just don't let her...."

Look at this. What Janelle's making them do. No good, any of it. Tweeter raises a hand, okay, let me see what I can manage, and leaves the room but, you know, it's not like it's a democracy.

Janelle's stashing a wallet in her purse, Woofer complaining that he can't do his breathing here because of the cordite smoke, he needs another room. Janelle looks down the hallway. "Well? Who's taking care of that? Do I have to do it all?"

Tweeter stalling for time. "Don't you think maybe he should have a last request?"

"What for? You think we're in the Foreign Legion? Does he even smoke? Just let him suck on the gun while you do it."

But he won't let this go, saying they owe the poor guy, it wasn't supposed to happen this way. Asking Woofer what he thinks.

"Whatever, whatever, if it doesn't take long." Like right at the moment Woofer doesn't want to be bothered. "Because I am *not* allocating another personal resource until I get my breathing in, and I won't get my breathing in until you stop fucking with me."

Janelle rolls her eyes. "Jesus, you two. And I suppose it'll be me who has to lug the phones back to the car."

Hardest thing he's ever had to do, go back to that proctology table and look at Stuart without really looking at him. Poor guy, Stuart's got to know what he's asking. It's either him or Janelle, no way she's leaving him alive. You can't just shoot Janelle and that's it. Have to shoot Woofer too and there's just no way.

So maybe he understands. Stuart taking the news pretty well, not begging like he was before. Resigned to it. And when Tweeter gets to the part about last requests, Stuart says what he wants, but Tweeter has to ask him to repeat it, make sure he heard right. Okay, Stuart's the one with the shaved ass and proctology table, but he still looks so normal, you know, how can his brain think up a thing like that at a time like this?

But they're deep into it now. Tweeter, keeping his word. He's in the kitchen when Janelle pokes her head in, got a box of phones in her arms, checking up on him like he's a two-year-old.

"What is it he wants?"

Tweeter shrugs. "Wine. He just wants some wine."

Janelle can't find much to argue with that so she leaves. If she only knew. Tweeter, walking back to the kinkroom feeling like he's about to wake up any second, start this goofy day over again.

He shuts the door, looking at Stuart, holding the wine bottle in both hands. Me and my big mouth. Any last requests? Oh, you bet, Tweeter, so glad you asked. All the millions who've ever been executed, and he's got to feel accountable to the first guy in the history of civilization who says he wants an enema. A *wine* enema.

"The bag's in that cabinet over there," Stuart says. "The plugs are right next to it."

Tweeter, hoping Janelle doesn't feel like a glassful herself, feeling parched from all that work she's doing. Walks in, sees a sight like this, her body count goes up another two for today.

Okay, how hard can this be? Open up the rubber bag. Wine goes in, cap goes back on, nozzle...not many options there. Gentle pressure, Stuart tells him. Not all at once. Steady flow.

"Give it a few minutes to work … before...." Stuart says. "Can you do that much for me?"

"To work, what do you mean?"

"To get me drunk, what do you think? You think I want to die sober? You think I want to die at all?" Stuart, stopping a moment. "Oooo … you're *good* at this, Tweeter...."

It's not like he's even minding it, nothing he could ever do for any of the women he's been with. All of them with this thing about their assholes, no-man's-land and that's the way they want to keep it. No no no, Tweeter, you stay away from there. Tweeter always assuming that vague dissatisfaction he feels with them to be just a phase he's going through.

The bag's empty, so he caps Stuart off with the plug, hides the bag in the cabinet. Tweeter, sitting with Stuart for a couple minutes, never been with anyone so sure to die in a few more.

Stuart telling him, "It's not too late. You know this isn't right. You know I could teach you things. We can go as rough or as gentle as you want, I think you've got it in you to do both."

Tweeter thinking there has to be some way out of this. But nobody giving him time to think, sort through the confusion. Still working on it when the door bangs open. Janelle leads the way. The gun in Woofer's hand and he's looking mellowed again but not happy about it.

This is when it starts to get real. Stuart's breath going fast and shallow, and he's shaking, so much sweat the purple-blue blotches start to run. Trying to say something but he can't.

"Get out of the way, Tweeter," his brother tells him.

He waits for Woofer to tell him again, then steps aside. Can't stand this. Better make some kind of move, make it fast.

Janelle saying, "Get this over with, we've got ninety-four phones in the car and they're not getting any more marketable."

"Don't rush me," Woofer says. "I've never done this before."

"Today was a first for me too, but you didn't see me hesitating, did you?"

Woofer takes another step closer, holding the gun out at arm's length. Lowering it. Raising it again. Aiming. Then not, just shaking his head.

"Oh, this is *so* pathetic!" Janelle cries. "What does this say about men if I've got more balls than anybody else here?"

"I don't know," Woofer says, "but I bet I'll hear all about it the whole drive back to Pasadena."

Giving her the gun.

She takes his place, like stepping up to bat. Janelle holding the pistol steady, leveled at Stuart's forehead and sure he's terrified, but he's got it under control. Lifting his head up high as he can with his lips pressed tight, looking straight at her so she has to look straight at him. Harder than it looks when the guy's not Sloane, being generous with the insults.

"I can do this," she says. Not wavering like Woofer, but not doing anything else. While everybody waits.

"Problem?" says Woofer.

"Well, look at him! Staring at me like that. Those big blue eyes. It's like shooting Bambi."

"Deer's eyes are brown."

"It's the Stockholm Syndrome again." Lowering the gun and glaring. "Goddamn you, Tweeter, now do you see why you should never have taken that blindfold off him?"

Woofer, throwing his arms into the air. "So walk around and shoot him in the *back* of the head. Or does his hair remind you of Winnie the Pooh?"

"So you don't think I can do this? You watch." And there she goes, hell on heels, Janelle and her plague-colored lipstick and Woofer's pistol. Clicking around to the other end of the table and stepping between its two forks, Stuart's ankles at either side.

He's starting to shake again, Janelle raising the pistol and thumbing back the hammer, no mistaking what that click means.

And next, well, isn't it just the capper on this whole day. Maybe it's Stuart's terror and he can't help it, or maybe he does it on purpose because he knows his ass is tilted at that angle, so why not give it all he's got. Look at the desperation. Look at the ingenuity. Look at the velocity. Stuart's toned body flexing in a heaving spasm to dislodge the plug, and it ricochets off Janelle's hand and with the sound of a horrible hydraulic gush she's slapped in the face with an entire quart of warm Bordeaux.

Janelle reeling back out of control, like who wouldn't, and now look, Woofer's caught a bullet in his eye socket. Flying back hard against the wall and sliding to the floor with a red splotch smearing after his head. Tweeter not much expecting him to get back up — you tend not to bounce back from a thing like that — so he reaches for the gun under his shirt before Janelle can wipe her eyes and face clean (and stop all that screeching and sputtering) and get back to what she does best, making life miserable. Tweeter draws a bead, pretending her head's a coffee can, just like in target practice with Woofer, and Janelle goes down slippery. All of it only taking five, six seconds' time, and now this has to be the messiest room he's ever seen.

Can't much blame Stuart for bursting into tears, then just as suddenly he's laughing like a loon, like he doesn't know *how* he feels. Tweeter able to identify with that, at least.

"About time you quit being so fucking passive," Stuart says. "Maybe there's hope for you yet."

Then he tells him where the handcuff key is. Tweeter unlocks him, wrists and ankles both, but Stuart can't move yet, just lies there atop the table with his wet, striped ass in the air.

Use it right, anything's a lethal weapon. Tweeter finds a towel and drapes it over Stuart until he quits shaking.

How do you even begin to clean up a mess like this? One body at a time, he supposes. Figure out some way to get Woofer cooked down to ash. Janelle, she can just rot, black and purple-blue.

Tweeter closes his eyes for a few moments, imagines riding out on that new Jet Ski, scattering Woofer's ashes with the clean salt spray in his face. Let the waves take Woofer someplace else in the world. Ride that Jet Ski back in, finally be his own man.

And if that's not a happy place, he doesn't know what is.

Brian Hodge is the author of seven novels, most recently *Wild Horses*, a lead title from William Morrow. He is currently at work on his next, entitled *Mad Dogs*. He's also written over seventy-five short stories and novellas, many of which have been forced at gunpoint into two highly-acclaimed collections, *The Convulsion Factory* and *Falling Idols*. He lives in Boulder, Colorado, where he's recently started a recording project called Axis Mundi, with an ever-growing arsenal of keyboards, didgeridoos, and digital gear, which very much want a room of their own. Web site: http://www.para-net.com/~brian_hodge

The Ghost of Her

by Trey R. Barker

She came with Jimmy James Cleave, riding high and fine in his brand new 1952 Caddy. While he talked to the station manager, I stared at her from the booth, and Sarah Vaughn sang about love.

". . . after hours," she sang, "while the whole town is sleeping . . ."

— *she checks her make-up. Her soft fingers blend it, smooth it; it has to be perfect, we're going out tonight. She plays with her dangly earrings —*

— a single earring, the other lost or sold —

". . . I find my heart keeping a rendezvous . . ."

— *her hands go to the plunging V-line of her red dress and then smooth the dress like a second skin. They touch her breasts; linger, invite —*

— raggedly thin, and it made the dress' V-line look like a tomboy's open shirt. The dress was no longer a second skin, but an extra skin —

". . . with the ghost of you . . ."

— *hands down to her hips and thighs, pulling the dress snugly over them. She grins. She likes the tight fit because I like to watch the sway of her hips, the dance of her ass —*

— legs were emaciated and her hip bones bulged through her skin as though they had grown haphazardly —

". . . after hours, haunting all of the old places . . ."

— *her tongue licks pouty lips as she turns to me. She walks slowly, rolling her shoulders subtly. At my pants, her fingers are certain. I long for her to kneel and use her tongue and teeth, lips and spit, but she doesn't. She believes it degrading to be on her knees —*

— tripped over her own feet and fell on her ass. Her giggle was a junkie's screech —

". . . I ask the same faces for any news . . ."

— her perfume is musky like a slow blues. Anticipation and desire rise in me. I want this woman. I need her. I love her —

— helped her up from the floor. She leaned into me for support and she smelled like a goddamned brewery —

". . . it's the same old blues."

— she decides we'll stay in tonight. Her tongue traces my ear and she whispers, "Make love to me." She removes the dress — her favorite — and a playful grin dances on her lips as she slides out of her bra, her panties, onto me —

Jimmy James Cleave called her back to my manager's office.

I released her thin hand and watched her go. She looked back at me, her eyes empty and hollow. Then she went in, knelt, and blew my manager while the Sarah Vaughn record skipped its way through a scratch.

KCCK; eight to midnight. That's me. Best jazz and blues disc jockey in the country. Or so I like to think. I've met all the great musicians and have been given "thank yous" on albums by Big Joe Williams, Speckled Red, Howlin' Wolf. Hell, I even got a Pat Boone mention once.

The rest of my shift was awful. I couldn't get Marilee out of my head. Everywhere I looked, I saw her eyes. Not the beautiful eyes I had known, but the empty ones I had seen tonight. At midnight, I left quick. Marilee, Jimmy James, and the manager were already gone.

I headed down to the Blue Oyster. There was some new cat in town and I wanted to catch his second set. But I wanted to drown Marilee, too. I wanted to drink and forget how I had once lost myself in her eyes; eyes that make a man want to settle down. Put a diamond ring on his finger, buy a little house, and stare into those eyes forever.

"Rory," I said to the barkeep. "How's it hanging tonight?"

"'Bout ten inches, bossman. But I ain't seeing where it's any of your business."

I chuckled. "And I'd just as soon not see that monster, either. Rum and Seven. This kid worth listening to?"

Rory shrugged, got me my drink. "Another kid, another guitar."

"Well, I'll just have to have a look-see."

"Don't count on it, bossman. His second set got bumped."

"The hell you say. Who's got that kind of clout?"

I should have known. Sitting loose and easy against the wall, Marilee by his side, Jimmy James Cleave. He smiled at me, a tight smile he probably thought women found irresistible. It turned my stomach.

"You gonna like this, bossman, oh, yeah, like it real good." Rory grinned. His gold-capped teeth flashing out of his dark-skinned face like beacons.

"My standards are pretty high."

"Oh, yeah, real high, like a pig in slop."

As he spoke, I watched Jimmy James. I hated him. I had known — in an abstract way — he and Marilee were tied up, but to see them like that, acting like they belonged together, set me on a hard edge.

I stared at Marilee and she looked back. Worlds of conversation passed between us. I apologized and she accepted. I told her I still loved her, she answered the same.

"Stay away from her," Rory warned. "She's a junkie."

"I know, Rory."

"And a whore."

"I *know*, Rory."

"And running–"

"Goddamnit." I banged my glass to the bar. "I know, Rory. Shut up."

He stared at me. Not many people talked to him that way. "Better watch that tone, bossman."

"Who's singing?" I asked, more harshly than I had intended.

Rory nodded toward the stage. Jimmy James Cleave, Junior jumped headlong into his first number.

"Junior?"

"He wants to be a star," Rory said. After a few notes he whistled quietly. "Whoooeee. He's worse than warm shit for dinner, ain't he?"

I nodded and closed my eyes. The music faded behind images of Marilee. She and I had split up a year ago and I'm sure Jimmy James thought it a hoot to bring her in to blow my station manager. Truthfully, we hadn't split up, I threw her out when she junked up.

On stage, Junior screeched an Andrews Sisters tune badly enough to shatter a deaf dog's ears. I gripped my glass, hoping Junior's voice wouldn't send my hand into a spasm that shattered the glass and cut me to ribbons.

I shook my head. "I've got to pee."

"I hope everything comes out all right," Rory said dryly.

"Your jokes suck, Rory."

"I know they do, bossman, I know they do."

He laughed as I headed for the can.

I hate public cans. Beer, piss, shit. All those stinks mixed up like stink stew. Add a little spice of come or blood and you got a real dinner treat.

I stood pissing at the urinal when the door opened. As much as I hate using a public can, I hate sharing them even more.

"Barnes."

A thin voice, clad in a red dress. Marilee.

Surprised, I turned to her.

"Nice dick," she said.

I glanced down. A tiny drop of piss danced around the tip. I shook it off and quickly zipped up.

"What are you doing in here?" Nice opening line. Not the one I had planned to hand her if I ever had the chance.

"Junior's singing."

I nodded. "You've got a pretty liberal definition of singing."

She giggled and her eyes darted from corner to corner, stall to stall, while her fingers played at her necklace. Her body shifted back and forth, foot to foot.

"What's up?" I didn't bother asking her to go outside. With Jimmy James' name hanging from her, she wasn't going to talk to any man in public except him.

Instead of answering, she stared at me, and I slipped away just like when I had first met her. Before the drugs, we had made love at Red Rocks amphitheater; we had played records together on the air; we had bought a puppy together. It seemed so long ago.

Still she didn't answer and I knew what was coming, it was in her eyes. They changed color; the green heated up. My blood raced.

"I miss you," she said. She wrapped her arms around my neck and pushed me backward.

We stumbled into a stall. Fumbling, I locked the door and she lifted her feet off the floor in case anyone came in.

"Marilee," I whispered, fear of Jimmy James thick in my throat. My fingers traced her ribs. The drugs had thinned her out. Her purse poked me in the gut. "Carrying?" I asked.

"Just a .38. For emergencies. And kneecaps." She bit my lip. "I miss you, Barnes." She kissed me and let her hand wander to my crotch. "Whoo, look at this. I guess you missed me, too."

She undid my pants and sank to her knees. An image of the station manager flashed through me and for a moment, I thought my dick would shrivel like a grape to a raisin. But her lips and fingers, her tongue, kept me hard. I imagined us on a desert island, making love under the sun as the sea boiled.

But when I opened my eyes, the island was gone, replaced by a blow-job junkie on her knees in a stall. I hauled her up by the arms. "Get up. You don't belong down there."

"Maybe I do."

"Bullshit."

She smiled and it erased an entire year of pain.

"Make love to me, Barnes."

"What?"

She stroked my penis. "Right here. In this shit-smelling, piss-covered stall. You'll make it better than this place. You'll make it good. I ain't had it that way in a while." She turned around and kneeled on the commode. With one hand she braced herself; with the other hand she raised her dress.

I stared at her nakedness, at her backside grin. "No panties."

"Junior's doin'. Wants me wet and bare so we can fuck whenever he wants." Her voice fell to a whisper. "He rapes me 'bout once a week."

I said nothing for a long time. This was the woman I had loved and there wasn't anything I could do to help her. Anger and rage welled up inside. I couldn't touch either Jimmy James or Junior. So I struck back with the only weapon I had: I took her. Defiantly, I shoved my pants down. I had been without Marilee for a year. To have her again, and to get back at the Cleave boys, I was willing to take her on a toilet.

She was warm and wet and moaned when I pushed into her. She grabbed my backside and pushed against me. I lost myself in her. She was a liquid roadway and I traveled her, seeing nothing else.

The end of the road built inside me, looming closer and closer. But before we reached it, Jimmy James Cleave.

"Goddamn, but my boy's good," he said, barging in and slapping his meaty hand against the urinal.

My stomach knotted up like a Boy Scout working on his rope badge. Marilee's eyes went wide. I squeezed her hand to calm her.

"Wha'd you thinka him, Barnes?"

I wanted to disappear. I was no hero and if Jimmy James saw us together — forget about my dick anywhere near her — he'd kill me right in that stall.

"You must have a helluva case of squirts, Barnes. You been in there a while. People ain't usually in bathrooms that long. 'Less they got business. Drugs. Sex."

There was another smell in that bathroom just then. Fear. Thick and pungent. I hadn't ever smelled that kind of fear coming from me before.

"Hey, Barnes? Got your dick in your hand?"

"Uh ... uh, no," I sputtered. "Just ... just ... uh...."

He laughed. Deep and dark and terrifying. Sweat broke out on my lip. There was nothing in the stall to use as a weapon. Unless I could manage to get his head in the crapper and then flush him to death.

"Bathrooms are scary places, no good for sex. I can't get off in one, too dirty. You gettin' off in there? Didn't think you were that dirty, but you never know 'bout some people."

He flushed the urinal and the sudden sound of rushing water scared me into a terrified yelp. Marilee gripped my hand so tightly I thought the circulation would stop.

"Like your manager. Hell, I thought he'd be a hard-ass about playing my boy's song, but he wasn't. I greased him with a little piece of ass. Wasn't even all that good a piece. I 'magine you'll be playing my boy's song tomorrow night."

Marilee closed her eyes. Her bottom lip trembled. Hero or not, right then I wanted to race out of the stall and slam Jimmy James' face into the urinal. I wanted to flush his blood down the sewer.

"Never know about people. Think they're happy 'cause of what you've done for them and turns out they ain't. Taking you down behind your back, stealing your money."

When he slammed his hand against the side of the stall, I screamed.

He chuckled, "Get that sex whenever you can, Barnes," and left.

I exhaled in small, stuttering breaths. "Christ."

"Shit," Marilee said. She sat on the commode, her dress still hiked up. "He knows."

I stared at her, confused and uneasy. "Knows what?"

Marilee licked her lips. "I'm skimming."

"What?" I was dumbfounded. I sagged against the stall door, my heart pounding louder than Junior's drummer.

She looked at me. Staring into those eyes, at the face I had loved, I didn't want to be angry. I wanted to love and help her. But we were talking about Jimmy James Cleave, not some shitty-ass neighborhood punk. This was the big time.

"His money," she said. "And his blow."

"Son of a bitch."

"And Junior's going to marry me."

I slid to the floor. "What in holy hell have you gotten into?"

"I don't *know*," she said, tears staining her cheeks. "It was just a few Bennies, that's all. Then it was a lot and then. . ." She laughed, dark and bitter like coffee with no filter. "From blow to blowin'. Jimmy James has me working off my debt.

I eat the drugs and some shitty trick pays it off by shooting his wad down my throat."

"Stop." I leaned my head back, closed my eyes. I couldn't hear any more. I had loved this woman and every day I kicked myself in a thousand little ways for ending it. Her drug stash had been small, but it was enough for me. I got as righteously worked up as any two-bit traveling tent-show preacher, shoved her out the door, and now she was whoring.

Angrily I stood, grabbed the stall door and banged it open. It missed Marilee's head by an inch.

"Where are you going?"

"Getting out of here. Have a great marriage."

I went to the door, stopped when I heard her crying. I should have gone back and held her. But I was feeling mean. "You better get your ass straightened out, Marilee; those guys don't fuck around."

"I know, Barnes, but I need some help." She stared at me and the last thing I saw as I left the shitter were her empty eyes.

"I don't know, Rory," I told him the next morning. We were in the A-1 Laundromat, listening to the steam hiss and the metallic bang of the washers and dryers. "Maybe I still love her."

Rory stuffed some old, battered underwear into the washer. "Sure as shit, bossman. And that shit'll get you dead."

I knew it, of course. Both that I loved her and that it might kill me.

"Besides that, bossman, she's a junkie."

The other customers mindlessly went about their laundry. I watched them for a while. "Yeah," I said finally. "How do I fix that?"

"You don't unless she wants it." He fed the machine a nickel.

"And if I do, Jimmy James is likely to kill me."

"Or Junior, maybe, for messin' with his woman."

"That's a load of shit, Rory, she isn't going to marry that slimeball."

"Prob'ly won't have the chance."

"What does that mean?"

He leaned against the washer. "Junior thinks they're going to get married. Great, wonderful, whoop-dee-friggin'-do. You all fucked up about it, doan' wanna lose a woman you tossed out. You jealous of her fucking Junior for the rest of her life. You got your priorities fuzzled, bossman."

"Goddammit, Rory, what are you talking about?"

He sighed. "How you so good on the air, dumb as you are? You worried about her sucking Junior's dick and she got a whole other worry than that."

He was right, and I was too blinded with hatred to see it. Chances were damn good she'd never walk down a church aisle because she'd be dead.

Stealing Jimmy James' money and drugs.

"Christ," I whispered. "What the hell am I going to do?"

Rory jammed his jeans into the dryer. "I don't like this laundromat. I got a cousin in Memphis owns a chain of 'em. They make this place look like shit. New machines, little vending machines give you soap, little carts to put your clothes in." He banged a machine with his hand. "Listen to that, bossman. These shitty machines don't even sing."

"Rory, I don't–"

"See," he explained. "You gotta hear the song inside. Get past the noise and the static, hear what's goin' on."

I frowned. "Uh, Rory … a little help here. I got a problem."

"Got some good radio where he lives. Hell, B.B. King was even on the radio there a couple of years ago … '49, I think."

I stood, angry at Rory. "Damn it, what the hell am I going to do about her?"

"Anything you do about her, you do about yourself, too, bossman."

I left him humming to the washing machines, singing along with the dryers. Fool was more worried about whether those machines sounded as good as his cousin's. Thanks for the help, Rory.

ℒ

At work the next day, I saw only Marilee. But every angle just gave me another view of Jimmy James. I couldn't seem to get around him.

"Play this," my manager said, tossing me a reel as he left.

"Telling me what to play now?" I asked.

He stopped. "And throwing your ass out if you don't."

With a scowl, I headed into the studio and pulled the records for my show.

Two and a half hours later, Marilee banged on the station door. I popped my head out of the studio, saw who it was, and went to open the door.

"Marilee," I said, "what are you doing here?"

Bloody and jittery, she stumbled in. "Lock the door, they're coming."

I twisted the key until it broke off in the lock, then hustled her to the small kitchen in the back of the station. "What happened?" I asked, wetting a towel and brushing it against her face as gently as I could.

She winced. "Jimmy James. He sent one of his goons to my place. Fucker wanted some pussy. Knocked me around. I managed to step on his balls with my heels."

On the air, my record ran out. "Shit. Hang on." I dashed to the studio, did a quick live break, and started a long jazz ditty.

In the kitchen, she sat at the small table, her face nearly cleaned of blood. Her make-up was smeared, as though she had put it on with a paintbrush.

I took her in my arms and hugged her tightly to stop the trembling. Her shakes rattled all the way through my bones. She began to cry. "Shhhh," I whispered. I pulled her head into my chest.

"I'm so scared, Barnes," she whispered.

I nodded. "Me, too."

Pulling her .38 from her purse, she handed it to me. "Help me, Barnes, please. I'll get straight, I promise. I been straight already."

I stared at the gun for a second, then shoved it in my pocket, and looked back at her. Cruel asshole that I was, I wanted to be certain she would keep that promise.

"Last night Junior gave me some Bennies. I palmed 'em." She stared at me proudly.

"Good," I said. That had been a hell of a step for her, I knew. To leave the safety and comfort of a pill haze; to clear her head enough to realize how bad things were. . . a big, dangerous, scary step. I was proud of her. "You did a good thing, Marilee. But it's not over, you know."

"Yeah." She'd been around junkies long enough. She knew the next few days would be the worst.

"But, if you want—" I hesitated.

Anything you do about her, you do about yourself, too, bossman.

Rory's words. As true as anything the man had ever said. I plunged ahead. "If you want, I'll be here."

She stared at me, still shaking, and her face was as close to happy as I had seen since before I threw her out. I kissed her tenderly, minding the cuts and bruises. She wrapped her arms around me. I expected her to move closer, to kiss my face and neck. I wanted her to unbutton my shirt and kiss my chest. I wanted her to take my pants off and love me.

Instead, she promised. "Straight," she said. "No booze, no pills."

I hugged her.

"Well, ain't that some shit?"

Jimmy James Cleave.

Startled, I shoved Marilee behind me. "How the fuck did you get in?"

He laughed. "My boy can sing and pick a lock. How 'bout that?"

I glanced at Junior. I had never seen a face so full of anger. My knees went weak. "I'm going to kill you," he said quietly.

"Fuck you," Marilee said from behind me.

Junior laughed and made a quick feint toward Marilee. At the same time, Jimmy James came at me. He pulled up short when the .38 barrel snapped up against his forehead. I cocked it and very obviously moved my finger inside the trigger guard.

"Barnes, Barnes," Jimmy James said quietly. "Don't do something stupid. Tell him, little girl."

"Don't you ever call me that again, you stupid fuck," Marilee said, her voice hard as gun steel. "You shitty puke, with your expensive boots and cars and those stupid damn cowboy hats. Don't you ever say shit to me again or I'll—"

"You'll what, sister? Have him shoot me? Neither of you got the balls. You're just lost little puppies. A couple of good, hard kicks is all you need."

I could have dropped him right then. Anger rose in me like a tidal wave and the other reason I didn't shoot him was because there was something better. I swiveled the gun at Junior's forehead. Jimmy James' face went white.

"Don't worry, Junior," I said. "I won't shoot your vocal cords. If you live, you can still sing."

"Drop that gun, you bastard." Jimmy James spoke very slowly. "Or you won't live long enough to regret this." His eyes bored into me.

"She's tired, Jimmy James," I said. "She's ready for another life."

"She's a junkie and a whore. There is no other life."

He was quick for a fat guy. He dashed across the room, slammed Marilee to the floor and was headed my direction almost before I realized it. Fear jabbed me suddenly like an uppercut and I fired.

As quickly as that, I became a murderer.

A bright red dot appeared on Junior's head. He looked surprised, then slumped to the floor. I jerked the gun around and jammed it in Jimmy James' face.

"Oh, you son of a bitch," said Jimmy James. "You killed my boy."

"Marilee, you okay?" I could hear her behind me, rattling around, getting to her feet, crying softly.

"Oh, Barnes, you killed him," she said.

I nodded. "Yeah." I pulled the hammer back. "And if you get in my face, I'll kill you, too, Jimmy James."

He stepped back. "I guess you do got some balls, boy."

"I guess," I agreed.

Inside, I had no balls at all. Inside, I was shaking, terrified of what I'd just done. The man I had killed had a daddy who bought cops the way I bought albums. I saw a surge of electricity in my future, one attached to a chair.

Marilee stared at me for a long time. Keeping the gun on Jimmy James, I looked at her, expecting to see the same empty eyes. But instead, they were alive, full of fear. They were scared, but it was something.

I knew then she'd keep her promise.

. . . got a cousin in Memphis . . .

The choice: run or stay. If I stayed, I'd have to kill Jimmy James. Did I want that much blood on my hands? If I ran, I had to outrun Jimmy James' cops and goons. And if I ran, I ran forever, no coming back. As long as Jimmy James was here, I'd be a marked man. Was I willing to give up everything for Marilee?

. . . hear the song inside . . . get past the noise and the static . . .

"Your car outside?" I asked Jimmy James.

"Fuck you."

I lowered the gun and pulled the trigger. His kneecap exploded.

He screamed.

"Try again. That Caddy outside?"

"I saw it, Barnes," Marilee said.

"Get in, I'll be there in a second."

"Barnes, I–"

I should have known. A man like Jimmy James Cleave doesn't go down easily. I turned my eyes just for a second, to give Marilee some confidence, and he was all over me. He slammed into me with a howl, and we fell backward into the sink. I dropped the gun just as I heard a giant crack and felt most of my world slip sideways.

"Barnes!"

When Jimmy James pulled back to hit me again, I fumbled and found a coffee mug decorated with the bright yellow KCCK logo. He stared at me only long enough to fall to the floor.

She woke up hours later. How do you feel?" I asked.

"Where are we?"

"Be in Kansas City in a little while."

"Pretty far from Denver."

I nodded.

"That's good, right?"

"Yeah."

She kissed me, sent her tongue deep into my mouth. It was warm and comforting and safe. I turned my head slightly so I could see the road. The shine of the headlights seemed to come out of the back of her skull. I reached an arm tightly around her. She was shaking.

"I need 'em, Barnes."

"No, you don't, Marilee. Those things are poison."

She nodded, white-lipped and scared. I turned on the radio — Chet Baker singing "You're My Thrill" — and when she began unbuttoning my shirt, I let her.

". . . you're my thrill . . ."

— leans over the bed, lips curled in a deliciously evil smile. Her breasts hang beautiful beneath her, the skin of her hips shines in the moonlight streaming through the bedroom window —

— make-up smeared, tear stains on her cheek —

". . . you do something to me . . ."

— her hands remove my shoes, socks, and pants. Next my shirt and my boxers. Her breasts are just above me. She touches me and them, lingering, inviting —

— impatiently slid my pants and shorts to the floorboard —

". . . you send chills right through me . . ."

— lips down my stomach and hips. She leaves a trail of smoldering kisses to my cock. She lays flat next to me, her feet near my face, and gently takes me into her mouth —

— hands shook as she went down over me. Her teeth rubbed along my shaft, and her head bobbed in agitated jerks —

". . . you're my thrill . . ."

Later, we stopped at a truck stop outside St. Louis.

"I — I'm glad you did — didn't kill him," she said.

I *had* killed someone. Had she forgotten?

"Jimmy James helped me, Barnes," she said, her voice edging into a whine. "When I was on the street, I didn't have anywhere to go."

"He raped you," I said, anger building in my bones.

"No, Junior raped me. Jimmy James pulled him off once."

"You were his whore."

She nodded.

I held her hand. "Listen, we left it all back there. Let's think about tomorrow, not yesterday, okay? I'm going to take a quick piss and grab some food, then we'll hit the road again. We'll be in Memphis before dawn."

She nodded, grabbed her purse, and climbed out of the car. I left her leaning on the hood and went to the can. When I came back a few minutes later, she was gone. Near where she had been standing, I found some pills spilled onto the asphalt. Reds, Bennies, goofballs. A fucking pharmacy.

Angry, I looked around and saw her climb into the cab of a big rig. "Marilee!"

For a split second, she looked my way. it was too dark to see her eyes, but I like to think that for that single moment, they were full and endless ... once in a lifetime eyes.

Then she climbed in, slammed the door, and the truck headed east, back toward Denver.

I jumped in the car and headed after the truck. I caught up with it quick, and drove behind it for almost ten miles, honking and flashing my lights to get the driver to stop.

He never did, and somewhere back in the confusion of my head, I heard Jimmy James. *Don't do something stupid ... won't live long enough to regret this.*

Angry, banging the steering wheel, I pulled over and stopped. I sat for a long time, wondering if she'd tell Jimmy James where to find me. Eventually, I turned the Caddy around, and headed for Memphis. I found Sarah Vaughn on the radio, singing about after-hours ghosts, and snapped it off.

Trey R. Barker's fiction, non-fiction, and poetry has appeared in a variety of publications, including *100 Clever Little Cat Crimes*, *Whitley Streiber's Aliens* (with Edward Bryant), *Terminal Fright*, *Midsummer Night's Terror*, *Epitaph*, *Night Terrors*, *Talebones*, *Cemetery Dance*, and many others. His written work for the stage includes adaptations of Charles Dickens' *A Christmas Carol*, and Agatha Christie's *The Mysterious Affair at Syles*, and an original one-man show based on the life of Edgar Allan Poe. Barker is also a musician with an affinity for African percussion and southern blues. He lives in Colorado with his wife LuAnn and three Canine-Americans.

Girls Are a Nuisance

by Alison Tyler

It was dusk. Or dawn. I'm not sure. I always get those two confused. Especially when I've been drinking. And I've been drinking, all right. For days now. Or nights. Depending on how you look at life, on whether you prefer moonlight to the glare of the sun. Lately, I've been a bit of a vampire.

The phone rang awhile ago, kept on ringing, then politely gave up. Then my head started to pound. Or was it the door?

"Katrina!" a voice shouted. "Katrina Loveless!"

"At your service," I mumbled, forgetting momentarily that it helps to open your mouth when you speak. Slowly, I untangled myself from the quilt, pushed up from the sofa, and stumbled toward the door. I honed in on the insistent knocking and as I finally reached the heavy wood barrier, the pounding stopped. I turned the knob. Outside stood my ex-husband, his suit disheveled, his face flushed.

"I need your help," he said, pushing past me and into the living room of the apartment we used to share. The place wasn't quite the same as when he'd left. But what stays the same in this topsy-turvy world?

"Kat..." he said, softly, "what's happened to you?"

A red light bulb glowed above our heads. A whip lay coiled by the foot of the sofa. Handcuffs were attached to the rack on the far wall. Empty bottles littered the floor, glistening beneath the crimson light. I caught sight of myself in the mirror. My black hair fell in loops and swirls past my shoulders. My eyes were puffy, the skin on my face so pale you could see the fine spider webs of veins beneath the surface.

"Happened?" I asked, falling back on the sofa and reaching beneath it for a bottle. The first was empty. The second held a drop, which I licked from the neck as if I were dying of thirst. The third was half full. You can tell I'm an optimist.

"What's up with the..." he waved his hands, as if hoping it would all go away, "...the paraphernalia."

"Nothing's up with it," I said, taking a swig. "If you look closely you'll see that everything's dusty."

"Where's Sandrine?" he asked next. This boy had too many questions and I didn't have enough answers. I shrugged.

He walked over to the torture wall and looked into the stand filled with bone-handled canes, a riding crop, a wooden walking stick. He moved closer and saw the fine spray of blood that patterned the wallpaper. He grimaced, but not because he didn't like it.

"She left me," I told him, finally. "A dick like you should have guessed that."

He ignored my dig. "Have you been working?"

I shook my head.

"You've been sitting on the sofa drinking... for how long?"

I could answer that one. "Days or nights," I said. "Depending on how you..."

He cut me off. "What ever happened to the Katrina I knew? The Katrina Loveless who always catches her man?"

"Didn't you hear? Front-page headline: Katrina Loveless Loses Her Girl."

"You're not a quitter, Kat."

I took another swig and watched as he inspected the different S & M devices. Russell has always been a purist. He doesn't stoop to toys or tools. He uses whatever is within his reach. While I watched, his fingers moved deftly over the handle of one cane. He stroked the wallpaper where I'd last pressed my face and sobbed.

"Broken hearts mend," he said, as if that made any difference. Or any sense.

"You should write fortunes for the Chinese place over in Hollywood. 'Good news will come by mail.' 'A forgotten friend will reappear.' 'Your ex-husband will come to your home and bother you.'"

"I'm serious. You'll get over her. You'll forget she existed. You'll heal."

"Not this time. I'm not giving it a chance. It's over. Everything is over."

"What do you mean?"

"I'm not feeling again. I am not even going to try. No more men. No more women. No more nothing."

He moved to my side, put his arms around me. I think he expected me to cry on his shoulder. He should have remembered what it takes to make me cry. I shoved him away, stalked down the hallway to my bedroom. I hadn't been in it since Sandrine left, and as I pushed open the door I got a whiff of her perfume. It made me dizzy with need.

He followed me down the hall. I didn't want him there. I stumbled as I tried to open my top dresser drawer. When I reached my hand inside, Russell came forward and grabbed my wrist, twisting it cruelly so I dropped what was in my grasp. He thought I was going for my gun, but when he reached in, he found the note.

"A Dear John letter?" he asked.

"Dear Katrina..." I started. I had the thing memorized by now. It made me sick, but knowing the words by heart was somehow comforting. I said them to myself as a sort of prayer each time I opened a new bottle.

Russell glanced at the note, at the pretty cursive writing, then paused and read it carefully from top to bottom. "She went back to her ex?" he asked.

"Speak English long?"

"I know that's what it *says,* but is that what *happened?*"

I shrugged and sat on the edge of my bed. "It's all I know."

"And you call yourself a detective?" he asked.

"No, you call me a detective. I'm retired. I don't work no more."

"How will you live?"

I opened my eyes as wide as they would go and stared at him. Didn't he get it yet? Had I really been married for seven years to someone this dense?

"Oh," he said, shaking his head. "You're not planning on living through this."

"Girls," I said forcefully, "are a nuisance. But this one, this special girl, was someone I wanted to be with forever. I thought we were perfect. I thought we had it made." I stood and paced, to the dresser and back again.

"No one's perfect, Kat," he came forward and tried to hold me. I kneed him where I knew it would hurt. He crumpled onto my bed.

"I know that, asshole," I said, remembering somewhere deep in my head that I can be a violent drunk and reveling in that fact. "I know that. But I thought we were."

He stared at me through pain-filled eyes. "So," he hissed. "You're gonna end it. But slowly, right? Why not take your gun and do a little mouth-to-mouth if you want it over so bad."

"Slow and steady wins the race," I spat over my shoulder, leaving the room to get my bottle. It was empty — again. I hate when that happens. I went into the kitchen where I had two full boxes of whiskey. The store on the corner delivers. Russell followed me, his steps heavy.

"You're not going to die of a broken heart," he said. "All you need is a little wake-up call."

He took the bottle from my hand and put it on the table, then grabbed me by the wrist and dragged me into the living room.

"What are you going to do?" I asked, "Fuck me better?"

"Such a dirty mouth," he sneered. "You talk to your mother with that mouth?"

"I sucked your cock with this mouth," I reminded him and he slapped me, hard enough to send me back onto the couch. Without changing his expression, he reached for me again and quick-stepped me to the torture wall. I was bound before I truly knew what was happening. Russell left me alone long enough to go back to the kitchen for scissors, and while I cussed him out he cut my robe off. The faded blue plaid hung in tatters from my naked body.

"You're still amazing," he said, stepping back to appreciate me. "You've got the most gorgeous ass."

I stayed quiet, listening as he rummaged through the stand of weapons. I heard the wood and bone clacking together, and then heard him grunt as he found what he was looking for. It was a bamboo cane. I knew it the instant it connected with my skin. He hit me with it once, as a way of introduction, and then let a series of blows rain down on my ass and thighs. The power behind the strokes left me breathless.

Sandrine had been a capable dom. Russell was born with the hot wire of a sadist alive in his soul.

"Feel that?" he asked, stopping for a second to press his palm against my heated flesh. "Waking up yet?"

I didn't respond. My mind was reeling. Behind my closed eyes, pictures rose like soap bubbles, bursting with each blow of the cane. Me and Sandrine together, in a clinch. The two of us, head to tail on a blanket at the beach. Her hands in my hair when she kissed me. The feeling of surrender as she locked my wrists into the cuffs. The rough flick of her tongue against my clit when I thought I would die if she didn't let me come.

"How many, Kat? How many strokes until I reach your limit? Until I break it?"

I pressed my cheek against the wall and looked into the mirror over the mantle. I could see Russell as he took off his suit coat and tossed it on the sofa, stretching his arms, getting himself nice and limber. He said, "Didn't she make you count? She must have. You know the secret number."

Fuck him for being a detective. I remained silent.

"Fine," he said, "we'll find out ourselves. It will be like a case that we're trying to solve. Together. The way we used to. The Case of the Pain-Deprived Female Dick. How's that sound, Kat?"

I bit my lower lip and waited. He stood back, raised the cane high, and slammed into me. "One," he said. I closed my eyes. He raised it up again, lined a blow directly beneath the previous. I had a feeling he was going to stripe me from head to toe.

I had a feeling I was going to like it.

The third blow landed on the roundest part of my ass. The fourth was right beneath it, a white-hot poker pressed into my flesh. The fifth wrung a sigh from my lips. The sixth, a moan. I promised myself I would not tell him to stop. But somehow, at some point, my hips began their indecent pounding against the wall. They beat out a staccato rhythm that relied entirely on the flick of his wrist and the track of the bamboo cane. It was a magic wand in his hand. He waved it and made me forget why I was sad. Why I'd been drinking. Who Sandrine was or what we had meant to each other. The pain obliterated everything else. Damn Russell for knowing me so well.

He said, "Pretty thing, I've always liked the way you look when you're hurting. Your eyes take on this hot glow, like a brush fire reflected in the ocean off Malibu. Your lips part hungrily. You look like you want it."

"Want...."

"It," he said, opening his slacks, pressing his cock against my throbbing flesh. "Do you want it, Katrina? Do you?"

"You're a P.I.," I hissed, "a private dick. Find out for yourself."

He dug his fingers into my shoulders and gritted his teeth. His cock went between my legs, knowing the familiar route by heart. Years don't erase that type of memory. He found my wetness, slippery, indecent. He knew he was right, thought he'd solved this case. He fucked me hard, pressing my face against the wall with his own, cheek to cheek, our eyes open and staring at our reflections.

"Loveless and Loveless," he said, never stopping the ride. "Together again." The red light cast a hellish glow over our bodies. The rhythm of his cock spoke a language inside me. It was a key that unlocked doors and let memories free. I responded to his touch as I always had, gripping him, swallowing him up. I knew each step, each frame, a second before it happened. He was brutal. As always. And I came from the pain — from the slapping of his body against my bruised flesh.

Then it was over, and he was pulling out, shooting over my welts, rubbing his come in good with his hand. He unchained me, waited for me to turn around. I pushed past him and went to the hall closet, getting another robe out, sliding into it and tying the belt around my slender waist.

"Better?" he asked, just like a man.

"You can leave now," I told him. "Case closed."

"But..."

"Leave," I repeated, and something in my voice made him realize I meant it. He picked up his jacket.

"I don't understand you," he said, "I'll never understand you."

"For a gumshoe, you sure are thick," I told him as I undid the chain. "Hearts mend, but they take time. Drinking binges happen, but they end. Women have moments of weakness and open themselves up to their exes. And life goes on."

Russell put his hat on his head and squared his shoulders in that manly way of his. As he pushed past me to get out the door, he said, "You know, you were right about one thing, Katrina."

"Yeah?" I couldn't wait.

"Girls sure as hell are a nuisance."

I smiled to myself as I locked the door behind him. It was late. Or early. Depending on how you look at things. On how you look at life.

I looked at the bottle. It was most definitely time for another drink.

Alison Tyler is a shy girl with a dirty mind. She is the author of several erotic books, including *Venus Online*, *Dark Room*, *Bondage on a Budget*, and the S&M mystery *Dial "L" for Loveless*. Her stories have appeared in *Playgirl*, *Midsummer Night's Dreams*, *Sex Toy Tales*, *The Unmade Bed*, and *Batteries Not Included*. "Girls Are a Nuisance" borrows its title from the Chandler short piece "Pearls are a Nuisance."

Private Dick

by Sukie de la Croix

Chicago can be a cold, lonely town, but Chicago is my kind of town. A toddlin' town. The name's Dick Fallus, though you may know me better as Dick Fallus, Private Eye. My job? To put right all those things that somewhere along the line got put wrong. I remember the case that paddled me out of shit creek with the taxman ... The Mysterious Case of the Missing Brit. *Huh! What a story that was!*

April 1. It was a Wednesday. I remember, I was killing some time, staring out the window, watching bags of stiffs being wheeled into St. Jude's Chapel of Rest, on the other side of the street. A light morning mist had given way to sheets of rain. Sheets so ugly, even K-Mart wouldn't stock them. Suddenly I heard a noise, and I turned to see Tommy Truetart, my private secretary, bringing in my lunch. A real man's lunch: a slice of vegetarian quiche, and a container of tofu salad from the Happy Bean Sprout Cafe.

"Gee boss," purred Tommy, in his trademark Lauren Bacall growl, "It's pissing down out there!" Tommy shook the drips from his no-frills, no nonsense, pink umbrella, and hung it on a hook by his desk.

There was a knock at the door. It opened slowly and in walked a dish. No, this was no Tupperware cereal bowl, but a cute blond guy, with more meat in his pants than a kosher deli window display. I stared at the kid's crotch, reached for the veggie quiche and salad, and dropped it into the trash. Suddenly I was feeling carnivorous.

"Good afternoon, Mr. Fallus." The dish was a Brit.

"Nice aftershave," I said, "What's it called?"

"Tearoom Romance," he answered, "I bought it at Bloomingdale's."

"Yeah! Thought I recognized it ..."

" ... You been out shopping again?" hissed Tommy. He could smell another man on my breath from 50 paces. It was uncanny.

The blonde shot him a glance, then dug deep into his pants and pulled out a wad of bills. Tommy stared the blonde straight in the eyes. "Is that Wells Fargo Bank in your pocket, or are you just pleased to see me?"

Huh! What a line! But the blond kid was a jumping cat, living off the tit ... smooth! He peeled a couple of C-notes from the roll and handed them to Tommy. "Here you go, sweetie, now toddle off and buy yourself something nice. I need to talk to Mr. Fallus alone."

Tommy snatched the money in his red varnished claws, lifted his black leather mini-skirt and slipped the crisp notes into the top of his stockings. "Just remember, boss, you owe me one."

Tommy headed out the door, and the blonde unzipped his briefcase, pulled out a green velvet drawstring purse and dropped it onto my desk. "Do you know what this is, Mr. Fallus?"

I opened the purse and looked inside. "Sure I know what it is. It's a butt-plug."

"Correct, Mr. Fallus. But it's not just any old butt-plug. It's Leonardo da Vinci's prototype Renaissance butt-plug."

"Da Vinci, huh! Wasn't he the old guy who painted *The Last Supper at the Jerusalem Hard Rock Cafe*? The one with the coven of Dead Heads oiling their tonsils on bottles of *Sangre de Cristo?"*

"That's right, Mr. Fallus. He also invented the helicopter, canal locks, snow-globes, leg-warmers...."

"...Whoopee cushions," I chipped in, just to show the kid I was no dumb-fuck. "And nodding dog heads, and didn't he write ... what was the name of that book?"

"*How To Host the Perfect Fondue Party*. That was him. He also invented the pubic wig, the fishnet umbrella, the male tampon, the stiletto sock, and the butt-plug. What you have in your hands, Mr. Fallus, is Da Vinci's prototype butt-plug. It belongs to my father...." The kid turned away and began to sob.

I hate to see a grown man cry. I don't mind when their eyes water a bit, but I hate to see them cry. "Hey, kid!" I said, "Just tell me what's up!"

The kid dabbed his eyes with an eggshell-blue handkerchief. I knew then that he blew both ways. "My father would never trust it to a safe-deposit box. He kept the butt-plug hidden about his person at all times, if you catch my drift. Two days ago I found the butt-plug on the table next to his bed. I realized straight away that something was wrong. And ... and Daddy's disappeared, Mr. Fallus. Gone! And nobody knows where he is."

"Hey, kid, you're telling me all this, but I don't even know your name."

"Binky-Raffles. Sebastian Binky-Raffles."

"Binky-Raffles! Isn't your old man Benjamin Binky-Raffles, the guy who made a packet out of chocolate-chip cookies?"

"That's him! Do you know him, Mr. Fallus?"

"No, I never met the guy, but I read about him in the gossip columns. Mixed with all the right people. Hollywood stars, the Sicilian set ... wasn't he bumping pussies with Scar Face 'Sissy' Petrocelli once? It don't matter. Anyone who can shove a kazoo up his butthole and play "Onward Christian Soldiers" at a Kennedy party is okay with me! But you didn't come here to talk about your pop's party piece. You want me to find him, right?"

"I'll do anything to get him back. Anything!" The kid dropped to his knees and buried his face in my lap. *Zzziipp!* "Anything, Mr. Fallus! *(Slurp!)* Please help me find *(Slurp!)* my father." I checked the calendar on the wall — all this, and it wasn't even my birthday.

The kid seemed pretty steamed up about his pop. Call me a sucker, but I'm a sucker for a man who's a sucker for a man. I opened the desk drawer, unscrewed the lid of my little brown bottle, and took a long sniff . "Sure, I'll help you," I said, "But I need some background. Take your time. No rush."

While the kid puffed away on my Pink Havana, I picked up the butt-plug and waved it under my nose. "Mmm ... Hey kid! There's something about this butt-plug that doesn't smell quite right."

Sometime later, I tossed the Kleenex into the trash, zipped up, and got to thinking about Tommy Truetart. Most guys you fuck and forget, but with Tommy it's different. After Tommy, you fuck another guy and you still think about Tommy. What a guy!

"Mr. Fallus!" The kid broke into my thoughts. The truth was, I'd forgotten he was there. Tommy does that to a guy. Tommy does that to a lot of guys. "Mr. Fallus, about my father ..."

" ... Sorry kid, I was just thinking about the butt-plug." So I lied. If people stopped lying I'd be out of a job. "So why come to me?" I asked. "Why don't you go to the cops? They deal with this kind of stuff."

"Oh, I couldn't do that! Think of the newspapers! We couldn't possibly have a scandal in the family. We're British, you see, and we don't like to make a fuss about things. If the press got a whiff of the business with my father's butt-plug, our cookie empire would crumble."

The kid's speech struck home. I remember when my own pop went AWOL with a transvestite cocktail waitress from Fort Wayne, Indiana. They hushed that one up. A Baptist minister can get a bad name for himself in a small American town, especially when he's playing around with a guy who looks like Oprah Winfrey.

"Okay!" I said, "So tell me a little about your father. Does he live alone?"

"Yes, he does — oh, except for Jesus José Augustín Maximiliano Farabundo Hernández Martínez Martí Duarte, his manservant."

"Quite a mouthful," I said.

"I wouldn't know, Mr. Fallus. I was brought up never to have oral sex with the staff. My parents were very strict about that kind of thing."

Yeah, yeah, yeah! I'd heard that one before. That's one thing I never figured out about the Brits; up front they're a bunch of slimy-faced snoots, but you don't hear those Dukes and Earls complaining when they've got nine inches of gardener shoved up their glory holes.

"Tell me something about this Jesus José ... er ... this Hispanic guy."

"Not much to tell. He's Mexican. He's been my father's manservant for three years now. On the night my father disappeared, Jesus José Augustín Maximiliano Farabundo Hernández Martínez Martí Duarte was out at his aerobics class. Oh, I nearly forgot ... he's only got one leg."

There was something about a one-legged Mexican manservant jitterbugging with the housewives at the local church hall that didn't quite ring true. I let the matter drop, but I had a hunch it would crop up again somewhere along the line.

"So, apart from the Mexican guy, can you think of anyone else who might know something about your pop's disappearance?"

"He knows a lot of people, but close friends? There is one. And that's another reason I want discretion. He's been seeing a lot of Miss Mimi La Trobe. She's a singer down at the Krazy Kat Kabaret. I'm afraid she's one of those trampy types. You know the kind — all fur coat and no knickers."

"And what about your mother? Where does she fit into all this?"

The kid's eyes misted over again. "I'm afraid my mother is dead, Mr. Fallus. She died last year, in a beauty parlor accident. Her head exploded under a hair dryer."

"Sorry to hear that. That's a tragic story."

I talked with the kid some more, and bit by bit I began to form a picture: priceless butt-plugs ... trampy cabaret singers ... an exploding mom; I could see the Binky-Raffles clan were a pretty normal, run-of-the-mill, nuclear family. But a whole bunch of questions were left unanswered: Why did Benjamin Binky-Raffles use Leonardo da Vinci's prototype Renaissance butt-plug, when he could have bought a new one for twenty bucks? What did the old guy see in Mimi La Trobe, a used-up piece of white trash, when he could have bought a new one for twenty bucks? And ... what kind of a God allows a woman to get rubbed out in the middle of a perm? It kind of gives you the creeps just thinking about it.

Soon after the kid left the office, Tommy returned, loaded down with shopping bags. "Gee boss! I got real lucky at Victoria's Secret. They had a sale on panties.... " Tommy sniffed the air and peered into the trash can at the wadded-up tissue. "I see you got lucky, too!"

"Quit flapping your gums, babe. It was nothing. Now drop those panties. We've got an appointment tonight with a songbird down at the Krazy Kat Kabaret, and with a little luck that songbird just might sing."

When you grow up in a one-fuck town like Fort Wayne, Indiana, the bright lights of the big city can look real pretty at night. And at the sleazy end of the strip, where angels, cops, and pizza delivery boys fear to tread, it can get real hot and sexy. That's why Chicago is my kind of town: the kind of town where a guy can get a hard-on and cream his jeans just walking to the store to buy a carton of milk.

Outside of the Krazy Kat Kabaret, Tommy stopped, drained his cigarette, then propelled his butt up into the night sky. "Hey, boss!" he said, "That Binky-Raffles kid was right about this place. It's a dump."

Inside the club, we ordered a couple of beers, then sat ourselves down near the front of the stage. On the next table, a couple of drunks had passed out cold, and propping up the bar, some guy playing pocket pool in pinstripe pants, was making goo goo eyes at Tommy. Like everyone else in this town, the guy was horny enough to screw the ass off a rattlesnake.

The show opened with a couple of chicks jiggling their jugglies and flashing their husbands' supper at the audience. This was followed by another chick, who paraded around the tables picking up coins with her tight-spot, then spitting them out into a can, all the time singing "Brother, Can You Spare A Dime?" When the stripping hermaphrodite hit the stage — I ain't never seen that kind of geography on a human being before — the joint started filling up. Every hustler, pimp, pusher, and lawyer in town was there — gab gab gab gab— but when a short guy in a white suit introduced Miss Mimi La Trobe, a hush fell over the room.

Oh, man, was she somethin' else! Tits and tushes like watermelons, all packed into a figure-hugging red-sequined dress, slit to the waist. Mimi ran her hands over the contours of her body, then pressed her lips to the microphone like it was the last cock on the planet.

"I wrote this little blues song myself," she said, "I hope you like it. It's called "I've Got The Hungriest Pussy In Town."

I've got a very friendly pussy
She smiles at everyone she meets
She's fluffy, and warm, and cuddly
But boy oh boy does she like her pussy treats

And that's the one bad thing about my pussy
The one thing that drags me down
Is that my pussy likes to eat, and eat, and eat
I've got the hungriest pussy in town

You see, I used to feed my pussy twice a day
Meat and a dish full of cream
But then she wanted more and more, and more
Her desire to masticate was reaching extremes

Then one day I solved the problem
The solution just came my way
How to keep my pussy satisfied
How to keep my pussy's hunger at bay

I was sitting all alone one night
My pussy curled up between my legs
When suddenly she started to moan
And then she started to beg

So I went out into the kitchen
Thinking there was pussy food to spare
I pulled open the cupboard,
... Oh dear, it was Old Mother Hubbard
For all of the shelves were bare

What was I supposed to do?
A hungry pussy, and I was clean out of meat
So I opened up the window,
And I shouted into the street

"Can anybody out there feed my pussy?
She's beginning to bring me down
My pussy likes to eat, large quantities of meat
I've got the hungriest pussy in town"

Well, there was a shipload of sailors in the street
They formed an orderly line outside my door
And they came in one by one and fed my pussy
'Til my pussy wasn't hungry anymore

So boys and girls at the Krazy Kat Kabaret
If your pussy purrs for cream
Just open up the window
Lean out into the street
And scream and scream and scream

"Can anybody out there feed my pussy?
Perhaps a soldier, or a sailor
Or even a Forest Ranger
My pussy relies on the kindness of strangers

Yes, my pussy likes to eat
Large quantities of meat
I've got the hungriest pussy in town

Mimi ended the song with a low tiger's growl, and the crowd erupted into wolf-whistles and cheers. When the show was over, I slipped backstage with Tommy, and found Mimi alone in her dressing room. "Oh!" she gasped, as we knocked and entered, "Who are you?"

"Didn't mean to scare you, Miss La Trobe," I said, dropping into a chair, "The name's Dick Fallus, and this is my private secretary, Tommy Truetart ... "

"Dick Fallus!" said Mimi, "*The* Dick Fallus? The Dick Fallus who solved *The Mysterious Case of the Anorexic Nun and The Eyebrow Pencil?*"

"That's me, babe." She'd heard about the pill-popping Sister Ejaculata of the Misconception. Geez! Now that was a weird case ... I'll tell you about it sometime.

"Well, I guess I'm honored, Mr. Fallus. And am I suspected of a serious crime?" She laughed.

I could see what the old guy saw in her. She was cute. But tough. "I'll come straight to the point, Miss La Trobe. According to my information, you've been rubbing bellies with Benjamin Binky-Raffles, so you might as well come clean about it."

The songbird threw back her head and laughed again, "Sure I know Benjy, but what's it got to do with you?"

"Maybe it's got a lot to do with me. Let's just say that I'm curious about it."

"Okay. He comes around here sometimes after the show. Picks me up, we go to a restaurant ... have a few drinks, have a few laughs, but it's not what you think."

"How do you know what I think?"

"Cuz you're *people*. You may be a Big Shot in this town, Mr. Dick-fucking-Fallus, but you're *people* just like everybody else. And *people* all think the same."

"So tell me about it."

"People are calling me a gold digger, a whore. But I'm not after his money, Mr. Fallus. I'm a woman of independent means. I'm a star! And one day, when I'm hosting my own TV talk show, those bitches are gonna regret what they said about me. The truth is that I love Benjy, and one day I'm gonna marry him."

"Like he loved his wife, you mean — before her head blew off in the hair salon?"

Mimi stiffened. I could see she was getting tired of me already. "So what's the BFD? She got herself what any girl wants. She got to end her days in a beauty parlor — like she ain't the first woman to lose her head over a bad perm. All I know is this: she's out of the picture, and I've ... I've had a hard life. Alcoholic parents, sold into the white slave trade at the age of 14, where I lived in the desert with Bedouin tribesman, who kept me in a cage for three years, beat me senseless every day, and fed me dung beetles—"

"Spare me the sob story."

"Mr. Fallus, I deserve a little bit of happiness, and Benjy makes me happy."

"Then perhaps you can tell me where he is."

"How the hell would I know?" The songbird was losing her patience. "I don't go around with my fist up his ass, calling him Lambchop. He's a man, Mr. Fallus, he's not a puppet. Try calling his office."

Whoo-whee! This girl had a mouth on her.

"He's not in his office," I said. "In fact, he's done a bunko — 'el disappear-o, hey, presto!' — vanishing act."

"What do you mean, he's disappeared?"

"Gone, upped and fled the nest, leaving Leonardo Da Vinci's prototype Renaissance butt-plug behind."

Mimi fell back against the wall, "He left his butt-plug behind?"

"Left it on the table next to the bed."

"But ... but he loved that butt-plug, Mr. Fallus. He never went anywhere without it. Something's wrong. He must be in trouble."

"Sure looks that way. His son came to my office—"

"Sebastian! That low-life, motherfuckin' piece of shit. I should have guessed he was involved in this. If he's laid one finger on my Benjy, I'll kick his balls into three different states, that cocksucking douchebag. That little cunt is so low, he could look up a snake's asshole and think it's the North Star."

Oh, man! I've seen a lot of horrible things in my time, but there's nothing so ugly as a lounge singer losing her rag over a man. I waited until Mimi's batteries ran down.

"So I guess you don't like the guy, right?"

" ... that fucking scumsucking dickhead sonofabitch ..."

I guess her mouth was plugged into a wall socket somewhere.

The next morning, I arrived late at the office to find Tommy reading one of those corny romance novels — *Love Down Under*, by Kay Duncible — a story of hot romance in the cold corridors of a New Zealand psychiatric hospital:

> *Sandra, a young nurse, is torn between the love of two doctors: Philip, the tall dark handsome psychologist whose life hangs in the balance after a near fatal accident with an electric lawn-mower, and her true love, Johnny, the tall blond handsome electro-convulsive therapist, who is more interested in his collection of antique oriental ironing boards than he is in her. Will Sandra marry Philip, and spend the rest of her life nursing a man with no testicles and a morbid fear of lawns? Or will she disguise herself as an 18th century Manchurian trouser press to attract the attention of her true love, the indifferent Johnny?*

Tommy read the last page, wiped a tear from his eye, then tossed the book into the trash, where it belonged. "So, boss, do you think Mimi La Trobe is stringing this Binky-Raffles guy along?"

"I don't know. Our little songbird's a tough one all right, but I get the feeling she's really fond of the old guy."

"So where do we go from here?"

"I think it's time we paid a visit to the Marcel Duchamp Beauty Salon, the scene of Cynthia Binky-Raffles' final perm."

"But what does she have to do with the old guy disappearing?"

"Nothing. I just thought we'd check out their prices on facials."

At the snooty Marcel Duchamp Beauty Salon, a creepy-looking guy with a D.A. rushed up to us with open arms; he was trying to hustle us back out the door. In the glitzy, ritzy world of glamour, we were about as welcome as a fart in a spacesuit.

"My name's Grayson," announced the D.A., as if somebody cared, "And I'm the manager of this establishment. I think you've come to the wrong place, gentlemen. Now, if you would kindly allow me to show you the door."

"Don't bother yourself," hissed Tommy, "We saw it on the way in."

"Nice door," I added, "We like it. We like it, don't we, Tommy?"

"We sure do."

"But you don't understand," pleaded Grayson, "We have a reputation here ..."

"Yeah, yeah, yeah. My name's Fallus. Dick Fallus, Private Eye, and this is my private secretary, Tommy Truetart. We're making some enquiries into the death of Cynthia Binky-Raffles."

"But that was over a year ago!"

"The sooner you tell us about it, the sooner we drag our sorry asses out of here. So cut a long story short."

Grayson sighed. "Cynthia was one of our regular customers. She came here once a week for a 'touch-up' — manicure, pedicure, the works."

"So it was a spackle-and-paint job, huh? She was no spring chicken, then?"

"Eighty-four years old. Anyway, she was only under the dryer for ten minutes or so, when suddenly there was a loud popping sound and her ears blew off. One landed in the cash register and the other was eaten by a Shi Tzu belonging to one of my other clients."

"Was there an autopsy?"

"Autopsy? No, one of the paramedics put his fingers down the dog's throat, and—"

"Not the dog! I'm talking about the woman! Was there an autopsy?" Dumb! This guy was so dumb he could lose a chess game to a Pop-Tart.

"No, there was no autopsy. Why would there be? The police said it was a simple case of spontaneous combustion. One minute she was sitting there, tightening her bra strap and reading Vanity Fair, and the next — POP! Then POOF! We were all running for the fire extinguishers." Grayson was interrupted by the phone ringing. "Yes, he's here. Mr. Fallus, it's for you."

"Who could that be?" said Tommy, "Nobody knows we're here."

I took the phone. "Uh-huh! ... Uh-huh! ... Uh-huh! ... Oh, really! ... Uh-huh!" The caller hung up. "Tommy, go back to the office and wait for me there."

"Where are you going, boss?"

"Something's cropped up."

As I stepped out of the elevator, two goons were waiting for me.

It was close to midnight when I got back to the office. Tommy was still there. "I was beginning to worry about you, boss. Thought maybe you'd got yourself into some kind of trouble."

"Just wrapping up some unfinished business," I said, *The Mysterious Case of the Missing Brit.* It's over and done with. They pulled Benjamin Binky-Raffles out of the river this morning. They say it was suicide."

"Suicide! But he had everything going for him! He had money, a dead wife, a sleazy fuck on the side, a one-legged Mexican manservant, a beautiful cocksucker for a son, and Leonardo Da Vinci's prototype Renaissance butt-plug stuffed up his ass all day long — what more could a guy want?"

"Who knows why people do that kind of stuff?"

"So who were those two guys?"

"What two guys?"

"The two guys who were following us. The two guys who knew exactly where we were. The two guys you spoke to on the phone at the snooty beauty parlor. The two guys you met outside. I was watching from the window."

" ... Er ... They were cops," I said, "Yeah, cops."

"Cops, huh?"

I knew Tommy wasn't buying this story, but I'd signed a big bucks contract with some very influential people, and I wasn't about to unbutton my lip to anyone.

Tommy calmly opened his purse, pulled out a pistol, and pointed it in my direction. "I'm sorry to do this, Dick, I really am, but my people need to know exactly what happened to Benjamin Binky-Raffles. And don't give me that bullshit about the old guy feeding himself to the fishes."

I fell back against the wall. I'd never seen Tommy like this before. "What are you doing?" I said, then trying to laugh, "This is a joke ... it's a joke, right?"

"Yeah, that's right, Dick ... it's a joke, and you're staring down the barrel of the punch line. Only it's not funny, is it?"

"So you sold out, Tommy. Sold out to the Sicilian boys ... I never thought you'd do it. Seems to me like everybody's got their price."

"Cut the crap, drop your pants, and bend over the desk."

"So now you want romance. You've got a nerve, Tommy. You want one more fuck before you blow me away. Don't you think that's kinda sick?"

Tommy sneered, "Yeah! It's kinda sick, Dick, but it looks to me like you got no choice."

I did what he said. I dropped my pants and bent over the desk. I figured I only had one chance of getting the gun away from him: when his defenses were down, while he was shooting his load. But instead of nine inches of meat in the seat, I got the barrel of the gun shoved up my gazoo.

"You move and I'll blow your fucking ass off!" spat Tommy.

"Hey! Calm down," I said.

"Okay Mr. Big Shot Fallus, spill the beans ... and then I might, I just might let you go." Tommy cocked the hammer.

I yelled out, "Okay, okay! The two guys were agents of the British Government — oh, Tommy, that hurts! Ease up a bit ... that hurts so bad...." Tommy pulled the gun out slightly. "They bumped the old guy off, and they wanted us off their backs. Benjamin Binky-Raffles was the illegitimate son of some royal person ... I don't know who. The old King of England, or something, and the old guy's mother, some two-bit actress, got paid big bucks to hush up and leave the country. That's how come he's in the States."

"And the money got invested in the cookie business, right?"

"Uh-huh! Well, the mother died a couple of years back, and Benjamin was going through her shit, and found out he was really the heir to the British throne."

"So the old sourpuss they got over there now, she's a fake, right?"

"Right! So the old guy starts wondering. Maybe he should get what rightfully belongs to him, and he tells his wife. Of course, she wants in on it — Queen of England, that's a big thing for a girl from Texas. And so they contact the right people, only they're the wrong people, because the last thing the Brits need is another Royal scandal. And so the wife gets wasted first. They give her these dynamite earrings."

"Dynamite? Don't you mean 'diamante?'"

"No, I mean dynamite, so when she adjusts her bra strap they detonate — oh, Tommy! That hurts so bad—"

"Keep talking!"

"Then the old guy starts getting sentimental over Mimi La Trobe, and so they waste him as well, just to shut him up. Then we come along."

"So how much did they pay you to keep your mouth shut?"

"$100,000. That's it, I've told you everything. I don't know who you're working for, Tommy, and I don't want to know. But I'll give them the money. I don't care if it's the mob, a Colombian drug cartel, or the Barbie Liberation Organization — just —"

Tommy laughed. "Thanks for the information, boss, and now, I'm sorry to say, it's time for you to say bye-bye."

I heard the gun go off, and I slumped forward onto the desk, as wave upon wave of ecstasy shot through my body. "Oh, Tommy," I gasped, "I love it when you play rough with me ..."

Tommy leaned over and kissed the back of my neck, "Honey, you can never keep a secret from me," he purred, then pulled the trigger again and again and again.

"Ohhhh, ohhhh, Tommy," I sighed, "That Jell-O enema gun we got at the Sexarama Boutique was the best thing we ever bought. I mean ... Oh, man! ... I mean ... THE BEST!!"

Sukie de la Croix was born in Bath, England in 1951. He is an internationally published journalist and columnist, has published a book of short stories, written for stand-up comedians, and regularly reads his work in cafés and beatnik bars. He lives — mostly — in Chicago, with his lover, two lesbian dogs, and enough Barbie dolls to choke Godzilla. His ambition is to be the first woman on Venus.

Hollywood Black

by Alex S. Johnson

I'm 34 years old and have no regrets. My career is blooming. I have a condo in the heart of old Hollywood and a rooftop pool where I float on my back on an inner tube, wearing Bermuda shorts and a ridiculous Hawaiian shirt.

Why strive to be original when the ugliest fashions of the recent past can become the trendiest gear of the moment? Dark chest hairs glisten in the sun. Little beads of water drip off my nipples. I've got my dad's Neapolitan good looks and my mother's winning smile.

At first it was only talk. I knew this girl from a screenplay job where instead of points I was basically "loaned" a sweet young thing. Not so sweet and not so young now, but definitely doable.

We met up at Screw, a floating fetish club in West Hollywood. In the laser-strobed darkness among the freaks you can be invisible. Balding businessmen and drag queens share floor space. We X-ray-eyed each other and even though she had been bought and paid for, I treated her like a lady. She never forgot. After that, we actually became friends. And that's why she chose me for the deed.

These days I spend most of my time in the pool, yakking with my agent on the cell phone. Jason is a man with constantly shifting dark gecko-eyes and no skin color. Except for the eyes, he could be a grub in an Armani suit. He only represents the best. His agency is "boutique" and he has affidavits from everybody who counts. He plays golf with Johnny Carson and bass guitar for Bruce Willis.

This is the vision that returns to me like bile when I'm alone. Acid reflux. It comes in saturated four-strip Technicolor, which is extinct now.

I am Tisa Hawn. I am dying her death. Rosebuds and fully-formed roses red and black float around her body, mixing their essence with my blood. The water is thick with it, and in the dark it looks black.

Death Scenes made it possible, although for years in magazines like *Details*, pseudo-death layouts have given us Siouxsie and other top stars sprawled on their carpet with the wine-glass spilled just so, eyes wide open and glassy, before rigor so therefore caught in the flash right after death. I think it was *Death Scenes* that made death fashionable for regular folks. I make it a point of studying these things.

Sweet Tisa Hawn just wanted to be loved. Love is the camera and glossy layouts in fashion magazines. The lights just so, for her. The pop of the flashbulb. Mink stoles and expensive perfume. Layouts in *Cosmo* and *Glamour*. Nights out on the Strip.

And me? My name is Walter Morotti. Maybe you've seen my name on the credits of your favorite shows. No matter how many hits I've had I still need to freeze-frame the credits on the VCR to see "Walter Morotti." I want to make a tape-loop of all my credits and jerk off to it. I may still.

Lately I have this dream where I'm drowning. I'm out in the pool as the sun rises over downtown office buildings, dead souls writhing under the job whip, their pain unheard behind blank walls with generic brass nameplates.

A huge hand shoots from behind me and topples me off my perch. The cell phone sinks to the bottom of the pool and I watch it go down, a postmodern sea-creature, still spewing out my agent's voice like squid ink.

The anonymous hand presses at my scalp and I'm going under, bubbles of breath tickling out of my nose and the corner of my mouth.

I press back against the hand, but the other hand has my wrists and it's a massive grip. Held down, the world is light blue. Struggling only increases the effort to drown me. This fact — that somebody would want to kill me as I lie there without a care in the world, that somebody actually cares whether I live or die and wills the latter — this makes me hot.

It gives me an erection like a steel girder. My cock pops through my shorts and it's trailing a cloudwhisp of come.

As the water floods in, my ears thrum and I can hear birds and helicopters faintly above my head as my vision becomes stars, spiral galaxies. My jism's a milky whey. I'm twisting and turning in the darkest reaches of space, just some flotsam, happy to be up here and unconcerned with the fate of the world.

My world no longer, thank Jesus. Last sight the scum of my seed mixing with dark blood, swirling up to the surface of the pool.

Immaculate nails rake the sides of the tub and there's a thin trickle of blood. Heavy, thick heart-blood and it's darker. Blue notes from the saddest sax in the world. A black and white loop where her head crashes against the faucet and blood squirts from a surface wound. Again and again. Dark blood like the Karo syrup mixture used in *Psycho*, swirling down the drain.

Now I can die like a star when people cared how stars died. I'm fucking Marilyn Monroe in her last barbiturate sleep. River Phoenix joins in and we toss around this four-poster bed, River taking Marilyn from behind while I cram cock into her mouth. A little dribble of my pearly come drips down her chin.

In the old days when people died and became legends — real legends, not the fluff-of-the-moment that passes for fame in this age of instant anonymity and direct-TV — in those days, movies could be monuments as impressive as any marble statue with an angel. More so.

Death could make your life complete. *Rebel Without a Cause* made James Dean a postmortem icon.

Over and over I'm going down and down until my lifeless corpse rests at the bottom of the pool. The gases will bring it to the surface.

Much like *Sunset Boulevard* only with a 21st-century, HD-TV eroticism. I specialize in derived mythologies. The secret to success in this town is not how original you can be, but how well you can mine pre-existing formulas.

The essential elements always apply.

I only wanted to be a porn star. I used to lie in my bed and be gang-raped by dream demons in black leather hoods. They'd use me until the come would dribble out of every orifice and I ached all over.

Blackmail? I had no moral compunctions about killing her, especially since I've never believed in standing in the way of people's wishes. She didn't have to bring up the screenplay deal or the vice squad. I would have done it anyway. I just had to gird myself. I'm a lover, not a fighter.

By the time I roll up her driveway in my silver Merc, the 'ludes have kicked in. I survey her one-story Spanish colonial with its brick tile roof, the cactus garden and gleaming quartz. The cacti wave to me with little green spiky fingers.

The shades are drawn and her eyes have rolled skyward. White limbs frozen in attitudes, like Greek statuary. Or maybe fake Greek garden statuary.

She didn't hire me for my talent. There are thousands of people in my position. I don't want to kid myself that I'm an original. But I'm repeating myself.

Tisa's grandmother's silver locket with its ancestral hair clipping tightly packed — she asks me to place the locket directly between her breasts.

Rosebuds and fully-formed roses red and black float around her body, mixing their sweet essence with her blood. The water is thick with it, and in the dark it looks black.

She wants to die as a starlet would die in the Thirties; none of this staggering out of The Viper Room puking and passing out on the sidewalk while trendies swirl past and around her. No nodding off in the john with a needle still hanging from her vein.

She remembers that star back when who also wanted a glamorous death but was found with her head stuck in the toilet. Some Latina actress now only memorable for her inglorious end. This was no good. She wants me to help her design the death. A death combining retro glamour and good taste.

Tisa took me on because I'm the perfect receptacle for pop culture. I'm perfectly blank. That's how I got all my TV jobs. I'll be walking down Melrose and hear something and write it down. Half an hour later it's a line from some vapid prime-time soap opera.

Now I walk through North Vermont, the "new Melrose," especially since Wacko and all the other trendy shops are disappearing. The Onyx coffee shop is here. I sip an iced cap and nod my head to the music of words.

It's a matter of being able to cruise along the surface, dipping in and listening only to the form of sounds, the waves of words that roll and roll. I bathe in it. It's my element.

If Johnny Hard-On can't deliver on his name, his career is over. Fluff girls can't get it started. So we can't finish it. I'm standing there in thigh-high black leather boots, my entire body glistening with oil. My vulva pulsing. His dick sits there like a dead worm on a log.

Outside the sun has just risen. Slanted light spilling through the bathroom shades at oblique angles, making thin golden designs on the white shag carpet. This precise moment to die.

My client had some modeling gigs and commercial work, but most of her acting hours had been logged in what we discreetly refer to as the Adult Entertainment Industry. Legendary for her ability to transform into the fuck-goddess of the moment.

She loves to imagine boys who wouldn't look at her twice in high school, pulling their twentysomething cocks to her latest skin epic. *Anal Invaders 2: The Second Coming* has just been remastered. It was her best performance. Maybe it wasn't Olivier in *Oedipus Rex*. But when she gets reamed, the little cry is the same.

She asks me for limbs like cold marble, legs strategically curled under her, head lolling to the right and thick dark tresses plunged into the water.

Tisa was the stuff you pour into the mold, and when it hardens, it's a wet dream crammed between work and parties and death. As much as we want to believe there can be glamour now, there's nothing new. It's all wasted, boiled down and cut up and poured into molds like Tisa who never wanted anything ordinary in her life and somehow had sunk below mediocre.

As she waits in the bedroom I run the water in the big antique tub with the claw feet. I adjust the temperature for a comfortable warmth. Then I place the razor blades on a bath towel and light three candles on the mirror dresser.

The light glints off the cutting edges. It's time.

Radio tuned to KLON, the Long Beach jazz station. Some endless dizzy solo in a Chicago nightclub long ago. And maybe standing right in front of the stage is a Tisa Hawn of the time, dressed in a stunning velvet dress, and the sax man is playing only to her. Only to her.

She stands in the darkened hallway wearing a silk purple nightgown. Her eyeshadow the same shade of purple and her lips lighter, violet.

I've taken two tabs of acid on top of the 'ludes and I feel like a jellyfish. But the stark realism of it — the act I'm about to commit — cuts through the drugs and keeps me from collapsing.

Tisa smiles ever so slightly and I take her right hand and kiss it. Trailing kisses up to her collar and then her neck. Her cheeks flush as I pass my lips up and down her neck. She sighs and begins to moan deep in her throat.

I taste her throat and kiss her right above the silver locket, caressing her breasts. Her nipples are hard beneath the gown. I take the right one between my thumb and forefinger and roll it. The locket has gone all mercury and spills down her dress.

She pulls the gown over her head and lets it fall in a heap on the deep-pile carpet. Then she passes me, walking into the bathroom and sinking her perfect body into the bath.

Plenty of room in there for me. My heart thuds heavily in my chest and the adrenaline pumps so furiously I think I will pass out.

Taking one of the new blades from the towel, I enter the tub and kneel over her, running the edge along her neck and down to her breasts. The flash of the blade ripples and repeats. The silver trails.

Experimental nicks seep blood and I lap at it, aroused at the metallic taste.

Her breasts large and appointed with gumdrop-purple nipples. I pass the blade over the top of her left breast, tickling the aureole and caressing her with the flat of the blade. Then I make a tiny incision above the nipple. Tisa's eyes get wider and wider.

I feel between her legs and she is liquid fire. I tease her pussy lips and expertly vise her clit between my right index and middle finger, while my left explores her labia. I've cupped the razor with my thumb.

While continuing the kiss of the razor up and down her arms, I enter her, timing the cuts so that the deeper wounds fall on the crest of some lesser pain.

By the time I've begun to inflict serious damage she is humping and bucking for dear life, grabbing my razor hand and driving it down her wrists. I nearly fall on top of her in an awkward sprawl.

Her lifeblood spills in waves and the tub gets slippery. Holding her hands above her head I make a series of lateral incisions to her forearms. Her head lurches back and hits the shower faucet.

Tisa's eyes milk over. I could drink from them. I lean in to give her a final kiss. As our lips meet, the force of her death spills out of her mouth and it's as if I'm inhaling her final moments. Tisa is in me now. And all her pathetic dreams as well.

Don't want to get old until nobody wants to come on my face or sink their head into ancient, skanky pussy. Bob on shriveled cock.

This is what the sax man on the radio says: the lady wants a silver laughing death, an end that will float out over the Pacific waters and carry her till she reaches the other side of the sun. I want to come with her death and pour out my sperm as her body relaxes completely and her head slides underwater.

I get out of the tub, balancing carefully. After drying myself off, I reach in and manage to hoist her body.

Sheer dead weight. She keeps slipping back down again. The position she'd asked to be placed in took a combination of art and engineering to arrange. But I would follow requests till the end. That was my job.

I'm 34 years old, an old man with his entire career behind him. I have no regrets. I always wanted to be a porn star and die fucking in a tub of my own blood. I have a condo in the heart of Hollywood and a rooftop pool where I take calls in an inner tube, floating on my back.

Lately I have these dreams of drowning.

Alex S. Johnson's nonfiction articles and interviews, as well as his short stories, have appeared in a wide variety of magazines, including *Bloodsongs*, *Implosion*, and *Juggernaut*.

The Gyrl with No Name

by Kate Bornstein

```
Doc No. H17764-23B, Seattle PD tape transcript (edited)
Re:        Case File SPD-H-17764, Donna Louise Tradore
Date/time:March 15, 1994, 7:15PM
Present:  Det. Sgt. Joseph Mendota (Mendota), investigating
          officer; Det. Sgt. Sandra Pell (Pell), assisting.
Subject Interviewed:    Jane Doe (JaneDoe)
Place:    Subject's residence, 1273 East Pike St., Apt 4R
          (formalities deleted from this transcript: see
          Doc. No. H17764-23A)
```

Mendota:	All right, you know this is an informal background check concerning your relationship with Ms. Tradore.
JaneDoe:	Uh-huh.
Mendota:	Right. So, could you please state your name?
JaneDoe:	(laughing) I could, but I don't have one.
Mendota:	Excuse me?
JaneDoe:	Look, the first thing she took away from me when I bonded myself to her was my name. That was four years ago. And when she left me, she didn't give me my name back. Simple.
Pell:	That checks with what we've got, Joe.
Mendota:	Uh, okay. Can you please. . .what are you doing with those?

Pell: For the record, the subject is attaching clothespins to her arms and across her chest.

JaneDoe: These? They help me keep calm. Believe me, you don't wanna see me hyper. 'Sides, they don't hurt goin' on, only when ya take 'em off — it's the absence that hurts. Isn't that cool?

Mendota: Uh-huh. It's your house, Ms. . .?

JaneDoe: (laughing) You can call me "gyrl." With a "y." She did. I hadda call myself "this one," like: "May this one fetch your tea, ma'am?" It was pretty cool.

Mendota: Concerning your relationship with. . .

JaneDoe: You really have to have this clothespin thing done to you to do it right. Donna, she would make these patterns all over my body when she did it. Donna, she would put me on display, and everyone would go ohhhhhh and ahhhhh; they would and I was so proud to be her work of art. I always say if you can't be a great artist, you can always be a great work of art, right?

Mendota: Uh. . .

JaneDoe: When I was a little kid, I never thought someone would really wanna do this kinda stuff to me. I always thought I'd have to do it to myself. Do you know what it's like to imagine your heart's desire, never really believing anyone would love you for who you really are? Not who you really are. So, you wanna know how we met?

Mendota: Please. Yes.

JaneDoe: Well, one day she just showed up at the food co-op where I was workin' the cash registers. I know she saw my hands tremblin' while I was ringin' up her stuff. It wasn't till later I found out she wasn't even vegetarian. . . She just bought stuff at the co-op so she could check me out! (laughter) By the way, if you leave these clothespins on too long you can hurt yourself. (laughter) Well, I mean seriously hurt yourself, OK?

Mendota: I see.

JaneDoe: The first time she touched me, she hurt me. It was right there at the checkout counter. She brought the palm of my hand up to her mouth and she bit me. She has these small, sharp teeth, and she kept on biting till she broke through and I was bleedin' right into her mouth. I felt like I was gonna come any second, but she left a second before I could! It was like she already knew my rhythms, ever meet a person like that?

Mendota: I. . .

JaneDoe: Oh! And then she left without giving me her name or number. "I know how to get ahold of you," that's all she said, and she walks out the door, laughing. The next woman in line looks at my hand, and she asks me, "Honey, are you all right?" All right? All right? I'm fine. I'm fine, thank you. Wouldn't you be fine if your heart's desire had walked into your life not five minutes ago?

Mendota: Uh, yes. Yes, I'd be fine.

JaneDoe: Exactly! Anyway, all I wanted to do was to belong to her. Not like her wife, I mean, Ewwwwww! And not like her girlfriend. I've been girlfriend to enough people. Not like a one-night stand, either. I wanted her to own me, like property. I told her that on our third date, when she had me tied down to her bed. Look, Mister, I loved her completely. I trusted her completely. I knew her and she knew me. She asked me what I wanted more than anything else in the world and I said I wanna belong to you, and she smiled and said "That can be arranged," and I started crying and I couldn't stop. You never know how profoundly moving the fulfillment of your fantasy is gonna be till it actually, finally, really happens to you.

Pell: Yes. Yes.

JaneDoe: I've got marks. (laughter) I got one right here. It's her brand.

Pell: Subject is indicating the inside of her upper right thigh.

JaneDoe: Right! Donna didn't do it, she had a friend of hers who knows how do it. They hafta heat the iron till it's white hot, didja know that? Any less hot than white hot, and you have to hold it down to the skin longer, and that makes the skin crack and get all blistery, and ya really spoil the mark. So, she got someone to do it, right, and they held my leg down to the table with four very tight leather straps. I couldn't have moved if I'd wanted to, but I didn't want to. I wanted her mark on me. I did. And when they touched the iron to the inside of my thigh, I felt like I was gonna shoot right out of my body.

Mendota: I don't doubt that.

JaneDoe: Some people remember how it smells, but I remember how it sounded. It was a bubbly sort of hissing sound. I was sick afterwards — for a few days I had a fever and chills. I was embarrassed, but the woman who branded me said, "Eh, that happens a lot." Y'know, even now, at night, when I'm alone in bed, I like to trace my finger through the brand. It's really deep.

Mendota: So you and Ms. Tradore. . .?

JaneDoe: We were madly in love, the toast of the leather community! We were the ones everyone looked to when they were so afraid ya couldn't find real love in sadomasochism. We got written up in all the leather journals. She had me, and we had it all. Then she stopped coming by every day. And I started to do this clothespin stuff to myself more and more. She started loaning me out to her friends more frequently. Hey, could you help me with this, please? Just take it off me, okay?

Mendota: I. . .

Pell: The subject has asked Sergeant Mendota to remove one of the clothespins from her arm.

JaneDoe: Oh, please? Ahhhhhhh! Thank you!

Mendota: Uh, you're quite welcome.

JaneDoe: She started loaning me out to men. I didn't mind that, not really. I mean hey, I was doing it for her. Could you get another one? Ahhhhhhhh. Yes! Thanks, this is nice. I usually have to do this myself. Thanks for doing this for me. I said to her, "It doesn't matter about the men, as long as you love me." She didn't say anything. Could you get this one right here? Thankyouthankyouthankyou. This one thanks you so much.

Mendota: Miss, please. . .

JaneDoe: 'Kay, okay. Four years we were together, and me without a name, and she comes into my room one night and says: "Okay, you're free to go now." Free to go? Free to go where?

"I belong to you," I said. "What did I do?"

"You didn't do anything," she said to me. "I just understand you."

"You understand me? Do you understand that I have given you the most precious gift I can give anyone? I've given you me!"

"I just understand you," she said to me.

"You understand me? Do you understand that who I am is that I live for your love? That is who I am. You understand me? What did I do?"

"You didn't do anything," she said to me. "I just really understand you." And she unbuttons her jeans, and. . .and she slides them down to her knees, and I . . .I can see this fresh brand on the inside of her thigh. It was really clean.

"Forgive me," she's sayin' to me. "You've taught me so much," she's sayin' to me, "and I understand you. You're free to go now," she says. "Call it my parting act of cruelty." (The subject is crying.)

That was about a year ago.

Pell: You want a tissue?

JaneDoe: Thanks.

Mendota: And two months ago, the night of. . .

JaneDoe: Huh? Oh. You wanna know about the killing thing?

Mendota: Please. Yes.

JaneDoe: I don't know anything about it. I was in San Francisco.

Pell: That checks, Sergeant.

Mendota: Thank you, Pell.

JaneDoe: Wanna know something funny? 'Kay, this is good. The old wizards and witches would never use their real names. They knew something we've forgotten: Whoever knows your real name holds the power of life and death over you. Whoever gets to name you gets to own you.

Mendota: Right. Thank you for your cooperation, Miss.

JaneDoe: (incomprehensible)

Mendota: Excuse me?

JaneDoe: I said gyrl. Just call me gyrl.

(end edited transcript)

Kate Bornstein is a performance artist and the author of *Gender Outlaw: On Men, Women, and the Rest of Us* and *My Gender Workbook*. Her stage work includes the solo pieces *The Opposite Sex is Neither* and *Virtually Yours: A Game for Solo Performer with Audience*. She has worked as a first mate on an ocean-going yacht, a salesman for an IBM subsidiary, and a phone-sex hostess.

Coke Call

by Michelle Tea

I said Marina deserved her own story, and I meant it. Her hair was as red and curly as Bozo The Clown and she dyed her pubes to match, though I don't know who she thought she was fooling. Marina was synthetic. Even her name might be fake, might be the name she adopted to whore with. It has been a long time and I don't know if Marina is living or dead. Her makeup was thick enough to make her look like an airbrushed mural on the side of a van — dark eyes, canyons of red up the side of her cheeks, lips drippy with thick red gloss. Marina's nails were claws, and she really did dress like a whore. She looked the part and it worked for her. You'd be surprised: A lot of men want the women they're renting to have a wholesome air about them. They really love the fresh-faced, I'm-Putting-Myself-Through-College shtick. It guess it makes it seem less dirty and disease-prone, more of a healthy, all-American male tradition. But Marina looked like a slut and she had lots of calls, and lots of regulars.

There was this one guy out on Cape Cod who loved her. He would have Marina drive all the way up there with a packet of cocaine to sit in a negligee and tell stories. Cocaine calls really reminded you why you were a whore. They were the best.

There was one, David Smith, all the whores were tracking his steady, drug-propelled demise. By the time I saw him there was hardly anything left in his apartment, just a clean, round table, a microwave, his bed, and his television. I sat on the bed in front of the flickering television and David clutched the remote — *flick, flick, flick*, never resting on a program for more than a few seconds. This went on for seven hours. It was my longest call ever, and the easiest. David was slumped on the bed looking really unhappy; occasionally he let the screen rest on a particular show — CSpan coverage of a Senate race in Virginia, a western, boring stuff. He would pass through something good, *Heathers* was on, and *Donahue*, lots of nature programs, and I would pipe up Hey That's A Good One, but he'd already zipped through it. *Nothing good's on, nothing good's ever on* David chanted, transfixed by the box. David was your average white business-guy, middle-aged, still in his button-down work shirt but without the tie. I may have run into him a dozen times before or since and I would not remember, the guy was so average.

This is how the call went: Under the bed was a round ceramic dinner plate dotted with little mounds of coke. I took David Smith's credit card and I chopped and chopped the stuff into a fine powder. I sculpted them into good fat lines. I presented the plate to David Smith who pulled himself up on his elbows, pulled out a rolled up bill and sucked it up his nose. *Take off your clothes*, he said, and the ritual began. Winter in Boston, way out in Newton I think he lived, and I had this tremendously long black velvet coat, looped all over with fancy black embroidery. It was a beautiful coat, a queen's coat. Under it was some kind of dress probably belonging to my girlfriend who was rich and owned lots of tasteful, feminine outfits, flowing rayon things with floral prints and gold buttons. These dresses were all too big for me, but since they never stayed on long, it didn't really matter. Black panties, black garter belt, black stockings, a tiny black bra.

When I was naked on David Smith's bed, he dove for my pussy, his fingers blunt and frenzied with cocaine. I kept my thighs clenched tight to protect my clit from his fumblings, arched my back and pretended to come, hollered a little, bucked his hands straight off me with my dramatic orgasm and David Smith went back to his television and did not touch me again. Seven hours I was there. I would lay out his freshly pulverized drugs, and smoke his cigarettes, Marlboros. I chain-smoked them. I did not do his other drugs. I walked into his empty kitchen and went through his cabinets. They were empty too. What did the guy eat? In his freezer were a couple of TV dinners for kids, and I found a full jar of pickles in the refrigerator. I took it back into the bedroom where David was attacking the remote control. Can I Eat These? I asked. *Uh*, he grunted.

David Smith was paranoid. *Sssshhhhh. . .* he'd start, muting the television. *Ssssh, ssshhh, ssshhh, did you hear that? Did you hear that?* We sat in the quiet. Nnnooo, I'd venture hesitantly, I Don't Hear Anything. *Sssshhhh, ssssshhhh, ssssshhhh. It's my ex-wife. It's my ex-wife.* The plate of coke went back under the bed. *Check the doors, check the house.* I padded naked through the empty apartment, double-checking the locks and peeking in the closets. His paranoia was contagious in the creepy vacant apartment. I rushed back to the TV. No One's Here, David. *You checked the locks?* Yes, I Checked The Locks, It's OK. I cut him some more coke and ate his pickles, smoked. Then it would happen again.

Sssshhhh, sssshhhh, sssshhhh. It's the cops, the cops are here. Want Me To Check The House, David? My voice was soothing. I made my rounds through the apartment. Every hour on the hour I had to collect the next hour's cash up front. David, Do You Want Me To Stay Another Hour? I'd ask him three or four times before he'd answer. *Yeah.* I Need The Money Right Now If You Want Me To Stay. *Sssshhhh, sssshhhh, sssshhhh,* he'd start that shit again. David, If You Don't Pay Me Right Now, I'm Leaving. He was a zombie, his eyes flashing with the television's reflection. He was spending a lot of money to have a really bad time.

Up I went, picking my bits of clothing off the floor, pulling on the stockings, hitching them up to the garter, snapping on the bra, the dress, the heavy coat, maybe even a scarf, my purse flung dramatically over my shoulder. Bye Bye David, I'm Leaving Now, Goodbye. *Here, here.* He reached into his pocket, his front pants pocket, and pulled out a tremendous roll of bills. Now that I was a whore I was able to really recognize what a lot of money looked like, and that was a lot of money. I nearly moaned. He peeled a couple off and tossed them at me, shoved the riches back in his pocket.

Oh, the thoughts that went through my head. Murder, duh, I could kill him, sure I could. A knife from the kitchen, or a frying pan if he had such appliances. Knock him out, grab the roll. The mind of a whore is a mind of hate and greed. At least mine was. I took my clothes off and sat back on the bed, hunkered down for another hour of manic channel-changing and paranoid outbursts. I sat and smoked and fantasized about David Smith dying. When the hour was up I'd ask for the cash, he'd get paranoid, I'd get dressed and threaten to really leave, he'd reach his hand into the golden pocket. I did this seven times. I made a bunch of money. I could have stayed the whole next day. I didn't want to believe it when he finally let me go. He had had a super paranoia moment, the TV got shut off, the lights went out, we had to lie motionless on the dark bed, the digital clock flicking its glowing numbers at me. David I Have To Go, I whispered. He grunted. David, You Have To Pay Me Blah Blah Blah I launched into the routine but David was out. Maybe asleep. But he was on all that coke, lines and lines of the stuff. Maybe he was dead. That seemed more likely than sleep. Was he breathing? He was quiet. Now was the time to steal his money, but I didn't. I just got out of that empty, creepy apartment. I had seven hundred dollars, I was rich.

But wasn't this about Marina? She would do those coke calls on Cape Cod, this guy who looked like the White Rabbit, kind of startled pink with white hair. Marina would bring a friend and everyone would do coke and talk dirty. The girls would, I don't know, eat whipped cream off each other's pussies, and the guy would jerk off. He wanted to hear incest stories. Eeeeh, I said. I stayed away from those calls. Once Lyn headlined my ad in the paper under "Teen Dream," and I wanted to kill her. I had every pedophile in the city calling me. I got them often enough with my tiny measurements, I couldn't believe she'd decided to capitalize on it without asking first. She took it out. Marina had been abused by her dad when she was a girl, and she'd do coke and tell this guy about it as he jerked off. I was astonished. She didn't really care. It was easy to feel superior when you learned things like that. Marina was a real whore. I had standards, boundaries and limitations that kept me sane. I would not lick a guy's butt. My friend Karina did, and I was horrified. Karina, Don't Do That! You Don't Have To Do That! *Really*? She thought she had to do whatever they wanted her to. After all, they were paying her. I saw the butt guy right after she did and he expected me to do it too, tried to bribe me with a fifty-dollar tip. When the boss set me up on a call with Marina's coked-out regular, I told her straight-up that I wasn't going to tell him stories.

I tried not to talk to them at all, tried to exert as little energy as possible. I could never be a stripper. You use so much of yourself, your brain, your muscles. It was exhausting just to lay there. Marina's regular didn't want me to tell him stories, he wanted to tell me stories, stuff about getting fucked by his big sister. I didn't want to encourage him, but I wanted him to get off so he would leave. I remember when he fucked me it felt pretty good and it made me sick, a thunder of shame and rage as full as any orgasm. The guy left and Marina was there, in the house, on the black couch that looked like leather but was actually this thin shiny cotton. Marina's boyfriend was a cop and ultimately that was a problem. He thought she just answered phones. They would go on double dates with Lyn who ran the place and her boyfriend Mark, the four of them hanging out at some awful, townie Boston sports bar, drinking beer and eating buffalo wings.

Across the street from the house we worked at was an alley which led to a lot, and the place was filled with pigeons. Often they were dead or really fucked up, and Marina adopted one of the sicker mutant ones. What did she name it, some long Italian name. It lived in a little cage on top of the TV, which meant you couldn't watch TV because you didn't want to look at the bird. It must've gotten hit by a car, it was just mangled. Head twisted back, feathers broken and it could barely walk. I don't understand how it didn't just die. Marina would take it out of the cage and cuddle it into her cleavage, coo at it. She would feed it with an eyedropper. once she left it out on the table and it was trying to walk and it could only move backwards and it fell off the table, hitting the floor with a thud and a squawk. I couldn't look. I heard it struggling to get up, a shuffling, scratching sound. Marina! I screamed, Marina, The Bird Fell! She was in the bathroom, getting ready for a call. She ran out in a teddy and put the thing back in its cage. Marina That Bird Should Be Put To Sleep, It's Miserable Marina, Look At It. *He's my baby*, Marina snapped, touching it through the cage's gold bars. *Don't you even think about killing him!*

It's all we could think about. Every whore in the house had her own fantasy of giving its wrecked neck a final twist, but no one did. Marina really loved it.

No one knew, but the whole time Marina was on a ton of coke. And she was moonlighting at this other whorehouse right down the street, getting men from Lyn's house to see her there on the sly which means she was fucking over Lyn, and they were friends. Lyn fired her and Marina went away and then a couple days later there was a call from the madam of her new house, Marina had been passed out in one of the rooms for days, going in and out of consciousness, would Lyn come get her? Lyn said *No way*, but gave the woman the cop boyfriend's phone number, which was wrong move number one, but how could she have known exactly how fucked-up and desperate Marina was? She told the cop boyfriend that it was all Lyn's fault, she had this crazy story about Lyn hooking her on coke and then turning her out, this really beautifully dramatic fabrication that the cop of course believed. I mean, he had believed that Marina was a *receptionist*, answering the phone in her scandalously short clothing, boobs spilling out all over the place. Anyway, the cop threatened to arrest Lyn who was, on the best of days, completely paranoid about getting arrested. So she shut everything down and no one had jobs and everyone was miserable. Lyn found a new space in an apartment building around the corner, and we all had to help her move, carrying all the fat, heavy furniture across the street at like five o'clock in the morning because she was breaking her lease so had to get it all out of there before the building manager woke up.

This was all around the same time that Lyn's boyfriend Mark tried to kill her. I guess he was on coke, too. Everyone was really freaked out about it, having mistaken Mark for a nice guy, allowing him to hang around the house, privy to all our whorey secrets. He tried to strangle her, left fingerprint bruises in a ring around her neck. She got a restraining order on him, but ultimately started going out with him again. He was sorry about it.

Marina I don't know what happened to. She was really young, like twenty-one, though she looked so much older with all that makeup. And she really loved that pigeon.

Michelle Tea is the founder of Sister Spit, San Francisco's all-girl open mike, which toured the U.S. in 1998. Her novels include *The Passionate Mistakes and Intricate Corruption of One Girl in America* (Semiotext(e)/Smart Art, 1998) and *Valencia* (Seal Press, 2000).

Faithful

by Michael Thomas Ford

I knew when Jake came in and sat on the edge of the bed, not moving, that it had gone wrong. He didn't say anything. He didn't touch me. He just sat there, his hands in his lap, swallowed up in the darkness while I waited for him to speak.

Usually he was the hardest after a hit — shedding his clothes as he walked in the door and slipping into bed next to me so I'd feel the length of his cock hard along my ass, his balls heavy against my thigh.

"Come on, baby," he'd say in his low, throaty voice as he moved his mouth over my neck. "Come on. I need to fuck you."

Before I could even wake up, his fingers would already be squeezing my nipples as he pushed inside me, a man possessed. His prick on those nights was strangely hot, like steel radiating heat from the inside, and as he thrust fiercely against me he seemed to be trying to outrun whatever fiery demons held him in their grip. It was as though everything he felt from seeing some man fall under his bullets needed a place to explode, before it burned him up from the inside and sent his soul scattering across the sky. He'd fuck me hard and quick, and I'd come just from the touch of his fingers on my tits, knowing that the last thing those hands had done was kill.

But this night was different. This time, there was only silence. I felt my heart beating, and the familiar rush of blood to my cunt that accompanied his return. But I knew from his stillness not to touch him, and I lay in the darkness, the sheets bunched coldly between my legs, as I waited for him to return to me.

"We made the hit," he said finally, his voice quiet as a stream of chill air.

The hit. Richie Marotta. They'd been planning it for a long time. "So, what's the problem? You guys have been after Richie for months now."

He rubbed his hands through his hair. "Yeah, well, this time someone got in the way."

I sat up, pulling the sheets around me. I could feel the coldness of Jake's mood against my skin like rain, and it made me shiver. "Who?"

"Corelli," he said softly, as though speaking the name any louder would invoke some kind of evil spirit.

Corelli. Jimmy Corelli. Head of the biggest syndicate on the East Side. He'd been in power longer than anyone else in the city. No one dared touch him. He let the smaller guys do their business uninterrupted while he looked after the big operations. In exchange, there was the unspoken agreement that none of them would try to get too big. Killing him was like spitting in the face of God.

"Corelli? Jesus Christ, Jake."

"We weren't even after him," he said, his voice close to cracking. "I mean, Jesus Christ, who the fuck would go after Corelli? We were just supposed to take out Richie. It was an easy hit. He was meeting with his guys over at the docks. All we had to do was bust in, blow their fucking heads off, and get the fuck out of there. Who the fuck knew he was meeting with Corelli?"

"What happened?"

"What happened? We stormed through the fucking door and started firing, that's what happened. Then when it was all over, we saw there were three more bodies than there should have been lying there with holes through them. Corelli and his goddamn sons. Both of them. Dead as shit. When Eddie rolled them over I just about pissed myself like a baby. All I could see was Corelli's face looking up at me with his goddamn eyes still wide open."

He started to shake. "We killed the whole fucking family," he said, his voice hysterical. "The whole goddamn fucking Corelli family. Do you know what the fuck that means? It means every one of our fucking asses is history, starting with mine."

Putting my arms around him, I held him as he wept. His large body fell back against mine, and my face was buried in his neck, surrounding me with the scents of his skin — sweat, excitement, and fear. Closing my eyes, I thought of Corelli lying dead, his blood pooled around him like a halo, and felt a familiar ache in my pussy. I undid the buttons of Jake's shirt and ran my hand inside. His heart was beating so fast I thought it might give out from fear. But still I couldn't help pushing my fingers down his belly, past his belt, and into his pants, where I wrapped my hand around his dick. It was rock hard.

Without a word, I pulled him back on the bed and unzipped his pants. Freeing his cock, I straddled him and worked the head of his prick into me. His eyes remained closed as I began to ride him, and I knew that he, too, was thinking about the way Corelli's eyes had looked up at him in wonder. After a few minutes, his hands closed around my ass and he shot deep inside me.

~

We knew running was useless. They always find the ones who run, and looking over your shoulder gets uncomfortable very quickly. Besides, it just wasn't the way things were done. Everyone who got into it knew that from the outset. The rules were bred into us from birth. All we could do was wait, wait and see what Corelli's men would do.

We didn't have to wait long. The phone rang less than an hour after Jake came home, while he was pacing the room and smoking and I was sitting on the bed, my cunt still sore from Jake's pounding. He grabbed it on the first ring, not even bothering to say hello. He was silent as he listened for a minute to whoever was on the other end, then he hung up.

"What?"

"That was Joe, Corelli's second," he said, his voice tight. "They want to see me."

"What do you mean they want to see you?"

"He said they know what happened, and they want me to come up to discuss it."

"Discuss it? You can't go there. They'll just kill you."

"I don't think so," he said. "If they wanted to do that, they'd just come over here and do it."

"I don't like it," I said. This wasn't the way things happened. Not in our world.

"There's something else," Jake said. "Joe said to bring you with me."

I looked over at him. "Me? Why?"

He sat down next to me. "I don't know. Look, you know you don't have to. I'll go alone. You can get the fuck out of here..."

"No," I said. "I'm going. You go alone, you're good as dead. With me there, at least you have a chance. You know I'm off-limits to them." Rule number two — women don't count for shit, unless they're pushing out more boy babies to add to the ranks. They wouldn't off me because it wouldn't get them anything except another body to get rid of.

We argued about it for fifteen minutes, but in the end I won, mainly because Jake was scared of being late and pissing off Corelli's guys. While he pulled on some clothes, I got dressed. Despite my fear, I sensed somehow that looking my best might be to our advantage. I pulled on a black velvet dress that Jake had bought me to wear to the opera. Sleeveless, it hugged my body tightly, pushing my breasts up and out. The black looked good against my pale skin, and with my long black hair pinned up, I looked like any other woman on her way to a performance of *La Boheme.*

We arrived at the house a few minutes before the time Joe had told Jake to be there. As befit his status, the seat of Corelli's empire was an imposing brownstone in one of the city's older neighborhoods. Surrounded by a heavy iron fence, it sat back from the street like a watchdog guarding its territory. I'd passed it many times on my way to and from different places, and every time I'd wondered what went on behind its curtained windows, what it would be like to walk its halls. Now, standing on its steps, I stared at the red lacquered door and wondered how I would get away.

Jake rang the bell, and a moment later it was answered by a young man in a white suit.

"We're here to see Joe," Jake said, the hand that held mine shaking so hard I had to squeeze it to make him stop.

The young man gestured for us to enter. Without a word, he led us up a staircase, then down a long hallway to another door. When he knocked, it was opened by another man, this one older, with graying hair.

"Joe," Jake said, nodding to the man as though we were meeting him on the street.

Joe nodded in return. "Come in." He didn't look at me.

We entered the room, and Joe shut the door behind us. To my surprise, I saw that we were in what seemed to be a bedroom suite. A large bed was in one corner, and across the room from it were several armchairs. In one chair sat a man in a dark suit, while two other men stood behind him.

Joe led us over to the man in the chair. When we neared, he stood and held out his hand to Jake. Jake took it, and the man shook. "Hello, Jake," he said, his voice low and pleasant.

He then turned to me, and again he held out his hand. When I took it, he closed his fingers firmly around mine. "And this must be Sofia. It's nice to meet you."

Not sure what to do, I smiled and nodded slightly. The man smiled back, and I was struck by how young he looked. His face was thin and handsome, with dark eyes and a mouth I couldn't help but think of as beautiful.

"Please," he said, indicating the chairs. "Sit down."

Jake and I sat, and the man resumed his place. He reached into a box sitting on the table next to him and pulled out a cigar. Taking great care, he trimmed the end, lit it, and drew in his breath until the end of the cigar crackled with heat. Taking a puff, he leaned back and let the smoke exit his lips in a dreamy, sensual cloud that drifted in the air between he and us. Then he turned to Jake.

"First," he said. "I should introduce myself. I am Nick Corelli."

Jake looked confused. "Nick Corelli?" he said.

The man nodded. "Yes," he said. "I know most people thought my father had only two children. But there are...were...three of us. My mother died when I was born, and I was sent to live with her sister in Milan. I then spent many years in school. I only recently came back to the city."

"Your father," Jake said. "You have to understand, I didn't mean to..."

Corelli raised his hand. "I have been told what happened," he said. "There is no point in discussing it."

Jake glanced at me, then looked back at Corelli. "If there's anything I can do to...."

Corelli laughed, his voice filling the room. "Jake, my friend, you know how it is. We all know how it is, don't we? I cannot just let you go without some kind of reparation. My father was the most feared man in this city. As the last of my family, I inherit what he created here. I think you agree that it would not be a fitting start to my reign to simply forgive the man who killed my father and brothers."

Jake was silent. I looked at him, waiting for him to speak.

"What is it you want?" I asked, when I saw that Jake wouldn't.

Corelli turned his eyes to me. "A game," he said.

"I don't understand."

"My father was very fond of gambling," Corelli said. "Horses. Cards. Women. He would often settle outstanding debts with a game. If his opponent won, the debt was forgiven. If not, then my father...collected what was owed to him."

"You want to play cards for your father's honor?" I said.

Corelli laughed again. "Oh, no. I have something much more amusing in mind." He took another drag on his cigar before speaking again. "Do you love your husband, Mrs. Gioconda?"

I looked over at Jake. "Of course I do."

"And does your husband make you come?"

"Excuse me?"

"When he fucks you. Does he make you come?"

I looked into Corelli's eyes defiantly. "Of course he does."

"That's very good," he said. "A man should know how to please his wife." He gestured toward the three men who remained behind his vacant chair. "Now look at these men. Would you say they were attractive?"

I looked at the men for a moment. "Yes," I said. I didn't know what Corelli was up to, but I figured lying wasn't going to get me anywhere.

"Good," Corelli said. "And would you say that you would enjoy making love with them?"

"Perhaps," I said after a moment. "It would depend on whether or not they were good lovers."

He smiled. "Do you think they would make you come, as your husband does?"

I stared into Corelli's eyes. "I don't know."

Corelli looked at Jake, then back to me. "The game I have in mind is a game of love," he said. "I would like to see you make love with these men."

Jake looked at Corelli. "What the hell do you think..."

I interrupted him. "And if I do?"

"If you do, then your husband goes free. If not, then I will have to take my payment."

"A man's life for watching me fuck?" I said, angered. "If you want a whore, Mr. Corelli, I'm sure you can easily find one."

"Very true," he said, smiling. "I'm sure there are some in this very house even as we speak. But it's not just about fucking, Mrs. Gioconda. As I said, this is a game of love. My father always said that a woman would come only for the man she truly loved. I've wondered for a long time if that's really true."

"I wouldn't know," I said. "My husband is the only man I've ever been with."

The corners of Corelli's mouth rose up. "Then this should prove very interesting. If my men can make you come, then your husband dies. If not, then true love wins, both of you go free, and all of this is forgotten."

"I haven't agreed yet," I said.

Corelli raised one eyebrow. "Then perhaps I should order my men to kill your husband now." He nodded, and one of the men ran over and grabbed Jake's head, putting the barrel of a pistol to his temple.

"It's up to you. Mrs. Gioconda," Corelli said, watching my face intently.

"Sofia, no," Jake whispered. "Don't do it. Don't."

I looked into Jake's frightened eyes. It was true, he was the only man I'd been with. He knew my body inside and out, and just thinking about his cock inside me made me wet. I turned back to Corelli.

"It's a deal," I said.

Corelli clapped his hands. "Very good, then. Alex, make Mr. Gioconda comfortable here."

The man holding the gun to Jake's head produced a length of rope, which he tied around Jake's arms, securing him to the chair. He then gagged him with a cloth. I looked at him and saw that his eyes were fixed on me, pleading with me.

I love you, I mouthed to him.

Corelli remained in his chair. "Oh, and one more thing. I think perhaps we need an audience for our little performance. Joe, if you please."

Joe walked over to the door, opened it, and went into the hall. When he came back, he was accompanied by Eddie and five of Jake's other main men.

"What the fuck is going on?" said Eddie when he saw Jake tied to the chair. "You said we were just talking here. What kind of shit is this?" He attempted to turn and knock Joe to the ground, but Joe punched him hard in the stomach, dropping him to his knees.

"Mr. Annarotti," said Corelli. "Thank you for coming by with your friends. I wanted you all to see that I am indeed a fair man. I know how stories can become...distorted...in the telling. This way, you can see for yourself, so that there are no misunderstandings afterward."

The same young man who had shown us in entered with six chairs, which he set up, three on either side of Jake's chair. The men sat down, Eddie holding his hand to his stomach.

Corelli turned to Eddie. "I have made Mr. Gioconda an offer," he said. "His wife has chosen to accept it. If she succeeds in the task I've set before her, your boss is free to go about his business uninterrupted by me or anyone else. Should she fail, then all that he has will belong to me. That includes you, Mr. Annarotti, as well as your men. Do we understand each other?"

Eddie looked over at Jake, who nodded slightly.

"Yeah, we understand," Eddie said. He looked at me then, his eyes dark with fear. I knew he had no idea of what was about to happen, but he was too frightened to ask any questions.

"Tony," Corelli said. "Perhaps you'd like to be the first to tempt Mrs. Gioconda."

Tony nodded. Walking over to me, he took my hand, and I stood. He led me across the room to the big bed. The chair with Jake strapped to it was directly opposite the bed, and he could see everything that was going on. Corelli, settled into his chair, watched as I turned to Tony and looked into his face. He was handsome in a rough way, but his eyes were the cold eyes of a man used to taking what he wanted.

Before I could think about what was going to happen, Tony grabbed me and kissed me. He was a big man, and his powerful arms encircled me tightly as his tongue forced its way into my mouth. His hands crept to the hem of my dress and pulled it up over my ass. I felt him tear my panties away easily, and then his fingers were gripping the mounds of my cheeks.

He pushed me so that I fell onto my back on the bed. Removing his suit coat, he quickly undid his tie and his shirt, tossing them onto the floor and revealing a well-muscled chest and stomach covered in a thick swath of dark hair. Another few tugs, and his pants followed. He stood looking down at me, his cock swelling between his legs as he stroked it to its full length. Then he climbed on top of me, his hands pulling my dress over my head. When my breasts were bared, he immediately began to pinch my nipples hard.

My body rose up against him as I jerked in surprise, and my pussy pressed against his balls, his hard cock slapping my stomach. Tony continued to pinch my nipples as he slid his body down mine, spreading my legs with his knees. Pushing his cock into my cunt, he slid all the way inside in one long thrust, making me cry out.

"So soon, Mrs. Gioconda?" Corelli's voice came from across the room, taunting me. "Is Tony so much bigger than your husband that he can make you come just from being inside of you?"

I looked into Tony's face. He was half smiling, and I could tell he was enjoying his part in the game.

"Give me your best shot," I hissed as I put my legs around his waist and tightened myself around his prick.

Tony groaned as he began to pump in and out of me. His big fingers worked over my nipples as I ran my nails up and down his broad back, scratching the hell out of him. I knew I'd be able to outlast him if I concentrated on making him lose his load. Every time he thrust into me, I pushed up to meet him, driving him as deep as he could go.

As Tony fucked me, I looked over to see how Jake was. His eyes were on me, and I could tell that, despite the gun that Alex was holding against his head, he was hard inside his pants. *Good old Jake*, I thought as I pulled Tony's cock into my cunt.

Tony fucked me mechanically, like a machine bent on beating my pussy into submission. Over and over he slammed into me, his breath coming in hot blasts against my face as he grunted in time with his thrusts. When his eyes shut and he began to groan, I knew I had him. He pumped into me a few more times, then I felt him explode inside me. He buried himself so that his balls were slapping my ass as his prick throbbed, spewing its load. When he was done, he pulled out and looked down at me.

"Nice fuck," he said, wiping his dick on my ass.

"Not nice enough, apparently," said Corelli. "Mrs. Gioconda barely broke a sweat over you, Tony. Perhaps Joe can do better."

Tony got off the bed as Joe came over. In his forties, Joe looked like any number of Italian men of that age. His gray hair was thinning, and his stomach was less than tight from all the pasta he'd crammed down his throat over the years.

As he removed his clothes, I thought of the times when, as a little girl, I'd watched my father undress after he came home from work. Like my father, Joe carefully folded his clothes and placed them on a nearby chair.

When he pulled his T-shirt over his head, I saw the scars. Three small, ragged holes near his navel. Bullet wounds. He saw me looking, and turned around as he removed his underwear.

"On your stomach," he said harshly.

I rolled over, and only then did he get on the bed. I felt his hand come down, slapping my ass hard. "Up on your knees," he ordered.

I pulled myself up so that my ass was in the air, my face lowered onto the pillows. Joe moved in behind me, and I waited for his cock to enter my pussy.

Instead, he slammed into my asshole, shoving his cock past the tight ring of muscle with no warning. I screamed into the pillows as he pressed himself tight against my butt. Before I could adjust myself to him, he pulled back, almost all of the way out. Just the head of his dick was inside me, and he began to fuck me in short movements, teasing my asshole until the pain subsided and I began to feel fingers of pleasure creeping up my cunt. Jake had always wanted to fuck my ass, but I'd never let him. Now, as Joe took my virgin hole, I began to groan into the pillow.

"Sounds like Joe is giving your wife a real ride," I heard Corelli say to Jake. "Perhaps our game will end sooner than expected."

I bit my lip, determined not to come. Even though Joe's cock was bringing me closer and closer to the edge, I wouldn't let him push me over. The harder he fucked me, the harder I bit down, until my mouth was filled with the taste of blood and I heard him breathing harder.

"Good girl," he said, slapping me with his hand as his cock buried itself in my hole. "You're giving daddy just what he wants."

"You fuck real good," I said through my teeth. "Bet you like ass a lot. I guess you've had a lot of practice with a lot of guys."

Joe slapped me hard on the ass, making me jump. He thrust harder against me, filling my ass with his cock as he continued to spank me. The combination of his rough hand hitting my skin and the pounding of his prick was making me crazy. Then, just as I felt the first small waves began to shudder within me, he came. Pulling out, he let his cum spray over my back in thick drops. I collapsed against the pillows, panting, and willed the stirrings in my pussy to subside.

When I opened my eyes, Alex was standing beside the bed. He didn't seem to be much older than nineteen or twenty, his body thin and almost hairless. But in his hand was a long, thick cock. Already a string of pre-cum was dripping from the engorged head, and the more he pumped himself, the more it oozed.

"Suck it," he ordered, grabbing me by the hair and pushing his dick between my lips.

I took as much of him in as I could, attempting to breathe. The thickness of him was choking me, but he kept shoving more and more into my mouth. I grabbed at his balls, trying to stop him, but he held my hands out of the way as he forced himself all the way in.

"Get it good and wet," he said.

I did as he said, slicking the length of him with my mouth until his shaft was covered in a mix of lipstick and spit. I was hoping I could make him come just from sucking him, and tried to keep him in my throat. But just as I thought he would lose it, he pulled out. Still standing at the side of the bed, he jerked my legs over his shoulders and impaled me on his shaft. My ass was still sore from Joe's pounding, and my tits ached from Tony's fingering. Now Alex worked on my cunt, spreading it wide with his thick cock.

Then both Tony and Joe were there again, their cocks hanging over my face. As Alex fucked me, they took turns sticking their pricks between my lips and making me suck them hard. As my mouth filled with cock, my pussy was being pounded by Alex's steel-hard dick. All around me I felt heat and skin and hard flesh.

"Come on," Alex said. "Come for me. Come for my big cock. I want to hear you come."

I slipped Joe's prick out of my mouth.

"You'll have to do better than that, little boy," I said. "I can't even feel you in there."

Pulling my legs tightly against him, Alex fucked me as hard as he could, his balls slapping against my ass. I knew that if I survived the night I'd be black and blue the next day. Even worse, my cunt was starting to ache like it did before I came. Every muscle in my body was tense, and I was on the verge of being swept away. Next to me, I could see Joe and Tony jerking off over my breasts. I started to moan.

"She's almost there," I heard Tony say. "Fuck her, man. Fuck her good. Make the bitch come."

I looked Tony in the eye. "Never call a lady a bitch," I said, and wrapped my hand around his cock. With three quick jerks, I felt him twitch, and his cum splattered against my tit. "You lose," I said.

Seeing Tony's cum dripping down my breast, both Joe and Alex lost it. They came together, one covering my chest with more jism, the other bucking against my cunt as he gasped for air.

"Very good, Sofia." Corelli was walking across the room toward us, his cigar filling the air with smoke. "You managed to outlast my best men. Your devotion to your husband is admirable."

"Looks like I win," I said.

Corelli smiled. "Not quite. You still haven't given me a chance."

The three men got off the bed, making room for Corelli. Alex went back and resumed his guard over Jake, while Joe and Tony stood watching. Corelli wiped his finger through the mixed puddle of cum on my chest. He brought it to my lips, smearing it across them.

"You look lovely in this," he said. "It's very becoming."

"Fuck you," I spat back.

Corelli laughed. "Why, that's exactly what I had in mind."

Removing his shoes, but keeping his clothes on, he stretched out on the bed with his head at the bottom of the mattress. "Come here," he said, patting his chest.

I turned around and straddled his chest. I was looking right at Jake as Corelli put his hands on my ass and pulled me forward. His mouth covered my pussy, and his tongue slid between the bruised lips. I put my hands on his shoulders to steady myself as he pushed up into me, eating the cum left behind by his men.

Jake's eyes were on mine as Corelli worked on me. I could see the fear in them as he watched my face for any sign that I might be about to come. Alex had the gun pressed tightly against his head, and I could see that he was sweating nervously.

I could also see that he was still hard. I doubted that he'd lost his erection through the whole thing. It struck me as funny, and for some reason I almost started to laugh. But then Corelli found my clit with his teeth and began to nibble softly at it. Unable to help myself, I ground my crotch against his face.

Reaching down, he unzipped his pants and pulled out his cock. Pushing me away from him, he looked into my face. "Sit on it," he said. "Feed my cock to your hungry cunt."

Crouching over him, I slipped his head inside me. Still keeping my eyes on Jake, I pushed down, swallowing Corelli's cock until I was sitting against his stomach. I watched my husband's face as I rode the prick of the man who wanted to kill him. I could tell that in spite of his terror, Jake was getting off on seeing me fuck another man, especially one who held his life in his hands. It wasn't about sex or even love. It was about power.

The truth was, I was getting off on it, too, and watching Jake was making me horny as shit. Looking into his eyes as Corelli's cock filled me, I knew that he longed to free his hands so he could jerk off. I imagined him sitting in the chair, his big prick gripped in his fist as he beat off. I pictured the head swelling, turning dark red as the blood filled it. I saw his balls pulling up as he came closer and closer. I saw the rain of cum splatter his belly as he went over the edge.

I couldn't help it. As Corelli pushed into me one last time, my throat opened and I began to cry out. My voice filled the room, and as I came in great, heaving gasps, my moans were echoed by the muffled sounds of a gunshot.

When I looked up, Jake was slumped forward in his chair. On the wall behind him was a red stain, as though someone had come in a great crimson splatter across the white surface. There was a smaller stain, darker, against the front of his pants.

"I win," said Corelli, pulling his cock out of me and pushing me away.

I lay on the bed, watching as Corelli zipped his pants and got up. He walked over to the mirror on the wall and looked at himself as he straightened his tie.

"Well, gentlemen, it looks like our little game is over. From now on, you report to me. If any of you don't like that arrangement, I'd be happy to give you the same chance Mr. Gioconda had."

He turned back to the bed. "As for Mrs. Gioconda, I think she showed us all just what it is she needs. For now she'll be staying with me. After all, a grieving widow needs all the comforting she can get."

Walking over to Eddie and the boys, he stopped before the blood-covered wall. "Any questions?"

Eddie shook his head. "No, sir." Jake's blood had speckled Eddie's shirt, as well as the shirts of the other men, and none of them could bring themselves to look at the body sitting between them.

"Good. Now why don't you boys go home. Joe will call you all in the morning to discuss your new positions."

He nodded toward Jake. "Get that piece of shit out of here."

Eddie and the other men left. None of them looked at me. Corelli's boys grabbed the chair with Jake's lifeless body still strapped to it and hauled it out of the room, leaving us alone. Corelli locked the door, then came back to the bed. Bending down, he kissed me deeply, his tongue as gentle as it had been cruel only moments before.

"You were good," he said, slipping the buttons of his shirt open and sliding it off. "I knew you would be."

"I had the easy part," I said, reaching behind to release the binding that held Nick's breasts in place. When they were free, I took one in my hand and ran my tongue lightly over the nipple. I bit. Nick jumped, drawing in a sharp breath.

"That's for making me wait so long," I said. I took the nipple in my mouth again, sucking gently this time and then releasing it. "You're so beautiful."

Nick laughed. "My father didn't think so. He never wanted anyone to know he had a daughter. He blamed me for my mother's death. That's why he sent me away. As far as anyone knew, there never was a Nicola Corelli. When I came back wearing suits instead of dresses, he didn't say a word to anyone. I think secretly he convinced himself that I'd been a boy all along. Even my brothers pretended."

"I knew the first time I saw you walking down the street that you'd be my lover," I said. "I went home and made myself come, thinking of kissing your face. When Jake fucked me that night, I thought about you holding me. It was the only time I was ever unfaithful to him."

"You meant the first time," Nick said teasingly.

She was right. After that day, I had looked for Nick everywhere. Sometimes I would see her on the street, or walking through the park. Each time, I would feel the dampness spread between my legs. Once, after catching a glimpse of her sitting a few tables away from me in a restaurant, drinking coffee, I had begged Jake to finger me under the table until I came watching her blow the smoke from her cigarette into the air.

We met, finally, at a New Year's Eve party held by a mutual associate. Shortly before midnight, I was going up the stairs to the ladies room, and Nick was coming down. She was dressed in a tuxedo, and when our eyes met, I held her gaze. She followed me to the bathroom, where she pushed me up against the wall and kissed me. Lifting me onto the edge of the sink, she fucked me for the first time. As the clock downstairs struck twelve, I came, moaning in Nick's ear as Jake looked around the room, wondering where I was.

After that, we saw one another whenever we could. It was as though Nick had entered my blood and flowed through my veins, filling me with her heat. I needed her every minute, and she needed me just as badly. All that stood in our way was Jake and Nick's family. One hot, wet summer night, while Jake was away on business and the thunder crashed around us as we lay in Nick's bed, we'd come up with our plan. Now, a few months later, we were together, as we'd dreamed of being.

"I remember seeing you at that party and asking my brother who you were," Nick said. "He laughed at me, telling me no woman would ever want me because I couldn't give her what she needed."

"But now your brothers are dead," I said, running my hands through Nick's hair and down her back. "And you're just what I need." I slid my hand into her open pants and felt the cock inside, the straps of the harness curving over her beautiful ass. "Jake used to be as hard as this after he'd killed someone."

Nick straddled me, pushing her cock against my belly. "But now Jake is dead, too, and you're mine. Poor Jake, he never should have told you where he was making the hit on Marotta."

"And you should never have told your old dear papa that Richie was trying to take some of his business away from him. Otherwise, he'd be safe and sound in his own bed."

Nick kissed me. "They knew the game was a dangerous one when they started playing it," she said. "They just didn't count on the players changing. But from now on, we're in control."

"Do you think we'll be able to pull it off?"

In answer, Nick entered me, and I enfolded her in my arms, drawing her deeper. As she began to fuck me, I knew that the game was just beginning.

Michael Thomas Ford's erotic writing has appeared under many different names in magazines such as *Paramour*, *Cupido*, and *Mach*, and in the collections *Best American Erotica 1995* and *1997*, *Flesh and the Word 3*, *Brothers of the Night*, *Ritual Sex*, *Flashpoint*, and *Leatherwomen III*. He is the editor of *Best Gay Erotica 1996*, *Happily Ever After: Erotic Fairy Tales for Men*, *Once Upon a Time: Erotic Fairy Tales for Women*, and *Butchboys*.

Stone Cold Perfect

by M. Christian

Yeah, they might swear, but they — the unders, the outsides, the beyonds — they don't have religion. Not like citizens, cops, or the big rich do. What they got are *names*.

You don't say *lucky*, for instance. You say *Brooks*, as in Jerome Brooks who was up for a dime and change for second-degree when a bank job went bloody. Was all set to hear the numbers, do the time, when the witness had a heart attack before he could give a deposition.

You don't say *stupid*, you say *Rosco*, as in Rosco Brown: A dumber-than-shit bagman who fell asleep in his car waiting for his pick-up. Car got towed with him inside, then he got popped "breaking into" the impound yard.

Small Tony blew it all in a war with Marco Giovanni, losing every inch of his territory, every soldier. Marco didn't fare much better, losing half his own turf and something like five mil in take when he put everything into hitting Tony. Marco didn't win, though, even after he torched Tony's Lincoln with Tony still inside — she skipped town with some mechanic from Queens. When you want to say *to die for,* you say *Jeena.*

Everyone tagged Isadore Durant for a idiot. Spent fifty grand putting together a heist on Newman Savings and Loan — a little Upstate pissant bank — all to replace a ledger. But over the next two years he got ten mil from the manager who'd been skimming — and didn't want the original ledger back. You don't say *smart.*

For getting set-up, for getting done — the kind of done that bites nasty and mean, you say *Toni Rivera.*

And when you want to say frosty death — someone stone, cold perfect — you say *Frankie DiNero.*

The hooker knocked twice — fast — just as, and where, Boxey'd told her. The door opened quickly, showing a room as faded and worn as the rest of the hotel: sour yellow curtains heavy and closed, thick and streaked by too many days uncleaned; a chipped and marred press-board dresser; a chipped gold-flake lamp; and a heavy, dark TV set rippled with scars from too many smoldering cigarettes.

"Hey, you here?" she said, dismissing the lamp as too unevenly balanced, not heavy enough to be effective. Maybe the cord — but only if she couldn't find anything else. "Boxey sent me, man. Said you wanted some '*com-pan-y.*'" She sang the last word making it jarring and strident, as if in a pathetic attempt to match a forgotten song —

Stepping in, she braced herself carefully in case he was going to try something rough. "Hey, man, you here or ain't ya?" She hoped he wouldn't, not because she couldn't handle him — because she could — but because it could be noisy … and noisy meant complicated. She didn't like complicated. She wanted to get in, do him quick, and get out.

He was standing behind the door, quiet as a piece of furniture. He swung the door shut just as quickly as he'd opened it.

It cost her just a second to weigh him: tall and broad, evenly distributed under a white T-shirt and black jeans. Simple black shoes. He was muscle, not just meat. His movements were even, careful and graceful. No heat, just bare, pale hands. She looked at his face, knowing before she did that all she needed to see were his eyes: cool cobalt never resting as he examined her. His features were hard and crisp from his unwavering concentration, sharp nose, thin lips, elegantly streamlined eyebrows. Dark hair, cut nondescript. He could be anyone in a crowd — save for his eyes. His eyes were sights and triggers — steel-jacketed.

She cracked her gum, looking him — broadly — up and down. "So, honey, you the guy looking for a date?"

He didn't say anything, just moved, and her purse was in his hands, then its contents on the floor in a glimmering cascade of cheap light. With every action — hand out, hand on the bag, bag upside down — his eyes never left hers.

"Hey, baby, I would have shown you–" she said, hands on hips.

He kicked her rat-tail comb aside, then the cheap switchblade. He didn't touch her little address book, the one with the utility blade inside, or the cheap necklace strung on piano wire.

She moved, acting impatient — trying to find an excuse to get close. Close enough. "Come on now, honey. I'm a gift. You know; a sweet little something wrapped up in a bow? You going to look me in the mouth, or you going to let me show you how special I am?"

"You know who I am?" he asked, stepping forward.

His reputation roared through her head, starting trained reflexes humming through her muscles: *Two fingers to his throat, knee to his balls. Necklace — and wire — close enough to loop it around his neck. Turn and heave him up by it.* Fear was unexpected for her, something burning and unpleasant. She wanted the job over and history, not in front of her and tense.

"'Someone big and very special, honey.' Boxey told me. Said I was to treat you right — *very* right. That's what I'm here to do — treat you very, *very* right." *I'm Boxey's reward, asshole: He's sweeping you under the rug. You've done your job and now you're gonna get ... retired. 'A little going away present,' that's what Boxey told me — told me to tell you.*

His jaw worked quickly, like he was chewing thoughts. She could almost hear them: fuck her or kick her out. "Go take a shower."

"Come on, honey," she purred, a practiced sexy rumble. "I'm clean — nice and clean and sweet. Good enough to taste ... and good enough to fuck." Lots to work with in the bathroom — towel rod, glasses, a razor if she was lucky — but that would take time: She wanted it over with. But she didn't move closer — getting it over with was one thing, walking into something she didn't know was another.

"What's the matter? Your meter running?" he said. His face was cool stone, unmarked by emotion, but his tones weren't granite.

"No way, baby; I'm here for as long as you want. I'm all yours. Every sexy inch of this gorgeous ass," she moved closer, adding a nice swing to her hips, a bounce that carried up through to her tits. She watched his eyes, saw them dip, a gentle drop down to them. "I just don't like to shower when it's light, baby. You know how that is — "

He actually smiled.

She was close enough — a beat, maybe two, and she could turn and slam her leg into his gut. Didn't have to be much, just enough to drop him, kick the wind out of him. Her knife, the address book, was still close enough.

Then she saw that his cock was hard, crammed tight against his thigh. His sights dimmed, became soft green eyes looking down at her tits. *Just* eyes.

Her mind stopped, frozen cold by that: his eyes — his cock. She let him walk by her, move into and through her range, and move toward the dresser. Too far away. "All right, but take that —" he waved at her clothes with a tight hand, but one subtly fluttering with nerves — "off first."

"You want to watch? That's sweet, baby. That's real sweet. I'll take it off for you nice and sexy — give you a real show. Just for you — "

She started a club-footed and clumsy strip, watching his posture and hands as she struggled with the black sports bra, hooking her thumbs into the springy, faded material then popping it up and off. His eyes blinked down, *just* eyes, not gunsights, grazing across her nipples — taking in the heavy weight of her tits.

Rocking her body with a heavy wave, she got them swaying back and forth. The room was cool, a winter bite leaking through cheap walls, so her nipples were at their best: fat and brilliant red. She shook them quickly back and forth as she rounded the bed and moved towards him, one hand low as if to go for his cock.

The reflexes, trained by years and lots of hotel rooms, spoke clear and loud in her head — *Grab and squeeze his balls. Elbow to the nose, aiming upward. When he falls back, get him in the throat with the heel of her hand. When he drops lower, kick him in the back* — but she didn't change her intentionally clumsy strip, didn't move to her bag, tense her legs for a kick.

He let her get close, damned close — his cock was hard all right. She could see it, a long shade against his leg.

Seeing it, she felt like laughing — the tension boiling out of her. Maybe powder and gun oil ran through his veins, but his little head still ran the show — another punk with gunslinger nerves and little-boy balls. She'd actually been *scared*, frightened of a reputation, a rumor. But what was under all that, what was he really ...?

She smiled at him, at the man. He was just a trick — just like so many others.

Her tits were out and free, beautiful full globes. She knew their effect, had seen it before: eyes glazing, mouths going slack at the sight of them. She watched the effect then, in that tired room: his eyes faded to mirrors, and in them she watched him stare at her.

No fear. Nothing but relief. She walked with a bounce, a practiced hooker's sway right up to him. Too close. Too close to hit him, too close to avoid being hit. But she wasn't thinking of that. She was drunk with laughter, giggles bubbling in her throat like cheap champagne.

"Come on, baby, let me suck that for a while," she said, soft and deep, standing in that too-close space where she could feel his body heat, smell the cheap hotel soap on his skin. She pressed her tits against his chest, and ran quivering fingertips down the length of his cock, feeling its tiny jerks, quiet vibrations.

She could almost see it, forced against his leg, a drop of pre-come oozing from the tip.

He was sweating. *He* was sweating —

"Fuck," he mumbled, hands lifting up as if to push her away — but ended up grabbing her tits. She'd braced herself, expecting a butcher's rough workings, but she didn't get them. Instead, he gently worked them, as if playing with their weight and shape. Fingers, tight and slightly stuttering with nerves, grazed her nipples.

The laughter again, tapping at the opening of her throat. She wanted to tilt her head back and let it out, a torrent of relief and scorn. *You fucking prick*, she thought, clear and strong as he lifted her tits and milked them forward — grazing her nipples across his chest, *you had me so fucking scared.*

You're just like the rest of them, aren't you? Little kid playing at being a big, bad guy. Playing with bullets but just wanting tits —

"Come on, baby," she said, pulling away, watching a flutter of disappointment travel across his face, "let me give you the rest of the show." Moving one step back, she started rocking gently back and forth on her too-high heels as she slowly crawled down the zipper of her jeans.

His eyes were riveted, drawn — magnet to metal — by her fingers, the zipper, the black Lycra panties she was slowly revealing. She watched him watch her, and felt her fear retreat, fall away. It was all so fucking easy: a gliding high. It was the easiest she'd ever done — well, *would* do, when she wanted to. There, *that* — that was it, the source of the high, the giggles that still threatened to spill from her painted-on smile: it was that she could, whenever she wanted to. Take him down, drop him fast and quick.

Whenever she wanted to. And, what the hell, she didn't want to — yet.

"Now, come on, baby, don't that look clean enough for you? Sweet enough to kiss?" she said, pushing her jeans down to her ankles with a little faster turn in her strip, showing him her black underwear.

He walked up to her, too fast and too hungry. She battled the reflex to smash his throat, break his neck.

He moved close.

She kissed him — and almost laughed down his throat.

When she broke away, she looked down, spoke: "Look at these — don't I have the damnedest tits, man?" she said, lifting them up, pointing her nipples at his chest.

"Fuck, yeah," he said, voice crumbling like a kid's, enraptured by the white skin, the silken beauty of her.

"*'Fuck, yeah,'*" she said, meaning it as mocking — but he was deaf, hearing only the words and not any hint of her real tone — as she stroked his cock through his still-intervening pants. His breathing was sharp and quick. "All me, man — no plastic in these." She took his hands and put them back on her tits, showing the boy how the woman liked it.

"All *yours*, baby — all *yours*. You wanna fuck me? You want some head? Whatever you want, baby. That's what I'm here for. Boxey's treat, man. All the lovin' you want," she said, cooing in his face, knowing that she could, and should, do him then, there — cold and icy. But she didn't.

It was because she could. That was it. *Whenever* she wanted to.

Not yet. A little longer. Not yet.

It was kind of a turn-on. Fuck that — it *was* a turn-on. "Come on, baby — get that cock out. I want to taste it...." she said, thinking her usual thoughts: planting her knee there, her fingers there, her knife there and there ... but putting it all aside as she kicked off her shoes — which thumped hollowly against the chest of drawers — rolled off her jeans, and clumsily reached for his fly.

"You want it?" he said, his voice low — as if he was speaking the words he'd always secretly wanted to say. Finally being able to, with her.

"You know I do," she breathed, hot and deep, getting down on her knees. "Come on over here and feed me that cock."

He crab-walked over to her, pants sliding down his ankles — and she almost lost it, there, then. Big bad walking like a duck, cock sticking out all hard and strong. But looking at him, she felt something rise in herself — something unexpected: a body surprise.

She pushed it, and didn't move — just let him shuffle towards her.

"You really want it, don't you." Not a question. A statement that he was praying, secretly, down deep to be true: that she did want it. Want him.

She had to admit it — that body surprise — she did. So she opened her mouth and let him ease his cock slowly in. He tasted of salt and bitter pre-come. The head of his cock was smooth, like silk, and she felt the shaft's texture as it slid over her lips, grazing her teeth.

Slowly, but then with more and more force, he started to fuck her face. That might have been the action, the movement between the two of them — but *she* wasn't getting her face fucked. She was on her knees all right, and, yeah, she had her mouth open and was stuffed with hard dick, but she was fucking *him*. It was royal, it was almost too much: Taking *his* dick, making him act like a cheap trick. She could take him anytime, slice him from balls to smile — but wanted to watch him fall, first. She wanted to watch him go all the way down....

She sucked him as he kept up a lame porno-movie monologue somewhere above her — and as he did she felt like giggling through her spit and his dick. She worked him, concentrating on breaking his prattle. "Oh, baby — um — oh, *yeah*, you're sucking — fuck, fuck, *fuck* — oh, yeah...."

"Come on, baby," she said, breaking her suck to smile up at him and wipe the drool from her chin. "Come in my mouth. I want to taste it."

"Getting fucking close," he said, smiling, looking more like a kid getting his cherry blown with every stroke she gave his cock.

"Or do you want my pussy? You can fuck my pussy if you want. If that's what you want — " she growled, hiding the heavy thoughts rumbling through her mind: *Beg for my cunt, baby. Beg for it. I want you down on your knees before I turn out your lights. I want you with your dick in your hand, jizz on the ground — before I do you.*

"Fuck, yeah!" he said, with a touch of hoarseness in his voice, grabbing her arm and lifting, slightly suggesting she get to her feet.

So she did, standing quick and straight. It appeared to her that she was looking down on him, towering above. She had one hand on his cock, holding him tight. "You want my pussy?"

"Yeah — yeah, I do."

Beg for it. Get down and beg for it. "How bad you want it, baby? Real bad?"

"Fuck, yeah," he said, touching her tits again — sweaty hands on her too-hard nipples.

"Then I guess I'm gonna have to give it to you." *Then I'm going to give it to you —*

She moved to the bed, stood next to the scratchy fabric of the bedcover, and hooked her thumbs in the waistband of her cheap black panties. Slowly, a fraction of an inch at a time, she brought them down, bending over as they slipped past her knees.

Kicking them off — bouncing them off the chest of drawers — she stood: She felt big, tall — fucking huge next to his tiny dick, his tiny balls, his tiny fucking rep....

He didn't move. Mouth slightly parted, he looked at her, was lost in her.

She scooted back across the yellow-ish, gold-ish, puke-ish bedcover — feeling the friction on her ass as a glowing warmth — and swung her legs wide, showing him her all.

"So," she purred, rough and tiger, harsh and lion, cold and cobra, "you want to fuck me, baby?"

Then he was — dick sliding into her surprisingly-wet cunt. "Oh, baby, give it to me — " she crooned, thinking of it as his last fuck, and getting jazzed. She felt her cunt respond, quivers of heat. "Fuck me, baby! God, yes, fuck me!" she cried, scraping his back with her nails, pulling him in deeper, slamming herself onto him as much as he was slamming into her. Their fucking made a wet, fast drumbeat in the room, a smacking applause that bounced off the walls and seemed to make them fuck ever faster — like an audience giving approval.

Distantly, she knew she could reach up and smash him across the face. He'd spasm and jerk away — then she'd kick a strong leg into his lower chest, aiming for his kidneys, spleen. A miss and he'd be down and out, a good hit and he'd rupture and be dead in hours.

Then she was coming — a rolling, churning come that surprised her with its brilliance and power. It came from somewhere surprising, from a corner she didn't expect. It set her teeth chattering and made her cunt spasm around his busy cock — as he fucked and fucked and fucked her into the bed. As she came, she felt herself lift up — it was all so perfect, so fucking perfect: *Fuck me, do me, you stupid prick. When you're done and you have that stupid smile on your face — I'll do you.*

Then he came. With a rattling groan, he came — a hot wetness that was almost invisible in her molten cunt. Panting, he dropped — flopping his sweaty weight on top of her.

Pushing him up, she rolled out from under him. "That was real good, baby. Now why don't you rest up a sec while I go take a splash," she said, moving quick and quiet, stopping only for a hammer of her heart (after-come, not fear) to neatly scoop up the book and the necklace.

In the bathroom she actually did splash, a sharp spray into the yellowing bowl. Getting up and wiping — and almost giggling from the feminine gesture — she caught her face in the mirror, felt and saw the smile brighten across her face. Then she pried the blade from the address book, cocked it behind her back, and looped the necklace around her other wrist — ready to grab.

She came out to him sitting on the edge of the bed. Not even noticing that she'd stepped away. Naked, he stared at the mumbling, glowing TV set.

As she walked toward him, moving on the balls of her feet — taking her time, knowing she had nothing, nothing at all to fear — a voice tumbled into sense from the warming set: " — earlier today. Reports are still coming in that famed Mafia attorney Howard Moscowtz — "

With the knife behind her back, the necklace looped in her fist, she moved around the bed ... *wire around the neck, he'll jerk away, but the knife is right behind, ear to ear...*

The set's glowing display caught her attention for a second, then held it for three: " — we have just heard that Moscowtz has been moved out of intensive care and is resting comfortably — "

She stood, stared. Her voice spoke without her, lazy with shock: "You fucked up. But you *never* fuck up — "

Then he stood up and walked with cool grace to the set, turned it off. "That wasn't the hit I was paid to do," Frankie DiNero said, bending down with calm precision, steel and gun oil accuracy — the trick gone, vanished as a professional pall fell over his icy face — to pull the belt from his discarded jeans. "I'm your 'going away present.' That's what Boxey told me — told me to tell you," he said to her, to Toni Rivera.

M. Christian's short stories have appeared in numerous anthologies including the *Best American Erotica* and *Mammoth Book of Erotica* series, and in his forthcoming collection, *Dirty Words* (Alyson). His editing projects have included *Eros Ex Machina, Midsummer Night's Dreams,* and *Rough Stuff* (with Simon Sheppard). He is a columnist for *Scarlet Letters* (www.scarletletters.com) and *Bonetree* (www.bonetree.com).

The Crush

by Jason Bovberg

When Etta Ruby first stepped into my office, I was looking at a nude picture of her. It was my favorite, the one that showed her with engine oil sluicing down between her large breasts. I'd taken it the night before, along with a dozen or so others. I was imagining the look on her husband's face when I showed them to him.

"Uh," I said. "You don't go in for knocking, huh?"

She lit a cigarette as I calmly slipped the picture back into the desk drawer. The flame of her small lighter lit up her face in a nice way. Her lipstick glowed crimson. So did the auburn hair framing that nice face. I noticed her hands shaking a little.

"You're McCallister." My name came out of her pretty mouth on a rush of smoke. "Jack McCallister."

I didn't answer right away.

The entire series of pictures was still fresh in my head. Etta Ruby in the arms of her mechanic, oil all over the place, smeared across her cheeks, swiped in finger-stripes across her thighs, shiny at her flared labia.

Etta cleaned up pretty well.

"My husband gave you some money," she mumbled. "To follow me."

"I don't know what you're talk–"

"Don't play the fool with me."

Etta Ruby was scared. Scared big. A white fluff of ash drifted from her trembling cigarette to the floor. I did the math. Hell, I was scared of her husband, too.

"What brings you here, Mrs. Ruby?" I leaned forward in my chair, concealing the erection produced by her photographs.

"*You* do, of course." She pushed some anger through her unease. "You and my husband. I feel like the mouse to you two Tomcats. Do you have any idea what that's like? I'm trapped, Mr. McCallister." She crossed her arms. The cigarette and her eyes smoldered.

"I'm just doing my job, Mrs. Ruby."

"Etta."

My mouth opened. Nothing came out for a second.

"I'm just doing my job, Etta," I repeated quietly. "A person gives me some dough and I have to do certain things."

"My husband and I don't make love anymore. You should know that. He doesn't love me and I don't love him. He's an animal. I need passion, Mr. McCallister."

"Jack," I offered. Something caught in my throat.

She stared at me with her big eyes. Then she came closer to my desk. I could smell her perfume. The scent matched her looks. She leaned toward me.

"I know you're supposed to be following me," she whispered, "but I beg you to stop. Give my husband a lie. I'm in love for the first time in my life. I don't want to jeopardize that."

"I'm not a liar, Etta."

"Then give him his money back. I can pay you, too. I can pay you more."

"I'm not in that business."

We stared at each other for a while.

"And I'm more than what's in that picture, Mr. McCallister." She straightened up and stubbed her cigarette out on my desk. Then she turned around and walked out.

I sat staring at the door. It said PRIVATE backwards.

When I thought about Ted Ruby, I couldn't see his face. We had met only that one time, in the back seat of his big '51 Caddy. In my head I only saw the brim of a dirty Stetson and a stubbled double chin. And a wad of money.

A big man with a small voice.

"You were recommended by Raymond Keller," he'd said.

"I've heard of him."

I could hear the smirk in his voice. "Told me about the job you did for him. The photos. You remember? Tiny Eddie, the bookie?" Ted Ruby's high-pitched voice could not hide beneath an attempted husky whisper. "Yeah, Ray took care of him. One of Tiny's hands has only two fingers now. You should see him try to count his dough. Like pincers. Big tears in his eyes." He chortled. The sound was unsettling.

"Why'd you call me?" I asked.

His sound stopped. "I can see you're a man who likes to chew right down to the bone." His voice was giving me head pains. He drew a roll of large bills from inside his dark suit and peeled off four or five of them. "Mr. McCallister, I don't trust my wife. She's a whore."

I just looked at the brim of his hat. Ted Ruby's fat little hand dropped the crisp bills in my lap. My gaze followed them. It had been a slow month. My last job, in fact, had been the one Ruby'd just mentioned. That was two months earlier. I still had Tiny Eddie's negatives hanging in my darkroom closet. In them he still had ten fingers.

I pocketed the money.

"If you know she's fucking around, what do you need me for?"

"I want pictures, Jack." His head moved up so that I could see his teeth. They were crooked and stained. The tip of his tongue touched his bottom lip, then withdrew.

"Why?"

"I like pictures."

Someone opened the car door, startling me.

Ted Ruby handed me a folded piece of paper. I reached for it, but he snatched it back. "This is the address. *My* address. Don't give it to nobody." I took it.

I stepped out and the car went away.

Those were the only words I'd exchanged with the man. Through the whole thing, I never saw his eyes.

I blinked, looked away from the PRIVATE sign. I opened the top drawer again and took out the pictures of Ted Ruby's wife. I spread them out on the desk.

They took me back a couple nights.

Etta had been a cinch to follow. I'd waited outside the Ruby home, parked across the street. She came out after dark and I perked up. She backed out of her private drive and headed south on Glendale, on her way out of the city with the same name. West on Beverly took her to her destination. She pulled into a dank alley and parked. I killed my lights and watched from the street. She got out of her fancy Nash Rambler and entered a small grease shop. I stopped my Plymouth, opened the door, looked both ways, and strolled over to a window. I peered inside the place. She was already in the guy's arms.

I knew the mechanic vaguely. He'd worked on my brakes once a long time ago. Didn't recall his name. Slim guy. Moustache.

I snapped my first picture of the evening. The only one, it turned out, that showed the two of them with clothes on.

I looked at that one now, fingered it.

I remembered the way things had gone after that. Etta Ruby's clothes had seemed to melt off her. Her breasts puffed out once the bust of her dress went down. She gasped. I watched her nipples pebble in the half-light of the garage. The guy's dirty hands were all over her.

Etta swiveled her hips and the dress slithered to the ground.

I raised my eyebrows and took another photograph.

Naked, they faced each other. The mechanic's long, thin cock poked at Etta's navel. She was running her hands over his chest. He was doing the same thing to her. He had the better half of that bargain.

She said something to him and he nodded. The mechanic shuffled over to his workbench and carefully opened a can of motor oil. I brought the camera down and frowned. Etta waited eagerly, running her middle finger between her thighs. Even from behind a grimy window, maybe twenty feet away, I could see the glisten of her sex. Her finger looked as oily as what was in the can. With her other hand, she manipulated one large, dark nipple. The mechanic turned, oil in hand, and went back to her. As if by design, she sat down on the garage floor, facing the door. Her wet labia pouted anxiously.

The guy stood behind her. His cock hovered over her head. He kneeled and began pouring the syrupy fluid over her shoulders.

"Holy smokes," I whispered, snapping a shot. I shook my head, laughing a little.

Etta closed her eyes and rubbed the oil all over herself. She glowed like one of those glamour girls on the Coca-Cola posters.

I took a picture.

She reached behind her with one slick hand and grasped the mechanic's penis, which angled like a divining rod over her auburn hair. He shuddered as she stroked it. He dropped the empty can and she pulled him around in front of her. He sat facing her. That's all they did for a long time. Stare at each other.

I waited for things to heat up, which they always did.

They scooted their naked bodies closer, finally, and started touching each other. Their hands slipped and slid all over the place. They got filthy with oil. The guy's hands were dirty and weathered, but she let him touch her everywhere. When he slid a callused finger down through the groove of her kisp, I grunted in distaste while I took another picture. Ted Ruby was going to go nuts.

That's all the two of them did, really. I couldn't figure it.

After, they wiped each other off with rags. Etta stepped into a tiny bathroom and used a blackened cake of soap to wash herself. While the mechanic stuffed away his cock, I watched her bend and twist, reaching with the wet rag for oily flesh. Her cunt, nestled between firm thighs, winked at me several times, and her full, round rear blushed.

I got one last picture and walked back to my car.

I earned the rest of the bills in my pocket when I strung up the photos in my darkroom. I studied them. They were good. I used them in a private way. I decided to make my own set.

Later, I collected them and wrapped them in paper, tied them up with string.

Now they sat on the ratty couch on the other side of the room. Etta could've snatched them up, negatives and all. She could have saved herself. Maybe she didn't want to.

I stared at the photograph that showed oil running down between her generous breasts. I scanned the rest.

The pictures seemed different now.

I climbed into my Plymouth and took off up La Brea. The streets were hot and empty. I thought about Ted Ruby.

He was the worst scum. And he was my employer. He was no one to me, and yet he was my means for living right now. Honor and honesty forbade me to betray him. I had to rat on his beautiful wife. I had to do it. I'd told him I would.

I took a right on Hollywood Boulevard. Whores bent at their little waists to peer into stopped cars. Etta wasn't one of those. No way.

Before I knew it, my car was idling outside the Ruby house. I glanced over at the pictures in the passenger seat. I wondered who would come out of the house first. I guessed that would decide it.

Two hours later, at dusk, Etta pulled out onto the street. She looked upset. I watched her wipe a tear off her fair cheek before she sped off.

I tailed her back to the garage. The car came to a jolting stop and she ran to the door. She knocked on it a few times. No one was home. She bowed her head, stared at the cluttered porch for a long moment. Knocked again. I wanted to get out of the car and go to her, comfort her somehow. Then I realized what a goddamn stupid idea that was.

I swallowed, looked over at the photos on the seat.

Dames play funny with your head.

I motored away from Etta Ruby. My heart was beating fast. I couldn't tell you why. The whole situation was trouble. I knew I should just drive back to Ted Ruby's house and fan the pictures out across his desk. I also knew I really ought to burn the damn things.

I cruised down Western. Took the left on Wilshire. My building stood, looking abandoned, at the corner of Wilshire and La Brea. Maybe I'd start considering another line of work. I pulled up to the curb and got out. The evening stood still and quiet.

I rumbled up the elevator, watched the numbers light up. I opened up the door and trudged into my office. I felt like maybe I was coming down with something. My stomach was all in knots.

I fell into my chair and looked out toward Santa Monica. Beyond it, the ocean, blanketed with haze. You could get lost out there.

Pretty soon I was asleep.

The second time Etta Ruby stepped into my office, I was looking at a nude picture of her. It was the one that showed the mechanic's cracked finger gliding along her eager kisp.

"Perhaps I'm overestimating you, Mr. McCallister." She strode in trailing a swirl of smoke. Under her hat, she looked at once purposeful and vulnerable. I liked both of those things. She wore a dark blue dress and heels.

I put the picture away clumsily.

"I could easily believe you've been sitting here since our last meeting, ogling that picture. May I see it?"

"No."

"Why not? Surely its negative is hidden somewhere safe. Perhaps all of your pictures are already in my husband's oafish mitts." Her voice broke just slightly and she shut up.

I reached into the drawer and took out the top picture. I handed it over.

She studied it for half a minute. Her red lips pursed. She gave it back.

"Has Ted seen this?"

"I haven't called him yet."

"I see."

"Not much there," I said. "Usually I take pictures of people fucking. I don't know how a guy'll respond to pictures of his wife splashing around in motor oil."

"'Fucking.' Not a nice word."

"Neither is 'adultery.'"

"There's more to fucking than a penis penetrating a vagina, you know."

"Not in my book."

"I'll forego a discussion of tantric sex. This is neither the time nor the place. Besides, I can't see how any of this is your business."

"Your husband made it my business when he dropped five large in my lap."

"Is that what you're all about, Jack? Money?" She walked over and perched on the edge of my desk. "There must be more to life than that."

"Maybe."

Etta Ruby took off her hat and tossed it over onto the couch. It brushed the package of photographs. Her hair spilled down past her shoulders like the oil.

"Does that door lock?" she asked, getting up.

"Mrs. Ruby–"

"Etta."

She slid the lock home and approached me. She reached behind her and undid something. The blue dress slithered off her. Her nakedness stunned me, and I sat back in my chair.

"This is the wrong thing to do," I told her.

"You prefer masturbating to photographs?"

"I mean . . . ."

"Shut up and take your clothes off."

I obeyed her. I stood up and loosened my belt, let my trousers pool at my feet. I stepped out of them and yanked my shirt over my head. Etta walked around my desk in her heels, and reached out for me. Her touch was hot. I whisked down my boxers and felt her fingers encircle me. Her breasts pushed against my chest. I felt the head of my cock burrow into her auburn pubic mound.

"Occasionally," she breathed, "I do like to fuck."

She had me in her fist. Not just my cock. I didn't care.

I reached behind her and took two handfuls of her rear. The cheeks were warm, soft and hard at the same time. My fingers delved deep, down and between. They found her sodden crevice and explored.

She slammed herself against me and I fell back into my chair. She came down with me, taking me into her mouth abruptly. I almost shouted. She braced herself on my thighs and went nuts. She had a talented mouth.

After some time, I urged her back up. She disengaged from her oral clutch with reluctance and climbed my body. She kissed the tip of my spittled cock with her wet labia. I took her by the waist and set her on my desk, spreading her legs. I scooted my chair up to her. She tasted like smoke and flowers. She leaned back, breasts heaving. She held onto the far edge of the desk for dear life.

"Mr. Mc-*Cal*-lister!" she panted.

"Jack," I muffled.

She flung one leg over my shoulder, then the other, and squeezed, pulling my face more firmly into her. I thrashed my tongue about.

I stood up and she opened her eyes. She leaned forward, smiling in a naughty way, and wiped my cheeks of her nectar. Then she licked her fingers.

I poked the head of my penis against her slippery cunt. Etta waited patiently. She seemed to prefer the moment over the suspense. It reminded me of her lazy oil bath with the mechanic.

I didn't go in for that kind of nonsense. I stepped forward, pushing myself into her to the hilt. She just closed her eyes, a kind of wistful smile playing on her lips. I started up with a deep rhythm, my balls slapping the middle desk drawer. I stared at her breasts, which moved in a voluptuous way as I thrust.

She just sat there with that dreamy look on her face.

Finally, she said, "Sit back down, big boy."

I withdrew from her and sat back into my chair. She stepped over me and steadied herself over my lap. I let her take hold and guide me into her. I closed my own eyes. She gave me her full weight. I felt imbedded. She started rutting back and forth in a surprisingly pleasing hip rotation.

Etta felt my release approaching. She knew what she was doing.

I convulsed and she rode it out, pressing down onto me even harder as I cried out into her hair. My cock buzzed and sparked, then calmed. I wrapped my arms around her and pulled her close.

Over her naked shoulder I saw the package, next to her hat. I was already imagining it in flames. When she was gone I'd douse it with lighter fluid and toss it in the metal trash can. Light a match.

Etta Ruby pulled away from my chest and stared into my eyes. I caressed one of her breasts lovingly. The nipple hardened between my fingers.

"Please lie to my husband," she whispered. "I'm a woman in love. I need passion, Mr. McCallister."

I let my hand fall. I felt myself go limp inside her.

Etta Ruby was a woman in love.

But not with me.

Ted Ruby's Caddy purred outside. I looked at it through dirty windows. I could see his Stetson. It wasn't moving much.

I took a breath and went out. The sun beat down hard. I squinted up at it, resigned.

A guy was suddenly there to open up the Cadillac's back door. I stared into the smoky maw and thought about turning around.

I stepped inside.

"You got the goods?"

"Sure."

"Well?"

I felt sick. I handed over the package and he ripped it open. The negatives fell out first, onto the seat between us, then the photos slipped out like cards. I looked out the window at people walking by. The pictures made rough sounds between his fingers.

"Whore," he mumbled. Then, louder, "What are they doing? Who the fuck is this?"

"Mechanic."

"No shit. What's his name?"

"How should I know? All you wanted was pictures."

"Yeah, you earned your keep. Now get the fuck out of my car."

I stumbled out and the door slammed behind me. The Caddy peeled out of there. I staggered up to my office and vomited into the toilet.

I sat behind my desk for three hours. I studied the stain directly above the middle drawer. What was that whiny-voiced slob doing to Etta?

There's more to fucking than a penis penetrating a vagina, you know.

I thought about what she'd said.

And there's more to love, I added, *than fucking.*

I grabbed my hat and jogged down to my Plymouth. I raced up the new Santa Monica Expressway to Glendale Boulevard, then high-tailed it north to the house. Everything was quiet and still. No lights. Leaving the car idling in neutral, I jumped out and pounded on the door. No answer. I listened for shouting, for crying. Nothing.

"Etta!" I called. My voice caught miserably.

I got back into my car and gunned it south, down Glendale to Beverly. I found the alley and squeezed in, then parked. This place looked deserted, too. I went to the door and found it open.

My body seemed to lose all its strength.

I pushed open the door. Something was wrong.

"Anybody home?" I called, stepping in.

A single bare bulb hung over a workbench, the only light in the place. I squinted, trying to make sense out of shadows. Desiccated hulks of automobiles looked monstrous in the corners. I felt with my hand for a light switch.

Something dripped. Could have been oil.

I found the switch. The place came alive. I felt like I'd stepped into one of my photographs from the other night.

I walked toward the lavender '50 Mercury in the center of the garage. It was right on the spot where Etta had —

I stopped.

Etta Ruby and her mechanic had been crushed beneath the Mercury. Naked and slick with oil, their bodies were flattened into the floor of the garage. The car's tires were wet with gore.

I sat down against the driver's door for a while.

Then I walked back to my Plymouth and drove back to my office.

Jason Bovberg is editor of Dark Highway Press, which published Robert Devereaux's *Santa Steps Out* and the forthcoming *Skull Full of Spurs: A Roundup of Weird Westerns*. He lives in the wilds of northern Colorado with his wife Barbara and his poodle Cujo. He is working on a novel titled *The Naked Dame*, which will feature Jack McCallister, smoking guns, cool cars, and, of course, a naked dame. Consider this story the prologue.

Night of A Thousand Fish

by Bill Brent

Shattering the silence of the deserted industrial district, the fire trucks raced through the dark to squelch the threatening inferno. Glass littered the street — glass bursting out of the nightclub's aquarium-style windows, glass shattered and hanging out of the unfortunate cars parked too close to the blaze. The alarm box still sounded from where the first of the few fortunate escapees had run to alert the department of this sudden, deadly blaze.

It was difficult to guess how many revelers were trapped inside — there'd be a bone-count later. It would take days to sort out the mess. Employees and roommates would turn up missing. The site would be sacked and looted. And that sign, that famous sign, one of the city night's boldest eye-catchers, hung limp, broken, extinguished.

It was one hell of a note to start the New Year of 1982.

La Notte di Mille Pesci. The Night of a Thousand Fish. You know the famous neon sign — a three-story-high martini glass filled with bubbles and dozens of multicolored fish, all tipsy-eyed and smiling. Night of a Thousand Fish. Burned to the ground, a formidable testament to the high price of reduced funding for the City's impoverished Fire Department, spread too thin putting out too many fires on the rowdiest night of the year. Night of a Thousand Fish. You know the rumors — a secret S/M palace after hours, catering to the kinkiest of the *hoi polloi*.

Night of a Thousand Fish. You know the sign. You know the rumors. Now know the story.

The odd name had come to the owner in a dream. Don Mariani ("Donny-Marie" to his gay comrades) was a second-generation Italian-American, first-generation leatherman. He still dreamed sometimes in the language that his parents had spoken while he was growing up. A few years back, his dad died suddenly and left him a hefty little sum. It was enough to wedge his foot in the doorway of his dream — to own a nightclub. Be the consummate showman.

Our paths first crossed when I hit lean times. In a desperate attempt to stay one step ahead of the collection agencies, I had signed on with Security Services. "The SS," as we temps bitterly called our sleazy employer, specialized in security guards and entry-level detective services. That's right Humiliating as it sounds, I was a temp detective. Hey, it was better than starving.

Don had been having trouble with vandals and with staffers dipping into the till, so he was using the agency's services to help keep an eye on things. Eventually, Donny-Marie had sent the other temps on their not-so-merry way and re-hired me, unbeknownst to my former employer. "Most of those guys just don't have a lot on the ball. You I like. I'd rather pay you more under the table, we just cut out the middleman. Sound okay to you?"

It sure did. It meant I'd be getting double the going rate for security temping. And no damned taxes on it, either.

"If you're going to hang out here, you might as well know *everything* that goes on here," Don told me. "We run a little sideline on the upstairs floor in the back," he grinned. "Come on, I'll show you."

"Now this is our cozy little dungeon-for-hire," Don explained. "Any time we get out-of-town visitors with a kinky streak, or if any of the local muckety-mucks want a place where they can satisfy their raunchier appetites, this is the place to come. We're totally discreet here. The room is soundproof. There's even a secret back entrance."

"Do you have this going most nights of the week?"

"I wish. It's damn good money, and completely off the books," he sighed. "Oh, you know how it is. This is the kind of shit that an out-of-towner would love to believe goes on here all the time."

I hefted a pair of fat, heavily padded wrist restraints dangling from the ceiling on a chain. "So how do they find out about this scene?"

"Word travels in all the right circles," Don smiled.

One of the unforeseen perks of working for Don was free access to the dungeon on off-nights. For my girlfriend Kendra's birthday, we arranged for her to be "kidnapped" by several of our play-pals. We dragged her off in a van to Don's dungeon, which then exploded in a flurry of restraints, strap-ons, and nipple clamps. Cocks, fingers, and breasts tunneled into every orifice she had, and maybe a couple she hadn't known about. I'd never seen her so turned on. All night, Kendra's lithe frame was one rippling, undulating, thrashing current of shrieking orgasms. Still, the real climax was lighting twenty-six candles — on Kendra — and watching them slowly burn down. And watching Kendra, delirious with pleasure and fright, go slowly out of her mind. Why blow out candles when you can blow out the birthday girl instead?

That was well over a year ago, damn it. Eventually Don had to let me go. Even gave me two weeks' notice with severance pay. A heck of a guy, really. Treated me way better than any of my so-called "legitimate" employers ever had. But these days, I'm happy to be working for myself again.

I got the call from Don a couple of days after the fire. "Meet me at greens. We'll discuss everything there."

greens: the popular vegetarian restaurant run by Zen monks out at Fort Mason, in one of San Francisco's many converted military buildings. greens: the only restaurant in town pretentious enough to avoid capitalizing its name. greens: yuppie grub favored by guilty meat-eaters in recovery.

Don was smoking at the restaurant door when I walked up. Don grinned broadly at everyone as a manner of greeting. We were opposites in many ways. Where Don grinned, I scowled. Where he was expansive, I was reclusive. But we were both shrewd and independent entrepreneurs, and this formed the basis of our mutual respect. "Dick, how ya been?"

"Things have been worse. I've even been pretty busy lately," I replied. "Several cases going, and I haven't had to call that smarmy agency since you whisked me away from them."

Don chuckled. "Well, that's good to hear. Let's go have a seat."

The restaurant was really one huge room. Its short lobby was separated from the main dining area by several enormous pieces of wood burl furniture.

The shaved-headed host seated us in a small alcove off to one side of the main dining area. It afforded us one hell of a view of the marina's harbor and the Golden Gate Bridge beyond. "Normally, you have to have a party of six or more to get this room," Don grinned. "Or you have to remind the maitre d' that you know about his shady past before he got all religious and shaved his head."

"I guess that would help."

"You seem a little uncomfortable, my friend."

"I'm just not used to places like this. Greasy spoons and Formica are more my speed."

"You should check out the men's room," Don chuckled. I looked at him warily. "Well, go see!"

There were two stalls. One was a fairly conventional Western toilet, while the other contained a Japanese-style squat toilet. My mind flashed to an image of two or more monks pressed into service to pry a large, over-indulgent patron off the narrow potty.

One other feature struck me, and that was the number of reflective chrome surfaces in the wash-up area. As I lingered, two other patrons stepped up to the urinals, and my suspicions were confirmed: if you stood at just the right spot, the reflective surface afforded you a full genital display of any guy taking a piss. Briefly I wondered which clever monk was responsible for *that* innovation. Then I realized it was really the machinations of some irreverent fag designer.

When I returned, there were several small servings of appetizers on the table. "That's a pretty unusual john."

"Yeah, I thought you'd get a kick out of that. My ex designed it." So I was right.

"Have something to eat," Don encouraged me. I searched in vain for something containing meat. I finally settled on some stuffed mushrooms. Slimy, but pretty tasty, after all. Maybe this wouldn't be such an ordeal.

"Well, Don, you seem pretty upbeat for someone who's just been burned out of business."

"Easy come, easy go," he replied philosophically. "I let my partner Philippe do the brooding. He's depressed enough right now for us both. Me, I'm just happy I got out with my skin intact. I figure anything else is gravy."

"Do they have a final body count?"

"Yeah. It looks like about sixty-five."

I gave a low whistle. A figure like that made this one of the biggest disasters in the City's history.

"Basically, it was anyone who was trapped upstairs and didn't know about the secret exit out the back of the playroom. That wooden stairway, the main one, must have gone up real fast. Plus, anyone who was on the ground floor, more than about thirty feet away from the exits, they never had a chance."

I knew the club's setup. Any of its usual deterrents to safety would have been exacerbated by a New Year's Eve crowd. "Large, unruly crowds don't behave," I began. "*La Notte* was full of people who don't usually get drunk. Plus, it was raining that night, so you'd be dealing with piles of wet coats, scarves, sweaters, and umbrellas. Flammable liquids — alcohol — and candles on cloth-covered tables. Of course, the place was packed beyond the legal capacity. SRO on the staircase for the shows — customers standing on the wall by the kitchen — totally illegal."

"Well, yeah–"

"I'm not judging you. If I were you, I'd have done the same."

"Feast or famine." He shrugged ruefully.

"When did you notice the fire?"

"I didn't. I was down in the basement, working on some bookkeeping, when my cook shouted over the intercom that the building was on fire. I didn't ask a lot of questions. I just grabbed my coat, a couple of important files, and the night's deposits, and got my ass out the fire door. I didn't even see a blaze until I was outdoors."

"And then what did you do?"

"Well, the fire department had already been called. My first thought was to make sure that Philippe and the staff were safely out of the building. Philippe I found fairly quickly, and we managed to track down most of the staff soon enough. Except for Eric and Hector."

"Dead meat?"

"Looks that way." He shook his head and stared out at the harbor.

"Are you gentlemen ready to order?"

"Yeah. I'll have the grilled red pepper polenta," Don replied. "Plus a garden greens salad."

The waiter looked at me expectantly.

"Uh, I'll have the same," I stated, hoping in vain that "polenta" was some kind of chicken or fish. "Dead meat," indeed. Not bloody likely at this inner sanctum of sanctimonious, flesh-free consumption.

"And to drink?"

"Bring us a bottle of Hop Kiln Chardonnay. And water," Don ordered, sending the waiter on his way.

"So what do you want me to do?"

"Poke around. Stir shit up. Stir some ashes up. Find the party who set my club on fire."

"What makes you think the City won't do that?

"Their agenda will be to deflect as much responsibility from themselves as possible. And try to dump it on us. Furthermore, when the place went up, we were hosting a very special guest in our dungeon, along with his favorite Mistress. Let's just say that he's prominent enough and paranoid enough to make sure that not too many of the details get revealed. My guess is that they'll chalk it up to a pre-code lighting fixture shorting out, or something similar.

"Let's just also say, for the sake of *argument*, of course — this being a purely *academic* assumption — that some of the City's dignitaries had been surreptitiously videotaped having a wild romp in the fun-room upstairs. If such tapes indeed *existed*, and if they were inadvertently leaked to the right sources, it could make life even *more* interesting for some people who already lead *extremely* interesting lives."

I smirked. "Lifestyles of the Rich and Famous."

"Yeah! The 'not-ready-for-prime-time' version, kind o'. Or, conversely, the existence of such hypothetical tapes merely could be *revealed* to the guilty parties, who would then do *a lot* to ensure that nothing painful and avoidable happened to us folks who ran the fun-room."

"And what about the class action suit that's going to be landing on your doorstep once the families of the deceased get together?"

"That's where you come in. I am almost positive that this fire was set maliciously. So I believe that all this hypothetical nastiness I've just described could certainly be *avoided*. I don't think this fire had anything to do with pre-code fixtures, and I don't think the City really believes that, either. But when your back's against the wall, whatcha gonna do? Anyway, we have several suspects. Your job is to pin the goods on one of 'em, if you can."

"Well, okay, then, what've we got to work with?"

"So glad you asked. Well, first of all, there's Lizzie's ex. Or, should I say, 'ex-con.' Miss Lizzie was the hostess that night. She'd been working for us about four months, came in once with a black eye, had bruises on several occasions. Anyway, she'd dumped her boyfriend a couple of weeks ago. But he'd been stalking her since. I was about to give her two weeks' notice since her continued presence meant *his* continued presence. Not very kind of me, but still, a perceived threat is better than an actual one. And this dude was *bad* news. The bouncers kept him outside the door, but he still could have started something on the periphery. Or sent in one of his buds to do the dirty work."

"Did she get out in time?"

"Yeah, barely. She was treated at S.F. General for burns."

I was taking notes as quickly as Don was guzzling the newly-arrived Chardonnay.

"Now, we're also looking at a group of ex-patrons — loud, boisterous drunk punks — who'd been bounced. We kept a list of names and descriptions, which we gave to the bouncers. New Year's Eve would have provided the perfect opportunity to settle a little grudge match."

"Then — let's see, there was Raymond. A disgruntled ex-employee. I'd sacked him for dealing drugs on the premises. Just not a great idea, y'know. *Way* too public about it." Don stared into his wine glass. "Now, if it'd been someone that the facilitator had sent in to 'manage' the place, and he was doing this kind of thing, there's not a lot I could do about it."

"Wait a second. What's a 'facilitator'?"

"Well, my friend, you're about to be educated in the highfalutin' lingo of grubby nightclub owners. A 'facilitator' is — well, he's a consultant of sorts — you pay a large sum of money to a facilitator, and permits are guaranteed. Facilitators have all the connections you need to get a club opened. And other kinds of connections. All handled through the big banks, all reported on the tax returns. A totally antiseptic way of making payoffs. This is the level where approval occurs."

"Is there any reason this 'facilitator' would have wanted to shut you down?"

"Naw. He was making too much money off us."

He was right about that. *La Notte* had the kind of protection it took to stay open, and it certainly made the kind of money to buy that. Protection in the form of people who would keep you from being busted by the cops at 5 a.m., even when they were called in to remove someone from a shooting scene.

"Is there anyone else?"

"One final possibility. The bouncer told me about some angry customer, very cracked-out, who'd apparently been given the brush-off by his girlfriend, who was still in the club. He may have come back, seeking revenge."

"That's sorta far-fetched. Wouldn't your bouncer have stopped him at the door?"

"Well, yeah, except that he was already distracted by a fight in progress inside the club just before the fire happened. So the fire could have got going, and the guy could have been gone, by the time they caught on."

"Jesus Christ."

"Well, you know how it goes," Don sighed. "At *La Notte*, a good, old-fashioned holiday brawl is just part of the price of entertainment."

"Don, have you ever considered a less stressful line of work?"

His eyes twinkled. "Well, y'know, at the moment, actually, I'm between jobs."

Just then, our polenta arrived. It didn't look as if it had ever laid an egg or bitten a fishhook.

I bit. "Hmph. Tastes like cornbread."

Don shook his head at the hopelessness of educating my culinary palate. "In a good way, though."

I stood in the lobby of the restaurant and put my two nickels into the machine. "Kendra, hi. How's it going?"

"Hi, honey. Okay, I guess. A little bored. How'd your meeting go?"

"Well, I took the case. Now all I have to do is figure out which of maybe six suspects started a fire that no one saw but killed practically everyone."

"Sounds like you've had a rough day," she purred. "Why don't you come over and I'll give you a little 'immoral support'?"

I smiled in spite of myself. "Horny, huh?"

"I just thought — ooh, I was just thinking that maybe you'd stop by, and you'd have that real authoritative manner you get when you're working on a case, and you'd sit down in that big, overstuffed chair in the front room, unbutton that sexy black trenchcoat, and drop your trousers. Then I'd crawl over on my hands and knees until I was nuzzling your nuts with my nose–"

My palms were starting to sweat, and my face felt flushed. "Kendra, I'm standing in the lobby. People can see–"

"Bullshit. You're wearing that coat. No one can see your hard-on. So why don't you reach inside your coat pocket and stroke that fat cock through your trousers. I know it's hard. Do it."

Shit, this was embarrassing, but she was right. "Okay. I'm stroking my cock."

"Aw, you can do better than that. *Squeeze* it now. Yeah, squeeze it till it hurts a little. I know how you like that." I groaned.

"So now I'm sucking your cock. Down in front of you, where I belong. Daddy's dirty girl. Making those smacking sounds you love. Your dick is really throbbing now, as I tickle your balls and run my fingers up to your nipples. Mmmmm...."

"Oh, yeah, sweetheart. Squeeze Daddy's nipples. Yeah, suck Daddy's cock like a good girl. Oh, fuck, Kendra — " Suddenly I realized there was someone close behind me, waiting to use the phone. "And let's have the lasagna. I'll, uh, pick up some sourdough bread at the bakery here."

Over the wires, Kendra's husky sex-voice erupted into giggles. "Oh, nooooo! I didn't know — oh, I am really such a bad girl sometimes!"

"We'll talk about that later."

"Oh, shit!" She broke into peals of laughter. "Now I'm in for it. So how soon will I see you?"

"Forty-five minutes?"

"I'll have the lasagna in the oven."

"You're an angel."

"Oh, by the way, how was the food at greens?"

"Edible, but not very filling. A little intimidating. 'Wholesomer-than-thou,' I guess. Like their karma ran over my dogma." She giggled. "Actually, better than I expected, but it'll never replace sirloin."

"See, vegetarian food's not that bad when it's done well."

"Listen, I gotta go."

"Okay. See you soon."

I couldn't resist one final peek into the john before making my exit. What can I say, detectives are creatures of curiosity.

My new client was standing at a urinal, sporting a full hard-on.

"Hmm. I'd say your ex designed this restroom with *you* in mind."

Don looked sheepish, but not really guilty. "And pervs like you, perhaps? Men in dark trenchcoats."

I was unfazed. "Nice cock." Amazingly fat, but mine was longer by a good inch. I sidled up to the second urinal and pulled out my still-hard dick. "So's mine. Like what you see?"

Don shook his head. "Fuck. I could just tell you had a big punk dick. All those months I spent fantasizing about that whopper of yours, wondering how it was shaped, how long it was, how fat, cut or uncut, and here it is, dangling before me like an invitation."

"Consider yourself invited."

He reached out and started stroking my now fully erect member. I moaned. "Ohhhh, god. How come guys always do that better than girls?"

"'Cause we know how it feels. Same reason we're better cocksuckers."

"That mean you're gonna suck mine?"

Don grabbed me by the handle, as it were. He led me into the stall with the squat toilet. "Hardly anyone ever uses this stall. That Jap toilet's too intimidating." I was glad the walls went all the way to the floor, thus averting detection. But still, the excitement of having sex in a public place was registering in a big way on my peter meter. "Enough of this vegetarian cuisine. Time for some meat!"

"Don't talk with your mouth full."

Don sucked like a dream. He had my dick so stiff it felt like it would break off. In fact, it was *too* stiff. I tried to relax, but I knew that I couldn't get off in here. Don, though, was whacking away furiously on his fat Italian sausage, and soon I saw his fist fill with a white torrent gushing over the top.

I exhaled hard. "Whew. Gotta put this away. Better save some for Kendra, or she'll be pissed. *What* a blow-job. Thanks."

"Thank *you*. I really needed this." He reached for a wad of toilet paper. "I've been a fucking wreck since the fire. Damn! That was fun. Any time you want a repeat performance, just say the word."

"Hmm. Remind me about that when I come by to collect my bill."

I looked over the folder of information that Don had given me. I knew how well-connected he was, and I wondered silently throughout our meeting what I could turn up that he couldn't, with a little well-paid effort. I reasoned that he was shrewd enough to keep his mouth shut for fear of incriminating himself somehow. Or maybe his lawyer told him to stay out of things.

The thing that bugged me most was simply that there were *too many* suspects. The whole affair seemed too complicated, and I realized now how Don balanced the multiple complications and distractions of running a borderline-illegal nightspot. Don lived on luck, trusting his instincts to guide him from moment to moment. On the other hand, I was a cynic. Sure, that's what he was counting on. My skepticism would worry this case to death. I would leave no piece of evidence unsifted, no statement unquestioned.

Start at the beginning, I thought. Let's call Miss Lizzie.

Her low-pitched black dialect rumbled across the wires. "You're not tape-recording this, are you?"

"Ma'am, I am required by the laws of the State of California to alert you if I am using a device to record this conversation, and such device must emit a beep tone periodically to remind you of such a fact."

Of course I had the recorder going. I just used an out-of-state model that didn't emit that guilty beep tone.

"I hear that you were burned in the fire. I'm sorry about that."

"Well, fortunately, it was just some embers that fell off the curtains and caught my blouse on fire. Except for some pretty painful blistering, everything seems to be okay." Her tone had softened. "Thank you for your concern."

"I'm just trying to do my job, Ma'am." I paused. "I understand that you were being harassed by your ex-boyfriend, and that he was stalking you at work."

"Yeah, he was. I was about to get a restraining order on him, actually. But I hesitated, since I knew an R.O. would fuck up his parole. I just wanted him to leave me alone, I didn't want to land him in jail again. I had just figured he'd give up eventually."

"How long had you been seeing him?"

"About six months. He met me at the club, actually. Started flirting with me right off the bat and kept coming back night after night until I agreed to go out with him."

"What caused your break-up?"

"He's extremely possessive. Can't stand to even see me talking with another man. Which is part of my job. I just got fed up. I finally went to a group for women in violent relationships, and that's what gave me the support to break up with him."

"Was he around the club on the night of the fire?"

"Now that certainly was *not* the case. I hadn't seen him for over a week. Oh, I'm sure he's still pissed at me, but he wouldn't have started a fire. His style is intimidation. Believe me, if he'd been lurking around *La Notte* on New Year's Eve, he'd have made sure that I knew about it. Before I dumped him, he'd said something about going up to Tahoe with some buddies over the holidays. He hardly loved anything more than skiing or gambling."

"Would he have sent anyone else to the club to harass you or start a fire?"

"It's just not his style. He'd do the job himself."

She must have seen everyone who'd entered the club that evening. "You know anyone else who came in who could have started that fire, Ma'am?"

"Any drunk could have started it accidentally. I honestly didn't see a thing, since I was on break then. In fact, I was almost trapped in the ladies' room. But that guy Don fired a while back, now he had an axe to grind. Raymond."

A couple of phone calls later, I crossed suspect number one off the list. Raymond got moved up a notch.

"Hello, this is Donny-Marie's message machine. No not the Mormons, the Horned Man's. Leave your message at the tone, and be sure to include your number, 'cause my address book is toast. Literally. Catch ya later...."

BEEP.

"Hi, Don. It's Dick Death. I'm calling to see–"

Don was screening calls these days. "Hey, Dick! I was just about to put my hand up some lucky boy's butt. How's it going? What's the news?"

"Well, so far, I've turned up more questions than answers–"

"I knew you were the man for the job." Don's unflagging optimism was beginning to grate on me.

"Listen, I've been trying to track down your ex-employee Raymond. His phone's disconnected. Do you have any other info on him — a mailing address, names of parents, social security number?"

I could hear Don sighing over the wires. "All on the employment application. All gone up in smoke." He paused. "Hey, wait a minute; I just thought of something. He filed for unemployment. That should be checkable, right?"

"Hey, that's good. Okay, thanks. I'll see what I can turn up."

Loud, boisterous, drunk punks. Now at least this was home turf for me. Of course, the names of all the obnoxious punks who'd been thrown out of someplace or other could fill half of San Francisco's white pages, but Don's talent for getting the dirt on everyone paid off again. Most of the punks he'd bounced hung out at a dive called White Lightning.

The jukebox was ruthlessly screeching out the Clash's "Rock the Casbah." I greeted the bartender on the afternoon shift. "Hi, Randy, how's it going?"

"Hey, Dick! Haven't seen you in months. Not so bad, how's it by you?"

"Okay. Glad the holidays are over." I admired the interlocking pair of antlers tattooed up to his left elbow. Not that it was common knowledge, but I knew of one sleazy punk dude who'd assimilated those antlers up to the crook of that elbow.

"So what'll it be? On the house."

"A Calistoga and a double lime squeeze is about my speed these days. Thanks."

"What ill wind blows you through these doors? Surely you're not stopping by for my world-famous Calistoga double-lime squeezes."

"Remember that custody case I helped you settle a couple years back?"

"Payback time, huh?"

I grinned. "What have the walls in this place heard about the fire at *La Notte* on New Year's Eve?"

"You into that fiasco?" he exclaimed incredulously.

"Let's just say I'm interested."

"Well, say. I've heard a couple of the regulars gloating about it since it happened. You know, 'It couldn't have happened to a nicer club.' That kind of bullshit."

"Any of these regulars have names?"

"I'd have to dig pretty far back into my memory to recall names."

I flashed an Andy Jackson under his nose. "Start digging."

"Well, say, there's Ruff Nekk. He got bounced from *La Notte* for throwing glasses about, oh, three months ago, right?"

"So what have you heard?"

"He was coming in on New Year's Day, all shit-faced, proclaiming, "To *La Notte*! Long may she burn!" Shit like that."

"So. Who else?"

"There's this real spooky chick — kind of a Siouxsie clone — calls herself Gwendolyn. Harry bounced her a couple nights ago. She'd been setting off little bonfires in the ashtrays, muttering incantations. Weird."

"Any indication she was connected with the blaze?"

"Just a hunch, I guess. Nothing specific."

I flipped out another twenty. "Well, give me a call if any of your hunches turn more specific, okay?"

I was looking over a copy of the police department's eyewitness reports — another piece of payback from a colleague with connections at Southern Station. Yet they were almost as useless as Randy's hunches. Apparently the police found no one who'd actually seen anything going on until the blaze was well under way. Lots of dramatic fragments from the lucky escapees — all of the "suddenly there was a giant ball of fire" variety. It seemed to enter from the front, which would explain a quick getaway. Not even the employees had seen or heard anything unusual until it was too late. They were all momentarily in other parts of the club, or just as distracted as the clientele, albeit less plastered.

So far, nothing could be proven. The ball of fire might as well have fallen from the sky. There was just nothing to work with. No real witnesses, no photos or videotapes, and no evidence like, say, an empty gas can with fingerprints. Of course, I was looking at the "official" police report — who knew what had been doctored, hidden, omitted, or "lost"?

Maybe the fire was just accidentally ignited by someone inside the club, and Don would have his ass in a sling. And not the one upstairs at *La Notte*.

I still hadn't checked out the site myself. I'd have been unable scam my way onto the property in the heady first days following the blaze — even Don and Philippe were kept behind a police cordon and kept from returning to the property for days. Basically, a private eye doesn't have any special privileges; he's just a private citizen who's probably a bit sharper than some of the cops.

At this point, though, I'd have easy access to *La Notte*.

When I came back, with a couple of rolls of flash photos in my pocket, there was a phone message from Kendra. She knew someone who'd been doing some programming work for the Employment Development Department, and had volunteered to do some snooping for me. "I've got some news on Raymond, the guy that Don Mariani fired. His last name is Walker," she told me breathlessly, "and the EDD lists an Oakland address for him. Call me for details."

I looked at the Coroner's Report for the final week of 1981. Some holiday suicides. Lots of deaths from the laundry list of natural causes. A few male casualties from some mysterious new pneumonia that was going around. A bunch of O.D.'s. And the long, long list of fatalities from the fire at *La Notte*.

A bunch of O.D.'s.

One particular name jumped out at me. Suddenly I knew what Raymond Walker had been up to on New Year's Eve. Nothing. Because he had been dead for four days.

With the last good suspect on ice before the fatal night, it looked like there was nowhere left to go. I wasn't doing Don or myself any good by continuing to work on the case. I thought of something my P.I. mentor, "Uncle Mike," had taught me about how to deal with frustrating cases. "If no fish are biting, go swim around in the pond for a while yourself." In other words, make something happen.

The next morning, I'd pasted together a flyer offering a reward for information on or witnesses to the fire. I figured I'd make some copies, run a few City Hall errands for other clients, and go by the site of the fire once more to poke around and see if any new ideas came to mind. Heck, I might as well put some of the flyers under a few windshields myself. Normally I'd pay Kendra's niece to do an errand like that, but why not me?

Once again, I climbed through the hole in the hastily-erected cyclone fence and started scanning. Not a clue for what.

I came around a corner of the building and was startled to find an old guy poking through the charred ruins. He wore filthy, olive drab trousers and a bright orange safety vest that sparkled in the dull, dwindling glint of the steely winter afternoon.

"Oh! Hey, there," he greeted me. "Scavenging, huh?"

"Investigating."

"Hey! Forgot your magnifying glass, huh?" He tittered at his tedious joke.

"This is still an unsolved fire. Maybe it's arson. Do you know anything about it?"

"Know anything! Came up from a good doze that night as soon as I heard the first siren. Livin' over there," he proclaimed, indicating a dilapidated shack that looked like a relic from the railroad era. "Guy was making a videotape of the whole thing."

"Did he say anything to you?"

"Sure could use a smoke," the old man replied.

For a town so self-righteously healthy, San Francisco has a whole lot of drinkers, druggies, and nicotine addicts. "Let's walk up to the store and I'll buy you a whole pack," I insisted. Christ, I'd get him a whole fucking carton if he'd keep talking.

"Okey-dokey."

"So did he talk to you?"

"Yah. Said he was taping the nightclub sign for some video project he was working on."

"Was anyone with him?"

"Naw. He was alone."

"What kind of car was he driving?"

"Wasn't. Came from over there." The old guy pointed to a huge military warehouse from the Second World War that had since been converted into an artists' co-op. "Seen 'im around before. Sometimes shopping at the day-old bakery a coupla blocks up. Kinda spooky guy."

"Oh, yeah? Spooky how?"

"Well, he's got real big — bug-eyes, like that British comedian on the public broadcasting channel."

"You mean Marty Feldman?"

"Yah! That's the one. But, like, also real secretive-spooky. Kinda mutters to himself sometimes and gets nervous if you approach him. Like he's scared o' something."

"Paranoid?"

"Yah! That's it."

"What does he look like? How does he dress?"

"Hippie type. Short, and kind of hunched over, with long, dark hair and a beard. Dirty clothes — spattered with paint. Don't take a bath too often."

An hour later, I was wandering the halls of the co-op. An arty-looking woman in a purple cocktail dress and lots of eyeliner was walking toward me.

"Excuse me," I began. "I'm here to see a guy about a videotape project, but I've lost his card. Maybe you can help me find him?"

"Well, there are probably eight or ten folks here who work with video."

"This guy has long, dark hair and a beard — not too tall, hunches over."

"Oh, you're looking for the guy in 109," she volunteered, a bit derisively. "John's his name."

"Yeah, right! John, that's it. Hey, thanks a bunch."

I knocked on the double wooden doors. Its laminated plastic sign curiously read, "SOME RE PRODUCTIONS." Then I realized the first word was "somewhere" with some of the letters knocked off. There was a peephole embedded in one door.

"Whoozair?"

"Hi. John? My name's Dick. I'd like to talk about your services."

An exasperated grunt emanated from behind the door. "Hold on."

A minute later, I was summoned from down the hall. "C'mon around."

"The main studio's all set up for a shoot, so I'm bringing you in the side door," he hissed at me. I felt less welcome than a Christmas carol in January.

The narrow passageway was a time warp, its walls lined with psychedelic rock concert posters from the old days. Maybe he used to do light shows. Hanging from the ceiling, I noticed various configurations of mobiles and giant versions of those God's Eye things that teachers had us making in grade school out of yarn and Popsicle sticks.

Something about the guy was downright unhealthy. Well, he stank to high heaven. He didn't take care of himself — a classic obsessive artist type. And paranoid he was. His gaze darted furtively from side to side, and he had a nervous twitch in his left cheek that seemed like a prelude to a full seizure or a manic rage. Maybe he was an acid casualty. Probably just a mean, angry drunk. That was the vibe.

"Siddown."

He motioned me into a wooden folding seat, part of a row of connected, theater-style seats. The stage was set up with lights focused on a perfectly to-scale miniature version of *La Notte*. My stomach dropped.

"So." A slight pause. Clearly I was to get to the point immediately.

"You take the camera out into the neighborhood sometimes?"

"Yeah."

"How do you tape at night? What do you do about lighting?"

"Depends. Sometimes, if I'm going for a grainy effect, I can do it on ambient lighting. I've also got a couple of portables. I fixed one of 'em so it attaches to the cam without making it too top-heavy. Sometimes I've even used my '64 Volvo's headlights. Why you askin'?"

I made sure he saw me glance at the set. "You were out taping the night of the big fire?"

"Who told you that?"

"Just a guy. Someone in the neighborhood."

"Are you with the police?"

"Do I look like a fucking cop?"

"Never know. Pigs could come dressed as anything."

"I'm not a cop. But, you know, if the pigs found out you had a tape of the fire, they'd seize it as evidence." Maybe if I talked like a fucking hippie, this guy would lighten up and we'd get somewhere. "No need to be uptight, man."

"Fuck that! It's my fucking property, man."

"That doesn't matter to the pigs. You know how they are. They can score anything they want, including your tape. You did tape the fire, didn't you?"

"None of your fucking business!"

"Hey, it's cool, man. I'm on *your* side, dig?" I felt like I was reading lines out of an episode of *The Mod Squad*, but since I estimated my time of departure at under one minute, what the hell. "I don't want a bad scene. I'm just helping out a cat who lost some of his own in that fire. And the pigs are out trying to cover it up 'cause the Chief of Police himself was out there drinkin' on duty!"

"You shittin' me, man?"

It was a fucking lie, but I'd just decided that I was gonna get me that goddamn tape if I had to tie this fucking degenerate scum's stringy hair to one of his set's pulleys and hoist until I yanked it out at the roots.

"No! It's for real. But, y'know, man, I've seen the pigs prowling around today, one block away, asking lots of questions. The vibe is real heavy. Sooner or later, they'll show up here." That was another bald-faced lie, but it sounded good.

"You know, it's like this, man. That tape is art. You get a shot like that maybe once in a lifetime. I was just tapin' the front of the building for this short. And that sign is so cool, I knew it would look real good in it. And I'd been there maybe ten minutes when this guy comes stormin' out, real pissed-off, and he marches to his car. Pulls it up in front of the club, goes into the trunk, and hauls out this huge coil of rope, drippin' like he dosed it with oil or gasoline, and he sets it on fire with his Bic and throws it through the front door. And the place goes up almost immediately. The whole thing happened so fast. It was so fuckin' groovy!"

"You got all that on tape?"

"No shit. I even zoomed on the license plate."

"And you haven't told anyone else about this?"

"No fuckin' way, man! I was *glad* to see that noisy fuckin' club burn. But I got the hell out of there when I heard the sirens."

There was a long pause while I remembered how to exhale.

"I want to help you out, and help my friend, too. That tape is gonna be much safer with me than floating around here, where the pigs can track it down and destroy it." He still looked skeptical. "I'll just dub it and bring it back, okay?"

"Art hurts, man. Art is expensive." Now we were talking! Everything boils down to fucking money.

"I dig. What can I lay on you for your holy art?"

"Um — about two hundred bucks?"

Sold.

Five minutes later, I was headed out of the parking lot and over to see the two queens at King's Video for several copies. I was relieved to be done with this sputtering, volcanic, disagreeable gnome.

It was so simple. The culprit was the one wild card in the deck — just some angry, cracked-out partier who'd been snubbed by his girlfriend. Based on the miraculous videotape, Tommy Fisher would be put away for life for the night he took sixty-five over the legal limit.

But it was harsh justice. Sixty-five partiers had lost their lives. Don had lost his club, and for what? Some violent club-goer in the heat of passion seeking instant revenge against his girlfriend.

"Here's a copy of the videotape and my final bill," I said to Donny-Marie. I was so happy I could almost smile.

"Well, you certainly fished this one out of the gutter," Don smiled. "Hey, sorry about that."

"Yeah. Enough of the fish jokes."

"You know, I really didn't think you'd get anywhere with this. This should reduce our liability by several million dollars."

"So glad you brought that up," I replied. "That brings up the question of my tip — or rather, yours. In my mouth. Turnabout being fair play, and all that."

"Well, I just made arrangements to rent a certain restaurant with a certain rest *room* for a private party, and I think that will be most possible. Even if our arsonist didn't return to the scene of the crime, we can return to the scene of *ours*...."

"One condition. That my girlfriend Kendra gets to watch. She gets super turned-on by watching guys have sex. She's got more gay porno than I ever knew existed."

"Well, bring as many of your friends as you like. Maybe we can make some porn of our own."

And that's how Don's next entrepreneurial move took him from "Night of A Thousand Fish" to "Night of A Thousand Dicks." But that's another story.

Since 1992, **Bill Brent** has operated Black Books, which publishes books about underground culture, including *The Black Book*, North America's foremost alternative sexuality resource guide. Black Books is bringing back to print the first two *Noiroticas* originally on Masquerade Books. He has edited seventeen issues of *Black Sheets*, a humorous magazine about sex and popular culture which he founded in 1993. His short fiction appears in *Best American Erotica 1997*, *Rough Stuff*, *Guilty Pleasures*, and all three volumes of the *Noirotica* series. He is co-editor of the anthology *Best Bisexual Erotica*, with Carol Queen. Recently he completed his first novel, *SOMA*. Current projects include *Brain Explosives!*, a survey of countercultural thought, edited with co-conspirator Doug Holland, and *The Ultimate Guide to Anal Sex for Men*, due from Cleis Press in Spring 2001. His favorite sexual position is open-minded. Learn more about his projects at www.blackbooks.com and www.billbrent.com.

Torch

by Amelia G

He was the kind of singer who could make you hit all the high notes. Beautifully sculpted face, vaguely Latin, a tumble of tuggable black hair shaved on one side, and piercing eyes whose green color I could discern from the table farthest from the stage in the dive he performed in. Not that any of that made much difference to me. I was there because I was either going to do a job or I wasn't. Depended on the job.

The singer's voice was very fine. Unfortunately, he was doing some sort of edgy folk music. I liked it better than most folk music, but after all was said and done, it was still folk music. I used to live with a guy who played heavy, heavy hard rock guitar. He called it groove-oriented guitar rock. The critics called it heavy metal. He was actually starting to become pretty well known for his musicianship at the time. Not that music was what paid our bills. The minor fame was turning him into a womanizing pig. If it was remotely female and roughly Homo Sapien, he'd fuck it. Or at least accept a blow job. But when he was home, I adored watching him practice. He had big, graceful hands with long, tapered fingers and I loved to watch his hands move over the guitar strings. His name was Johnni and he used to practice for hours on end, sitting on a straight-backed chair in our kitchen, hunched over his electric guitar with the amp unplugged so he wouldn't make the neighbors more crazed than our infamous parties already had.

Watching this beautiful boy play his folk music, or whatever it was he considered himself to be playing, made me think of Johnni. I shook my head impatiently to clear it. Business, business, got to keep my mind on business. After his set, the singer strolled over to my table and sat down with a sly smile and no invitation.

"Maybe that seat's taken."

"Pardon me, is this seat taken?

"No."

He smiled lazily like I was being charming even though really I wasn't. "I hear you are an artist," he told me.

"Went to school for it and everything." Two years at UCLA before I ran out of money, but the customer doesn't need to know the specifics.

"I hear you are the best." He stretched his lanky legs out under the table in a calculated sexy sort of way which I imagine would make a lot of women inclined to beg or at least brag. But not me.

"I'm not the best. I'm just good enough. Let's face it, almost is not good enough in this business, but good enough is just as good as perfect."

"That is very honest of you," he said wryly.

"My prices don't suck either," I told him, "for people with your kinds of problems."

"Are there people your prices do suck for?" He had the kind of smile that could charm the frock off a nun, and I wished he'd quit pointing it at me.

"There are some people who couldn't come up with any amount of money to make me help them. So I guess priceless is a sucky price. I used to do some work for Tobias' people. But that was a long time ago."

"Who is Tobias?" he asked, leaning toward me.

Now this is the part where I should have gotten suspicious. Sure, the singer had a reference from the bartender at my favorite dive bar, but *everyone* in our neighborhood has at least heard a bunch of bullshit stories about Tobias. Certainly everyone who hung out in this set of rotating dive bars should have had an accurate clue. Innocently wondering who the man is should not have been on the menu here. Why did I travel in circles that felt compelled to rotate a series of dive bars? I could have afforded better, but I think it is a trickle-down from the movie industry. It is terribly L.A. to be constantly in search of a divier dive in which to hang out and do shots while hiding out from your theoretically copious fans. Or from any outstanding warrants. Whichever.

"Tobias is a former employer of mine."

"I'd like to hire you, but your resume is, you must admit, rather vague."

"This ain't corporate America. You've got a personal reference says I can do it. I've got a personal reference says I won't be fucked if I do it for you. I imagine your family wouldn't like it if I gave their names out at a future date. Assuming I do the job, consider my vagueness your personal security."

He reached across the table. "My name's Paoulo. Let me buy you a drink." He touched my hand and I jumped like he'd put a fork in it.

"What's wrong?" he recoiled.

"Nothing. I just don't like anyone to touch my hands. I need them for my work."

"Okay."

"Yeah, thanks, I'd like two double shots of Cuervo Gold and a big pair of lemons." I could tell Paoulo was a nice boy because he didn't make any rude innuendo. Then it occurred to me that maybe he just spoke English as a second language and hadn't thought of any rude innuendo. "You speak really good English," I told him when he glided back from the bar. He was the kind of guy who glided or maybe strode, rather than simply walking.

"I should. I was born here and I've lived in Southern California all my life."

"And they still won't let you petition for your mother? Fuck."

"They'll let me petition all I want. I just keep getting turned down or put off."

I shook my head. I think that we should sandblast that shit off the Statue of Liberty if we don't mean it, but hey, that's just me. I shook some salt into the crook of my left thumb and forefinger, caught Paoulo watching me lick it off, tossed back the first shot and jammed one of the lemon wedges in my mouth. Talking around the peel, I told him I'd do it. "I'll need two photographs of your mother. She should be able to go into any passport photo place and get the right kind done. The pictures should cost somewhere between eight and twenty bucks depending on where she goes. They need to be identical and I'll need an example of her signature and the information for how she wants her name to appear. I will need half my fee up front and half on delivery. If she wants to show up right in computers if anyone runs the ID, then it will be an additional $1,200 which needs to be paid up front in its entirety, because I outsource that and my markup is minimal. Can you have that taken care of by, say, eight p.m. Thursday? We could meet back here then."

"Why don't we meet at your place?"

"Because you don't need to know where I live."

"Can you repeat those instructions without the lemon in your mouth?"

I did the second shot and repeated myself.

When I think of what happened to Johnni, I always think of it in terms of what They with a capital T did. Of course, at least in an indirect way, the capital T stands for "Tobias" rather than "They." But the personal relationship was with Victor, this burly surfer-dude who I don't think really knew what he was getting into until it was much to late. But ignorant of his future or not, Victor could have chosen not to do what he did. I know the moron always thought I was a cutie (his expression, not mine) so maybe he thought if he proved himself somehow more manly than Johnni, I would be attracted to some turnip-IQed enforcer instead of my talented musician boyfriend. Not that I was working for Tobias as a cutie; I was doing the same art gig then, just for different sorts of clients. Johnni was doing more traditional (i.e. lower-paid) bagman work. To Victor's way of thinking, I should have been attracted to him because he brought home more green than Johnni. I shouldn't even say Victor had the IQ of a turnip; the Turnip Anti-Defamation League will get after me.

They made Victor, because he was Johnni's regular connection, do it. "Nothing personal, man. I like you, but this is business." Then to me on his way out of our apartment, "I'm sorry, Celene, I can't express how much. I've always considered you and Johnni my friends."

"As a general rule, Victor," I purred, "friends don't go around breaking one another's fingers. or any other appendages for that matter.

"Women," he said, shaking his head of dyed blond surfer curls, "they just don't understand business. Talk to Johnni. He'll set you straight."

I waited until Victor had the door to the hallway open before I spoke. "Hey, Victor."

"Yeah." The motherfucker actually had the gall to look hopeful. Like we were going to be pals again, even though I could hear Johnni screaming at 911 from where he'd locked himself in the bedroom telling me to leave him alone. Screaming into the phone that he had tripped and broken one finger on each hand catching himself falling. From the sound of Johnni's side of the high-volume conversation, even the 911 operator could tell that, actually, Johnni had been interacting with someone who was not his friend.

"Victor, I just wanted to tell you that we're having a party this Saturday night."
"Cool."

"I'm going to tell everybody to show up around nine, but it probably won't be hopping until around eleven."

"So you figure ten-ish is the best time to show up?"

"You don't really need to worry your pretty little head about that, on account of how you're not invited."

Victor actually looked hurt. After Johnni killed himself, pulled a straight razor across his own throat when he realized he couldn't play guitar any more, Victor didn't have much expression on his face at all, on account of how I emptied a seventeen-round clip into it.

When I hooked up with Paoulo the following Thursday, he brought a bottle of Cuervo Gold and a pair of shot glasses with him as a gift. In the interest of fucking up my life, I consented to drink it with him in the parking lot in my car. I drive a red Chevy Cavalier. I used to have a black vintage Cadillac with tailfins, but it got stolen a couple of years ago and I could never bear to have a car I liked afterwards.

"Where's your car?" I asked him.

"Uhm, I walked." He did the first shot without benefit of salt or lemon.

"Nobody walks in L.A."

He shrugged and I couldn't help noticing that he appeared to have some nice muscle definition under that black T-shirt. He was wearing it tucked into tight black pants which were, in turn, tucked into black jackboots. I thought maybe he was kinky and did another shot. Normally, the salt and lemon makes the first few shots easier, but I can face the first few painful slugs if I must, as I know that after the first three or four, somebody could really swap battery acid for my tequila and my cauterized mouth and throat probably couldn't tell the difference.

I put the key in the ignition and turned on the radio. I flipped stations for a few, hoping to get a sense of what Paoulo would like to listen to, but when he didn't volunteer any opinions, I just settled on KROQ out of inertia.

"So," I said, "what do you do besides sing and play guitar in bars?"

He looked instantly as tense as the last dove at a crack-whore convention. Like I was gonna eat him or something. Which, come to think of it.... Well, I figured he was probably a dealer or hustler or some such on the side and it made him uptight. I don't really understand people who let their circumstances push them around until their lives are just tapestries of regret and self-recrimination. Tapestries of regret and self-recrimination? Wow, but I love what tequila does for me.

"What makes you think I do anything besides sing and play guitar in bars?" Paoulo asked me, his expression tight-lipped and anxious.

"Down, boy. Everybody has a day job in Los Angeles. No shame there."

"So what do you do besides making fake passports and birth certificates?"

"Sometimes I make driver's licenses. I wholeheartedly support underage drinking."

"That doesn't really sound like a day job."

"I'm also an assistant manager at Pearl."

"The eyeglass place?"

"No, the arts and crafts supplies store. My parents had hoped I'd do more with my life, be more successful; I was a promising little artist. But at least having a day job means there is something I can tell them."

"I hadn't really thought of you as having parents." Paoulo regarded me thoughtfully.

"Everybody has parents. I'll tell you the details when you're older."

"You'll show me the details when I'm older?"

"Tell, tell, not show, pass the tequila."

"Here. Maybe everybody has parents, but I only really call mine on birthdays and see them on holidays and you struck me as the. . ."

"Yes. Go on."

"I don't want to be rude."

"We all dig our own graves."

"Well, you just seemed like the sort of person who would be estranged from her family."

"Hey, I am a specialist at reuniting families."

"But you get paid a lot for that."

"You complaining about the price?"

"No." Paoulo gave me a winning smile and a nice flex as he reached for the tequila. "I just meant that it's not like you do it for love."

I decided that I was probably getting too chummy with this customer no matter how truly fine he was. "There are types of customers who could and would pay a lot more, but I choose to do my art for what I believe in, rather than where the biggest dollars are. The other advantage of having a day job, even a shitty one, is that it means I'm never so broke I have no choice."

"So you don't usually do work for smugglers?"

"No. No, I don't. Not usually. Not ever."

"I'm confused."

"About what?"

"I'd just heard that that was your thing."

"Well, what you heard is out of date by about four years." I gave him the best chilly glare I could muster through the rapidly encroaching tequila fog.

He seemed to visibly shake some negative feeling off as he mustered his charm. When he smiled at me sheepishly, his teeth were bright against his bronzed skin and his eyes were sexy, almost animalistic in the glow of the lone street lamp in the parking lot. He ran his left hand through his black hair; it was glossy and the shaved side of his head that his hand uncovered seemed, somehow, to indicate sweet vulnerability. I even noticed, in the small confines of my car, that he smelled good.

Paoulo was giving it all he had and what he had was considerable. Not that I was impervious to his charms, but the fact of the matter was that my days of doing stupid things for beautiful boys are long past. I'm twenty-six years old and that is quite simply old enough to know which cock my bread is buttered with. "So," I said toughly, "you think if you seduce me, I'll give you a discount?"

"No, no, no, nothing like that. I've got the money right here." He flashed me a wad of green far bigger than he ought to be showing in a place like this. Even inside a car in the dark parking lot. "I'm not trying to seduce you at all."

"Oh, well, that's okay then." I did another shot of tequila. "You too." I pointed to his shot glass.

"I think I might be past my limit."

"Do you think you are too drunk to get an erection?"

"What? No, I. . ." Paoulo smiled lazily. "Okay, do you want to, uhm, here." He began to slide toward me on the seat.

"Ugh." I made a show of suppressing a shudder and did another shot. "Eau de Dumpster has limited erotic appeal for me."

"I'm wearing Drakkar Noir."

"Let's go back to my place."

"I thought you didn't take anyone back to your place."

"Could we please refrain from reminding me that I'm doing something stupid?" I took the car out of park.

"You're not going to *drive* right now, are you?"

"Die young and leave a repulsive corpse penetrated by the steering column, I always say. Didn't I ask you to refrain from reminding me that I'm doing something stupid?"

Fortunately, I didn't live that far from the parking lot in question, so we lived to make it to my apartment. Once I got Paoulo naked, I realized it would have been a terrible waste for me to have died horribly in a fiery wreck before fucking him.

When we first entered my apartment, he got all shy and nervous. It was kind of cute to see him go from the assured predatory sexy charm he had exuded in the parking lot to shyly pretending he was just at my apartment for a low-key social call. He started asking me about where my drafting table was and where did I keep my laptop and other dorky work-related nonsense. But when I unzipped those tight black stretch-pants, that sure put a stop to the chatter.

He wore black and white bikini briefs that did nothing to conceal his interest in me. I led him to the bedroom and pushed him down on my single bed. I helped him pull off each jackboot in turn and then tugged his pants from around his ankles. His dick was the same smooth coppery color as the rest of him, crowned by blacker-than-black glossy pubic hair, and hard as gunmetal. Actually, the gun I keep under my mattress is a Glock 17, so I suppose I don't have that much experience with actual metal guns per se, but his dick was hard and ready.

He looked up at me speculatively as I peeled off my own jeans and T-shirt. I don't get laid nearly as often as would be good for me, but I know I'm a good-looking girl and I could tell through the tequila that he was impressed. I straddled his body and ran my hands down his chest. He was lean but more ripped than most guys I've been with. I traced his twitching muscles with my hands, marveling at his beauty. He was obviously ready for me and I felt ready for him. Besides, even if I wasn't 100% wet when we started, I wasn't going to be feeling any discomfort with this much tequila in me.

I had my hand on his cock and I was arched up to guide him into me, his soft moans sweet in my ears, when a little voice in my head started saying irritating things. Now, if the little voice had pointed out that this whole exercise was a bad idea and I should kick Paoulo out and probably move shortly thereafter, well, that might have been useful. But all my conscience had to suggest was that I should use a condom. I wanted to whine that I associate with gangsters, I drink to extreme excess, I drive drunk, I let strangers into my home, why does my sex have to be safe? But I knew there was no point in arguing with myself because there was no way I was going to enjoy the act if I didn't get a fucking condom immediately. Of course, I don't have sex often enough to stock the things myself.

"Do you have a condom?" I whispered urgently.

Startled, he said: "Actually, yes, in my pants pocket. I'll get it." He tried to get up from under me, but I hopped off and picked up his pants.

"You sure have a lot of junk in your pockets." Rooting around for the condom packet, I felt the wad of money he'd brought, some rubber bands, paper clips, a pen, a bunch of other stuff including something metal that made me unaccountably uncomfortable, but I didn't take the time to examine much of any of it as I had more pressing business to attend to.

I hurriedly rolled the condom over Paoulo's rigid shaft and pressed myself against him. He flipped me over on my back and penetrated me without further assistance. I was entirely wet enough to accommodate him immediately. He held himself up over me with his arms. The muscles in them flexed and relaxed in an entrancing rhythm as he thrust in and out of me. I watched his arms and chest as I felt the orgasm build in my gut. I came sooner than I expected to given the amount of alcohol I had ingested. Paoulo stopped for a moment to let me breathe. "You're beautiful," he whispered, "a perfect fit." Then he began thrusting again in earnest.

I inhaled his musk and cologne and spread myself as wide as I could for him. The jackboots had made me think that maybe he was kinky, but while this might be a straightforward missionary fuck, it was a really excellent athletic straight-forward missionary fuck. We were both slick with sweat by the time I came a second time, sharper and more final, and just as I began to spasm around him, Paoulo began shaking between my thighs as well.

I lay there for a moment, blissed out in the afterglow. All of a sudden, I was struggling to get out from under his hot body. With the desire to come no longer clouding my brain, I had suddenly realized what the metal object in his pocket was.

"Badge!" I burbled, pushing him away from me. "Fuck me, you're a fucking cop, fuck, fuck, fuck me."

He tried a charming smile on me while still holding me down. "I think I just did," he said lightly.

I had to bang him on the head three times with my gun barrel before he lost consciousness. Glocks are great for a lot of things, but they are too damn lightweight to administer a proper pistol-whipping.

Paoulo slid off of me and I sat up in the bed, clutching my own knees with the gun between them and shaking a little. I thought to myself that for a girl who normally could take care of herself, I certainly was slipping.

I was further alarmed when the door of my bedroom abruptly sprouted a policeman's billy club and then came crashing inward to the floor. Behind my destroyed door was a cop in uniform. Overweight and swaggering and doing severe damage to my apartment.

"Well," I said, attempting as much dignity as possible under my naked circumstances, "I guess they don't make all of you particularly fine-looking."

"I'm sure his girlfriend will be sad to hear that he died in such a situation, but at least she'll be glad to know you appreciated him."

"You can't arrest me for murder. He's not dead. I just knocked him out. L.A.P.D. has nothing on me. Nothing."

"I have no intention of arresting you for murder. I don't think the Department has any interest in you, either. Although I do suspect my unfortunate former partner thought he was doing his job for them."

"What do you mean?"

"I mean, I work for Tobias."

"Not the Police Department?" I was starting to shake for real now.

"Mmm-hmmm," he nodded, "I work for them too. Double-dipping at the taxpayers' expense, but the cost of living just keeps going up in this city and what's a man to do?"

"So, what exactly are you doing for the money?" I thought that perhaps I could bargain with him, convince him not to hand me over to Tobias' people. At least find out whether Tobias actually knew about Victor or only suspected. Or whether Tobias had some other fucking problem just over the fact that I wouldn't do work for him any more.

The fat cop winked. "Actually, although the money is nice, my late partner's girlfriend is a very nice girl who deserves someone who does not cat around on her."

I felt my eyes go wide as I realized what this creep intended.

"Are you upset that he has a girlfriend?" Paoulo's partner asked sympathetically.

"Yeah," I nodded back at him. "I'm really looking for a relationship right now, some commitment, a picket fence, maybe a couple of kids. That's why I keep fucking musicians."

Even though I didn't take time to aim when I pulled the Glock out from between my thighs, I drilled the leering scumbag perfectly between the eyes on the first try. It was a beautiful shot and I was tempted to leave him like that because I was just so damn proud of my marksmanship. After I caught my breath, though, I thought that maybe I should make it clear to Tobias that he should leave me alone. So I introduced the other 16 bullets to Mr. Crooked Cop's cranium. I figured that if Tobias knew about Victor, then he would know that this was me, too. Of course, if he'd wanted to see me about something else and his dead little pal had only been planning on killing Paoulo and not me. . .well, then I had told him something that he would probably take as a challenge. But you know, omelets and eggs and all that. Regardless, I would have to move.

I heard Paoulo begin to stir on the floor. His body still looked beautiful to me. It had been very nice getting to have sex with him. I was kind of sorry he turned out to be a big liar, but it had felt good and I'd even remembered to use a condom. No regrets. That's just what you get with a certain sort of guy. Carry a torch if you like, but they just can't keep it in their pants. Not that I apparently can, either. So perhaps stone-throwing is out of order.

I put my hand up to my forehead to steady myself. As my adrenaline died down, I felt my inebriation beginning to return.

I had to think quickly. In my neighborhood, the neighbors might or might not call in the gunshots. But eventually the body would be found. Tobias might be after me anyway, but I didn't need to have the cops on my tail, too. I realized what made the most sense.

I hated to lose my gun. You can still get a Glock 17 (named for Gaston Glock's seventeenth patent), but due to an irritating law passed in 1994, it is really tough to find a clip that holds more than ten rounds. Still, it was unregistered and Paoulo would have to be holding it to really convince anyone that he whacked his own partner.

I wrapped a hand-towel around Paoulo's partner's gun when I carried it over to the singer's prone body. Paoulo had seemed like such nice boy; I thought maybe I couldn't do it at all. Well, he had kept his day job undisclosed. Maybe I should shoot him in the leg. Then he could claim self-defense. If ballistics showed it was his own dead partner's gun, then a shoot-out between the two of them might just seem more plausible than any true story the young cop might tell. On the other hand (I'm an octopus), he did have a girlfriend he was cheating on and if I just put a bullet in his brainpan, then there could be no stories about me.

Decisions. Decisions. Sometimes I have myself almost convinced that what is wrong with me is what happened to Johnni. But that is probably not it. Sure, it hurts. I loved him. But then, so did a lot of other girls. Really, it is just the daily harshness of the world I cannot handle.

Amelia G is the editor-in-chief of *Blue Blood* magazine. Her fiction has also appeared in *Noirotica* and *Noirotica 2: Pulp Friction*, Circlet Press' *Sexcrime* and *Blood Kiss*, Cleis Press' *Dark Angels*, and a variety of alternative press publications. She recently launched blueblood.net and gothicsluts.com. Amelia G's anthology *Backstage Passes* features work by many of the same authors you have no doubt enjoyed in the *Noirotica* series. She can be contacted c/o *Blue Blood*, 8033 W. Sunset Blvd. #43, West Hollywood CA 90046-2418.

Candy Man

by Carl Wheat

Rain and two wheels just don't make me feel easy. It's bad enough trying to stay out of the oil and grease from all those four-wheelers when the sun's got it baked into the asphalt. Put the first Southern California winter rain down on the city streets and it's like driving on glass smeared with fresh come.

The fuckin' water coming out of the sky is black with L.A. smog. It feels just like someone is driving needles into my face. I can't handle it any longer; my leathers weigh closer to a hundred and fifty pounds than the thirty or so they normally do. I got enough coke in my pocket to put me in jail for a long time and don't know this neighborhood for shit. I got to find a place to hole up.

This is an older part of town, back a ways from the beach, and when it was new it was probably a ways to most anything. This neighborhood was on the outskirts of the oil-refining trade back then. The good part about it is there's several small taverns with friendly names like Rocky's, Sherry D's, and Antoine's lining the streets. I pick the one with the side lot. The bar shares the parking spaces with a laundromat and TV repair shop. My scoot might not cause as much interest from the law setting up against the back of the building.

Antoine's is dim with a long dark bar off to the left of the side door. Directly in front of me is a small pool table that has seen better days. The cuts on the green felt let the eight-ball slide into the corner pocket from a strange angle. The hard-looking broad holding the pool cue is either lucky or knows the table well enough to count on the imperfections in the surface to win. If the rain keeps up long enough I might even learn which one.

Taking a bar stool close to the pool area, I slip a ten on the bar top and wait. The broad's hair flips off the front of her shoulder in a wide arch, flaring out into the dim light and showing off a full tit cuddled in stretch cotton. The shirt is slashed in several places from her shoulder, across the swell of her breast and into the right lower rib cage. Her every move makes the size of her hooter more evident. I'm not complaining.

"Beer?" she asks. The lady's voice is smoky. Too many cigarettes and too much whiskey? Her eyes are wide and the brows above them shaved or plucked into an exaggerated arch. Her waist pinches in nicely and the butt cheek she raises and settles onto the bar stool is prime. I just might enjoy the afternoon after all.

"Yeah, beer will do. Get busy around here?" I want to find out what this place will be like in an hour or two. If it fills up with guys from the refinery at quittin' time, this is gonna be the wrong place to lay low.

"Not that ya'd notice. We get excited by the plants growing in the flower boxes," she smart-mouths.

"House ever play dice with a person for the music?"

"You bet. Horses?" She jumps down off her stool, her pointed tits bouncing with the action.

"I don't care. Just so you play some music." I watch her back side-slip down the bar toward the darkened end of the room, swayin' a lot more than it would to walk over yonder most times. I take a moment to check things out. I've been places only to find people there I didn't know about. Things like that can get disconcerting. But the place is almost empty this time, far as I can see. There's one rummy propped against the wall at the back. At the moment he's snoring. Loud. Not another soul in the joint. The juke box sets at the end of the building in a corner and the bar itself makes a horseshoe sweep, only going as far as the beer cooler in the center of the room.

Miss Beer Tender picks up the dice cup and sashays back toward me. She ain't moving fast, but the body language is making my cock hard. She's got on a pair of jeans so tight I'd be willing to bet she sat in a tub full of water while wearing them and then dried them right on her butt. "What's this chick want? I hope it's my cock." The thought puts a smile on my mug which she picks up on in a heartbeat.

"What's so funny?" she wants to know.

"Nothin'. Forget it. Best out of three?" I ask about the game. My tone is automatic. This chick's got to know I don't take kindly to nosy.

"Sure." She ain't too happy getting told to hold her mug, but she keeps her mouth shut about it. All I see to confirm her mood is a little pout flicker across her face.

I slam the dice cup down on the bar surface and watch her eyes. No eye action from this lady. Not even a flutter. She just looks up into my shiny blue eyes with a slight question in her own. I pull three sixes out of five dice and since I stop now, she only gets the first roll to beat 'em. Her threes aren't worth a lot and we go on to the next round. My eyes drift to her half-exposed tit as she brings the dice cup down on the bar top. I see the darkened skin at the very end of her tit slide into view and disappear as quickly as it showed itself. When my eyes look up into hers again, she's watching mine. The smile crossing her faceiasn't put there to have me stop watching.

I stand up momentarily to strip my leather from my body. I fold the heavy coat on the bar beside me and ease back into the barstool.

"Last chance," she says.

My next roll is all fours. She simply slips off her stool and prances to the cash register. On the way to the jukebox her hand sweeps down the bar, then lifts to run the back of my shoulder. In moments the country song about being a 'Diamond Some Day' rolls out of the speakers. I walk down the bar behind her, enjoying the sight of her bent over the jukebox, the cheeks of her ass making a smile across her butt. Maybe she knew I was coming up behind her, then again maybe not, but the sight of her running her hand up from her waist and cupping her own tit stops me. I stand about ten feet behind and off to one side watching her play with the nipple until it's rock hard. She seems to notice my presence for the first time as she turns back toward where we were sitting.

"Oh. . . ." Her eyes are dilated and her mouth opens slightly, letting me see just a hint of tongue. In the dim light it looks to me like she is flushed.

"Where's the head?" I ask.

She lifts her arm in a sweeping motion that swings her finger right past her impossibly hard nipple to indicate where I thought I'd find the toilet in the first place.

"Use nose candy?" That nipple just drug that out of me. She wasn't a cop and if she liked "go fast" I was gonna have a blast this afternoon.

"Of course, doesn't everyone?" Her reaction is not real surprising. Shit. Just about everyone uses coke.

"Okay, I'll leave a line on the bathroom cabinet."

"Don't use the men's. Nobody can get it clean, no matter how much we try. The women's isn't near as bad."

Her comments say it all. The building is old and has been a bar for years. How many times the walls in the men's head have received a spray of beer and puke can't even be counted. The rummy picks his head up off the table as I pass. I hear him order three whiskeys, straight up. I push open the women's rest room door and step into a sparkling white room with a remarkably clean floor. The smell greeting me is clean . . . right out of a bucket. I do my thing then open my stash of white powder, tapping the lip of the glass rim to the vinyl top of the cabinet. I sure as hell don't want the broad to know how much I'm carrying.

After sealing my coke back up, I remove a razor blade from my wallet and scrape the white powder into two lines. My glass straw slides from its hiding place in the cuff of my pants and I snort the poison deep

I damn near run into the broad as I step out of the bathroom. She is standing right in the hallway, dancing from one foot to the other. She greets me with a brilliant smile, pulls her arms tight against her body, the fingers of her hands interlaced and held just beneath her chin. She's fucking quick on her feet. I can't even clear the door frame before she passes me. I hold the door open and extend the glass tube to her, watching her face as she drags in the drug lined up for her.

"Thanks! I'll be right out."

The rest of the morning goes pretty smoothly. Western music, and the bar maid giving titty shows. The rummy is nursing his drinks now. Still three at a time. He's easy to ignore. I keep the conversation with the girl pretty tame but enjoy how she's trying to get my attention with her body. Finally, after a couple hours of just her and me sitting there talking, she must figure I'm about to leave.

"Got any more of that fancy 'go fast'?" She doesn't surprise me with her direct approach.

"What's it worth?"

"I'm not much on giving pleasure for goods, but then, I don't mind pleasuring the people that give me things I really like. And like I said, ya got good stuff." Her way of putting things doesn't say it all, but what the hell, I was going to pack her nose before I left anyway.

"Okay. I'll line you out again."

The bathroom door bumps into my shoulder as she squeezes in with me. I've got the coke on the counter and I'm lining it out with the razor blade. The rest of my stash is already back in my pants pocket. I let her in and offer the tube so she can get back to the front.

The white powder is quickly inside her head and I'm about to bend to my share when I feel her fingers at the top of my zipper. I go ahead and take my snort while she's loosening my pants. She wants to undo the belt, but I stop her. If the belt and waist band of my pants aren't in place my piece won't stay at the small of my back. I'd just as soon she doesn't know I'm packing. She's surprised when I yank her hand away from the buckle, but goes with the flow. Her hand slips inside the fly of the leather pants, seizes the shaft of my cock. She shows off a tongue flicking snake-like against her teeth. Her fingers drag the lengthening shaft of my cock through the zipper-teeth opening in my leathers. I watch her eyes drop, taking in the awesome sight of nine inches of rigid cock grasped in her fingers. Her palm slides along the length of the shaft. Measuring? She's not the first to be fascinated with my rod.

I figure she's opened the door. I reach out and grip the tit she's been shaking at me all afternoon. I'm pleased. The nipple is as hard as stiff rubber and the darker skin surrounding it crinkled. She's hot.

"Oh, baby. Gimme...." she starts. That's as far as she gets before her knees fold under her. She crushes herself against my front as she drops. My cock throbs. Her hand grips me at the root of my pipe of flesh, holding it up and squeezing with palm and fingers. I'm not happy about her dicking around.

Finally, her mouth lunges. Her tongue takes my cock's crown, catches the pre-come at its end and pulls back to savor the taste. Then her mouth opens wide, wider, and she struggles to take in the full length of my cock. But she's good. She doesn't gag when my rod hits the back of her mouth and pushes into the top of her throat. She doesn't stop until her nose presses leather. Even then, she works her way past my fly and shoves her nose into the hair at my crotch. She's taken it all, right down to the fuckin' root. I feel her lips press against my balls as the tightness of her throat grasps the head of my cock. Now that she's sure she can swallow the whole thing, she pulls away until only the meaty crown is still inside her mouth, then rams my rod home, right back down to the root.

"Jesus Christ, girl. Where'd you learn to suck cock like that?" It's the hottest fuckin' head I've had in a long time. I'm gonna come, and soon.

Pulling away enough to speak, she answers, "I get your cream. Okay? When I suck cock I get to swallow." She doesn't wait for a response. She's already taking another dive on my cock.

She doesn't have to worry about my giving up my juice. I'm gonna come any moment. She asked for it.

I'm hanging at the edge of letting off a load, my breath hard and quick. Then, I'm there. "Fuckin' shi-i-i-i-i-i-t-t-t-t!" My hand grabs the back of her head, almost shoving my pulsing rod right down into her stomach. The explosion taking off from behind my balls tightens the shaft of my cock for a split second, then, wham, shoots my load into her throat. Four, five, then a sixth spurt of white-hot juice forces itself down her throat.

Slowly the feelings ease, and I let up on the pressure at the back of her head. When I let her escape my hold, she slowly pulls her mouth away, sucking at the shaft even as my spent cock shrinks. She can suck my cock whenever she's in the mood. A mixed stream of saliva and come bridges between my cockhead and her eye-tooth. With a slurping lap of her tongue she recovers even this small string of cream. I get a bit more satisfaction in seeing the girl's eyes are moist with the effort of swallowing my cock and load.

"Do you think we could do that again sometime?" she asks, regaining her feet.

"I don't really know if I'll be around, but I'll give it a thought," I tell her.

It only takes a moment to rearrange my clothing. For the girl's part, she acts as if nothing has happened at all. The rummy is conscious again. He curls his lip at me as I follow the girl out. I ignore him. He's not worth messing with. We go back to the bar where we sit talking, listening to the music and the soft patter of rain on the roof.

I'm sitting there peaceful as can be when I feel the rummy breathing down my neck. He's just a rummy. I would gladly ignore the dude. I would have too, except for the Saturday Night Special he shoves me off my stool with.

"You're a fuckin' bitch, Darla," he snarls at the bar maid. Spittle flies with his slurred words. The gun's barrel swings between the girl and me. "Fuck anybody but Steve, right? I ain't good enough for ya, am I? I'll teach ya. Teach Jerry, too. Goddamn son-of-a-bitch waters the liquor and don't share his cunt."

The dude's obviously cranked up and ready to let fly with that gun. It ain't time to be arguing. It ain't time to be doing anything except giving him what he wants.

"Give, bitch," he swings the barrel at the register. "Don't give me any crap about there not being any money. I know Jerry ain't picked up last night's till yet."

Darla doesn't even bat an eye. She simply comes up from the shelf below the register with a canvas bag stuffed with cash.

"This is all of it," she says as she holds out her hand, offering the money to the souse.

"Bring it here. And you. Don't be a hero!" His last slurred sentence is directed at me.

The dark-haired girl moves cautiously towards where he stands at the end of the bar. She's a little nervous, but not nearly as much as I'd be, looking down the barrel of his piece.

I don't move. I don't even try to flex the muscles of my arm resting against my hip. My gun is only inches from my fingertips but as long as he's looking this way, I remain still.

He grasps the canvas bag and pulls Darla into a bear hug. He leans over her, surrounding her in the stale sweat of his shirt and the stale whiskey on his breath. She doesn't go getting nuts or anything. No sir, she keeps her head about herself. She does a little two-step and turns the drunk so his back is to me. I see the hand holding his gun go to her chest. He's trying to cop a feel and hold his gun at the same time.

I don't need an invitation. My hand snakes up under my shirt at the small of my back and comes up holding four and a half pounds of hard steel. When I bring the piece down on top of his head, his lights go out.

Darla doesn't freak out then, either. She reaches down and grabs the money out of his hand. Then she brings the heel of her boot down on the back of his throat in a perfectly delivered karate kick. When she looks up at me, there's just a hint of the tiger in her eyes.

"Creep," she announces.

"Honey, this ain't the place for me," I tell her, grabbin' my leathers.

"Where you off to?" she asks.

"I've got to see my man down in Long Beach. Then Vegas maybe, or San Antonio. Who the fuck cares?"

Hefting the bag in her long, slim fingers she says, "There's three grand in here. Want a partner?"

Her question is a bit sudden, but I'll be damned if I can see anything wrong with the idea. The way she gives head is worth the coke she'll use. And she sure showed she's got heart.

"I'm outta here one way or another, anyway." She kicks the drunk in the side of the head to make her point.

"Fuck 'em then. Let's get out of here." While she's pulling a light jacket and fanny-pack out from behind the bar, I wipe the prints from my glass and move it a stool or so down the counter.

I've lived this long by keeping my head. I try to stay shy of quick decisions, but can't say I've ever wished I'd made any other. She can sure suck-start a Harley, and I enjoy the way she gets off when I'm stuffing her other holes. She's my main squeeze now. I'm her Candy Man.

Carl Wheat's work has appeared in *Penthouse Letters* and other magazines.

Phantom Lover

by Maxim Jakubowski

I had a history, a bad habit of always wanting what I couldn't have. This time it was her.

You know how it is. You know how it goes, sometimes: the sad ending is already in the sights of your periscope, but you forge ahead regardless. Just in case. Hope against hope and all that.

It was the summer of '97. Don't ask me about the weather, I can't recall it well, it was neither too hot nor too cold, that's all I remember of it. Because of the time we spent naked in alien rooms, I suppose. Just once I had seen her shiver and passed over my overlarge gray T-shirt as shelter from the momentary chill. I still wear that T-shirt from time to time; it brings back memories. Of the color of her bare flesh. The concealed shape of her drunken body.

I was on a job. As it is, meeting her was wrong. Very wrong.

But then the rules of this private eye game are ill-defined. Even more so if you're British. We can't carry guns like the ones in America and all the books and movies. Takes some of the glamour away already.

I do my best, though. I don't do adultery, debt research or repossessions. My field's more refined: industrial espionage, corporate shenanigans. Pays well, limited risks. Quiet and unspectacular, just my style, I reckoned.

That's how I first came across her.

A customer called the agency. Basically, the agency is me. And a few freelancers. And lots of names in a computer database. People who could be bribed. British Telecom engineers; bookkeepers for brokerage firms; disenchanted clerks with City banks; underpaid and exploited staff in the despatch departments and post-rooms of large corporations. The indispensable human tools of the trade in my business.

The Labour party had come in a few weeks before and were threatening the privatized utilities with the windfall tax. One of the larger utilities was mounting some form of legal defense against the government plan. But their counterplotting was somehow making it into the national press. As soon as something was discussed at a boardroom level, it arrived in print on the financial pages of one of the large national newspapers. Inconvenient. You can't play chess when your opponent always knows your likely response to his movements. I was hired over the phone by a Mr. Jones in Corporate Planning. Money no object. Find out who was leaking the minutes of the secret meetings, and stop them.

Piece of cake.

The annoying columns were penned by the business correspondent of the newspaper. One I used to read, but had recently given up on. I soon had a tap on his South London mews house telephone and 24-hour surveillance in operation. He operated from his Canary Wharf newsroom; unfortunately, because of the other year's IRA bombing in the vicinity I couldn't get access to the paper's offices and his phone there. Not to worry. I would just have to be patient and more thorough than usual.

Motive was quickly revealed: the guy's wife was a member of the local Labour constituency. Bloody idealists. So now it was just a question of pin-pointing who at the Utilities was passing him information. At first I assumed it was also a local party activist, passing information to the press for what he or she thought were all the right reasons. So I left a couple of freelancers to keep a close eye on the Canary Wharf and City jaunts of the damn journo, and decided to concentrate on the South London connection personally.

And met her. The wife. Callie.

And my problems began.

And the joy.

Turns out I was on the wrong trail, anyway. The division at the Utilities that had called on my snooping services didn't know what another division on another floor was up to. It seems that they were aware there was no legal chance in hell of reversing the government's new tax, even if they had spent months and mountains in cash taking their case to the European courts of wherever, so they had leaked the stuff to the newspaper themselves to put the frighteners on the politicians in the hope of discouraging the Exchequer to set the windfall tax too high. Manipulating the media, and my business correspondence target was just the patsy they had unwittingly used. He was fairly new to the job, an arrival from TV and radio who didn't realize he was being manipulated. He probably thought all along he was God's answer to investigative journalism. I never did like him anyway.

But I didn't know all that then, and I also thought I was doing a damn good job. Did I say patsy?

Early bright late May morning, parked fifty yards from the couple's semi-detached, I munched on a chocolate biscuit in lieu of breakfast, aware that this job was playing havoc with my expanding waistline. Mark, the journalist, had left half an hour ago for Canary Wharf, and a reliable acolyte had followed him. I'd planned to keep on the wife's trail. Already knew quite a bit about her. Second generation Irish, Epsom grammar school and Cambridge, a second in English, a few dead-end jobs on regional newspapers and now a reader in the drama department for one of the new television cable channels; married eight years, in the chapel of the Cambridge college where they had both been undergraduates. No children. Canvassed for the local branch of the party. Must have had her first orgasm in months on the night Labour won and they fucked whilst blinding drunk. On paper, a common type. Somehow, I hadn't summoned a mental picture of her, wasn't really expecting anything surprising. She was just a pawn in another very ordinary case.

The house's front door opened.

I was blinded.

Within a week, I had contrived to meet her at a launch party for a balti curry cookery book in a Central London art gallery. Her voice, the way the thin material of her blue dress hung over her shoulders, her dark eyes peering inside me as we spoke inconsequential gossip, it all made the longing reach unthought-of agony.

Within two weeks, we were in bed together.

I had crossed the line.

Cookie, my old mentor, had always warned me never to mix business with pleasure, get personally involved in a case. But all the wise precepts were quickly forgotten as her lips engulfed my vile meat in a kiss of fire, unabashed by the fact that I had just retreated momentarily from the wet furnace of her innards and was still dripping with her juices.

On the first hotel bed, it was lust. Extraordinary. Venting the frustrations of our respective lives. Reinventing the lovemaking that our respective partners no longer sought with the same intensity as before. Drinking at the tap of life all over again. Reminding ourselves that our bodies still held untold beauty that was elsewhere being taken for granted or perused for growing imperfections.

Oh, my Callie.

Crossing the thin line. She had never been unfaithful before. Accidents hadn't happened. I had. Opportunities. Not very often. One-night stands. The job made it easy. But none of the affairs had lasted long; enjoyable distractions on the journey to middle-age. She was younger, the thought had sometimes occurred, there had been other men making passes; she was pretty in her unconventional way, but it had never been the right time or place, she supposed.

But when I asked for details of her nearly past adventures, she was always reticent and invariably changed the subject quickly. And I had more immediate priorities. Mapping the pale color of her skin until the morning came when we would have to go our own way. Using her shocking pink lipstick to enhance the blood-engorged color of her private parts before I licked them clean. Maneuvering her body into impossible contortions and positions to make my thrusts ever deeper until she screamed loudly, scaring me, "No, it's okay, it's pleasure, not pain. More, more." Tracing the bumpy texture of her cunt walls with the probing tip of my tongue. Inserting my fingers past the resistance of the invisible muscles protecting the heart of her moon-shaped arse.

Think of hardcore pornography and add unthought-of perverse trimmings and we did it.

She brought out the worst and the best in me.

And vice-versa.

"Do you know? I've never done it that way...."

"We can try it, I suppose."

"I'm not sure it's even possible."

"No harm in trying."

"I'll be careful."

"I know you will."

And as we sunk in free-fall to the very depths of uncontrollable lust, my heart broke. Just like that. One moment we were fucking with abandon, our wetness mingling, our bodies intimately joined in at least three different areas, blissfully unaware of the world outside the pulled calico curtains. We were in her bed; Mark had gone to Oxford for the day: "Remind me to put the sheets in the washing machine as you leave." I had parked a few streets away by the Park. I could feel the sweat bucketing down my forehead onto her cheeks, my tongue embedded in her mouth, my cock growing harder with every forward movement and her insides melting as she jesused away while the pleasure grew within. Just then, I opened my eyes. And looked into hers.

And I walked with the angels as I realized, right there and then, that she was the one, the one I had always been looking for without knowing if she even existed. It was love at second-hand sight, no longer lust. I knew, as I fucked her with untold rage, that I had to have her. Not like this, mere copulation, sweat and secretions, but forever. She could belong to Mark no more. I wanted all of her. Sharing was no longer a possibility; nor was a mere affair of the flesh.

By now, I knew she wasn't involved in the leak of information from the utilities company, of course. I had reported accordingly to my paymasters and my sidekicks were still tailing her husband, although there was little evidence of him being in contact with anyone suspicious. At any rate, it was useful to know his whereabouts at all times. Maybe I was secretly hoping he was conducting his own affair somewhere. It would have given me the right impetus to force her permanently into my arms. Sadly, he was a boring man and never strayed. Too ambitious and mindful of his career prospects, I assumed, from what Callie had told me of him.

Later that evening, we were having a drink in a pub somewhere along the South Bank, far enough from her home, we thought, to be safe. I couldn't tell her that I was aware Mark was still on his assignment in Finchley, where a large theater chain was opening a new multiplex.

"I love you," I said.

"I know," she said, sipping her gin-and-orange.

"No. I mean, for real, I want us to be together. Leave him. I'll move out, find us a place. We could travel together."

She knew I was married too. Somehow I'd have to explain what my job actually was, explain earlier white lies. I was confident I could.

"You're going too fast," she replied, surprising me. "We've got to give it time."

Right then I had the awful feeling we were not going to make it.

That things would not work out.

And it began to kill me inside.

Back home, I carefully composed a letter to her husband, revealing our affair. It was illogical, I knew, but it was a compulsion I could not resist. I slipped the letter into an envelope, and the next day at my office, stuck the letter at the back of a drawer, knowing that one day I would use it as a weapon of vengeance.

We stayed together, so to speak, another three months. Every time we made love, I drew a small star with the letter C in my diary. Looking back at those pages today, it's like a monotonous parade of distracted graffiti strung out between cryptic notes of things to do or telephone numbers, a private Milky Way leading to my own death by a thousand shards of longing.

The sex became even more frantic, as the despair inside me took a firm hold and her coldness became more apparent every time the subject of our future was broached.

All the time, the ticking bomb inside my desk was on its fatal countdown.

But the sex was good, oh yes, Callie. As if the contact of our skin turned us into incredible two-backed beasts capable of reinventing the flesh like no one had ever done before. With all the energy I was putting into our encounters, I no longer had to worry about my waistline. And sweet Callie bloomed into a sensuous flower of the night, sex vibrating all around her as she walked away to her night train, still full of my seed, her long legs eating up the station concourse, the eyes of every man in the immediate vicinity automatically turning toward her, this creature of sheer lust. Mine.

One day. summer coming to an end, in another pub somewhere in the no man's land that separated both of us from our real lives and relationships.

"Joe?"

"Yes?"

"It's still going too fast … I need some time to think. I don't want us hurting anyone, you know."

"What do you mean?"

I had carefully not raised the subject of our getting permanently together for a few weeks now, hoping she would naturally come to the idea.

"I think of you too often. It's not good. It's affecting my work. I just don't know how to act when Mark's around. We don't talk much any more. He's going to suspect something soon. . ."

"So what?"

"We must spend some time apart."

"No."

"A few months maybe. Then we'll see how we feel about each other."

I knew all too well this was a recipe for disaster.

We negotiated. I pleaded. The time apart, its length, remained unsaid. I begged. We agreed on a final fuck the next evening. Sentimentally, I even asked her to wear the same outfit she had on the first time we met. Well, if this was to be the last time....

That afternoon, I posted the letter.

It was after the final postal pick-up from that particular letter box. Mark wouldn't get it until the morning after next. Or later if the mail room at his newspaper was slow in distributing things.

Which left me one evening to make love to her so well, so badly that she would change her mind and stay with me forever. I had to find the imagination, the words to sway her. Usually, I work well against deadlines. A sad gamble, I realize now.

She never appeared for our clandestine meeting.

There was no answer from her phone. They had no answering machine, but even if they had I wasn't in a position to leave a message.

A few days went by without news from her.

Puzzled, saddened, I tried to phone her at work. Her private line was dead. I hesitated, then decided to phone Mark at the newspaper.

"Did you get my letter?"

He sounded genuinely puzzled.

"What letter? Who are you?"

He must have thought I was some madman, some crazy guy with a bad grudge against business journalists.

Not only had my letter not reached him, but he wasn't even married, let alone living with any woman right now.

"Whoever you are, you've got the wrong man, Mate," he concluded.

I slammed the phone down before he did.

Felt cold sweat all over.

I phoned directory enquiries to get the number of the cable television company where she worked. Why would she have pretended she was married to Mark? It made no sense at all. Made the reservations she harbored throughout our affair meaningless.

The woman on the switchboard swore they had no one called Callie working there, neither under her married name nor her maiden one. Sensing my increasing desperation, she even checked through the list of all the freelancers who occasionally used a desk at the company.

"No. I'm absolutely certain. She does not work here," she assured me.

"Are you positive?" I asked again. "It is so important."

"There ain't that many of us here, you see. I know every one. Nobody answers your description. Are you sure you're not confused? There are a lot of independent TV companies in the area."

I had often accompanied her in the morning to the building, seen her from afar walk through the building's portals.

I spent the day being a dedicated private eye. Checking things I should have investigated before. Local property registers: the South London mews house I had first seen her leaving, luminous, was in Mark's name only. Caught a cab to Somerset House to check again on the damn marriage certificate where I'd learned about the Cambridge college chapel. Yes, it was there: eight years ago, maiden name Callie Edwin. Collected my thoughts. Then visited another room in the large official building. And found the divorce papers: Mark and Callie had separated four years ago.

The hole in the pit of my stomach began twisting its spear through my heart. Was her name even Callie?

Who was she?

A million questions whirled frantically through my brain.

But the main one was "Why?"

Why, Callie?

I went home late, torn apart by conflicting emotions. My wife was still awake. Angry, inquisitorial. She had received a letter in the mail that morning accusing me of having an affair. She had repeatedly phoned me throughout the day, but it was always engaged, and in my mixed-up state I hadn't bothered to answer her messages.

"Who sent you the letter?" I asked.

"That's not the point," she answered. "Is it true?"

"Who wrote the damn letter," I shouted back at her.

"So it is true," she remarked.

"Who?" I asked her again.

"Someone called Callie," she said.

"Yes, it's true," I admitted. I didn't have the energy to argue or fight.

My whole world had just been shattered into lots of small, desolate pieces and I just had no answers.

In the days that followed, I could not summon the will to lie or apologize, and my marriage collapsed, while I still desperately followed every conceivable lead that might take me to the invisible Callie, her motives and her warm body again. I was in denial. Couldn't accept the unexpected and puzzling rejection. Hitchcock stories surely didn't happen to real people. I tried to recall every conversation we ever had, to remember any name that might have been mentioned by her in passing, any clue to her identity or someone who might be aware of her or even her whereabouts. And all these memories could not help invoking every little thing we had done, the curve of her breasts, the color of her lips, the feel of her tongue on my trembling skin, how her throat turned pink as pleasure took hold of her senses, her moans, her sighs, her soft, gentle, almost shy voice when she whispered my name with such awful delicacy as we lay entwined in bed. Constant torture, it was. But it got me nowhere.

Not only had she disappeared from the face of London, but there was no evidence she had even existed.

Apart from the deep tattoo she had carved in my errant soul.

Visions of her kept me awake at night for months on end. Fleeting visions of other women in the street recalled a lock of hair, a swish of material, the simile of a smile, but of course it was never her. Just a pale imitation, a fuzzy piece of the overall puzzle that Callie had become.

Time passed.

I still couldn't forget her. Kept on wondering whether she would have disappeared if I had not posted the damn letter. But knew, deep inside, that the scenario had already been written the moment I met her, and nothing I had done would have changed the outcome.

I was a mess.

Single life didn't suit me and there was no way my wife would have me back; she sensed that I had given my heart to Callie and would not tolerate its absence if we resumed our relationship.

For months I haunted the places we had been together. The pubs, the restaurants. I even stayed a few times in the same hotels for a night, always insisting on the room we had originally occupied. And invariably jerked off, screaming her name out loud as I came over the starched sheets or the bed cover, evoking mental images of her body, her sex, her royal rump. Talk about sad!

I tracked the real Callie down, once Mark's wife. She now lived in Brixton with an Irish loft extension builder. She had long, straight, brown hair and round glasses, prettyish face but bad legs. There was no resemblance. But then, I had to try every possibility.

By now — I still kept watching him on a regular basis — Mark was shacked up in the South London mews semi-detached with a small redhead, who also worked in Canary Wharf. I had actually witnessed their meeting over the lunch break in a sandwich bar. Mr. Cupid, that's me.

The windfall tax was passed and the official side of the Callie case came to an end. By then, Office A had found out about Office B's plans; I was called in and my services dispensed with, with minor apologies and a reasonable check for my efforts.

My nights were still empty with the despair of longing and the image of her face at rest on a shared pillow began to lose its intensity, its focus. But still I grieved inside. Badly. On the anniversary of our first fuck, I wrote her a postcard I never sent. Where could I send it? Another on the next Valentine's Day. On what she had told me was her birthday. There were still people out there, paid by me, who had her description, looking for traces of her. But nothing ever came up. I lost myself in work. Expanded the agency, and finally agreed we should now take on adultery cases. Why have scruples any longer? Business boomed.

Two years had gone by. The pain still buried like a tumor in my previously-unfelt depths. Trying to grow old gracefully. I enjoyed an affair with one of our new operatives, Lucy, a small, curvaceous, auburn-haired young woman who broached no sentimentality and preferred a no-strings attached relationship. She was good for me, uncomplicated, defiantly cheerful. What she didn't know was that most times I had to conjure up the ghost of Callie to stay hard when making love to her. But I suppose you wouldn't call that being unfaithful, technically speaking. Just a sex aid. Even took a holiday with her. Rented a white stucco villa in southern Portugal where we shared our time fucking nonchalantly and eating too much. Which only served to remind me that I had never managed to go anywhere with Callie further than a few uninspiring, furtive-dirty-weekend, coastal hotels, and hadn't seen her on a beach, by the pool or even in a swimming costume.

Time, like a slow, slow river.

August 1999

Waiting for a train at Paddington Station, I was browsing through the newsstand and spotted a Paul Klée postcard. The second anniversary of our first time together was just a few days away, evoking balmy sensations of my fingers slipping through her curls and the oh-so-tender softness of her uncovered, shivering breasts. I bought the card. Wrote "I miss you still" on the back, and then, lacking an address as usual, buried it in my pocket, there to gather oblivion again, until the next absurd celebration of her continuing absence.

Missing her was an understatement.

Every day and every night.

Still.

Always.

The station's tannoy system announced a fifteen-minute delay on the arrival of the Cardiff train. I had to sign for some documents a junior clerk was bringing up to London from a Bristol solicitor. I backtracked to the newsstand, searching for a magazine to kill the time, but none caught my attention. Moved over to the book racks.

At first, it was the cover illustration that I noticed. A photographic close-up of a woman's leg, the constricted flesh bursting through the fishnet patterns of a stocking. An image that struck a responsive chord inside my dormant libido.

The Man Who Didn't Understand Women, by Katherine Blackheath.

I seldom read women's fiction, but the back cover blurb intrigued me. Something about a man and a woman, London, anonymous hotel rooms, three months of forbidden passion.

Standing at the center of the station concourse, I began reading.

I finished the book at two the following morning. I'd canceled an evening with Lucy earlier.

It was all there.

Our story.

With subtle changes: Did I really never smile? I was no longer a private eye but merely an insurance investigator. But then I had never revealed my occupation to Callie; I had indicated I was a freelance journalist. It wasn't Eastbourne, but Brighton, and there was no mention of a husband but now I had two children … wholesale chunks of conversations we had had, in our usual pub, in bed, were accurately evoked. The fateful letter I had written. She even described the sounds I would make when I came, the words I would say, those she would herself whisper. The ritual of undressing and kissing. And the woman in the book was also called Callie.

I can't say I was shocked. Surprised, maybe. It was strange to see myself in print like that. Or, at any rate, a character whom I could recognize as me. Possibly angry that she should steal our story in this way.

Toward the end of the novel, after the two lovers had badly betrayed each other, they both traveled a lot, enjoying rather sordid adventures. Mine, I didn't mind. Hers, I winced at the thought that she might actually have fucked all these other men, it was so realistic. Difficult to know where the fiction and the reality took divergent paths. She wrote well, Callie — or was it Katherine — did. I could sense the emotions, the feelings oozing from the pages as the narrative developed.

But nowhere was there an explanation for her actions, her disappearing act, all the obvious preparations she would have had to undertake to fool me in the way she did about her very existence. And neither was there a reason why the character in her novel did what she did to me, to him, the somewhat passive, seemingly spineless male protagonist.

"Because she thought she loved him," she wrote somewhere in the book.

Which made the whole affair no easier to understand.

The novel ended with a melodramatic shoot-out straight out of a hard-boiled noir movie, in which most of the characters, including the two of us, perished. Gave things a sense of closure, but felt all wrong.

I was tired. It was dark outside. I was puzzled. I was hungry.

Another mystery confronted me now: *The Curious Case of Katherine Blackheath. Or the Detective Who Always Drank Coca-Cola.*

The next morning I contacted the publicity department of the book's publishers in an attempt to obtain information about the novel's author. They promised something in the mail. All I received was a flimsy press release, which clumsily summarized the plot and promised oodles of promotion and reviews. About Callie, all it said was that she lived in New York.

When we were together, my unfulfilled fantasy had been to take her to America. I couldn't quite picture her in the Manhattan hustle and bustle.

I tried to get more specific details through a junior in the publicity department, but there was nothing of substance to be had. The manuscript had been bought from a literary agent, through his British counterpart, and the author had been unwilling to provide any biographical details, let alone a photograph.

Within a week, I landed at Kennedy.

As my cab raced down Van Wyck Expressway toward the inevitable traffic gridlock beyond the Midtown tunnel, I wondered what to do next.

I'd never operated in a foreign country. The rules were different.

Here, private dicks used guns.

My hotel on West 44th Street was undergoing renovation and Polish builders tramped up and down the corridors, peppering the lift and the lobby with white dust. The television set in the room wasn't working. I called out for a Chinese meal. By the time the under-spiced food arrived, it was lukewarm. By now I had jotted down on a pad my course of action. The art of detecting is to be methodical, organized, and, most of all, patient. But I'd never been a patient person. Maybe that had been my undoing with sweet Callie?

Call the New York agent. Arrange an appointment. Have some bogus business cards printed up to present some sort of front. I'd brought over an assortment of glossy British magazines with some of the bylines I'd be borrowing for the occasion. I was confident few, if any, of the journalists involved would be known here. Small risk involved, really. Change travelers checks for lower denomination dollar bills. For transport, tips and bribes when necessary. Tomorrow, contact the local agency with whom my outfit had sometimes collaborated on the technicalities of past cases involving transatlantic connections. Visit the *New York Times* cuttings library to assemble American reviews of the book, which might provide information as to the author's whereabouts, in the likely absence of interviews. Determine how regulated British residents are in America. Was she here on a visitor's visa or did she have a green card? Government offices were a weak link where the right amount of money spread around might earn me some valuable information.

That would do to begin with.

If, as I expected, this failed, the second angle of attack would involve more illegal methods to trace financial records at the publishers or the literary agency. This was problematic, though, as I still had no precise indication of her real name.

The biggest risk would involve breaking into her agent's offices to check their records.

Not something I was looking forward to.

But, if it came to that, I knew I would do it. I could sense it in the air, Callie was in Manhattan. Probably no more than a mile or two away. I had to find her. I would find her.

September 29th 1999

Finally managed a meeting with her agent, a perky preppy twerp with regulation red braces and an insincere smile. No, Miss Blackheath is quite adamant that she wishes to retain her privacy. Did you know we've a Hollywood option for the book? Gwyneth Paltrow is being lined up. Personally I'd have gone for Anne Heche, you know, but she's a hard sell for romantic stories now, of course. If it were up to me, I'd love her to consent to an interview. Would help sales. The absent author lark has its drawbacks, you see. He relented slightly, assuring me he would contact her and strongly recommend she agree to seeing me. Absolutely loved the magazine I was pretending to write for. Really. But that's all he could do. He did have this other client, an ex-stripper and dominatrix who lived in Alphabet City and now penned very erotic books. Great angle. Wouldn't a feature on her be great? She wouldn't mind being photographed in the nude, you see. He would get in touch, one way or the other, when Katherine Blackheath responded to my request. No, he didn't know how long it would take.

I tried to squeeze some more information out of him. Background stuff for my piece. How had he come to represent her? In fact, it was another agent who had since departed from the agency and he had only just taken over her affairs. Had never actually met her. Loved the book. So funny. I noted the previous agent's name. He'd moved to Los Angeles to be a reader for a film company.

In her novel, Callie's character had decamped to California and become involved in the making of hardcore porno films. Jotting things down on automatic pilot, in the agent's office with its panoramic views of downtown Manhattan, I recalled the feel of her lips, in London rooms, caressing the dangling sack of my balls, teasing my rigid stem before tenderly devouring me whole.

"I don't think I can really tell you more," the agent said, rising from his padded chair. On the way out, I smiled broadly at one of the young women at a nearby desk. Asked if she was his assistant. No, just an intern. I smiled again. English accents are popular here. A possible future contact?

October 12th 1999

"I know it's you," the letter said. "Do not try and find me, I implore you, if you have any decency left in your body. Let me be."

"Who cares about decency? What the fuck does it have to do with us? I must see you, Callie, or whatever your name really is or was, or is now, Katherine. Please," I answered, sending the letter in care of the agency.

At night in my hotel room, I read her few lines a thousand times over. Smelled the paper, desperately attempting to retrieve even a trace of her scent. Two years ago, I had mentally catalogued every one of her fragrances, from the bitter sweet smell of her breath on awakening in strange, sordid hotel rooms, which she always tried to obliterate with mints, to the pungent aroma of her underarm perspiration following our exaggerated sexual exertions, to the unique perfumes of her inner secretions which I would greedily suck from her as she spread herself open for me.

"I still love you madly," I wrote her with a distinct lack of originality. "And whatever I have done wrong, I beg for your forgiveness. I must see you. At least, let's talk. It kills me that I don't know the answers."

October 24th 1999

"No. I swore it was over, Joe, and nothing you could say or write could make me change my mind now.

"Stop stalking me. It doesn't suit you. At all.

"It will soon be the year 2000. Can't you understand once and for all that I have rejected you and call an end to this sorry episode?

"Do not write again. I will not answer any more."

She signed the letter Katherine Blackheath. It was just addressed to Joe. Not even "Dear Joe."

How definitive she could be in her vindictiveness.

And, no, I didn't understand women.

Her words both pained and angered me. I swear we shall meet again before the bloody year 2000. Just wait and see.

November 2nd 1999

I'm seeing Stevie for drinks tonight. She's the young woman with the kind smile back at Callie's literary agency. Exploring another avenue.

Have given out almost five hundred bucks among various contacts I've been given at the immigration offices to track Katherine Blackheath down. None of them asked questions. They took the money and made vague promises.

Now, I wait.

November 3rd 1999

Stevie allowed me to kiss her briefly, as we reached the door to the flat she shared with two other ex-Bennington graduates in a Lexington Street brownstone.

I'd laid on the charm like a real hypocrite, never even hinting at the reason for my attentions.

We're eating out tomorrow night.

Her freckles make her look even younger than she is.

November 8th 1999

Stevie and I are now sleeping together. The first night was good; I didn't even have to pretend she was Callie to maintain my erection.

We went to the Hamptons for the week-end. I hired a car.

She talks too much. But then maybe I'm too quiet, and it balances out in the order of things.

But London nights are, so quickly, back in my mind again, as I wish Stevie's fingers might move a little further, a bit harder, differently, as we make love between crispy white sheets and she catches her breath in spasms under the weight of my body.

November 14th 1999

A month and a half to the millennium. All the papers and TV news (the hotel management has finally put my set right) and chat shows are already interminably rambling on the parties and celebrations on New Year's Eve. Times Square will be a killer.

Six weeks left to locate her.

It will be strange seeing her again. I know there's no point in rehearsing a speech or something. I'd forget it in her presence anyway. I'll have to overcome her initial anger, of course.

She's not here on a green card. I have managed to determine that. Expensively.

Next Sunday, I intend to ask Stevie an important favor.

November 20th 1999

No, not there, Stevie screamed as we fucked. I'm sorry, I told her, but I know she didn't believe me.

But I *am* sorry. She's just the wrong person at the wrong time. I'm too rough because she's not the woman my whole body screams for in an act of madness. I don't like hurting people.

She's agreed to look up the Katherine Blackheath file some time next week, when she gets an opportunity to get into the agent's office during a lunch break. Probably Wednesday, as he's booked for lunch at the Metropole Hotel for a meeting with some Bertelsmann top brass.

November 26th 1999

Stevie's provided me with an address. On Varick Street. In the Village. Must have passed the building on countless occasions.

Stevie has also said it would be better if we didn't see each other any more. She knows I have used her.

November 28th 1999

It's a small three-story building. There's an ansaphone by the front door; there are no names on two of the bells. I tried all of them. None answered. This was in the morning. Same again in the afternoon. Maybe she's working during the day. Has to make a living. I returned in the evening and the building was still empty. I lurked outside until three in the morning. couldn't stand it any longer. Felt like a fool. Major caliber idiot. Freezing. I gave up for the day and returned to the hotel uptown.

This weekend, I'll go to Varick street again.

December 2nd 1999

They are already spreading decorations throughout the island in preparation for the festivities. Twinkling colored light bulbs adorn the trees around Union Square. I'm the one who's anything but cheerful.

I've finally made contact with the other two occupants of her building in the Village. They know little of her. Very quiet. Keeps to herself. Hasn't been seen around for a few weeks. The merchant banker from the top floor thought he remembered her catching a cab, holding a suitcase. Maybe a trip to the West Cost because of the film rights to the novel, I wondered?

I try her bell every two days.

Surely she'll be back for Christmas?

December 10th 1999

Callie has returned.

But I managed to miss her.

She knew I'd been, though.

There was an envelope with my name hastily scrawled on it, cellotaped to the bell.

"How dare you follow me the way you do," Callie said. "Just go away. I can't stand it any more, Joe."

She had vacated the apartment the same morning. I contacted the letting agent and visited the premises, maybe hoping she had left something, papers that might provide me with a clue to where she had decamped to.

This was the bed in which she had slept. "No, I think it's too small for me," I told the realtor.

I was back to square one.

And needing her was eating me up inside like a cancer.

December 20th 1999

At last, I'm no longer running around in ever-diminishing circles. I'm back on the trail. Through her erstwhile agent who had moved to L.A., I discovered that she had accepted an invitation to dine on New Year's Eve at the 42nd Street Brewery that now overlooked Times Square. She will be with some studio executives who are developing her novel.

I tried to make a booking there, but it has been sold out for months for such a momentous evening. No doubt for the view, rather than the food.

December 29th 1999

My final contact in immigration at last provided me with an address. Varick Street. A bit late in the day. I already knew she had left no forwarding address.

The *New York Post* kindly outlined the crowd control measures being put into operation for the Times Square Millennium party on New Year's Eve.

I knew from one of the waiters that her booking was for 10:30.

The only access to the Brewery would be down 42nd Street, coming from 5th Avenue.

December 31st 1999
I await the year 2000 standing in front of the Fun City sex shop. Its neon lights turn my skin a sickly shade of pink. The end-of-century sales advertise 6-hour all-anal gangbang tapes for only $9.99, but tall blondes with shaven snatches and extreme amateur debuts go for $12.00. A few yards further down, there's a security cordon of cops who check people's passes to Times Square venues.

Everything around sounds too loud.

Artificially joyful.

The sky is clear of stars.

10:15. Here she comes, sashaying down, her long legs lime metronomes, her strawberry-blond hair shorter than I remember, walking too fast as usual, her eyes full of sadness peering ahead in a myopic trance.

The crowd of revelers parts slightly as she moves nearer.

She sees me.

Not a sign of emotion.

My heart beats like the onset of a major symphony.

She approaches.

Glares at me.

"Hi," I say.

She stays silent.

"We were bound to meet eventually," I clumsily say, by way of excuse.

"I told you not to," she finally answers.

The crowds whiz by on their way to the party of all parties.

"I had to see you."

"Why?"

"Answers."

"You know it's over. It can never be the same again."

"You owe me some explanations."

"No, I don't."

"You just disappeared..." I mumble.

"You can't take rejection, can you?" she says.

"You're right. It's physical, mental, whatever, I just can't accept there's not even a diamond of hope you might listen to me again, remember the way we felt...."

"The way *you* felt."

"Please, Callie."

"It's Katherine, now."

"Please."

"No, Joe. Life is not like fiction. There are no second chances."

"So why did you write the book?"

"A way of finally putting it all behind me, I suppose."

I see her lips, I look into her eyes, I can feel the warmth of her body just a few inches away from me. In the cold air, her breath smokes away from her mouth. Is this really the way it ends?

"Walk away now," she asks me.

"No."

Her features stay blank as her hand moves to the small black handbag and pulls out a small, silver gun. I don't even recognize the model.

"You wouldn't," I say.

And move closer to her, to the familiar pale skin now shielded by winter clothes. The gun is now all that separates us.

"I would," my sweet Callie says, a vision of terrible pain taking control of her face.

"So do it," I order her.

She shoots me in the heart. The bang of the small gun is surprisingly unloud.

As the century recedes slowly, I see the cops move towards her in slow motion, their own weapons drawn.

Everything blurs around us. We are imprisoned in a pocket of time.

Callie raises her hands as the cops approach her.

"The guy was stalking me," she says.

Not content with appearing in the first 2 volumes of *Noirotica*, **Maxim Jakubowski** pursues a life of crime with his *Mammoth Book of Erotica* series (five to date) and his own romantic version of pornography. Following *The State of Montana* (1998), he is soon to prolong his life in the slave galleys of the erotic field by committing *On the Tenderness Express* (2000).

Second Chance

by P.D. Cacek

The room stank of sweat and beer, whiskey and testosterone, cigarettes and cheap cigars. It was the smell of money — heady, intoxicating and t ripe for the picking.

And Chloe McAlister considered herself one of the prime pickers of that kind of fruit.

Clutching the brass pole with both hands, Chloe arched her back and pressed the front of her g-string against the cool metal. The smell in the room changed, the musky-sour male scent suddenly rising above the rest. She smiled, open-mouthed, and ran the tip of her tongue over the glossy, never-smudge lipstick. She leaned back even further to shake the rosy peaks of her naked breasts the way Gennah had taught her when she first came on the circuit as a green runaway from Duluth.

The roar of approval momentarily drowned out the sound of heavy metal music screaming through the speakers behind her.

Chloe shook them again. For good measure.

No silicone in these *babies*, she thought proudly as she released one hand and swung, gracefully down and around. And she probably wouldn't need any until she hit, oh, twenty-five or twenty-six. But that was years and years away.

Swinging back to her feet, Chloe stopped thinking about growing old and pretended she could see through the thick haze to where he was sitting.

At the bar. Last seat. Far right side.

Back where the light had been broken so long Chloe wondered if there'd ever been a light there in the first place. Or maybe he'd had Pete, the club's owner, take out the light because he liked it dark. He could have. Because he was an important man. With connections.

Probably the most important man Chloe had ever ... "dated" on a regular basis.

Another wave of male-smell crashed over her as she began strutting down the runway — hips waggling, black stiletto heels clicking, shoulders back, breasts bouncing in time to the hard-driving beat. Tiny white lights, like the ones she used to help string on Christmas trees back when she was a kid, the ones her Grammy called "Fairy Lights," outlined the runway. Pete had stapled them along the edge after one of the dancers, a "Specialty Act," had walked right off the end and sprained an ankle. The poor jerk she landed on sprained more than that.

Chloe liked the little lights. They made the sequins on her costumes, what there was of them, sparkle like diamonds, rubies, and emeralds.

Tonight they were emeralds in the shape of a butterfly. Chloe had chosen that particular G-string because she knew *He* was going to be there. Green was his favorite color.

Hers, too. Especially when it was in the shape of a twenty and being held out by a blurry-eyed, red-nosed, wet-faced man in a rumpled business suit.

Time to weed the garden, Chloe thought and pivoted in mid-step toward the offered bill.

The musky pre-cum scent rising off the man was enough to overpower the smell of whiskey and sweat. For the moment. But it was enough. Pouting, finger to mouth, Chloe blinked eyes she'd been told looked like clear blue pools and acted coy. Like she didn't know what to do. The crowd shouted instructions and red-faced man hooted and waved the bill, enjoying being the center of attention. She pretended innocence for a moment longer before straddling the upraised hand (an inch over the crisp ATM twenty) and pulling down the front of her G-string.

Offering her own special "TM" for him to slip the money into.

There was a some kind of city ordinance or something that prevented her and the other dancers from going full buff, but as long as she kept the G-string on (more or less) it was okay. In fact, it was more than okay ... it not only showed everyone that she really was a true blonde, but allowed her to keep all the tips she got like that out of the "Community Chest" which got split six ways when the club closed.

Gennah had once figured she made more that way, even if the bills were a little damp afterwards.

The businessman was even drunker than Chloe originally thought. His hand went left when she went right, right when she shifted left. It was frustrating as hell, but at least the crowd loved it. When he finally managed to stuff the bill into her "snatch purse" the cheer swallowed up the music again.

Always mindful that she was a professional (Gennah had told her that), Chloe pretended to struggle with her costume before spinning on one needle-thin heel and fanny-fanning her way off stage. She got to the stage curtain just as the music ended.

And bowed.

Then squealed when the rain of fives, tens and twenties started flooding the stage. Chloe fanny-fanned all the way back down the runway, making sure everyone got a good look at her bare, sweat-glistening breasts (as a thank-you) while she hurriedly picked up the communal tips before scurrying off. She knew *he* was waiting. And *he* didn't like to be kept waiting long.

Besides, Sheila the She-Bitch's number was next ... and Sheila hated waiting even more than *he* did.

Chloe was grinning from ear-to-ear as she wove her way between the drunks and ass-pinchers to the shadowed last stool at the far right side of the bar. Not only had she managed to stuff another twenty and two tens into her "secret cash drawer", but she liked the way the front of her short, almost genuine silk robe felt against her skin.

It tickled. Made her nipples hard.

Made every man in the room think she wanted him.

Especially the *him* currently sipping down a whiskey sour.

Mr. Roland "Call me Rollie" W. Spelman, Jr.

He grinned back when Chloe slid onto the empty stool next to him. Even though the club was full to bursting and the line at the bar was three-deep, no one had had the balls to take the empty stool she was currently occupying. *That's* how important he was.

Chloe giggled as she crossed her legs and one of the bills poked her. In the nicest possible place. She giggled again, remembering how they'd met, the shock-delight/shock-terror after she got back to the dressing room and removed the folded bill he had stuffed up her pussy purse. She'd thought he was just another businessman — maybe a little more rumpled and blurry-eyed than the rest — until she pulled the damp hundred dollar-bill from her snatch.

One-*Jesus*-hundred-*freaking*-dollar-*Christ-on-a-crutch*-bill!

Since she'd never seen a real hundred-dollar bill before — hadn't even seen a fake one, for that matter — she'd stopped jumping up and down just long enough to hold the damp C-note out to Gennah and ask if the fat, bald headed old guy with glasses who discovered lightning was really supposed to be on it. Or if it was just, like, Monopoly money.

But when Gennah, silver and gold glitter-stripes decorating her naked cocoa-caramel colored body (she was billed as "Tiger Rose — Queen of the Urban Jungle"), took the bill and smiled wide enough to show the three gold molars, Chloe knew she'd hit pay dirt.

That had been the shock/delight part. The shock/terror part came after Gennah shook the bill open and a small ivory business card decorated with the unmistakable gold-and-black *badge* shaped symbol fluttered to the floor.

Chloe had gotten as far as the words, *Investigation Division — Criminalistic Unit*, when *he* walked in. Roland W. Spelman, Jr.

"I'm not a criminal!" Chloe had screamed at him, one hand trying to cover her naked breasts with a face tissue, the other snatching the bill from Gennah's hand and waving it like a flag of surrender.

But he laughed and told her the money was only in appreciation of her ... unique talents.

Gennah hadn't laughed. Not then. Not when Roland ("Call Me Rollie") suggested all three of them go out for coffee after the club closed.

Gennah never did laugh when Rollie was around. Not even after they all became lovers.

"*Don't trust no po-lice,*" Gennah had answered Chloe for the millionth-and-a-half time when asked why she didn't like Rollie; even after he'd explained that a Criminalist was only a fancy name for an Evidence Technician ... the guy who takes pictures and fingerprints dead bodies *for* the police. "*Maybe nice, maybe no. No can tell until it too late. I know. I see many times before I get 'dopted.*"

After a while Chloe had stopped asking and just accepted that Gennah's past was against her. She probably had seen a lot of shit go down. Probably all over her more than once.

But that was okay, because Chloe loved Gennah.

Even after she came home from a "date" to see her with Rollie's dick so far down her throat it looked like her eyes were about to pop out.

Even then.

Chloe didn't realize she'd stopped giggling until she noticed Rollie staring at her. He looked mad.

A chill that had no business being in the overheated club jabbed its icy finger up her ass. She squeezed her legs tighter together.

"Something the matter, honey?" Her voice quivered. Pretending to cough, she accepted an iced tea from Pete that looked like an iced tea (Rollie was too important a man to try the ol' iced-tea-for-whiskey switcheroo) and took a long sip. "Didn't cha like my number?"

His grin came back — but only a little and only on one side.

"I loved it, baby," he said, his voice so deep it sounded like it was coming from somewhere in his belly. "You've got more talent than you know what to do with."

Chloe let the front of her robe slip open so he could see some of that talent. "Then why the sad face? Your boss givin' you shit again?"

Rollie started to say something, then took a deep breath and stared into his real whiskey sour. Chloe sucked in a mouthful of tea through the thin red bar-straw and waited for the chill to go away.

It never did.

"I assisted with the autopsy on Gennah this afternoon."

Chloe pushed the tea away and held her breath. Her Grammy, the one who strung "Fairy Lights" on Christmas trees, had told her that if she held her breath long enough that whatever pain she was feeling would magically go away.

Holding her breath had never worked when she was little... and it didn't work now. Maybe because she couldn't hold her breath long enough.

When she finally let go, it sounded like a sob.

"Oh."

Chloe hadn't worried when Gennah didn't return to their studio apartment the night before. Sometimes the "trips" she made for Rollie lasted longer than he said they would. Sometimes they were shorter. Not that it mattered, because Rollie was an important man with connections and when he said jump, Gennah had always asked "How high?"

Then stuck her tongue out when his back was turned.

And Gennah always brought Chloe back a souvenir from the places Rollie sent her even though she wasn't supposed to — cheap, touristy things like pink-plastic sunglasses with flamingos on them from Miami or fake voodoo charms (also of plastic) from Trinidad.

Or the gold-plated hair-pin she'd brought back from Bangkok, six inches long and with two intertwined hearts carved into the knob. Two hearts — hers and Gennah's.

Stuff like that.

Even though she wasn't supposed to.

"*He fuck me,*" Gennah had always said, "*but he no own me. It just work. Just to make money so we can live more decent.*"

Chloe reached up and touched the twin hearts on the lapel of her dressing gown. They felt as cold as ice. As if the chill she felt was real.

As a rule Chloe didn't read the newspapers except for the funnies and didn't watch the news, local or national, because it was just too damned depressing. So she didn't know about the headless, handless cocoa-caramel-colored Jane Doe someone had tossed in a dumpster behind the *Thai-Hi Deli.*

Didn't know and wasn't worried.

Until a tall Italian with black hair and eyes and almost olive skin appeared at the door of the dressing room, flashed a badge similar to Rollie's (but not quite) and asked if she could identify the body of one Gennah Thuy Watkins.

Not that there was much left to identify.

That's what held up the investigation, the Italian detective whispered as they looked at the naked, mutilated body on the other side of the morgue's observation window. Without fingerprints or dental records it had been practically impossible for their man in Forensics to make a positive ID.

Even though he was *supposed* to be the best.

It wasn't until they found a small tattoo, high on the inside of the right thigh. A small red heart with the words "Gennah W loves Chloe Mc."

Chloe had one just like it, in the same place, only the names were reversed.

No one had known about the tattoo. No one. That was why whoever killed Gennah had missed it when they cut off her hands and head to make it impossible to identify the body.

No one knew. No one had ever seen them.

No one.

" — wish I'd been there, at the Station, when you came down," Rollie was saying. Giving her a look that could melt sequins, if she were wearing any. Chloe blinked hard and tried to remember to breathe. "That must have been tough ... identifying Gennah like that. The way she looked, I mean."

"It was murder," she said, without thinking.

But for some reason he laughed, long and hard, before finishing off the sour. Pete had another in its place before the empty hit the bar.

"Sure would have helped if I'd known about that tattoo," he said, "would have saved you from having to see ... that."

Chloe ran her thumb down along the shaft of the pin, feeling it play hide and seek with the almost-real silk. She dropped her hand to her lap and noticed a single drop of blood where the pin had penetrated the soft flesh just under her thumbnail.

It didn't hurt.

"So," Rollie asked as he played with the condensation on his glass, "you got a tattoo, too, I don't know about? Something that'd make it easy to identify you if someone cut off *your* head?"

For some reason the chill disappeared and Chloe felt warm. Strong. Important.

Almost as important as Rollie was.

But she kept that to herself and just shrugged.

"Yeah, real sorry I wasn't there. Mighta been able to keep you away from Ranieri." The ice tinkled in the glass as Rollie exchanged the second empty for a third. "Tight-assed wop's been trying to get something on me for years. Don't know why. Probably just doesn't like me."

Chloe glanced to where Pete had been standing a moment before, but he'd already moved to the far opposite end of the bar yakking it up with a couple of guys in matching hockey tees. Ignoring her, and the important man she was talking to. The rest of the audience was just as oblivious.

And, half-turning toward the runway, she figured out why.

Mistress Sonya was strutting her stuff, black leather cut-out bra and thong gleaming in the golden light that drenched the stage. She was on the prowl, black riding whip slashing the air as she looked for a victim to humiliate.

The piss-colored air pulsated with man-scent.

Chloe knew she could set off a bomb at that moment without anyone in the club even looking up.

It was now or never.

Chloe turned back to face Rollie at the same time she pulled open the front of the dressing gown and spread her legs. Gennah's hair pin lay comfortably against her right palm.

"What are you doing?" he hissed, but didn't seem too surprised when she reached over with her left hand and began unzipping him. "Someone might see ... oh, God."

He groaned when she fumbled his cock through the slit in his jockeys and scooted back on the stool, his spine pressed against the wall.

The pin grew warmer in her right hand as her left hand stroked him rigid.

"Hmmm," Rollie sighed, eyes closed, thinking he was still the important man. With connections. Thinking she was nothing more than some blond bimbo who liked to shake it for money. Thinking that Gennah was nothing more than some piece of trash he could use and toss out. With the garbage.

"Christ, baby ... what's got into you tonight?"

"Nothing ... *yet*," she whispered, low in her throat. They used to practice saying those things in front of the bedroom mirror, her and Gennah; laughing that men could be so gullible.

Laughing in each others arms and mouths.

Laughing.

Chloe spread her legs wider to keep Rollie's attention and leaned forward, letting the tip of one breast graze the head of his cock ... and the tip of the needle graze....

He was moaning harder, eyes closed to slits, the piss-colored light reflecting off them. Like marbles. Like glass.

"Why'd you kill Gennah, Rollie?"

His cock went limp at the same time his eyes popped open.

"What the hell are you talking about?" he hissed. His eyes were moving now, back and forth, checking to see if anyone was looking at them, was listening.

Only the pin in Chloe's hand moved. Closing the distance between them.

"Are you *on* something, bitch? I don't know what the hell you're talking about. You're either crazy or that damned Ranieri put you up to this ... either way I'm outta here."

He tried to stand, tried to pull his cock out of her hand. Chloe tightened her grip and he sat back down.

"Wh-what do you want?" he said when she released him enough to catch his breath.

"I want to know why. I already know it was you, so you don't have to lie about that part."

He smiled. But there was nothing happy about it.

"And how would you know that, sweetheart?"

"Because you're always bragging about how good you are at finding evidence," Chloe answered. "Even Ranieri was surprised when you said identifying the body would be impossible. Besides, you would have known that was Gennah even without her arms or...."

She squeezed her eyes shut and tried to swallow back the sob before it escaped. Tried and failed. He was laughing when she opened her eyes again.

"Yeah, guess I did leave myself open for that, didn't I?" He looked down at his lap. "No pun intended. So what? You think anybody's gonna care if a half-gook stripper got killed? Shit, it's not like she was Mother Theresa or someone important. You think anyone'd care if you ended up the same way? Think anyone would find evidence leading back to me if you did? Shit, I'm *the* criminalist in this town, sweetheart. Detectives want a case solved, they come to me ... doesn't matter if they got evidence or not because they know *I* can provide that. They don't want to find any evidence ... I can do that, too. Just like I could lead a trail right back to our old friend Ranieri if you happened to wind up dead. Easier than slitting a throat, believe me."

Chloe's stomach tightened. The pin felt white-hot.

"But you still didn't tell me why you killed her."

He was angry now, despite the hold she had on him.

"Because the bitch tried to hold out on me." He said it like he was ordering a cup of coffee. No sugar. No cream. The pin inched forward. "Came up three bags short from her last trip ... said it was a mistake when I found them stashed up her cash box. Like after seeing your act I wouldn't look there. Christ, you teach her that trick or was it the other way around?"

Chloe jerked the pin out of the way when he suddenly leaned forward, his hand snaking into the pocket of his jacket.

"Look, tell you what ... you take this and we'll call it even." Chloe looked at the three rubber balloons — red, yellow and green — he dropped on the bar next to her iced tea. "For your retirement. Keep Ranieri off my ass and you can have ... two."

She stared at the bags. Three bags full. Just like the nursery rhyme.

"Two'll be enough to leave this town and start someplace new. Yeah," he pushed the green and yellow balloons toward her, "two's enough for a whole new life."

A whole new life. A second chance.

The pin trembled in Chloe's hand.

Roland W. Spelman, Jr., chuckled.

"Take them and get the hell out of here before I change my mind and do to you what I did to Gennah. And believe me, this time I'll make sure *nobody* will be able to identify the body — "

"An eye for an eye," Chloe said as the pin pierced silk, cotton, flesh and cartilage; sinking until the carved knob lay flush against his tie. "And a heart for a heart. No pun intended."

She left him sitting there — in the dark, last seat at the bar, far right side, with his cock drooping out over the front of his pants, eyes wide open and staring at the stage ... the smile still on his lips.

Ranieri was waiting for her in the dressing room. She was the most beautiful woman Chloe had ever seen. Besides Gennah.

"Did you remember to take the pin?" she asked, her voice low and smoky. She was dressed more casually than she had been at the station, jeans and a loose-fitting top that kept sliding off one shoulder and clung to her high breasts. Any man in the club would have thought she was just another stripper-wannabe.

Chloe nodded and touched the entwined hearts nestled in the hastily done French knot.

"Good," Ranieri said, smoothing back a wisp of hair from Chloe's forehead. "A little shampoo will take care of any residual blood. How about the drugs?"

Chloe pulled two balloons from her pocket and held them out. "I-I left the red for Pete ... like you told me to."

Ranieri covered Chloe's hands with her own and smiled. The chill she'd felt back at the bar — with *him* — disappeared.

"Good. Good. Now stop looking so worried. Needle marks are inadmissible evidence, Roland told me that himself when I tried to get him to verify evidence on a homicide that used a needle filled with air. Pete'll take care of everything ... your name won't even come up."

"But...."

The dressing room door swung open and one of the dancers, a new girl Chloe hadn't really gotten to know yet, hurried past on her way to the bathroom. Still holding her hands, Ranieri pulled her toward the rack of costumes at the opposite end of the room. Chloe took a deep breath. Ranieri was wearing Chanel No. 5.

"But everybody *saw* me with him tonight," Chloe continued, lowering her voice to a whisper.

"Yeah, they did ... but I doubt there's a man out there right now who'd be able to describe anything besides your ass and tits. Typical male observation." Without warning, Ranieri leaned forward and kissed Chloe lightly on the lips. She tasted like cherry liqueur. "Don't worry, I have a lot of connections."

Nodding, suddenly feeling shy, Chloe backed up a step before looking up into Ranieri's doe-soft eyes.

"I ... I never asked your name."

Ranieri cocked her head to one side and smiled.

"Louise," she said softly. "Lou, for short."

Still nodding but no longer feeling shy, Chloe moved in close.

"Lou," she whispered, "I think this is the beginning of a beautiful friendship."

Specializing in tales of "twisted reality," **P.D. Cacek** has won both the Bram Stoker Award and Word Fantasy Award for short fiction. The author of both a collection, *Leavings*, and a humorous vampire novel, *Night Prayers*, P.D. is currently finishing a modern-day ghost story set in New Hope, Pennsylvania.

Pat Sterling, P.I.

by Edo van Belkom

John Knowles read the name on the card, and checked the name against the one etched on the door's glass.

PAT STERLING
Private Investigator

Satisfied he had the right address, he opened the door and entered the office. From the look of the decor it was obvious that this Pat Sterling guy was a top-notch detective. The floor was covered with old hardwood floorboards that creaked with each step he took. The walls were covered with old panels of oak and were decorated with all kinds of awards and citations. There were even a few celebrity photos personally signed with thanks.

When some of the other insurance adjusters recommended using Sterling on the case, Knowles had balked at the guy's fee, figuring no one was worth that much cash. Now he was of a different opinion. Someone who did this well had to have something going for him.

He walked up to the big oak desk and the gorgeous secretary behind it. The nameplate on the desk read "Marcie." She was a bouffant-blonde with a figure that made Barbie look like some pre-pubescent schoolgirl.

She smiled at Knowles and the room seemed to get brighter. "Can I help you?"

"My name's John Knowles. I'm here to see Mr. Sterling."

The secretary smiled at that and said, "Pat will be with you in a minute."

Knowles sat down and leafed through a dog-eared men's magazine sitting on top of the pile on the table. As he admired the nude models draped across the magazine's pages, he wondered why more waiting rooms couldn't be fully stocked with similar reading fare. This Pat Sterling was Knowles' kind of guy.

"Pat is ready to see you now," said the secretary, standing up to reveal her slim, yet buxom, figure.

Must be a real ladies' man, thought Knowles as he watched the leggy secretary walk over to Sterling's office door and open it for him.

"Thanks," he said as he passed her.

The woman just smiled.

Sterling was seated in the big desk chair by the window. With the chair's back facing him, Knowles couldn't see Sterling, but judging by the size of the chair, he figured the detective to be a big, bone-crushing sort of a bruiser. Just the sort of ape this case needed.

Slowly the chair turned.

And Knowles caught sight of one of the most gorgeous and voluptuous women he'd ever seen in his life. "Have a seat," the woman said in a voice sultry enough to melt vinyl.

"Uh, thanks," stammered Knowles. "I think I will."

"I'm Pat Sterling," she said, leaning forward as she extended her hand across the table.

Still in shock over the fact that Pat Sterling was a woman, Knowles found himself somewhat mesmerized by the inviting dark line of cleavage beneath her blouse.

"John," he sad. "John Knowles."

"You can call me Patricia. I use Pat because some people still think being a detective is man's work. As we both know, some cases require the touch of a woman."

Knowles was silent while they continued to shake hands. When they were done, her hand lingered in his and her fingers traced a gentle line across his palm.

"You told my secretary Marcie over the phone that you had some sort of job for me?"

Knowles blinked and shivered, then finally realized he'd been asked a question. "Yeah, that's right." He gave his head a shake and busied himself with the files in his briefcase. "It's about a claimant insured by my company. His name is Richard Daley. He was involved in an accident a couple of months ago in which his car collided with a truck belonging to a cartage company we insure. He didn't suffer any physical injuries, but is claiming post-traumatic stress disorder. Seems the psychological stress of the accident has left him … uh … impotent."

Sterling laughed. "Sounds like my kind of case."

No doubt, thought Knowles. With a package like that, there was no telling what kind of response she could solicit if she set her mind — not to mention her body — to it.

"We've offered him what we think is a generous settlement, but he's asked us to double it. We're reluctant to go to court since disproving his condition was directly caused by the accident could turn out to be more expensive than the settlement he's currently asking for."

"I don't know who recommended me to you," said Pat, "or what they told you, but my services don't come cheap."

I'll bet, thought Knowles. "I'm aware of that."

She scribbled something on a slip of paper. "This is my fee. It's standard in a case like this," she said, sliding the paper across the table toward him.

Knowles took a look at it and checked himself from displaying any outward signs of surprise. Even though it was less than the settlement offered to Daley by the company, it was still a lot of money, and far more than he'd ever paid an investigator in this type of case before. There was no way he could justify the expense if she failed. He cleared his throat. "If the amount is payable only upon the successful closing of the case, then you've got a deal."

She walked around her desk and sat on the edge of it, crossing her legs to expose a generous amount of thigh. "Deal," she said.

As they shook hands, all Knowles could think was how much he envied Richard Daley.

ঌ

Knowles had said that Richard Daley frequented a downtown bar called *The Falcon's Nest*. It was a dimly lit place where singles and other people looking for some company came to meet after the sun went down. It was decorated with movie posters from the '30s and '40s and looked as if it might have been the setting for a Dashiell Hammett novel or two.

Pat had a snapshot of Daley in her bag and took it out for one last look as she stepped inside. A quick check of the room located Daley sitting at the bar next to the draft spigot, just where Knowles said she might find him.

She took a deep breath, adjusted her skirt against her hips and thighs and undid a third button on her tan silk blouse. A final, quick tussle of her raven hair and she was ready.

She walked over to the bar and stood next to Daley.

He looked over at her and nodded a non-committal hello.

"Hi," she said, smiling warmly. "Is it all right if I sit here next to you?"

"Free country," said Daley.

She sat down. "It's just that I thought a good-looking man like you would be expecting someone. If you know what I mean?"

He looked at her again, this time with a more inquisitive gaze, as if he were sizing her up.

Pat crossed her legs, making sure most of her thigh was exposed. She also leaned forward slightly so that the lace of her bra cups peeked out from beneath her blouse. Daley noticed that, and Pat let him look all he liked.

"You always play so hard to get?" said Daley, lighting up a cigarette and tossing the pack on the top of the bar.

She laughed. "No, not at all. Sometimes I walk right up to a man and slide my hand down his pants."

He smiled at that, and some of the tension between them was gone. "I bet that gets a rise out of them."

"Honey," said Pat. "If it don't, then they're dead."

"Would you like a drink?" he said.

"Whatever you're having."

Daley signaled the bartender for two more drinks, and they talked for a while. As they chatted, Pat smoothly slid a hand onto his leg and leaned forward as if she were interested in what he had to say.

She'd seen his type plenty of times before. He was a career criminal, stealing just enough to keep him in booze and cigarettes while he waited for the big score that was always just around the corner. Obviously, this insurance claim was supposed to be his ticket onto Easy Street. Too bad it was going to turn out to be more like a speeding ticket.

As they continued to talk, Pat moved her hand casually up and down his leg. To her surprise he seemed not to notice her touch, and when her hand was practically on his cock, there didn't seem to be any activity there.

Maybe he really couldn't get it up.

"Another drink?" he asked her.

"No thanks," she said, taking hold of his hand and placing it on her leg. Under her skirt.

There was no expression of surprise or excitement on his face and for a moment, Pat thought about getting out and recommending Knowles pay up. But then, after a slight hesitation, Daley moved his hand higher on her thigh until he felt the lacy top of her stocking and the straps of the garter belt holding it in place. "Um, nice," he said.

She brushed her hand over his crotch again, but there was nothing going on there — a dead zone.

He looked at her and smiled apologetically. "Sorry, but I was in a car accident a while ago and I haven't been able to get it up since." He looked down at her hand, which was in the process of giving him a gentle squeeze. "It was a pretty bad crash and I came out okay … except for that."

She took her hand away and sighed. "I understand," she said, turning to the bar to take a sip of her drink. As she did so, she deftly undid another button on her blouse, allowing it to fall open to reveal even more of her lacy black bra. It was a push-up demi-bra that left most of her breasts bare. In the cool air of the bar, her nipples pressed against the thin fabric of the bra cups like the barrel tips of a couple of snub-nosed revolvers.

She turned back around to face Daley, and said, "You know, it's really too bad, because you remind me a lot of a guy I used to date. Every time we got together there was nothing he liked more than for me to wrap my tits around his cock and to fuck him that way until he came like some volcano erupting between two mountains of flesh." As she spoke she wrapped her arms around herself in a hug, pushing her breasts together until they threatened to spill out of her bra and onto the top of the bar.

"After that, I'd slowly suck and lick him back to life, and then we'd fuck like crazy into the small hours of the morning." She ground her rear against her seat, then crossed her legs to reveal even more of her stockinged leg. "God, he knew a lot of different positions."

At that, Daley licked his lips. "Okay," he said, a little out of breath. "I might not be able to get it up, but that doesn't mean I'm not willing to give it another try."

"Hey," she breathed. "That's just the kind of spirit I like in my men. My apartment's just down the street. Want to come?"

"Oh, yeah," said Daley.

Pat slid the key into the lock and opened the door.

"So this is your place?" asked Daley.

"Do you like it?" she said, moving into the living room, turning on the lights as she went. "Have a seat on the couch."

"You like to do it with the lights on?" asked Daley as he made his way to the couch.

"You could say that." Pat went off to the corner where she pretended to fuss over a potted plant. When she moved away from the corner, a faint red light glowed through the branches of the fern.

She walked over to the couch and stood there facing him. "Don't you look good," she said.

"Likewise."

"I tell you what. Why don't we take off our clothes, each of us removing one piece at a time?"

"And when will we stop?"

"We'll just keep going until something, uh ... comes up."

"All right," he said. "With the way things have been going these past few weeks, I'm willing to try just about anything."

Pat wondered again if Daley had been telling the truth about his problem. If he was, then she was helping the insurance company get out of paying him what he rightfully deserved.

"I used to do chicks like you all the time before the accident," said Daley, as he made himself comfortable on the couch. "But it's been a while now."

Then again, thought Pat, *maybe he deserves to get stiffed.* Besides, it wasn't like he wasn't getting anything out of the deal. If he could get it up, he could have her — any way he wanted.

"Then you'll be more than ready." Pat winked, then began the game by running a hand over her blouse and pulling it tighter against herself until her long nipples poked stiffly against the fabric.

Daley took off his shirt.

Next, Pat undid the last few buttons, her fingers lingering over her breasts as if she couldn't leave them alone. Finally, she pulled away her blouse, revealing her plump nipples standing stiffly out from her demi-bra.

In response, Daley hurriedly pulled his undershirt over his head.

Pat played with her breasts for a while, running her hands over the tops of them and fingering the hard, stiff nipples. "You ready?" She said.

Daley nodded.

She undid the clasp holding her bra in place and slowly pulled aside the cups. Her breasts sagged slightly, then settled into place on her chest.

Daley's mouth opened in a gasp.

Pat cupped her tits in her hand, squeezing them and massaging them as if she felt liberated to have them hanging free. Then she raised one of the breasts to her mouth and lapped at the nipple. The dark teat seemed to distend to meet her flitting tongue before her lips closed over the flesh and sucked it deep into her mouth.

Daley undid his belt and slipped out of his pants.

Pat looked down between his legs and let out a sigh of disappointment. He was as limp as a cold, dead fish.

Still, she continued on, undaunted. She let her hands slide down from her tits, over her belly and hips. She undid the zipper on one side of her skirt and moved her hips from side to side, sliding the skirt down to her ankles. She was left standing there in her heels, stockings, garter, and thong.

Daley lifted himself off the couch and pulled his underwear off, revealing the short stub of his cock.

Pat chewed her lip in frustration at the sight, but decided to carry on. Her fingers glided over her belly once more, this time their destination being the lips of her pussy. With a practiced hand, she slid her fingers under the waistband of her thong and began fingering herself.

"Mmm..."

After a moment, Pat opened her eyes and saw Daley taking hold of his cock. This lifted her spirits and she began rubbing her fingers harder over her clit.

"Oh, yeah..." muttered Daley, his cock growing slightly in his hands.

Pat moved her finger harder and harder over her moistening pussy, reveling in the power she had over Daley and the imminent success in disproving his claim.

She looked at Daley again and marveled at the eight solid inches of cock growing up from between his legs. "I thought you said you had a problem?" she breathed.

"I do," he said.

"I don't know where you're from, but where I come from we don't call that a problem..."

"Well, it's a problem if you're aching to put it somewhere hot and wet."

"Then let me offer you a solution." She rose up and climbed onto the couch. After straddling Daley, she took his cock in her hand and guided it between the waiting lips of her pussy.

"No more problem," said Daley, grinding his hips against her.

Pat smiled. "No, not any more."

Daley laughed at that and began to thrust with slow and sure strokes.

Pat was beginning to enjoy this assignment, and let out a long, seductive moan while she grabbed her breasts in her hands and lapped at her hardened nipples.

Daley quickened his pace.

Pat ground her pussy harder against his cock in response, rising up and down to help maximize the length of his strokes. Eventually she was riding him like a horse, her sweaty buttocks slapping against his body like an open hand.

She'd been ready to climax for a few minutes, but no matter how much she was enjoying herself, the job came first. She would only allow herself to orgasm when she was sure that she had more than enough evidence on tape. Business before pleasure was a motto that had served her well over the years and she wasn't about to change things now.

"Oh..." she gasped in perfect rhythm with Daley's pounding cock. "I'm coming!" she lied.

"Me too!" he said.

"Let me see it," she said, climbing off him and grabbing his cock with one hand and fingering herself with the other. She stroked him several times before he arched his back and erupted in orgasm.

The sight of Daley firing off bolt after bolt of hot cum, and the knowledge that she'd gotten all the evidence she'd need, was more than enough to help her finish her own climax.

Her body shuddered, and she came.

Minutes later, Daley was stroking himself contentedly. "That was great," he said.

"Not bad," said Pat with a smile.

"Can we do it again?"

"I don't know," said Pat. "*Can* you?"

"Uh … I think so," Daley said.

Pat looked over to the corner where the video camera sat hidden behind the plant and wondered if she had enough tape to last the night. But then she saw Daley beginning to get hard again and realized that she really didn't care.

"Great," she said, moving her hand down between his legs.

They'd do it until they ran out of tape.

And then some.

👠

"Come on in, Mr. Daley, have a seat," said John Knowles, welcoming the bogus claimant into his office.

Richard Daley shuffled into the room.

"I imagine it's been hard for you these past few months, Mr. Daley?" he said with mock sympathy, struggling to contain his delight over the pun he'd made.

"Well, I wouldn't use quite those words," he said. "But yeah, it's been kind of rough. Not to worry though, the settlement money will go a long way to making my life easier for me to bear."

"Oh, I'm sure it would," said Knowles. "But before we get to the subject of dollar amounts I'd like to show you a videotape belonging to the company."

"Sure, okay."

Knowles went to the VCR in the wall unit and pushed *play*. He'd previously cued up the tape to the most damning part, the spot where Daley came for the first time in full view of the camera.

When Daley saw himself caught on tape, his face turned a pale shade of yellow. Then, as the tape continued to play, he straightened up in his seat and leaned forward for a closer look.

"I'm no doctor, Mr. Daley," said Knowles, placing a hand on top of the television. "But judging by what I've see on this tape, I'd say there's absolutely nothing wrong with you. As a matter of fact, I'd say that there are many men out there who would love to be as virile as you obviously are."

On the tape, Daley had climaxed and was slumped back onto the couch, exhausted.

In the office, Daley was slumped back in his chair, defeated. "You know, it was almost worth it."

Knowles fought off the urge to say, "That good, eh?" and instead said, "Oh, I can imagine. Miss Sterling is a very attractive woman."

Daley sighed. "So I guess that's it, then. I end up with nothing."

Knowles shook his head. "Well, not quite."

"What do you mean?"

"There's still some money coming to you. If you sign this release form, I can give you the check in my desk that is made out in your name."

"A check? For what?"

"Well, a friend of mine is a packager of amateur porn videos. I showed him the tape and he's made a rather generous offer for the rights to it. The check is your share of the purchase amount."

Daley thought about it. "Do I get a copy of the tape?"

Knowles nodded.

"Got a pen?"

Again, Knowles nodded.

And Daley signed.

Edo van Belkom made an auspicious debut in the horror field when his first short story sale, "Baseball Memories," was reprinted in *Year's Best Horror Stories 20,* edited by Karl Edward Wagner. Since that first sale in 1989, he's sold over 100 stories. His first novel, *Wyrm Wolf,* was published by HarperCollins, in 1995 and was a *Locus* bestseller. His other books include the novel *Lord Soth* (TSR), *Northern Dreamers*, a book of interviews with science fiction, fantasy, and horror writers (Quarry Press), and the chapbook *Virtual Girls: The Erotic Gems of Evan Hollander,* a collection of five erotic science fiction stories published under the Evan Hollander pseudonym by Circlet Press of Boston.

Autumn Diary

by Joy Robertson-Maciel

September 5, 1988

There is something up with Christine. I noticed it this morning while I watched her from my easel at the edge of her garden. The chill in the air bit my nose and heightened the color of Christine's cheeks. Around me I could see touches of gold and vermilion in the maple trees. What was it I saw in my wife's eyes? It was just a glimmer. No one but an artist as sensitive as myself would have detected it. I will keep a closer eye on her. A man in my situation has no choice.

September 7

My painting is coming along well. Everything about September lends itself to inspiration. The air is robust. The colors grow more vibrant with each passing day. Christine spends her mornings in her favorite garden. She waits until the dew disappears before she begins to cut and gather the herbs and flowers she will sell in her shop. I watched her again today. She toiled until noon, then set her baskets in the shade, curled up next to me, and sunned herself. A potpourri of scent — rosemary, verbena, sage, and mint — lingered about her hair and clothes. The smell of her brings me great pleasure.

September 10

She is restless. There is no mistaking it. Today I spied on her as she worked in the drying shed. For most of the day she only paced among the bunches of herbs and flowers hanging from the beams. She seemed preoccupied with something. Or someone.

When we married nearly five years ago, I had hoped that I could keep her. But a war veteran with his legs scarred and his manhood crippled has to expect that one day his woman will try to wander. Women are that way, particularly young ones such as Christine. Like the whores in Vietnam, they add a certain beauty and fragrance to our lives, but they can never be trusted.

September 14

I gave Christine's shop a fresh coat of paint today. The fall business is beginning to pick up. Most of her customers are tourists. They come to Vermont every year about this time to savor the brilliant colors; to take deep gulps of the country air. Her shop sits on the winding country road next to our home. The walls inside are covered with floral and herbal arrangements of every shade and shape. Bins of dried rose petals, lavender, and geranium fill the center of the room. The oak drawers behind the counter are stuffed with packets of seeds and spices. Oils, perfumes, and fixatives sweeten the air. Near the Christmas season she hangs pomanders of orange and clove from a tree in the window.

This shop, this little world unto its own — belongs only to Christine. She spends hours and hours working on her creations. I am but a bystander, an unwilling assistant who occasionally attends the customers and takes their money.

September 22

Cool days have given way to frosty nights. Brilliant orange and yellow leaves have transformed the countryside into a spectacle of light and color. My painting is finished and I have started another. Business in the shop has been brisk, so Christine has little time for me. I spend much of my time painting. I keep a flask of whiskey in my pocket to ward off the chill. The liquor helps dull the pain in my knees, and my suspicions about Christine. I watch for local men who might be visiting the shop too often. I also make sure that she is never alone.

September 25

There is yet more work to be done. Next to the shed looms a huge pile of prunings. Christine expects me to set my painting aside, start up the shredder, and transform it all into a carpet of warmth for her tender perennials during their winter sleep. Why can't she understand how important my work is? I can't be bothered by meaningless chores. No wonder my work is not selling.

October 1

Christine went for a walk today. "We have a new neighbor," she said at the breakfast table. I asked if he was the one who had bought old man Groggin's place.

"It's a she," Christine replied. "She came into the shop the other day and bought a laurel wreath for her front door. Been back several times, just to visit. We agreed to go for a walk this afternoon. The trees are so glorious now. You'll mind the shop, won't you?" Watching Christine lick the plum butter from her fingers, I asked if the woman was from around here. "She's from the West," Christine said, "Oregon, I believe."

I asked if she had a husband. "She's quite alone, John," Christine answered.

Funny thing, a woman moving to the country by herself. She must be the independent type. When the going gets hard, she'll find herself a man soon enough. I asked Christine if she didn't think so. "Perhaps she will, John," was her reply.

"You bet she will," I said.

October 5

Christine asked me to help out in the shop again today. It was busy until mid-afternoon. At three o'clock, the new neighbor woman came in. A cold gust of wind accompanied her. I took a drink from my flask as I looked her over. She was a curious sight. Her hair was cut in a bob, too short to be fashionable. She wore gray wool trousers and a red checkered mackintosh. I asked if I could help her with something.

"No, thank you," she said without a smile, her small eyes darting around the room. "I've come for a walk with Christine. Isn't she here?"

Before I could answer, Christine was at her side. She introduced us. The woman's name is Ann. "I'll be back before dark!" Christine called on her way out. Dead leaves blew in as the door slammed shut.

October 10

Last night it froze so hard that even the pumpkins were left with a veil of white. Christine complained bitterly because I hadn't found time to put the mulch down for the winter to protect her precious herbs. It's too cold to continue my work at the easel. Business is tapering off at the shop. It will pick up again toward Thanksgiving. Christine asked me to mind the shop today while she went for a walk with Ann. I refused. She closed early and went anyway.

October 16

The days are growing shorter and shorter now. Christine's eyes only grow brighter and brighter. When she came home from her afternoon walk today her scent was different. She smelled of molding leaves and ground yarrow. There was also a smell about her that I didn't recognize, yet it was a familiar odor. It disturbed me. I'm still struggling to recall its origin. She and the bitch Ann have apparently become the best of friends. I've got to find a way to put an end to it. Christine is spending too much time away from home.

October 20

I turned fifty today. How disgustingly depressing. I was in no mood for a celebration, not that I have anyone to celebrate with. No family, no friends, only

Christine. She surprised me with a gift. "Manly" scented sachets to put in my shirt and underwear drawers. God, she makes me want to puke. The evening was horrible. She had the nerve to invite Ann over to share pumpkin pie and rum with us.

October 25

The last three days are a complete blank to me. I ran out of whiskey early this morning. This evening, my aching head cleared enough to allow me to walk to the field next door and snap off a pumpkin for Christine. She's out in the back porch now, carving it. I asked her to go into town to buy another bottle of whiskey. She refused. She says I get mean when I drink. She doesn't know what mean is.

October 29

I've been dead right about Christine. This evening she didn't return from her walk until after dark. I was sitting by the fire waiting for her when she burst through the door. Her long black hair was flung behind her in a tangled mess. She was breathless and flushed. From the doorway, her eyes met mine momentarily. They were glazed and wild.

I asked her to come warm herself by the fire as I moved closer to the grate with the pretext of warming my hands. She moved to the fireplace and stood at my side, still breathless. It was unmistakable. Intermingled with the musty fragrance of damp grass and leaves was the pungent odor of passion, recently spent.

October 30

This afternoon, I followed them. I kept to the woods at the roadside as they walked along the damp pavement. High above my head, flocks of birds flew about frantically in swirling formations against a darkening sky. I kept expecting the two of them to part. Christine's lover, whoever he may be, would be waiting for her somewhere. Ann surely would turn back, once her usefulness was served.

After a mile or so, they left the road and entered the woods. I crept along behind them, keeping a safe distance. Their pace quickened as they came to a clearing not too far ahead. Briefly, I lost sight of them. On hands and knees, I crawled to the edge of the clearing and peered through the bushes. There stood those two filthy sluts under the gnarled arms of a huge oak. Their lips and arms were locked together. I watched them with a hideous fascination as they fell upon their forest bed. Their ardor revolted me. Overcome with nausea, I retched. The minutes passed and their frenzy increased. I continued to watch until I could take no more. I left them mewing like wild cats.

October 31

I spent last night in the den with the door locked from the inside. Christine called my name and rattled the door knob a few times. She didn't try for long.

The phone rang early this morning. Christine answered on the first ring. I picked up the extension and listened. It was some nurse calling from the hospital in Essex Junction. Christine's mother had suffered a stroke last night, the woman said. Would she come right away? Glad to be rid of her for a few days, I offered to drive her to the train station in Waterbury. We made the trip in silence while devilish fantasies danced through my head. The scene I witnessed last evening passed through my mind over and over again.

Christine purchased her ticket while I waited on the platform. An icy wind numbed my face. As soon as she joined me, I turned to go. "John," she said suddenly, "Ann will be coming by this evening sometime to pick up a book on herbal medicine that I borrowed from her. Would you see that she gets it? I left it on the mantle."

I forced myself to speak. I told her I'd give Ann the book. Then I said, "By the way, Christine, I may have a surprise for you when you get back."

"How nice, John," she purred.

I lit the jack o'lantern at dusk. Christine had washed a few apples and left them by the door in a basket. By seven o'clock, the handful of children who live around us had come and gone. I blew out the jack o'lantern and sat down to wait for Ann. It wasn't long before she walked up to the house, her heavy boots clumping up the porch steps. I opened the door before she could knock. She looked startled. "Where is Christine?" I told her Christine had to leave town. "I came for a book she borrowed," Ann said. "I'll come back another time." She started to turn around.

Before she could leave I told her that Christine had left the book for her in the drying shed. I explained that I'd been expecting her and suggested that she warm herself a bit before going out to get the book.

She came in. I poured us both a whiskey and invited her to come closer to the fire. She refused the drink, but she did not decline the warmth of the fireplace. We eyed each other for a moment or two. I broke the silence by saying how glad I was that she had come along — that Christine had needed a companion like her.

She seemed to relax a bit. I offered her the whiskey again. She refused, but accepted a shot of rum. I asked her how it was that a woman as attractive as herself hadn't married. She took a long swallow from her glass. The fire crackled and snapped. "My Prince Charming just hasn't come along yet, I guess," she replied.

I began to sing softly, watching her face. "Someday my prince will come . . . Someday–"

She interrupted me. "Look, I've got to go," she said, heading for the door. "Can we get the book now?" I protested her leaving so soon and asked if it was because she didn't like my singing. She made no reply.

A heavy mist was seeping up from the ground as we made our way across the back yard, past the wood pile to the drying shed. I unlocked the door of the shed and pushed it open, stepping aside to allow Ann to enter the dark room alone.

Quietly, I picked up the ax. She must have sensed my movement, because she sprang back from the door like a frightened cat and disappeared into the mist. If I were a whole man, a strong man, I would have chased her down like the animal she is. She knows now. Later tonight, I will pay her a visit.

November 1

It is done. You are all mine now, Christine. And to think it was so simple. What sensuous pleasure it gives me to lie here in your bed, knowing that in a few short hours you will join me. I will never have to share you again.

I must finish this journal and share it with you, Christine. I can almost see your dark, languid eyes as you listen to me read. Your graceful hands will grip my arm, your legs will wrap themselves around mine. When I have finished, we will cling to each other and make love as we have never made love before.

For a few brief hours, I doubted you. When I came to the house last night and found him alive, I was afraid that you had lost your nerve. But no, he just hadn't started drinking until I arrived. You didn't fool around, Christine, and the herbal medicine book served us well. I wonder, how many doses of Foxglove digitalis did you add to his whiskey bottle?

He was going to kill me, Christine. If it weren't for his gimpy legs, he might have. My lungs were burning by the time I reached home and bolted my door. I spent the night in a terrible fever, Christine. Between the fear that he might try to stalk me in my home, and my craving for your presence, I felt mad with anticipation. At dawn I crawled out of bed and jogged across the soggy field, back to the house. The lights were on. I crept up to the front window and peered inside. There he sat in front of the fireplace, the whiskey bottle shattered on the floor beside him. I banged on the door, but he didn't stir. I felt as if I were in a slow motion film as I opened the door and moved across the chilly room. I could see this pathetic diary in his lap. I reached for his neck. He was a cold and hard as marble.

John, or what's left of him, lies in a heap, ground together with the prunings and refuse you left next to the shed. He will do nicely as a mulch for your gardens, don't you think?

Joy Robertson-Maciel's poetry and short fiction have appeared in numerous literary journals and in the nationally-circulated *Changes Magazine*. Her work was also included in the 1994 *Best of Writers at Work* anthology. She lives with her husband and three sons in Vancouver, Washington where she is on the verge of completing her first novel.

The Gaff

by Simon Sheppard

Rattler liked to live on the edge. He knew that's what would get him in the end. Always knew. He'd been living out in the desert, out on the Interstate, for years, for nigh on a decade. And he'd always walked the darkside nimbly as a cat.

Every so often he'd hop in his old truck and cruise out to the nearest city, looking for suckers, for easy long green. As mile after mile of barren rock whizzed past, he'd think of the marks to be fleeced in the city: their stupid, bovine faces, their utterly boring souls. Shit, those solid citizens were fairly begging to be taken. He was performing a public service.

He depended on the usual hustles, the classic ones. Mostly he worked variations on the pigeon drop, leaving one sucker after another with a sack full of nothing and a temporary grin on the mark's greedy face. Twice, maybe three times a year, he'd go into town, get a room in a rundown motel, and set to work. He'd scout out fresh meat, out-of-towners who'd have to go back to somewhere else, leaving behind nothing but their money. Failing that, he'd find some local woman, old, alone, and desperate. Clean her out so thoroughly it wasn't worth picking over the bones. A couple of weeks of scams and he'd have made enough to go back to the desert, back to his frugal, lonesome life in the middle of nowhere.

He was heading out to the sunset now, out to where smoggy air hung over the city like a poison veil. He stomped his boot down on the gas pedal, squeezing out whatever speed he could. Whenever he went into town, he always wore his lucky snakeskin boots. Maybe that was it, why he was called "Rattler." Or maybe it was because he was long and lean, no hips to speak of, and he kind of glided through the world. But probably it had to do with his dick, which, like the rest of him, was long and lean, with a shaft that was startlingly white. Like that fancy asparagus that's grown under sunless bushels, so it'll turn out real, real pale. Like Rattler's dick.

About sundown he hit the edge of town, cheesy buildings on half-lit streets. His stomach was rumbling crazy with hunger. He pulled up next to where a couple of kids were torturing a cat, walked into a greasy spoon and ordered a club sandwich and a cherry Coke. Which is when he saw her. She walked out of the ladies' can, great tits and a painted face, the attitude of a queen bitch. She spotted him, stared him right in the eye. A queen bitch in heat. She walked past him, looking back over her shoulder, trailing cheap perfume. He knew he should have left her be, but he always had an appetite for disaster. So he called to the waitress to cancel his order and he followed the sickly sweet smell out the door.

She was waiting on the sidewalk, her weight shifted to one hip, her tits sticking way the hell out.

"Everybody calls me the Countess," she said. "But my real name is Velma."

"Everybody calls me Rattler. You can call me that, too."

"That's my place," she gestured with her too-blond head. He followed the gesture to a crummy storefront with a fizzing neon sign that read "Fortunes Told." Some kind of mystic eye was painted on the window. "You want your fortune told?" She moved her hand over her tight sweater, stroking those great big tits.

What the hell. He followed her into the storefront.

Tatty curtains filtered the feeble light from the street. Not much worth taking. A jumble: crystal balls, mystic eyes, cheap shawls on the walls and tables. The usual crap for the racket. And some knickknacks, the slum they give away at cheap carnies. A souvenir shot glass from Tijuana. Rattler collected shot glasses. He looked around: the broad was busy lighting candles stuck inside cheap glasses with decals of the saints.

It was easy to imagine her, bandanna on her head, piles of flashy jewelry around neck and wrists, leaning over the table, tits nearly brushing the tabletop. Saying to some mark, "Now wrap the money in this handkerchief." Getting ready for the switcheroo.

Once the candles were lit, the Countess cornered him, drowning him in a swamp of perfume and lust. She shoved herself against him, boobs pouring out of her sweater, ass working overtime. Her tongue pried open his lips while one hand shot down to his still-limp dick. The broad didn't waste any time.

Rattler's stiffening cock was crawling down the leg of his pants when he heard a noise in the rear of the place. "What's that?" he said around her tongue.

The Countess pulled away, rearranging the cashmere over her big milky chest. The dusty red curtains at the back of the room gave a shudder, and out walked an odd little man. He was, what, maybe thirty, thirty-five, but his face still had something of the nine-year-old about it. Thin lips, thin nose, big blue eyes. The face was maybe cute, but it didn't quite fit. And a couple feet south of the face, the thinnish body swelled into a perceptible paunch. If the boyish face had an expression, the semi-darkness kept it a secret.

The Countess didn't seem as embarrassed as she might have been. "My brother, Jerry," she half-explained, half-introduced. Rattler could still smell himself on her breath.

"You'll have to pardon Velma, Mister," said Jerry. "She's a real big whore."

The Countess' face turned alarmingly red, red as her painted-on lips. She started to say something, then turned on her heel and walked out the front door, her stab at dignity sabotaged by the sway of her juicy ass.

Rattler was at a loss.

"Quite a girl, our Velma is. Hey, what's your name?"

"Rattler."

Jerry started to say something, then thought better of it. "Drink?"

"Bourbon?"

"Gin."

"Gin."

Jerry went to a fake-wood cabinet, poured two, handed one to Rattler. "Where you from?"

"Down the road a piece."

"That's a good place to be from." Jerry laid a hand on Rattler's shoulder and kept it there, squeezing softly, then slowly edging down his chest. Jerry's blue eyes were blank with lust. His face asked a question. So that was the game, then.

"You can go ahead if you want," Rattler said, not knowing why.

Jerry's face didn't move, but his hand did, sliding into Rattler's shirt, finding its way to a nipple. Now his face looked like a kid's for real, all soft and full of surprise. Rattler let him continue.

The little man slowly unbuttoned Rattler's shirt, then bent over and rubbed his face up against the mat of hair. Up against Rattler's heartbeat. His mouth found a nipple, licked it, then sucked on it, got it harder, sucked harder, hard enough to make the lean man moan. His teeth nibbled down. Rattler hadn't made a move.

Teeth still on the leathery nipple, Jerry reached down and found the man's crotch. This was it; if there was going to be trouble, it was going to be now. But trouble didn't come. He kind of gasped when he felt the piece of meat, long and hard. His hands pulled down the zipper and dodged inside, dragging out hot cock. He played with the foreskin and squeezed the cockhead till Rattler began to buck his hips.

His hands on the prize, Jerry spit out the nipple, stood straight up, and looked into the man's cold gray eyes.

"You wanna touch me?"

Rattler nodded. Still not knowing why.

"My dick, or the rest of me?"

"Don't matter to me."

Jerry let go the cock, which would have been white if there'd been enough light. He unbuttoned his own shirt and let it fall open, then took Rattler's hands in his own, guiding them over his pudgy torso like he was teaching a blind man. Over his hairless chest, brushing against his flat nipples, then down over his belly, smooth and sweet as a baby's. He let go of Rattler's hands, expecting them to draw away. But the hands kept moving, propelled by curiosity, unbuckling the belt, sliding down into Jerry's pants, finding the boy-man's small, hard, hot prick. Jerry smiled as a hand closed around his sticky dick, pulled it out. When Rattler looked down at their dicks, he smiled too. Now they were both surprised.

"You wanna fuck me?" Jerry asked.

Rattler nodded. Jerry struggled out of his clothes. Rattler kept his on. Both men's cocks were still good and hard. "Here, let me lube you up," Jerry said, and got on his knees. Rattler's crotch smelled good and strong. Jerry liked that. He didn't waste time. His moist mouth closed around Rattler in a gulp.

"What if your sister. . ." Rattler gasped, but Jerry didn't talk with his mouth full. The kneeling man did his best to swallow the long, skinny cock, but when Rattler's hands went around his head and shoved him down on the shaft, he nearly gagged. Tears came to his eyes, but he kept on going, sucking and sucking, massaging cockflesh with the muscles of his throat, and Rattler was glad he did. Because it felt so goddamn good.

"Wet enough," said Rattler at last, and Jerry stood up and lay back down on the fortune-telling table, his ass hanging over the edge. Rattler stood between the little man's upraised legs, his cock homing in on the heat of Jerry's hole. Jerry rested his heels on Rattler's shoulders, grabbed hold of the long, hot shaft and guided it inside him. No resistance: the little man knew what he was doing. Rattler felt himself drawn into the boy-man's slippery insides. It felt real good. He pumped, tensing and relaxing the muscles of his lean, furry butt. Jerry started pushing back. Sometimes their rhythms meshed and sometimes they collided, till eventually they moved as one and the table shook so hard it sent tracers of fear across Rattler's mind. But the shawl-draped table withstood the pounding. The strokes grew more violent, deeper. A deck of tarot cards scattered to the floor: The Lovers, The Hanged Man, Death.

"Oh fuck, I'm gonna. . ." Rattler gasped, and Jerry grabbed his own hot little cock and pulled at its hardness.

When the crystal ball fell off the table, it missed the edge of the threadbare carpet and struck concrete with a crash. The noise of splintered glass startled the men, but they were too far gone to care, riding a dark and sweaty orgasm till neither could come any more.

And then the most startling thing of all happened. Rattler bent over and kissed Jerry's thin lips, and the kiss lasted a good long time. Then they disentangled. When Jerry stood up, he cut his foot on a bit of crystal ball, and he went to fetch a broom. When he returned, comically naked with broom and dustpan, Rattler said, "I never done this before."

"None of it?"

"Nope, not with a man."

"She's not my sister. She's my wife."

"But I liked it. I surely did."

"Yeah. Give the shot glass back."

"The cunt has gotta die."

They were lying in a soggy post-coital bed at the Tip-Top Motel, Rattler absent-mindedly stroking little Jerry's soft, sticky paunch. Over the past week, when Jerry could sneak away and Rattler wasn't busy fleecing the life savings from a widow that he'd found, they'd met in mildewed Room 109. And when they'd finally had enough of fucking, Jerry would talk about Velma. How they'd met when she was running a raw-egg scam. How he'd fallen hard, but she'd always treated him like a chump. How she was cheating on him with some slicked-back gigolo named Ripstein. And how she was holding out on him, saving up a nest egg in a place he couldn't touch, keeping the little silver key, day and night, dangling from an anklet that she wore. "A lot of the money's from her last husband's life insurance policy. They *said* his death was an accident. But I always watch my back."

Rattler, for his part, had never killed a woman. Had never even considered it. But then, he'd never thought he'd fall for another man, either. His fingers moved down to Jerry's pretty little cock. "I dunno, Jerry...."

"Rattler, it's perfect. Nobody would suspect you. you only been seen with her once, and then only for a second. We'd be rich. I'd be free of her. We could get the hell out of here and settle down somewhere, just you and me."

Rattler loved to watch Jerry's thin lips moving, wrapping themselves around his dreams. Almost as much as he loved to feel them moving over his dick and balls.

"But killing her? I know you told me she's a bitch, but. . ."

"All that dough. No more sucking up to wrinkled old bags. Just you and me. You and me."

Rattler didn't say a word. Just twisted his fingers through Jerry's silky dickhair.

"Lie back, Rattler. I wanna show you something."

The tall, lean man relaxed onto his back and closed his eyes. Jerry squatted at his feet, grabbed his ankles, and pushed his bent knees up to his chest. Was he gonna get fucked? He didn't want to get fucked.

Instead, Jerry stuck his tongue out, began licking Rattler's asscrack, zeroing in on the tightly puckered hole. Rattler had never felt anything like it before. It was almost too much, almost too dirty. But then he imagined Jerry's babyface between his thighs, his thin nose pressing at the ballsac. His thin lips rubbing against his hole. And he relaxed, letting Jerry's tongue into his chute. The boy-man was right: the Countess had to go.

Rattler had already overstayed his plans for the city. He'd delayed making off with the widow's dough so he wouldn't have to blow town. He'd begun to dream of Jerry. Once he stole the little man's underpants so he could stroke and sniff them when he was alone. But it wasn't hard to get time with Jerry; Velma, it appeared, was spending more and more time with her inamorato Ripstein. So the two of them had plenty of time to finalize plans for killing the Countess. And whenever Rattler raised a qualm, Jerry's talented tongue made him melt again. *Fuck*, Rattler thought, *I got it bad*. But knowing that didn't relieve the ache when Jerry wasn't there.

One evening, after an afternoon of sweaty screwing at the Tip-Top, they were driving back in Rattler's truck. They were driving past the storefront, *en route* to the spot a couple of blocks away where they always met and parted, when Jerry drew in his breath and stiffened. Rattler followed Jerry's glance. A too-handsome man with a pencil-thin moustache was walking away from the fortune teller's. "Ripstein," Jerry said.

Once, Rattler wouldn't have blamed the Countess for cheating on Jerry with the almost-suave Ripstein. But now, now Rattler was a sucker for his friend's pudgy vulnerability, his sullied boyish innocence. He hated Ripstein on sight.

"Velma."

"Yeah?"

"This is Rattler. Remember?"

"Sure. Who could forget a guy with a name like 'Rattler'?"

"Velma, I think we got some unfinished business." He was trying to make his voice real, real seductive.

"Could be." Silence. "And?"

"And I want to see you."

"Howdja get my phone number?"

"Wasn't hard. It's on the window of your place."

"Yeah."

"So?"

"Yeah." She was damn near purring.

He picked her up a couple of blocks from the storefront "so Jerry can't see," careful that no one was watching. He double-checked before they went from the truck to Room 109.

"Only got this one glass," he said, pouring her a bourbon. And that glass had the remnants of toothpaste around the rim. She gulped down the booze anyway.

"Jerry's an asshole. Y'know?"

"Yeah," Rattler said. Rattler was lying.

Velma unbuttoned her tight blouse, contorted till she could unhook her bra. She stood there in nothing but tight Capri pants, her tits swinging straight in his direction. Then the pants came off. She wasn't a real blonde. But he already knew that.

"Well, c'mon big boy, I don't have all day."

As he screwed her, he tried not to think about Jerry. He tried not to think about her. He tried not to think at all.

Her well-used pussy was nowhere near as tight or talented as Jerry's hot little hole. But he managed to spew inside her and rolled off her, panting and sticky.

"He's not my husband, you know. Did he tell you that? He tells everybody that. He's my fucking brother."

"Get dressed."

He drove her back, silence sitting uneasily between them like a bad Mexican meal.

"I'll call you," he said, and watched her big ass swing into the distance.

"She says you're her brother."

"She's a liar. She's a lyin' bitch. A lying bitch slut whore. You know that."

"Yeah, I guess I do."

Jerry pulled off his briefs. His stiff little cock stood straight out beneath his pretty paunch. Rattler had the now-familiar feeling of being sucked into something beyond his control.

"...so it'll be better if we get it over with soon," the little man was saying.

Rattler wanted to voice his objections, the qualms he'd felt in the middle of the night. But Jerry's mouth was on his balls, licking and lapping, then moving up the underside of the shaft, swirling around his dickhead. At moments like this, Rattler figured he would do anything for this man. Even kill. Even kill Velma.

"Hey, Jerry," he said. "Would you like to try to fuck me?"

The plan was to go to the storefront late one night when Jerry was away, when the wind swept trash down the deserted sidewalk, when nobody with eyes was around to be a witness. And the thing, Rattler now knew with certainty, was going to happen, whether he wanted it to or not. Because that's what Jerry wanted.

He tried to imagine life with Jerry, the two of them having all the money they needed to buy a little house somewhere and. . .do what? Whatever it was, was it worth having Velma's blood on his hands?

For days, he tried to think it through, to see a way out. But there was always a dead end where his brain stopped thinking and his hunger took over. And no matter how many times he told himself he was being a sucker, the hunger remained. Because, Rattler knew, when it came to easy things like robbing widows or running a game of three card monte, he was a pro. But when it came time to deal with the important things, he was as weak as a fucking faggot.

Which is why one night, after Jerry had phoned him, Rattler called the Countess and pretended to be pleased to hear that the coast was clear. He parked his old truck in the alley behind the storefront, belted down some Wild Turkey from the bottle, then walked around to the front door and, making sure no one was watching, knocked.

She was wearing a pink rayon robe hanging half-open at the tits, nipples clearly visible through the cheesy fabric. She had on some of that perfume of hers. The joint was pretty dark, lit by a few candles and a lamp with a red scarf over the shade. He wanted to feel scared or happy or something, anything. So he looked at Velma, and tried not to think of Jerry.

"Whatcha lookin' at, Rattler?" She had that big, dumb look cows get as they're herded through the slaughterhouse. She threw her arms around his neck. Close up, her tattered, over-made-up face seemed more deserving of pity than anything else. *I'm not gonna do it,* Rattler thought. *I just can't kill this broad, no matter what.*

Her lips were on his now, sighing booze-breath into his mouth. Her flattened-out knockers pressed against his skinny chest. *Heart to heart,* he thought, inappropriately. But he had to think something, anything to keep him from being sad, sad in the knowledge that after tonight Jerry would know what a loser he really was, what a Judas. And Jerry would kiss him off. And then he'd finish Mrs. Murphy and slink back to the desert with his tail between his legs.

"Penny for your thoughts. Dollar for your dick." Her hand zoomed in like a horny bird of prey, grabbing hold of his long, limp dickmeat through the crotch of his pants. She licked her lips lewdly, then gave a funny little laugh. "Here, baby, I know what'll get you going." And she backed away a couple of steps and did an awkward sort of striptease, popping one breast from the robe, then the other, squeezing her nipples and winking, then undoing her belt and letting the robe fall open. She was naked beneath the pink rayon. But Rattler had seen her snatch before. He tried very hard not to think of Jerry.

With a clumsy twirl, Velma shed the robe and dropped to her knees in front of him, fumbling at his fly till his long, white dick hung out of his pants. Her brightly-rouged lips closed around him. Jerry gave better head, but the Countess wasn't bad; Rattler felt his reluctant cock beginning to swell. He thought about little Jerry eating out his ass.

Velma gagged a little, spit out his dick, and stood up. She wrapped one arm around his neck, spread her legs, and tried to guide Rattler's half-hard shaft into her pussy. Unsuccessfully. The softening dick slipped out. The Countess spit in her hand and grabbed the soft meat, stroking and pulling with increasing desperation.

"Whatsamatter, baby? Doncha like your Velma any more?" Her tongue lunged into his mouth. Their boozy breaths mingled, but no sparks were lit. Rattler pulled away from her, and thought about escape.

"Christ, you're not even as good as Jerry." Realization dawned on her face, a comic book expression that only needed a thought balloon that said "*Aha!*"

"It's Jerry, isn't it? He got to you, didn't he, Rattler baby? The two of you ... God, it makes me want to puke. You're nothing but a faggot, arencha?"

"Shut up, Velma."

But there was no stopping her. Her bright red lips writhed like snakes. "You're nothing but Jerry's little fairy-boy. Did he fuck you, huh? Did he make you into his girlfriend?"

"*Shut up!*"

She was shrieking now. Shrieking and laughing. Laughing in his face.

He grabbed her and shook her. Shook her hard. But she wouldn't stop laughing. He had to stop that laughter. He slapped her across the face. She shut up and looked surprised. Then, deadly serious, she hissed out, "That's right, hit a woman, you fag." He shoved her up against a wall, against a chart of the zodiac, and slammed his fist into her face. This time the surprise froze on her features and she crumpled to the floor. He picked up a big crystal ball, brought it down hard on her head. Again. A thin red serpent of blood slid from her ear. She groaned, stopped moving, stopped breathing.

Suddenly Rattler felt very, very tired. He picked up the robe and placed it over the dead woman's face. Dark blood began soaking a stain into the garish pink.

He lay on the floor, staring up at a chart of a great big hand. The life line. The fate line. His eyes began to close.

"Jesus Christ, you really did it, didn't you?" Jerry was standing over dead Velma, a big grin on his boyish face. He reached down, tore the little silver key from her anklet, put it in his pocket.

Rattler wanted to explain how he hadn't meant to do it. A lot of good that would do now. So all he said was, "What do we do now?"

"Well, there's no fuckin' way we're gonna make *this* look accidental. Your truck out back?"

Rattler nodded.

"Then let's get her the fuck out of here."

They wrapped the naked body in a tarp that Jerry pulled from the closet, then carried what was left of the Countess out the back door and threw the corpse in the back of the old truck. "I'll drive," said Jerry. "You look like shit."

They drove out of town and headed for the desert. The full moon bleached the vastness white beneath an empty sky. Rattler wanted to feel something, anything, but he was as empty as the dead land stretching off to nowhere. He glanced at Jerry. The little man had a little smile on his too-young face, and he was humming softly to himself. Rattler tried to remember how he'd felt when they were together in bed. Twenty minutes outside town the truck turned up a dirt road, jouncing over the washboard surface till they reached the crumbling ruins of an adobe mission. They pulled around back, safely out of sight. Jerry switched off the ignition and killed the lights. The moon would be enough.

They dragged what had been the Countess out of the truck, into the roofless remains of the mission. Jerry went back to the truck for shovels. Rattler stood there, staring down at the tarp-wrapped parcel.

It didn't take long to dig a shallow grave, to dump in the body, to cover it back up.

"Shouldn't we say something?" Rattler asked, standing over the unmarked grave, the moon casting crazy shadows.

"Yeah. Good riddance." Jerry patted Rattler on the back. "Let's get the fuck out of here."

Back on the road to town, Rattler was startled to see a man standing in the middle of the interstate, hat pulled down over his face, gesticulating wildly. His late-model car was half of the road, headlights on, hood up. Jerry pulled the truck to a stop.

"What the fuck're you doing?" Rattler said.

"Just helping a stranger in need. Don't worry. We're okay."

Jerry got out of the truck and walked over to the stranger. Rattler couldn't see the man's face, but his gestures made it obvious he was upset. Jerry gestured back to him to get out of the truck. Rattler didn't want to, but he did anyway.

"Car trouble," Jerry said. "Maybe you could take a look."

Rattler shuffled over to the car and stuck his head beneath the hood. "Moon or no moon, it's too hard to see. If you've got a flashlight. . ."

At that moment, a blow with the force of fire tore through the back of his head. Rattler crumpled to the ground. Above him stood the stranger in the hat, holding a tire iron, getting ready to strike again. Just before his eyes slammed shut, Rattler saw the man's face. It was Ripstein. And Jerry was smiling at Ripstein, hungry as a mouse at cheese.

Rattler came to long after dawn. He'd been dumped in the middle of nowhere, desert all around. Searing pain: his legs had been broken. His snakeskin boots were gone. He felt faint. And nauseated. And well and truly used.

Ripstein and Jerry were headed somewhere. Together. They would be rich. And he would be dead. The sun was already hot as hell. His thirsty tongue was already swelling up. The sky was white and getting whiter. As white as Jerry's ass. His beautiful, pudgy little ass.

In the endless hours that followed, Rattler's hearing grew more and more acute as his other senses dimmed. But all he heard was silence. He had plenty of time to reflect on the awful things a man's heart could get him into. Even so, his last words, whispered to no one who could hear him, were "I love you. I love you."

And that was that.

Simon Sheppard is the co-editor, with M. Christian, of *Rough Stuff: Tales of Gay Men, Sex, and Power* (Alyson Books), and his collection *Hotter than Hell and Other Stories* is forthcoming from Alyson, as well. His work has appeared in the two previous *Noirotica*s and in many other anthologies, including *Best Gay Erotica 1996, 1997, 1999,* and *2000,* and *Best American Erotica 1997* and *2000.* He may not be bad to the bone, but he has done an unforgivable thing or two.

Stiletto

by Lucy Taylor

The night was frigid and the coffee so strong you could use it to flush a carburetor. I sat at the counter of the L.A. Diner (That's Last America, not Los Angeles, by the way) and checked out the only other patron, a balding, thick-waisted guy sitting with his back to the wall, going over some books. Tried to calm my nerves by making a game of guessing how big his dick was.

I started with his hands, which were big, thick-wristed, and peppered with dark hair. Full lips and the kind of proboscis people usually buy in a dimestore on Halloween. And when he'd got up to use the restroom earlier, I'd noticed a cowboy jut to his pelvis, like he was either hauling some serious cargo or trying to give that impression.

I figured him for an eight- or nine-incher.

But what the hell, even though I was dressed for the possibility, I didn't plan on fucking Barney McGuire.

Not if I could possibly avoid it.

I glanced at the clock above the door. Ten after one in the morning. Not a lot of time to accomplish what I needed to.

Outside snow drifted past the window, small steady flakes that would add up to a foot or more by daylight. Detroit winters can be brutal. I was thankful to be wearing the full-length fur coat that I'd been nagging Donny to buy me next time he got paid for a smack shipment. He always said no dame needed such an expensive coat, but on a night like this, maybe he would've understood.

The counter girl, Myrna, was coming out of the kitchen with a pot of coffee in one hand and my breakfast in the other. There was a sway to her walk and a droop to her lids that gave her that freshly-fucked look. Which, since her boss Barney was here doing his weekly accounting, she might well have been.

Long witchy-looking black hair, a valentine-shaped butt, tits that, from the two inches of cleavage showing at the neckline of her uniform, must be perched on some serious underwire. As usual, she was painted up like a ten-dollar whore — crimson lipstick, kohl eyeliner, gold shadow — and hobbling around in a pair of towering spike heels that gave a succulent jut to her ass.

I'd had the hots for Myrna since we both waited tables at one of Donny's nightclubs and sneaked opportunities to make out in the ladies' room when we could. Then I got a chance at better things with Donny and, not long after that, Myrna went to work for Barney McGuire. Funny, huh? Two nice Detroit gals ending up in the employ of rivals in the numbers, whore, and drug trade.

Myrna slid a plate of grease-drenched eggs and hash browns in front of me. As always, my eyes went to the pattern of raised red scars on the back of her wrists — reminders that Barney, like his buddy the Marlboro Man, had a thing for branding.

"So when do you get off work?"

"When Barney says."

"Which is?"

"Depends on whether or not he's in the mood for any dessert." She seemed to want to change the subject. "So how's Donny? He okay with you bein' here?"

"Donny don't need to know every time I take a piss."

Myrna shrugged. "Your neck."

She reached over and ran her hand over my fur with the mingled lust and timidity of a girl about to give her first blow-job. "Mink?"

"Sable."

"Lucky girl. Donny must be a generous guy."

"He can afford to be. Every few weeks, he does a transaction, he takes in fifty or sixty grand."

She picked up my cup of coffee and refilled it. I reached for it just in time to let our fingers brush, nails clinking lightly together. Then I couldn't stop myself from glancing at the clock. Myrna saw me, and her scarlet mouth pouted up like maybe I'd hurt her feelings. Maybe she thought I had a hot date. Night like this, most people aren't in a rush to be anywhere.

I looked around the empty diner. "Weather keeping people home tonight, I guess."

She nodded. "Yeah. Everybody but Barney, I guess, but he's gotta finish the damn books."

It was common knowledge how grumpy Barney got if he had to deviate from any of his comfortable routines. Going over the books at the Diner Saturday night was one of them. Arty Cohen, Donny's right-hand man, used to say Barney would wait to take a shit if it weren't written down on his schedule.

"He's been checkin' you out since you got here," said Myrna. "You don't want him to hit on you, you better leave."

I sipped my coffee. I didn't care what Barney did, as long as he stayed where he was a little longer.

When I set the coffee cup back down, I let my hand stray across the counter and brush hers. She jerked her hand away and glanced over at Barney to make sure he hadn't seen.

"You know what, these eggs just ain't doing it for me this morning. What I really want is something hotter, sweeter."

Underneath the make-up, her cheeks actually darkened to a deeper shade of pink. "Jeez, Viv, this ain't the time. He'll kill us both."

"Nobody lives forever. Don't you have a storage room or a basement? And stop lookin' over at Barney, he'll think somethin's goin' on."

She giggled, scowled and glanced at Barney all in the space of an eyeblink. "No shit, Viv. We can't. Barney, he don't like games if he ain't winnin'."

I was ready to risk scribbling something on a napkin or whispering in her ear when Barney yelled, "Hey, Myrna, what the hell's going on over there. Do I pay you to make out with my customers?"

Myrna jumped back like he'd jabbed her with a cigarette.

"Fuckin' broads."

He pushed back his chair and strode over to the counter. He was dressed like a banker who had a thing for Liberace. Nice suit, silk tie. Gold cigarette holder and a diamond big as a chicklet on his right hand. Smile rehearsed and phony as a Fuller Brush salesman about to fuck the farmer's daughter.

Shit. It was almost one-twenty. I didn't have time for this crap.

"Ain't you one of Donny Marshak's girls?"

I nodded.

"He know you're here in my establishment?"

"Me and Donny, we had what you call a partin' of the ways. We're not so close no more, you know."

"He let you go? The man's a bigger dickhead than I figured him for."

"He got a short attention span, Donny does."

"So you're a free woman?"

"You could say."

Barney's expression went cool as a corpse. Like if he let anything show, his skin would crack. But I saw the tiniest, secret smile. Nothing you could even swear for sure was there. Like the smile of a man who's just seen his mistress across the room when he's got his wife on his arm.

He whisked out a card for Jules' Liquor Store and scrawled a number on the back. "Look, hon, I'm takin' off now before I get snowed in. You call me, though. Beautiful woman like you never has to worry where her next meal's comin' from as long as Barney McGuire's around."

I stroked the collar of my fur. "You don't gotta go right now, do you?"

He shrugged, looked almost embarrassed. "My daughter's gettin' baptized tomorrow morning. Don't wanna run the chance of missin' it, you know. Disappointin' her and her mama."

A kid? Funny, but I never thought of guys like Barney havin' kids. Not legit ones, anyways. Or going to baptisms, for God's sake.

"Hey, don't worry, though. I'm a man of my word. You want a job, doll, you got a place with me."

I imagined I could hear the clock over the door ticking. Like it was daring me to do something.

I put a hand on his lapel. "Before you go promising to buy the merchandise, ain't you gonna ask for a sample?"

"Hey, do I look like a guy who'd ask a woman to elope if I didn't plan to marry her?"

"I don't know. What does a guy like that look like?"

The bags below his eyes puckered with irritation. "Look, honey, Donny may go for pushy broads, but—"

I opened the fur coat and let it slither onto the countertop behind me. All I had on underneath was a garter belt and black stockings. I heard the sharp intake of Myrna's breath. Barney's eyes got big as my nipples. His gaze went to my tits, then did a quick up-down of my silk-clad legs and platinum snatch.

He glared at Myrna. "What you starin' at? This is between me and her. Go clean out the freezer. Scrub the john. You *work* here, don't you?"

I couldn't tell if Myrna's eyes were green with jealousy or if she was just pissed because he might get cum on the floor. If it was jealousy, that came as a shock. Barney was as sadistic a bastard as Donny. I hadn't known she cared.

Barney unzipped his fly, grabbed my hair, and shoved me to my knees. His cock sprang out like a party favor, not as outstanding as I'd guessed in the length department, but thick as a rolling pin. When I took him in my mouth, it was like trying to suck down a rolled-up copy of *The Detroit Times*. I risked a look at his face and saw his eyes. They were mean and greedy, like his cock. Full of venom and guile.

You don't work the streets, then become the girlfriend of a mobster, without developing a throat like a vacuum pump and a gag reflex so numbed-out you could swallow swords.

I knew I was doing a great job on Barney. His cock was swollen and stiff and he was ramming himself past my teeth the way men do when they're ready to come. But nothing was happening.

I came up for air. "What do you like, baby? Tell me what you want."

"Hey, take your time. Now that you got my interest, I ain't in *that* big a rush."

He pushed me down onto the grimy floor, my legs up over his shoulders, bending me back so far that I thought his cock would ram into my tonsils.

A door slammed and I got a glimpse of Myrna disappearing into the kitchen. *Good*, I thought. *Just stay there.*

Meanwhile Barney was fucking with workman-like concentration, grunting and sweating and pounding away like a carpenter hammering nails with my feet in their four-inch stilettos up over his shoulders.

I thought how I'd been thinking about Barney when I'd gone into my closet to find that pair of silver fuck-me pumps last night. Shoes, everybody knew Barney loved shoes.

I leaned back and arched my pelvis so his cock popped out of me with a sound like a cork leaving a wine bottle.

Before he could reinsert himself, I pulled off one of my pumps, held it to my mouth and ran my tongue, long and strummingly, up the heel. Put the heel in my mouth, sucked on it.

Barney sat back on his ankles. Bug-eyed and unblinking.

I slid the saliva-slick heel up my pussy and twisted it around. Pulled the shoe out so he could see that the leather was shined with my juices, and popped it back inside. He licked his lips and squeezed his dick so hard that the veins on the back of his hand showed.

I bucked my hips and fucked myself faster. I wanted to look at the clock, I wanted to see if Myrna was still in the back, but to know either of these things would distract me, break my rhythm.

Barney groaned and clenched his jaw. He was one of those men who would split a gut before he made a sound during orgasm. Then his cum spurted forward, not onto my pussy or tits as I was expecting, but onto the bar stool where I'd been sitting.

He grabbed me by the hair and jerked my head up, positioned my face over the chair.

"Lick it up, doll. Get every drop or next time I'll cum on the floor."

Not exactly my idea of dessert, but I did what he wanted, lapping the pearlescent ooze while faking little noises of enjoyment.

"You wait here, baby," I told Barney.

"Where you think you're goin'? You don't go nowhere until I tell you to."

"I want to go find Myrna. Make it a three-way."

"Oh." He looked surprised that such an idea could originate from a woman. "Okay, then. Tell that slut she don't act nice, then I won't act nice, either. And, believe me, she don't want that."

"Sure, baby." I paused just long enough to pick up my fur from the countertop and put it on. "Cold night huh?"

"Make it quick. I still gotta get home."

I searched the back room, but didn't find Myrna, so I followed some rickety stairs to the basement. She was slumped on the floor next to a shelf full of canned goods. Tears tracked her face and smudged mascara blackened her eyes.

When she saw me, she grabbed a can of baked beans off the shelf and threw it at me. "You bitch, it's bad enough seeing you again after all these months without having to watch you fuck that scumbag."

I dodged another can. "Stop it! What's wrong with you? I thought you hated Barney."

"I do."

"Then—"

"What is this, your revenge because I didn't trot after you the minute you winked? What are you doing down here, anyway? Why aren't you with him? He needs cream for his coffee, tell him to jerk off in it."

"I told him I was gonna bring you back for a three-way."

"Are you fuckin' crazy?"

"I wanted an excuse to come talk to you."

"We got nothin' to say."

I reached over and tried to wipe away the tear stains. She pulled away.

"Fuck you, now what kind of game are you playing?"

"It's not a game. It's serious."

"Fuck you. I'm going back upstairs."

"No, wait." I grabbed Myrna and forced my mouth against her darkly-painted lips. She tasted of mint and just the faintest after-taste of Marlboro.

"Leave me alone."

I started unbuttoning the black plastic buttons on her uniform. Yanked her bra up and buried my face in her cleavage while I ran my other hand up underneath her skirt. She wasn't wearing panties — probably a concession to Barney's need for instant gratification. I found her clit and rubbed it with my thumb, while I slid my fingers up inside her pussy.

"Don't you know why I came here tonight? I came to get you."

"What d'you mean?"

"Didn't we always talk about gettin' out of here? Going someplace warm? Maybe Mexico. Tahiti."

Upstairs I heard the front door open. Footsteps.

"Don't kid yourself. We'll be stuck here till the day we die."

More noise above us. A chair scraped back across the floor. Then shattering, as though a glass had fallen.

"What the hell is that?"

She started to get up.

"No! Stay here!"

I bit down on her nipple. She stiffened, gasped and then relaxed. I hurt her just a little bit, then moved up to her ear, tonguing the lobe, exploring the folds and whorls inside while I moved my fingers up inside her cunt.

She started to lean back and thrust her hips against me. "Oh, God, Viv!" My first thought was that this was a comment on my pussy-eating skills, but then I saw her eyes.

I twisted around and saw the blood trickling down from the ceiling. First a single stream, then two more. The streams split as they slithered toward the floor, candystriping the grimy, pockmarked wall.

Myrna began to cross herself. "Holy Mary Mother of God..."

I put my hand across her mouth and we held onto each other, watching the crimson rivulets come down the wall.

When the front door shut, we waited a few minutes before we went upstairs.

They'd used silencers, Donny's boys, and they'd been right on time. One forty-five, just like Mac Cohen had said they'd do it when I told him how I'd walked into Donny's place last night and found him dead with one of Barney McGuire's calling cards up his ass.

"We can't let that fucker get away with this," Mac had said, and thank God he had meant it.

Barney's body was laid out across the table where he'd eaten his last meal. His face and chest looked like they'd been run over by a streetcar and then snacked on by vultures.

And then that little touch of humor — the heel of a silver fuck-me pump plunged into Barney's eye. Maybe even the same one I stuck up Donny's ass right after I shot him.

Everyone knew that Barney's trademark was a high-heeled shoe — in the eye, up the ass, puncturing a ballsack. Nobody in Detroit finds Donny Marshak with a shoe heel up his ass got any doubts that it was Barney McGuire done it.

"Come on," I said to Myrna. "My car's up the street. We gotta *go*."

"How? Where'll we go? We don't have any money."

I squeezed her hand. "Hey, would I ask you to elope if I didn't think I could support you?"

I drove. Even wearing a fur coat, with nothing else on underneath, I was starting to get cold. Detroit winters can be brutal, but then, so can Detroit dykes.

Donny hadn't understood why I needed a full length fur, but on a cold January night, holding Myrna's hand and knowing the coat was lined with fifty grand of Donny's money, it went a long way toward warming my heart.

Lucy Taylor's works include *Close to the Bone*, *The Flesh Artist*, *Unnatural Acts and Other Stories*, *The Safety of Unknown Cities*, *Dancing With Demons*, and *Painted in Blood*. She lives in the hills of Colorado with her eight wonderful cats, her partner, and a shepherd/rottweiler named Bear.

Hack in the Poontang Jungle

by bart plantenga

I was the nocturnal hack, psycho-topo joyrider, romantic speedtrap dodge, Zen cartologist & eternal pioneer of the poontang jungle.

I was still reeling from encounters with a dazzling Deutschland fraulein who reeked of beds made in the Black Forest. She climbed into my cab, told me she'd surveyed my slightest gestures for weeks, had analyzed my smile, had gleaned much ado about something in her eye. She spoke of April dips in cold Bavarian lakes, a hole in the ice like her grey eyes, & the use of rare fish air bladders for flotation in the Adriatic, while the top heavy portion of her torso listed & leaned into me in front of the Flame Bar, site of many clandestine consummations.

She navigated me away from my appointed function to the Subterrain where we flattered one another into a drunken stupor shoved in a corner. She played with my fly, made it hum like a jazz instrument as we descended the inebriated steps into the Dankenkeller.

There she leapt up on the dark oak table & pounced into my embrace. & I walked her around in the murmurpheric irreality. I placed her stern up on the edge of the table where she lifted her skirt, said, "Look, no panties, in your honor!" & there she unveiled me into the cup of her caress with a moan. Held me like a little girl would hold her first Easter chick. & suddenly I was lost in the space between suspire & sigh. & this is how we made love, her big toes barely touching the stone floor, her haunches sliding off the varnished oak, her suspensory body hovering between 2 horizontal planes. While the footstomping patrons kept time to Tuscaloosa Slim & his Blues band right above us.

Then she laid her intrepid body urgent across the length of the table with a half bottle of Gamay between her legs & her breasts bursting out over the edge of the table. Thusly she siphoned the last vestiges of spunk from my scrotum, at one point talking with her mouth full of me, at another stretching the foreskin over her nose; "Look, der nosen varmer."

Sleeveless humming patrons came down to piss, half-missing the bowl at the moment of our crisis, with her hauling spunk by the bucketful from the furthest reaches of my feet. & later, with her grope gripped to my charm, we drove her home, wending wildly, skirting shoulders, sending up veils of dust. In front of her home she vowed to "strafe by periodically & make it so that life & desire are indistinguishable. When I sleep you will be the lanky incubus on my belly."

Thus it was moments like these that nourished me on slow nights, watching the dull noctuids make their final pilgrimage to the heart of the streetlight.

I was leaning back, on such a night, knees on the wheel, mind full of Ilke's flanks fiddling with the FM out of Detroit when in tumbled a distraught frazzle-haired dame. "Turn on the meter. & drive. Just drive. Out to Dixon Hills. I'm Debbie. Sometimes it seems I'm not. Don't tell me yours. I don't wanna know." We combed the windy lanes of Dixon Hills dense with the arrogant hush of privilege.

"Look for a late model Camaro. Red. Grey interior. I got the plate number in here someplace. DAMN!" Her ex had skipped out on her & alimony "in utter defiance of the law as stipulated." & the more likely we weren't going to find him in his inamorata's neighborhood, the more furiously she began to chew her gum.

At $6.30 we pulled into the Brew & Burger. "I'm hypoglycemic. I've got to eat or I go wacko. Go into convulsions." She ate like a nervous rodent made of carveable wood. She blabbed on about the many conspiracies that drove him from her, that were meant to undo her, periodically revealing clumps of half-masticated burger. Eating as if food was merely designed to stave off certain negative aspects of delirium. She wiped her mouth & belched. "I feel better. Now my mind can focus like an aimsight. That bastard's tryin' to eliminate me by ignoring me. It's too late for that! That'd be too easy!" Only later did I find out that her mouth had been wired like a marionette's after a head-on in a PA fog.

"True Joe Football Flake. Rather male bond, wash his car, have tailgate parties than spend time with me. Handsome as a soap star. & he knew it too, the bastard. Pardon my French. Even kept scrapbooks of scalps."

"What was he, a headhunter?"

"Sorta. He kept locks of hair of all his conquests."

"Your husband?"

"I spit on you! My ex, Ex, EX!!" Spit & bits of bomburger hit my cheek. She was livid. "Kept'm in chronological order. & I was special only in as long as I was the last."

"Seems kinda sick."

"Kinda!? Had I only known. Made me feel so special when he took that first pubic lock." She pointed down under. Domelight on. I imagined a tuft missing from her poontang jungle.

"The tall pompous bitch. Anthro prof. Dixon hills. Swedish, atheist & tan, Tan, TAN! & blond, Blond, BLOND!" Debbie was nervous as a horsefly before a thunderstorm. We made one more disconsolate sweep through Dixon's leisurely dips full of mist & crickets. & then we headed empty-handed to her room at the Busy Bee Motel, a shack-up place called affectionately "The Busy Bee Jay" in hack parlance.

We pulled into the diagonal parking spot. & as we got out I spotted a mangled smirk inside the blur of mussed hair & weeping skin. A smirk soaked in the heightened emotions of sadness which brings fever to the blood. A smirk that only much later said, "I've found a patsy go-fer to chauffeur me through my many melodramas."

She spotted the distinctive wheels parked out in front of Room 12A. She was 13A. 36D. 30-40 years old, had a $2,500 credit line. She mistook the wheels for a Rolls.

"It's a Bentley. Yuh can tell by the grill." & suddenly everything seemed to reverberate with sexual innuendo-13A, thick shake, nice grill work, etc.

Inside I unzipped her dress only because she'd instructed me to do so. But despite the utilitarian nature of her request I allowed myself the pleasure of listening to her zipper fleeting down tailbone like a siren's mantra.

Later she had me towel her back but not too much of her back. My duty (which I thought would lead to immense pleasure later) did not take me up & over her shoulders (yet). I watched her shave her legs with her foot perched on the edge of the tub. Watched her rub oil deep into the skin. Saw the scars on her face. Food caught between her teeth. & I imagined she'd belch just at the moment of orgasm.

"I'd like to meet who owns those wheels." She sprayed a confusing bouquet of scents across the exposed portions of skin. "Let's go out, look at them wheels o' fortune." She shimmied into a tight wrinkly wad of presumed class. Wiped a gaudy red onto & beyond the true contours of her lips to give the impression that her lips were more full & voluptuous than they actually were. She ran her fingers across the black fender. Ogled the crushed-velvet seats, black marble bar in the back seat, the ivory steering wheel. She kicked the tires.

As if by instinct I retreated to my cab, (the ticking meter up to $12.50) & hid the jar of tips under the seat, even ran my hand across my back pocket for my wallet.

Two grinning fellows stood on the opposite side of the car observing her with leering delight. They greeted her in fine pleated slacks & 5 o'clock shadows. One of them was short enough to be called a midget — in platform shoes. He had a failed swagger that yearned to insinuate him as taller than facts allowed. The other was a ruddy sort of Henry Fonda who twisted a silk tie that perhaps only weeks earlier he hadn't known existed. They looked like the kind of guys who could've dug graves during the Spanish Civil War or done messy hit jobs for the mob. In any case, the elegance of their cut of threads betrayed them more than complimented them.

"I guess we're neighbors." They swayed inside their wingtips, telescoping in on her. & if looks could kill, I'd've been an abortion stat; i.e., I did not exist.

"This is a true work of art. It's gorgeous! Whatchu guys do anyway?" They, nouveau suave, picking at the vestiges of factory calluses, circled around us-or HER.

"Real estate." said the midget hoping the term could be insinuated far enough to stretch across her body.

"You want we should give yuh a tour?"

"Gee, yea, sure!" Wide-eyed as a Dr Pepper ad. They crawled into the back seat. From under the bar they grabbed an erotically-shaped amber bottle & poured her a soda glass of something exotic sounding. Her nipples were erect. A sucker for silk & anyone who knew what a Tahiti Typhoon was.

I focused on the dash. 40,923.4. I wondered if it might've been 140,923.4 miles. I kept my thoughts — the ones that figured they were NOT the Bentley's owners at all but merely its chauffeurs — to myself.

They dragged Debbie with her pink barrettes, her exquisite daintiness & bomburger stuck between grey teeth, across the seat, across themselves, their urgent hands assisting her at every step & into their lair. Where they sipped more Typhoons, gulping flaming shots of who-knows-what as their bravado grew bold & loud. "You have zee lovely curves more zan Le Mans."

Video equipment lay strewn about with cords snaking over cheap furniture. This caught her eye. She touched the knobs. Bent provocatively to read the fine print. "How's it work?" I sat on the edge of the bed close to the door, looking at the lint between my toes, ready to make a discreet vamoose.

"It works when we say 'go.'"

Debbie had always wanted more than ANYthing, yes ANYTHING, to be in movies or on TV. She'd do ANYthing. So they crawled into her action like dream merchants lugworming their way inside her unrequited yearnings. They flattered her beyond recognition. & she went on about plays in high school. & they said they'd probably be able to get her something in a sitcom.

"REALLY?"

"Why not? We know talent when we see it. That's our livelihood." As the midget zoomed in with his equipment. Double entendres abounded. There was great zest & zeal & more promises. She suggested songs from *Hello, Dolly*, *Oklahoma*, *Mary Poppins*, & a Dr Pepper spot she'd seen that she really liked. They zoomed into her teeth & caught close-ups of her heaving assets.

On the second take they had her jiggle her breasts for 6 takes & as a token of her enthusiasm lifted her skirt to show her slip & more. The slip absolutely shimmered on the replay. The midget went gaagaa into somersaults. He regained his composure, combed his geek hair back further anointing her ego with promises of a possible appearance on *Star Search*.

The Fonda guy was running his finger down his tailbone mumbling on about modeling as she lay transfixed across the bed, legs in the air, high heels precariously dangling from her toes, watching the screen — *Star Search*, Broadway, *Folies Bergeres*!

Both heels fell to the floor as our dapper dagger turned her over on the bed, mumbling fatuous advice in her ear. He managed to pull her bra off without removing her blouse. "I am une amoureuse magicienne." She was too enthralled to be taken aback.

He mounted her like an adult on a supermarket kiddie rocking horse. The midget caressed her feet, salivating, catering to her every whim & fart.

Then just as suddenly he was off of her & all was business again. & she was banging out strange octaves, giving it her most earnest. Whereupon the midget was encouraged to go up her skirt with the camera — just for fun, of course — which she began to hump. & now they knew she was theirs. & primed to be flattered into all sorts of compromising positions. Because they'd allowed her to think that they were HERS.

I read the *TV Guide*, saw that *Hogan's Heroes* was on every afternoon at 4:30. I just didn't exist & so I played the part.

The double-jointed midget danced a crazed fertility dance around the bed with a brandy snifter on his balding head. As our dapper blade lapped away at her pouty grotto, her back arched & her voice sang along to something from *Jesus Christ, Superstar*, something that sounded like a rooster on Quaaludes with a farmer wringing its neck.

The midget doused the lights. But in the blue of the TV I could see him still wagging his gnarly truncheon under her nose. As she tried to recruit them to help her get back at her ex. This kind of proposal made them even more erect.

"Anythink you desire." & that she was now sobbing no one — not me, not even her — attributed to sorrow. It's always the drink, too-much-too-soon, the excitement, the...

The dapper Fonda geek kneeled amongst the blossom of her ripe hindsight where he undid his underpants which were held together with Velcro, at the hips, for easy-out-easy-in. He had the flair of a toreador or a carnival performer as he massaged her kidneys ("Old World erogenous zones") with the handles of 2 Romanian knives.

"You are a flower yearnink to blossom." I should have puked then & there but did not. *Hollywood Squares* every day at noon. She was breathing like a character in a Harlequin novel, like a steam engine in a cartoon. She was ready for him to breathe fire.

"I feel so ... so different."

"But that you are indeed." She knocked a glass of Tahiti Typhoon off the nightstand as he lifted her by the waist & impaled her atop his quiver. The midget meanwhile with video camera on his shoulder was lapping the Typhoon off her shoulder as he continued shooting.

On the screen her version of "Let's Get Physical" as I made my discreet slip out the screen door. I could hear our dapper blade trying to convince her to hoist her buttocks in the air into the light & to let him go "backstage." So she could become a star — at stags in Cheboygan, bachelor parties in Hazleton.

"No, no, not inside!" The video camera still humming away.

"You vill be something of a star." This hastened my retreat as I saw her struggle with the web of the midget's sperm in her hair.

I pissed like a race horse, against the door, up on the door handle of the Bentley. Small revenge. Big thrill.

I stopped the meter at $26.10, her smell still caught in my cab. I opened my windows to air out my interior. So I could be someone I remembered being — only 6 hours earlier.

& later I lied about my experience down at the cab office, as the dispatcher divvied up lines of coke to fortify us for the pre-dawn hours of a slow summer night. I had made nothing but chump change thus far that night. Thought of going back to the Busy Bee to make her make good on the meter. But I didn't care. I got what I wanted. Or deserved. Later my cabbie pal, Jim, said I'd been the 3rd cabbie stiffed by her. We thought of designing a wanted poster. Thought of a reunion of stiffed cabbies. But neither of us could get beyond the anguished blur of her face, a face full of too much motion. No definite lines save the scars.

& this story, nonetheless, being nothing but the truth, is nothing like what we told the other cabbies up in the office that night.

Bart Plantenga is the author of *Wiggling Wishbone: Stories of Pata-Sexual Speculation* (Autonomedia) as well as *Confessions of a Beer Mystic*. He has been a DJ for 12 years in NY, Paris and now Amsterdam. He has been widely published in venues perceived to be eroto-pornographic: *Pink Pages, Paramour, Screw, Batteries Not Included, Yellow Silk* and *Best American Erotica*.

Inside the Works

by Tom Piccirilli

Art, sex, and madness crawled and spun side by side down deep inside the Works; the walls dripped with drama, floors covered in genius, soul, and a phalanx of talent. Torn pages of poetry lay strewn in the halls beside broken guitars and drumsticks, soiled ballet slippers, condoms used and unopened, splatters of paint and blood as rats squeaked in the shadows.

The door to Fruggy Fred's suite was open. He lay in bed with a couple of empty bottles of tequila, crushed lemons, and two sleeping members of his band, the Wrong-Faced Babies, saw me coming through the door, but he was far too wasted to do anything more than grin and mumble. Most of Fruggy's 400 pounds were in the bed, with only a few of his outer pale and bloated rolls hanging over the sides of the mattress like tumors. His tongue lolled onto one of the Babies' shoulders, their hairy, sweaty chests sliding against one other with each breath.

I slapped his door shut and kept going, amazed at the amount of renovation d'Outremal had put into the Works in the months I'd been gone. It didn't take long to realize he'd not only bought out the entire warehouse, but the whole city block, even the rubble of the projects at the end of the street where a vast twisted vegetable garden now crept among the brick dust and dog shit. From what I could see, he'd split the place into nearly thirty separate areas including communal living quarters, private suites, a small museum and showroom, theater stage, sound rooms, and a bar. I couldn't see it, but someone had mentioned there was now also an abortion clinic. A combination tattoo and piercing station was packed with clients. Small classes were being given in rape prevention, tap dance, horticulture, and how to correctly camouflage a cannabis garden.

Scattered in the darkened corners and corridors of the Works, people were sleeping, sketching, going through scenes of Edward Albee plays, dropping acid, masturbating and making love. Two women, hands locked behind their backs, leaned forward kissing passionately, murmuring sonnets; I watched for a while. d'Outremal had opened the doors wide but the chemistry hadn't changed much. Keyboards clattered and whispers of music rang in the studios, which still hadn't been properly soundproofed. The remaining Wrong-Faced Babies, drummer and bassist, were laying down some final tracks, and the bass thrummed.

This type of artistic coalition hadn't been seen since Warhol's Factory, and though the Works wasn't so self-indulgent as that, it reeked of the same posture. Retro-sixties counterculture meets Generation X, Y, and Z, along with a stew of malcontents, curious voyeurs, lost souls, and geniuses.

I cut across the show room, surprised at how much more art had been added, the amazing quality of some of the pieces, set side by side those composed by the blatantly insane.

Hiding behind a statue of Kali, the death-mother, entwined with Moses, her four hands stroking an erection that peeked out between the stone tablets, sat Brandenburg. When he saw me he grinned and stuck his pen between his teeth, licking, orally fondling it in mockery of me. His even white teeth bit down until his incisors were tinged with blue ink. Cancer hadn't quite wasted him completely away, his natural slim physique and pallor now an unhealthy yellowing gauntness, and it would kill him long before the HIV turned full-blown AIDS. His Yale sweater was prominently displayed upon his pointed shoulders and sunken torso. Still, he smoked, dry lips skinned back like a leering wolf, a cigarette dangling and stuck to sores in the corner of his mouth.

"Lazarus has arisen," he said, gingivitis rotting his gums away. "And come unto us again. Hey, nice hair, Paynes. Natural, yes? You're not simply going for the prematurely-gray, distinguished look?"

I smiled, and he held up a notebook, covered with his illegible handwriting. "Shall I read you my latest work in progress? Ah, it's about you, of course, but then again, what around here isn't? I call it, uhm, ah, *Broken 'Neath the Weight of Love*. Catchy, eh?" He cleared his throat, threw on a haughty European lilt, and made up something pretty wretched on the spot.

Brandenburg handed me the page of meaningless scratches. I folded the paper and put it in my pocket. He was a masochist and pinned his rejections from the *New Yorker* and *Atlantic Monthly* to his mantle like medals. Each time he handed one of his poems to someone who crumpled the page and threw it back at his feet, his confidence would build. I said, "Thank you. I appreciate the effort."

He stared at me like he'd love to beat me to death with a hammer. "We're having bad problems with the rats. I doubt you care, but if you're going to stay, even for the night, make sure you keep an eye out, set up away from the east alley side. That's where they're worst. They still think this place is a meat-packing plant. We'll never get the smell of blood out of the walls." I thanked him. "And Kendra's been looking for you."

"I'll see her later."

"So, exactly what are you now? I can never tell anymore. A writer, is it? Playwright? Keeper of the eternal flame of romance? You've failed at so very much."

I shrugged and held my palm up over my mouth. "How about an Indian chief? Woo-woo-woo."

"I've got a better idea," he said, the drama in the air something he couldn't forsake. "How about a ghost?" I nearly burst out laughing. After a moment, as he rose and coughed and started to limp off, now with a shade of fear in his shadowed eyes turning back to face me, I nodded.

Whoever the woman was, she had been yanked onto her toes, hoisted by chains that went up over the rigging of a delicate set of pulleys, and came down to thread through her cuffs and clip to her nipple-rings. She'd been dressed in dominatrix togs, gagged with a short, pink dildo, and drool spilled down her chin. I wondered what she found in doing this, what all of d'Outremal's models found in this. Veins in her neck and ankles bulged blackly. Streaks of mascara sliced through the abundant rouge on her cheeks. She occasionally grunted and squealed, dripping wet with piss, as d'Outremal ignored her sobs, working the canvas. He painted slowly but efficiently, as if he were capturing each drop of sweat filming her brow, every pore on her large, dark aureole, the hue of that creaking leather, all the exciting details of her pain. Instead, he drew a vase of roses resting behind her on a shelf.

The proximity of the tattoo and piercing booth had been a temptation he couldn't resist — his arms and neck were covered with Kabbalistic symbols and Egyptian glyphs, faces out of religion and mythology, rings edging around both ears, running along his eyebrows. Twin studs punched through his lips, and a large brass ring had been stationed in the septum of his nose, so that he looked something like a bull. Once he'd been a great painter, careful in his craft, but the modern Impressionists had given him an excuse to exercise his laziness, and the first bad LSD trip had torn wider holes in his talent, and now everything he drew looked like a red seascape. The roses in the vase behind the crying leather-deather looked like radishes in a red seascape.

On his wall resided a nude portrait of Jeanne he'd done in his prime, less than a year ago. Seeing it again made my breath hitch, as shards of memories stabbed and slashed in my brain. There was embarrassment in her trustful, childlike blue eyes, that and something more. Thinner than she should have been, Jeanne had always battled her childhood trauma of anorexia, with small and somewhat sagging breasts, chest speckled with freckles, legs already bruised with hatchings of varicose veins. Her blond hair had that wild and rangy look that always excited me. Her usual, large, say-cheese smile is missing, and so her slightly crossed front tooth can't be seen. Her upper lip is tucked into her bottom, as if she were pouting. d'Outremal, to his credit, at the time did not toy with the reality of his canvas. Her pose is not fuck-me erotic in the least, although it made all my lust and love run through me again like rabid animals in my blood.

The model grunted — veins in her neck throbbing as she gagged, exhausted at the end of her limits. She'd started to slip off her toes, the rings stretching out her nipples until I thought her flesh might tear. A lot of girls had become scarred before the empty easel of d'Outremal.

"Kendra told me you were finally out of the hospital," he said with an air of admonishment, like a father disappointed by a sickly child. "Are you still writing?"

"No."

"You can't stay here if you're not out on the edge."

Even his diction had fallen into the puerile. "I've been out on 'the edge,' Doot. Call me creator of the Works."

"Co-creator, and no, that's not good enough, Paynes."

Money from my first two novels went to paying for the warehouse, and after the movie rights sold, I managed to incorporate and fund the Works. Deals were cut with other established artists. But d'Outremal was right; if he hadn't pressed me in the beginning, I wouldn't have started it. "Okay, then I'm a ghost."

He liked that a little better, showing his teeth, but said, "Still not good enough."

The model started to bleed, her stretched nipples splitting as her body sagged. I went over and unclipped her breasts, untying the pulley wires. She sank to her knees and dropped into my arms. When I pulled the dildo out she went into a coughing fit that brought up crimson-flecked phlegm. The portrait of Jeanne stared down at me. d'Outremal snapped his paint brush in half, a groan rising in his throat that quickly turned into a growl. I looked up at my lost lady a final time and left, knowing that no matter how deep inside the Works I had been, I needed to go down deeper.

Prostitutes rallied and blocked the doors, waiting for the kids and weary artistes to take their edges off in the surrounding maze of alleys. Between the bass beats of the Wrong-Faced Babies could be heard the caterwauls and cries of the neighborhood. Half-and-half's were cheaper in this section of town, blowjobs going for only ten bucks, around the world for fifty. Some of the whores took classes, usually the self-defense seminars. The homeless congregated at the west side of the warehouse, away from the rats, hoping for handouts, although the artistes owned even less than they.

Wandering through the Works, I discovered the new bedroom where they were continuing the Flick; I walked in and found a man and woman engaged in anal sex, her face buried in the sloppy, stained blankets. d'Outremal had invested in better cameras and lighting. The tapes on the library shelves were neatly stacked, labeled, and numbered. A lot of people were curious, but a firm rule had been that nobody gets to look at any of the film until the Flick was completed. When that was, no one, certainly not d'Outremal, nor I, knew. He considered it cinéma vérité, the ultimate in truth. He'd been filming for nearly two years. Three months ago, when I went into the hospital, d'Outremal had had about forty-two hours of film. Now I could only guess how long the Flick had grown, what kind of a life it had taken on. There were a lot more tapes, as though they were filming in a frenzy. Everyone who came to the Works had to get into the Flick. Kendra and I were in the first ten minutes, directly following d'Outremal's masturbation scene that opened the Flick.

The woman on the bed was Kendra.

I sat and waited in the corner near their clothes until they were finished, and after they'd slept for about an hour, he rose and left while Kendra lit a joint. It took a few more minutes before she realized someone else was in the room.

Staring at me, as though not finding my face, she asked, "Paynes, is that you? My Christ, you look so different. Why did you come back?"

"I wanted to see you," I said. "All of you."

Maybe we'd been in love once, or perhaps our madness simply meshed. She was a writer too, and we'd found a sick and happy place together delving into the white empty pages of our books and minds. We'd discovered succor and solace there, until Jeanne entered my life and pulled me up from the mire of my sorrow and talent.

Kendra patted the dry side of the bed, urging me to sit beside her. "Be with me." I shook my head and threw her clothes, and, reluctantly, she began to dress. "You still holding a grudge? She wanted to join, Paynes."

"I know."

"She said you were finally allowing her to come and be a part of us."

Those shards in my head ground together and I winced, splinters sticking in up and down my mind, thinking about how Jeanne had entered the Works, and how she'd left. "But you realized it was a lie. You knew I would never have let her become a part of this. She was free, and she made me free. You knew it was a lie, Kendra."

"Maybe, but what difference does it make now? She got what she wanted. She wanted to understand, and once she understood, she wanted to die." Kendra stood and kissed me, grinding up against my groin, once again in my arms. "I knew she was doing it for you. Even hanging herself, Paynes, even that was for you."

"Let's walk."

We moved against the flow of traffic in the halls; people now seemed to be revolving on a track, moving in one direction around the warehouse, in some kind of race. She asked, "Where are we going?"

"Outside."

The thought troubled her. I wondered how long it had been since she'd been outside the Works. "Why?"

"I want to show you something."

We hit the exit and she froze, gathering her courage, then took a step into the alley. Whores flashed their tits and called me by name. A number of cars, limos, and cabs had parked on the street, drivers getting head.

"God," Kendra said, "this is going to sound so horrible. But in a way, I'm glad she's out of your life. You just became so goddamn boring after you met her, Paynes. I mean, listen, even after everything, I love you too much to see you so cut off from yourself, from the real you. Believe me, I saw what was happening, what Jeanne was doing. Loving her was killing you." She sighed and pressed me back against a cab's bumper, as the driver moaned inside. She touched my face. "Look, I never told you, but you've always been the only one for me, really. I've...."

I snapped the antenna off a cab, turned and whipped it across Kendra's face. Her first cry was more like a laugh. I smacked her again and again; falling to her knees, beautiful body folding angle by angle, she cackled and lifted her bloody head to look at me. She smiled. Two teeth were already gone. I spent another minute smashing in her face, then threw the antenna in the gutter and walked back inside, leaving the whores whispering my name.

I needed a dolly, and needle and thread. I asked a woman I'd known since high school, and though she didn't recognize me, I was directed to the appropriate places.

Fruggy Fred remained unconscious — I jumped up onto the bed and, using all my strength, managed to pry him away from the other Babies, shoving at his bulk until he toppled off the mattress with a resounding "*ka-boom!*" Tequila bottles shattered. The room shook, but he landed perfectly on the dolly. Fruggy snored quietly.

The noise woke one of the Wrong-Faced Babies. "What are you doing?"

"I'm killing him."

"But....?" His words caught in his throat, eyes spinning in panic. "What about the band?"

"You'll do sell-out memorial concerts for the rest of your lives."

He thought about it, and while thinking, passed out again.

I picked a broken guitar string and snapped drum stick from the floor, covered Fruggy with a sheet and rolled him to the other side of the warehouse into one of the unused meat lockers, where only a few stragglers sat reading and tap dancing. Nobody said anything. Once inside, I carefully sewed his lips shut, locking that slimy, slug-like tongue into that froggy mouth. There was little blood, and apparently even less pain. I slapped him, hoping he'd at least look at me, and understand what was happening, and why. He started groaning but didn't wake up, not even when I got the chains around him and hoisted him into the air. In that position, with all his weight pulled by gravity, his lungs would probably give out before he woke up, but I hoped not. I wanted him to think about all the rotten meat in the Works.

I shut the meat locker and found Brandenburg on the floor outside, staring at me. He'd seen what I'd done, started to run, and had slipped on rat turds. Frail as he was, he'd probably broken an ankle. I grinned. His mouth sores were bleeding, infection soaking his cigarette. He should have just screamed, but even that wasn't dramatic enough for him. He swallowed thickly, the stained cigarette dangling, pen and poem in his hand. "I know why you're doing this," he croaked. "What ... what kind of punishment do you have in store for me, Paynes? What are ... ?"

"You I've been thinking about," I said. "Brandenburg, I think cancer and AIDS is punishment enough." I punched his shoulder gently, like two buddies talking about high school football, and snatched the pen from his hand. "You get to stay and be the ghost now." I actually considered it, letting him just shrivel up, cancerous and putrefied, internal organs turning to liquid, and then I thought about the Flick again, and Jeanne's scene.

He almost smiled in relief. "Look...."

"Let's forget I said any of that," I told him, reaching out to grab his throat, pulling him to me in with that same kind of embrace he'd swallowed her in. Feeling the solid warmth flowing through my shoulders and back muscles I strangled Brandenburg, forcing his lips tighter and tighter around that cigarette until his teeth broke, green ooze leaking from his mouth, the soothing clicking noise of the tap dancer floating down the hall.

A new woman and man were making love in the film room. I shut off the camera and lights, and said, "Get out."

Riding atop him, she smiled and asked, "What, honey?"

Pulling her by the wrist, I dragged her off the bed, the guy beneath still squirming and thrusting until he realized she was gone. He bolted upright ready to spring at me, the woman hopping angrily about now, slapping my face. At once, they recognized me; everyone could recognize me if I wanted them to. All it took was throwing the heat back into my eyes, showing my teeth, the usual pose from my book jackets, releasing just a hint of the madness. It felt good to resume form. They backed out of the room.

I had to search for awhile until I found the correct tape, one of a hundred, with nothing outstanding to differentiate it from any of the others.

Watching the Flick:

As Jeanne, blinded by the glare, raised a hand to cover her eyes and was met by a bark from d'Outremal. She dropped her arm, squinting. Fruggy Fred's fat shadows fell upon her first, rising up behind her from the floor to link with her own shadow, and then his flesh entered camera range, that inhuman paleness almost blue in the light like an asphyxiate. He spun Jeanne to him, and Brandenburg too reached for her shoulder, opening his arms wide in that warm-hearted embrace, cigarette dangling almost into her ear, each of the men now lightly touching and kissing her in the best places — small of the back, her jawline, now moving to her breasts — smiles flashing, like dogs nipping, her lips set firm and eyes narrowed in an effort to control panic, and they drew her down to the bed. Soon d'Outremal left his post behind the camera and moved into the scene, so clearly taken with the concept of director directing himself, becoming one with the documentary of libido, joining in the fuck of the Flick. It was nearly seventeen minutes before Kendra entered the room and, tentatively at first, plied Jeanne's wet thighs as well while the others swarmed my lady, and then Kendra fell against Jeanne with a gruff moan of lust and began biting her, too.

Jeanne had gone this deep inside the Works to find me, my origins, my nucleus. Somehow, I'd failed in my love for her — she knew I couldn't quite make it in the regular world anymore. I'd left too much of myself behind and went to find and regain it for myself. To discover and try to understand what comprised the real me. Whatever she'd found, it had been too much.

I found d'Outremal in his studio. He was painting me — the me he remembered before Jeanne, the me I'd become again now that she was gone. He turned and started to say something, and stopped. On the floor lay the broken brush from before. The proof of my life was in his paint; he already knew why I was here.

"I loved you, Doot," I said.

"Then why are you killing me?"

"Why did you kill her?"

"I didn't. She asked to join us."

"But I told you to keep her away."

"The idea was to let everyone in."

"I know," I said. "It was my idea."

In the rape seminar area I heard women empowering themselves, shouting, as they learned the art of smashing scrotums.

"What in the hell are you going to do?"

"Give you what you've been lacking," I said. "It won't take long."

And it didn't. After the first few minutes of struggle, he gave up; he was stronger, but had less power, here in my inner sanctum. I dragged him to the filming room, tied the guitar strings around his testicles, plugged the snapped paint brush and drum stick into his rib cage, stuffed the pen in his eyes, his screams only another song being sung here, another affirmation of art, until his body was twisted and laid out across his easel, and the portrait of the real me.

"Verite," I said. "That's what it was all for, wasn't it? Honesty? Well, here's our truth. I am the Works."

I set the lights up to shine perfectly across his body and filmed the proper ending to the Flick. He mouthed words at me, dribbles of blood and gore running down his face, a false messiah crucified by a real one, drawing in further into close-up. I tied the other ends of the guitar strings around his broken fists, so that when I pulled them his hands rubbed at his crimson crotch in a mimicking of his masturbation scene that began the Flick.

Before he died, I cracked open the tape case and wrapped the film around him, winding it tightly, layer by layer until he was mummified. No flesh could be seen except for his face, and then I dragged him out through the corridors in front of everyone, who recognized me and watched in silent, rapt fascination, to the east side of the warehouse. I threw him down. After a few hours the rats came out, and it didn't take long before another red seascape opened beneath us. I was beginning to like my new work of art. I would leave it for all to admire.

Tom Piccirilli is the author of eight novels, including *Hexes*, *Shards*, *The Night Class*, *The Deceased*, and his "Felicity Grove" mystery series consisting of *The Dead Past* and *Sorrow's Crown*. An omnibus collection of 40 of his best stories entitled *Deep Into That Darkness Peering* is available from Terminal Fright Press.

Open Season

by Thea Hillman

I push my way in the door. Mad shuffle panic. Foot door jamb. Push. She loses. Shove in. Denial. Panic. Nowhere to run. Panic. Knife? Phone window. I can see it in her eyes. Options. Eyes. And once I see it, I see it all. Her options are my options. Grab her by the back, gasp, of the head, short hair slides through my fingers, grab throat, hold, jerk back. Twisted half-Nelson. Find her knives. She recoils fast from the knife, almost escapes, grasp, smack. Hit her face hard, gasp. She starts crying, don't do this. What is this, I ask her. I don't know, she says. Right, I say. I'm gonna fuck you. I'm going to fuck you and then I'm gonna kill you.

I pull at her clothes. Ripping them off, pushing her, pulling. The kitchen knife isn't so sharp. I have to hold it in my teeth, and tear. Tie her hands in her shirt. You're going to die under me, under my hands. She's looking messy now. Naked. Red scratches, snot, clothes scraps, whimpering. Push her down on the floor. She's lying on her tied arms. Tie her one leg to the bed with the phone cord. Sit on her other leg to keep her still. Feel her. I'm going to feel you die.

She feels my hands on her, jumps, jerks, like everything tickles and everything hurts. She jumps and jerks as far away from my hands as she can. She twists her face from side to side as if it makes a difference. I grab her face and makes her look at me. I'm the last person you're ever gonna see. Knee on her leg, hand searching, probing her pussy. She's wet. I tease her. You're wet, slimy cunt. I silence her refusal by placing my free hand on her throat and squeezing. Pulse, squeeze. Red squeeze, pulse, pounding. She jerks away but can't get loose. Can't breathe. Squeezing throat. Jerk. It's like jerking off, getting red, veins pulsing.

I hear pounding and I don't know, I'm not sure, I don't care if it's at the door, in my head, or in my throbbing cock. Everything is throbbing, jumping out, jerking off. I'm gonna fucking kill you, I say, as I shove my cock in. Jerk, thrust, squeeze. Her eyes are looking surprised, popping out like veins in my cock, hot, and I'm pumping, ripping, squeezing, tearing. There's bubbles and spit and froth. Like jerking off and fucking at the same time. She's my cock. Red. Hard. Wet. She's my pussy. Red. Slit. Wet. I'm spilling into her. She's spilling onto me. She's mine. I come.

```
Case No.:    0459335
Date/Time:   01-05-98
Location:    74 Dolores St., Apt. 13, San Francisco
Crime:       Homicide
Report:      Respond  to  911  call  at  1300  hrs.
```
Disoriented, vague caller, "there's blood all over. I don't know what happened" (tape enclosed), unable to provide address, location. Call trace to pay phone on Market St. Met at scene by unarmed caller, Caucasian female, approx. 6', 28 yo, blond short hair, blue eyes, blood on hands, face, clothing, abrasions on face (appear to be from fingernails, inconclusive), lump on back of head, repeatedly stating, "I think she's not okay." Provided identification (Melanie "Mel" Levant, Petaluma, CA) and identified victim as Thea Hillman of San Francisco, CA. Says she gained consciousness and found Thea "all bloody," called 911. Lt. Robranov commenced medical and mental health procedures (see Robranov, same case no.).

Proceeded to crime scene, third-floor studio apartment, two cats. Approached victim: Caucasian female, approximately 27 yo. Victim found naked, wrists bound with clothing, ankle with phone cord. Multiple contusions, abrasions, signs of struggle apparent by visible trauma to skin on face, neck, hands, wrists, ankles. Checked all vital signs, DOA. RM onset. Return to vehicle, report apparent cause of death: bled to death from multiple knife wounds (possible hunting knife, inconclusive) including incision at throat and eviscerated genitals. Request coroner, homicide backup.

Scene search: Presence of various sexual aids including dildo, harness, latex gloves, and condoms. Presence of sadomasochistic paraphernalia—wrist, ankle restraints, nylon rope, leather face mask. No murder weapon found.

"Annie! Oh, my god...." Sandra rushes in to hug Annie as soon as her friend answers the door.

"I know, I know," says Annie, taking Sandra's hand and leading her to the couch. "Are you okay?"

"I can't believe it. I just can't believe it. After you called yesterday, I kept crying. I couldn't hold it together. My boss sent me home. Sometimes I'm fine and then I just start sobbing."

"I know, it's the most horrible thing imaginable. I can't believe she's really dead. I keep expecting to hear her upstairs running for the phone or her door closing. I've got Barley and Saul here." She glances down at the big white cat that is rubbing against her leg.

"Okay, so let's sit down and you have to tell me everything you know. God. Can I smoke? I mean, in here?" Sandra is talking through the fingernail she's biting.

"Yeah, fuck it. It's a special occasion, right?" Annie glances quickly at her ceiling, then looks for something else to focus on. She passes Sandra an empty wine glass for an ashtray.

"That's better. Okay. Tell me. All I've heard is what you left on my machine and what Ruby told me. I mean, can you believe her? Saying she dated her—they went out on *one* date—and saying Thea shouldn't have been 'sleeping around' so much!?"

"It's the classic 'blame the victim,' like she was asking for it. And this from a dyke, don't you love it? She's pathetic. Speaking of pathetic, Ricky has called me three times today. She's out of control, completely distraught. I know she never stopped loving her, but it's like this is her personal crisis now." The cat jumps on Annie's lap and she pets the cat on the head, hard, over and over in the same spot.

"She's just gotten sober, I heard. Marnie saw her at a meeting."

"I know, this brings up stuff, but I am, shit, was, her best friend. I can't handle this whole thing in the first place and then on top of it I'm supposed to deal with all her freak ex-lovers? God bless her, but we both know she picked fucking weirdos. And I know everyone's in shock and freaking out, but shit—" Annie looks at the ceiling again, looks down at the cat, resumes petting.

"This must be really hard on you. Is it really weird being in the building?"

"Yes, it's really fucking weird. I can't think of anything else. I know it's irrational, but I keep thinking what if there's something I could've done, what if I had been home that night, maybe I would've heard something, been able to call the cops, something. I keep seeing her body, the way her Mom told me about, upstairs, the walls . . . I haven't slept here since it happened. I can't. I just don't feel safe in the apartment now." Annie fills her second glass of wine.

"What did they tell you about how it happened? I mean, you don't have to tell me if you don't want, but I feel like I need to know, you know? Like it'll make it more real or I'll believe it or something. I don't know." Sandra alternates between smoking the cigarette and biting the same fingernail, lower and lower.

"It's sure real to me right now. Oh, and I have to show you this stuff I found in her apartment. I haven't told anyone I have it. I remembered Thea had read me this story she was working on about her and Mel. It's really intense. Just like her, all intertextual, raw. I guess I'll give it to the cops. I wanted you to see it first. I didn't want her parents to find it. You want tea or something?"

"Got any more of that?" Sandra gestures to the wine glass with her cigarette. Her other hand has finally come to rest on the arm of the couch. Bitten below the quick, her finger is bleeding. She is getting blood on the fabric, but she doesn't notice.

"Yeah, here take some of mine. So they found them because Mel called the police. That's the part I can't get over. She — her words — gained consciousness, saw Thea, all bloody, next to her, and called the cops. She says she didn't even know she was dead yet. Doesn't remember anything before that. The cops found Thea, dead — god, it's really hard to say that — and Mel, who was kinda beaten up too." Annie's eyes move in sequence: ceiling, cat, Sandra, ceiling, cat, Sandra, ceiling, cat, Sandra.

"So maybe she didn't do it."

"Mel's lying, I think. I think she beat herself up. She's psycho. I never trusted her. Thea told you those stories, didn't she?"

"About the restraining orders and the screwdriver, yeah. I'm the one she called after the first time they played, you know, when she started asking around and got all that dirt about Mel." Sandra lets out a gust of air in a moan. "It's awful to think about what she asked me then, about whether she should even think of playing with someone who had a reputation like Mel's. God, you know what I told her? I told her I thought it was just gossip and oh, god, this is so scary, I told her I thought all the stories made the whole thing kind of sexy."

"Yeah well, I believe that dirt. Mel's violent. She used to drink a lot. She smoked pot, too. Those stories about restraining orders are true. From what I've heard, she was in a couple of relationships that got pretty rough, domestic stuff where neighbors called the cops. Usually there was alcohol involved. I mean, Mel and her girlfriend were both drunk, but Mel was usually the one throwing stuff around or breaking things and threatening to beat up the girlfriend. Anyway, after the second restraining order, she decided to get clean, and that's why she left town."

Annie pauses as she glances up at the ceiling. Staring at the white above her head, she continues, "Do you think blood soaks through the floor, like movies, where the person in the apartment below the murder knows something is wrong when blood starts leaking through into their apartment? I keep thinking the blood is going to make this stain that spreads on my ceiling. I woke up last night dreaming that blood was dripping on me. They found Thea with her throat slashed, her face totally cut, bruised. And she was, ohhh . . . she was torn open. Her mom didn't tell me the details fully, but it sounds like she was really mangled. I can't even tell you how horrible it was talking to her parents last night. Her dad kept reaching for Saul, like he just needed anything to hold on to. Her Mom never stopped shaking the whole time. And I felt guilty, 'cause I never liked Mel, and I didn't ever tell Thea not to see her. Like that was my role, right? She was always telling me what to do in relationships, not the other way around."

"You really think Mel did it, then?"

"I'm positive."

(Article 57-2847, Case No.: 0459335. Found by Annie Femme in victim's apartment. Surrendered to police custody 01-08-98):

I remember the first time I met Mel.

I'd never seen him before.

I remember the orange jump suit and the smile, wanting to know all about my writing. I saw tight bun huggers covering her round ass, noticed the way her hands cradled her cock, loved her impish grin, and heard her growl as she got beaten, the bad boy. Had heard she played rugby and I could tell; as she got flogged on the St. Andrew's cross, I could see the muscles rippling in her back, flexing and getting tighter to steel herself against the blows. Her long arms shook the chain restraints, threatening to rip the bolts clear out of the ceiling. Her legs were spread open and bared down to her work boots, muscles standing out and clenched in frozen rebellion.

He followed me onto the bus.

Saw her look at me. Saw her watch me watch her. Knew she liked to be topped by queer men and that she liked to play fag and I knew none of that was me. Knew I couldn't get with her because I couldn't be the boy too. And also because all I saw when I looked at her was a gorgeous woman. But it was my arms she fell into after that scene on the cross and my lips that soothed with ice on her stinging ass.

He was looking at me. Like he knew me or something.

Next time I see her is when I take part in a hospital scene where she's the patient; I am one of the nurses. She's the naughty boy patient getting a rectal exam. She tires of the scene and we go smoke out in her car. We return to the club and start eyeing each other, weaving in and out of the dark corridors, following each other around chain link fences and glory holes. She finally pushes me against the wall and starts kissing me. Too stoned to do anything intense, she asks me if I'm interested in bottoming.

I saw him look at me as I got off the bus.

I say yes. Slapping. Biting. Choking. She lays the emphasis on, restates: heavy bottoming.

Shit, he got off the bus, too. Doesn't necessarily mean anything.

And I want to know what her definition of heavy is.

It does mean something. I look over my shoulder and he's following me. The street is empty, besides us. Drop boxes, shards of glass, mirror, discarded office furniture, and yellow caution tape from the construction going on in the empty buildings. I pick up my pace, walking faster. I start running.

Heavy, the epitome being rape scenes. Chase you around, she says, making me run, ripping my clothes off, making it look real. She says she'll tell the monitors ahead of time not to do anything no matter what I scream unless it's my safeword. I tell her I'm scared already. She says she's hard already. Next time I see you in a setting like this, she says, it's open season.

Open season.

(Article 57-2848, Case No.: 0459335. Found by Annie Femme in victim's apartment. Surrendered to police custody 01-08-98):

May 7, 1997

Dear Mel,

Your cock and my taste for getting what I want compel me to write you two requirements and a thought.

Seems like if we are both interested, we could end up in the same place in a situation where processing and/or negotiation might be in the way. We didn't decide on a safeword. In order to simplify things, my safeword will be Safeword. If I say it once, it means slow down; if I say it twice, it means stop. In order to play the scenario we discussed, I need some indication that you recognize my safeword.

My second condition is that we play sober. I don't have a problem with drugs, and while I very much enjoyed our negotiation, I know my thinking was dulled and slowed in a way that I wouldn't be comfortable playing with in the future.

The thought is that, although it's probably obvious, I am a novice. I am thinking about starting off with a less edgy scene and building to heavier play. I'm of two minds, though, because much of the excitement of the scene we negotiated comes from not knowing you well and fucking with boundaries around comfort, trust, and control.

"She's not okay, is she?"

"No, Mel, she's dead. I know you're upset, but we need to keep talking about what happened. I shared the transcripts of our last meeting with your regular therapist. We both agree that it's crucial to your case that we get as much information as possible about your relationship with Thea. Can you do that? Good. How did it start?"

"We saw each other at parties. I always thought she was cute, we'd flirt, but I was always there with someone else. I loved talking to her about her writing; she'd get so excited about it. One time we were both at some S/M party, watching an intense scene, and she started telling me about her thesis. She was so great. We would talk about stories she was writing. We negotiated a scene once, and she called me to talk about doing it, but I was in the middle of a breakup, so I didn't call her back for a while."

"How did you reconnect?"

"I called her out of the blue one time when I was in the city. I apologized for not calling for so long, explained why I hadn't called, and then asked if we could hang out some time. Our first date was really hot. We went to dinner at some Thai place. We both kept smiling, the buildup had been going on for over a year at this point. We both just wanted to go home and fuck."

"So things were good?"

"Yeah. We were in the same place. She didn't push my buttons like some of my other girls have, so it was mellow. We both wanted to play around. She definitely brought out my top."

"How did she do that?"

"What she wanted made me hot — piercing, edge play, choking. And she was bratty, a challenge. She'd crack up at the weirdest moments when I was trying to be serious. I think I surprised her."

"How?"

"I never got pissed when she didn't stay in the scene. I would set everything up, turn down the lights, light candles, wouldn't smile. I think I was the first person she ever played with who really got into setting a scene. One time I finished piercing all around her nipples and had spread her legs to pierce those tendons right on the side of your pussy. It's a form of restraint, the person can't move once you've stuck the needles in or else they poke themselves. And she started laughing. I think she thought that I would stop or get pissed or something. So she was surprised, impressed maybe, too."

"Tell me some more about your scenes."

"I don't know. I guess I always topped. We didn't even end up playing that much. We talked a lot about a scene we both wanted. This is where I'm going to get myself in trouble."

"Trouble, how?"

"We wanted to play rough. We wanted to play with Evan."

"Evan. Who's Evan? Does Dr. Kathy know about Evan?"

"Yeah. He's the rough one, plays real nasty."

"What does nasty mean?"

"Evan scares people. He can't help it. He likes it."

"How does he scare people?"

"Well, one time he and Thea played and he knocked her around and she liked it."

"She liked it?"

"She said 'no,' but she liked it. She'd asked for it and agreed to it."

"Mel, was this real or was this play?"

"This was play. Thea was with me because she wanted to do some edgier play."

"Why would someone want to do edgier play?"

"Thea was a very typical Capricorn. Capricorns are stable, in control at all times, or at least think they are; creative but restrained, practical. She wanted someone to shake her out of it, out of that feeling of always being in control. Taken down, that's what she called it, she wanted someone to take her down."

"And that was a turn-on for you?"

"Hell, yeah. I hate feeling like people are scared of me. I like when people want to take chances. Not real chances, nothing bad would happen, but when people want to go somewhere, push the boundaries of supposed safety."

"And that's where Evan comes in?"

"Yeah. Evan pushes the boundaries of what feels safe, what's real and what's play. He doesn't come out and play often, though. Not many people understand him. They're scared of him, especially girls."

"Would Evan hurt someone who didn't want to be hurt?"

"No. He would never do that. Sometimes I'm scared he could, but he never would do it. It's just that sometimes he believes other people when they think he is dangerous."

"What were Evan and Thea going to do?"

"Evan was going to follow Thea home one night, do a push-in robbery kind of move, and rape her. He was going to wear a mask, force himself on her after a struggle. Thea was going to struggle, fight. It was going to seem real except it would be quiet, we didn't want neighbors calling the cops."

"So you discussed all this with Thea beforehand?"

"Yeah, we'd been talking about it every time we saw each other."

"What night was this so-called rape supposed to take place?"

"January fifth."

"Can you remember anything about that night? Did things go according to plan? When did things go wrong? Can you remember opening the door? Arriving? Getting in? Anything like that?"

"No . . . nothing after walking to her house, getting to her door. Nothing. Until after."

"Mel, is it possible, completely by accident, that things could get out of control and maybe Evan could hurt someone badly, maybe even kill someone, by mistake?"

"No, I don't know. Is she really not okay?"

Thea Hillman's writing has included *Nuts and Chews*, a chapbook of poems and stories, and short fiction in the first *Noirotica* and numerous other anthologies. She holds an MFA in writing from Mills College.

A Walk in the Rain on the Wild Side

by O'Neil De Noux

Judy was plenty scared. Two seedy-looking men leered at her legs as they sat across the aisle of the narrow streetcar. She looked up at the only other person on the car, the driver, and tugged nervously at the hem of her tight silver minidress. The driver was too busy driving through a tropical New Orleans rainstorm to notice anything else on the streetcar at one in the morning.

Judy told herself to calm down. This was what she'd planned when she climbed into the shortest dress she owned earlier that evening. Checking herself in her full-length mirror, as she built up confidence to leave her house dressed like that, she felt excited. The slightest bend at the waist gave a clear view of her thin white panties. Her dress was so short, she had to pull her black thigh-high stockings all the way up to her ass, to keep the top of the hose from being seen when she walked.

Finishing her make-up, Judy had rolled dark red lipstick over her lips and took a look again in the full-length mirror. She'd run her hands down her hips to straighten her dress and turned. Not bad, she thought. At thirty-two, she still had a good figure and damn nice legs. She just wished she could tan, so her skin wouldn't look so — white. She ran a final brush through her long brown hair and slipped her Smith and Wesson .38 snub-nosed revolver into her purse. After a third glass of wine, she decided to go braless.

Judy squirmed in her seat and realized it wasn't fear that made it difficult for her to breathe now — it was her dress. Her dress was *shrinking*. She should have known better. Everyone knows, never wear crêpe in the rain. It shrinks.

It hadn't been raining when she walked over to Carrollton Avenue to catch the streetcar. She'd immediately flashed a well-dressed man with green eyes when she sat across from him. She felt a blush cross her face as she crossed and uncrossed her legs, watching him stare at her legs every time she uncrossed them. She told herself this was all part of the plan. She felt him looking up her dress, and liked it. The wine helped.

Getting out on Canal Street to wait for the return trip, she didn't notice the clouds overhead. The rain caught her just before the streetcar arrived. It was a typical, late summer rainstorm that came down in torrents. It ruined her hair and drenched her dress. Stunned, Judy climbed aboard the streetcar.

Sitting on one of the bench seats that faced the aisle, near the rear of the streetcar, she wiped the water from her face and arms. It was then she felt someone staring at her. She watched two young men move directly across the aisle from her. The black one was tall and wore a wild African shirt. The other, a ruddy-looking man with a reddish face, looked like a Portuguese pirate. They stared directly at her legs. She crossed her legs immediately. The way she'd been sitting had given them more than a good view up her short dress. She felt a flush on her face again. These were the type of men she was looking for, but hadn't expected them so suddenly, nor they way they were looking at her — as if she was dinner. She stole glances at them as she wiped the rain from her arms. Pulling her purse close, she was soothed by the weight of her .38.

Younger than Judy, the black man looked to be in pretty good shape, with bulging biceps. His companion, also in great shape, was about Judy's age and wore a gray T-shirt and torn jeans. His complexion looked as if he'd spent years under the hot Louisiana sun or on the deck of a tramp steamer. Judy felt nervous as they ogled her legs, and fought to calm herself.

The streetcar slowed as the rain increased, slamming against the side windows in sheets. Judy struggled with her dress; it was getting tighter around her waist by the second. Tugging at the dress did little good. She looked down; it looked as if it had been painted on. The tops of her stockings were completely exposed. The dress pressed so tightly around her breasts, it hid nothing.

Judy looked up at her two spectators and saw that they had noticed her dress was shrinking. Judy had to uncross her legs to pull her dress down as much as she could; but even holding it down failed to cover her panties now. Looking at the two men, seeing them staring at her crotch gave her another flush. Excited and frightened at the same time, it was a rush, sexy and dangerous. She felt her heart beating. She looked out at the rain, feeling the cool damp air through the cracked window while the men stared between her legs, her dress shrinking by the second.

Then the streetcar stopped. The driver called back to them. "There's some cars blocking the tracks 'cause of the flooding. I'll be right back." He bolted out the door before Judy could say anything.

The rain slammed against the streetcar. Outside, St. Charles Avenue was flooded.

The dress was so tight around her chest, it was cutting off her breath now. It must have been on her face, because the black man said, "Say lady, that dress is shrinking you to death."

"It's crêpe," she answered nervously, then deepened her voice immediately. "It shrinks when it gets wet."

He leered at her crotch. Judy looked down and saw that her dress was half way up the front of her panties.

"How do you wash it?" The man asked.

"Huh? Oh, I have to send it to the cleaners."

"Oh."

Both men grinned.

It was then the black man said, "My cousin lives right over there." He pointed to a two-story wooden house down Euterpe Street. Euterpe? That was the very street she'd planned to get off at and walk down in her daring dress, to find someone, anyone that would talk along the block between St. Charles and Prytania.

The wind howled loudly and shook the streetcar.

"Look, y'all," he said, "I ain't staying on this streetcar. Y'all better come with me to my cousin's. I think there's a tornado out there."

At that moment, a gust of wind slammed against the streetcar, rocking it so hard Judy almost fell out of her seat. The man reached over and grabbed her arm. Then he pulled his hand away quickly and said, "I'm sorry. I didn't mean to touch you."

Judy watched him move to the open front door and step out. Standing now, Judy realized her dress had crawled halfway up her ass. The thought of being left alone on the streetcar was scary enough — but she wasn't alone. The pirate was still there. She looked back and saw his dark eyes staring at the her rear end. Composing herself, she moved forward and looked out at the darkness of Euterpe Street. The man stood out in the rain, in knee-high water, his hands in the pockets of his jeans as he looked back at Judy.

She gulped and told herself this was where she was supposed to get off. If he had a cousin who lived on Euterpe, then she was half finished with her mission.

Overhead a lightning bolt flashed, followed by a roll of thunder so loud Judy jumped and followed her movement right out of the streetcar, right for the black man. With her heart pounding, she followed him down Euterpe Street. She lost both high heels and was completely drenched by the time they made it to the back porch of a three-story wooden tenement. Pausing to wipe themselves off, the man told her his name was Donnie. Judy told him her name was Marsha. From below, she heard a voice call out.

"I'm Sam!" It was the pirate. He'd followed. Shielding his face with his hands, he said in a heavy accent, "Can I come up on the porch too?"

Donnie told him to get up before he drowned. Then Donnie quickly excused himself and went up a flight of stairs. Judy heard him moving on the wooden stairs above, then heard him coming down.

"Damn, he ain't home."

Judy couldn't breath anymore. She wanted to just ask him the question, but felt herself going lightheaded. She had to unzip her dress. Tucking her purse under her left arm, she reached back and tried unzipping the dress with her right hand. Her purse fell. She bent over and grabbed it. Standing, she felt faint.

She struggled with her zipper again and managed to get it down a couple inches but then it stuck, so she asked Donnie to help. He moved around and tried, but only managed to get it down another inch. Judy wiggled and looked up at the bright porch light they stood under. The men would get a good view in about a minute. She had to get out of that dress, braless or not.

"Let me," Sam said.

Donnie stepped out of the way and Judy felt Sam's strong hands on her zipper. After a few seconds of struggling, he said, "I'm trying not to rip this, but–"

"Rip it," she told him. "I can't wear it again."

She felt Sam's knuckles now, digging against her back as he ripped the dress completely off. Instinctively Judy put her arms over her breasts. Donnie, who as standing in front of her, got a good look before she covered them. He looked up at Judy's face and smiled .

"What do I do with it?" Sam said, holding up the ruined silver dress.

Judy grabbed it and threw it off the porch into the rain.

Donnie removed his shirt and threw it out in the rain too. So did Sam. Before long, they were all standing in their drawers. Judy pulled her hair out of her eyes and watched the men stare at her breasts. Her nipples were erect as she stood there, half-naked with the two strangers.

Turning to Donnie, Judy said, "I could have used your shirt."

"Want I should go get it?"

It was lying in mud, so she told him no. The rain seemed to increase. Aided by the wind, it blew in on them in waves. They edged to the wall of the building. Donnie, always the leader, had another idea. He told them to wait a second and then went back up the stairs. He scrambled down a moment later.

"Come on," Donnie said, "we can get out of the rain."

He led them upstairs and around the side of the building and pointed to a high window. "It's vacant. I just climbed up there." He held his hands together to give Sam a boost. Judy was next and a moment later, found herself tumbling into Sam's eager arms. His hands conveniently ran across her breasts and caressed her ass momentarily.

Judy tucked her purse against her breasts and pulled away. Donnie climbed in a second later. She looked around the room and saw that they were in a empty apartment, illuminated only by the bright street lights streaming through the windows.

"I thought your cousin lived here," she said.

"He lives in the next apartment. This one's vacant." Moving next to her Donnie added, "You're bleeding."

Looking down at her panties, Judy saw a dark stain of black grease along the rear of her panties. Away from the light, it looked like blood. It looked gross.

"Take it off," Sam said, as he pulled his drawers off and threw them across the empty room. Donnie followed suit.

Looking into Donnie's eyes, Judy heard herself say, "Just don't hurt me."

Donnie's large brown eyes widened as he spread his arms and said, "Lady. Nobody wants to *hurt* you. That's for sure."

Turning her back to them, Judy pulled off both stockings and used them to try to wipe the grease from her panties and rear end. She only succeeded in spreading it. So she sucked in a deep breath and slipped out of her panties and used them to wipe the remainder of the grease from her ass. Then she threw the panties and stockings across the room, too, and stood there stark naked with two strange men, in the middle of a storm, in the middle of an empty room, in the middle of a night that was anything but empty.

Craning her neck around slowly, she saw them standing in the window light, their bodies glistening from the rain. She saw the erection between Sam's legs as he stared at her naked ass. Donnie, wiping the rain from his arms, was completely erect. He had a long, thin dick that stood straight up.

Judy felt a weakness in her legs as she stood there. Her stomach bottomed out. Looking down at the floor, she saw that it was fairly clean, at least by the window. So she moved to the wall, put her purse down and sat, pressing her purse against the wall. She pulled her legs up against her chest and waited, her chest rising with each breath. After a moment, Judy leaned her head to one side and began to wring the water from her long hair.

Without a word, Donnie moved up, took her hair and wrung it out, gently. Sam moved on the other side of Judy and sat cross-legged, his dick sitting up stiff between his legs. When Donnie finished with her hair he sat next to Judy, also cross-legged. In the ensuing silence, Judy looked at Donnie and then at Sam and watched the two men examine her. Slowly, Judy let her knees down and leaned back against the wall, her arms falling to her side. She crossed her legs and closed her eyes and felt their gaze tracing their way up and down her body. Slowly she moved until she sat cross-legged between them.

Opening her eyes, Judy saw Donnie on his knees, leaning close and staring at her face. Hesitating, he leaned closer and moved his large lips toward hers. She felt her heart thundering in her ears. He parted his lips slightly and leaned even closer. Judy felt her head turn one side and they kissed. Donnie kissed her ever so softly at first. She felt his tongue probing hers as the kiss became more intense. Judy frenched him back long and hard and felt his fingers on her breasts.

Donnie pulled her away from the window, lying her down, just beneath the window. Kissing his way down her neck, he kissed each of her breasts as his fingers found their way between her legs. Then she felt Sam's hands on her ankles as he gently moved them apart, wide, wider, until she was completely open. Donnie's fingers slipped inside the folds of her pussy.

It was unbelievable. Judy felt so many emotions as Donnie climbed on her and pressed the tip of his long dick into her. She sighed at the penetration and curled her back and almost came immediately as this lean young man began to fuck her.

"Oh!" She reached down and grabbed his ass.

Donnie pressed his tongue hard into Judy's mouth as his dick plunged into her, his balls slapping against her ass. Judy came in a rush and came again just before she felt him explode inside, felt the gush of his climax as he pounded her. He pumped a full, hot load into her and cried himself as he came. Kissing her softly again on the mouth, Donnie moved off. Judy kissed him back and felt Sam move between her legs and press his wide cock into her.

Sam fucked her long and hard and came in spurts. Moving off, he curled up next to Judy and said, "Man, you are a beautiful."

She smelled their semen mixed in with her pussy-juice, smelled their sweat on her chest as they lay there catching their breaths.

When Donnie was ready again, he asked her to stand up and put her hands on the window sill. Spreading her feet wide, he moved behind Judy and sank his dick into her doggie-style. His hands on her hips, he rocked against her and rode her, moaning and grunting as he jammed her. Judy could hear the sloshing sound of his dick moving in and out as he fucked her again.

Rubbing his hands over her ass, he gasped, "White girl, you got one great pussy."

Sam moved beneath Judy and began sucking her nipples as Donnie fucked her. She didn't think her legs would hold out until Donnie came again. But she held up and he came once more.

Then Sam pulled her down and mounted her and screwed her again. He rode her a long time, kissing her neck and mouth and breasts, working his large dick in her until she came again. When he came, he cried out something in Spanish.

Judy watched both men lying on their backs after, their dicks flaccid and spent. She watched their breathing decrease. But — she was still hot. Moving over Donnie, she pulled her hair back with her left hand and took his dick in her right hand and kissed it and licked it and sucked it until it was up again. Then she climbed on it and rode him to another spurting climax. Then she did the same with Sam.

Curling between the men, she felt Sam when he rose and climbed out of the window and left. Much later, with the rain subsiding, Donnie told her he lived a couple buildings down. Judy picked up her purse and asked the question as casually as possible.

"I know a guy who lives on Euterpe. Jimmy Walker."

"Yeah? He used to live in my building, just downstairs." Donnie's brow was furrowed now. "Jimmy's bad news. How you know him?"

Judy pressed herself against Donnie and french-kissed him again.

"That's my secret," she said.

"Well, he stays on Prytania now. Atop that food store painted green and yellow. But he's bad news, lady."

Donnie took Judy's hand and led her, naked, into the night to his apartment. Judy felt so naughty and sexy walking naked in the light rain, right on the sidewalk of Euterpe Street. Just before turning to Donnie's tenement, two men sitting on a porch across the street whistled and Donnie waved to them.

After a hot shower, they went to sleep in Donnie's bed.

The next morning, Judy awoke with Donnie's big dick pressed against her stomach. Donnie was awake and looking at her. He rolled Judy on her back, climbed on her again and gave her another good long fuck.

Later, he gave her a pair of shorts and a T-shirt after and led her down to his beat up T-bird. Passing around the corner, on streets still wet, Donnie pointed to a wooden building painted green and yellow and said, "That's where Jimmy stays now. But he's bad news, lady."

She made note of the address. She had him let her out on Carrollton. As she started to climb out, Donnie reached over and fondled her breasts once again. She walked home after he pulled away. Going straight for the telephone, Judy called Homicide and waited on the line for the lieutenant.

"Lou, this is Judy Wilson. Third District Patrol. I have Jimmy Walker's address."

"You do?"

She gave the lieutenant Jimmy's address.

"Good work. I'll let you know if we get him."

Judy took another long shower and climbed naked on her bed. She lay there with closed eyes and remembered the excitement, the feeling of getting gang-banged by two strangers.

She must have fallen asleep; the phone woke her. It was Homicide.

"We got him," the lieutenant said. "I don't know how you found him, but that was good work, officer."

"Thanks," Judy said, hanging up and feeling so good that they'd finally caught that no-good, rotten cop-killer Jimmy Walker. Closing her eyes again, she thought about that, about how she had found Walker when no one else could.

Then she thought about what she'd done and her breathing increased as she lay on her back on her bed. Her eyes snapped open. She felt hot again, very hot. She replayed her walk on the wild side, replayed every scintillating moment. And it felt delicious.

A former homicide detective, **O'Neil De Noux** writes realistic police novels and stories. His latest novel, *The Big Show*, has been lauded for its riveting portrayal of police work. His short story collection, *LaStanza: New Orleans Police Stories* was released in 1999 from Pontalba Press. Mr. De Noux is currently working on a book chronicling his exploits as an undercover bra fitter for Interpol and the Sureté.

Some New Kind of Kick

by Clint Catalyst

The X begins to hit me, tingle in my groin, inner thighs.

Ten after eleven and I'm leaning against the sheetrock of my usual Saturday night spot, the right-hand wall of Lillith's dancefloor. Silhouettes of dark figures sway in the fog of the room, the features of nearby dancers discernible in the faint red overhead lights.

The club's actually attractive tonight. Reminds me of the way it seemed when I started coming here around a year back, the excitement I got from observing impeccably dressed people before I could predict their outfits, the rush I got from listening to mysterious music before it became routine. As the bass of "Love's Secret Domain" by Coil vibrates the room's foundation, seeps into my skin as if it were liquid static, this place seems new to me again. Magic.

And big fucking deal if it's drug induced. Jeffrey gave me the hit over a month ago, but I didn't take it 'til tonight, didn't resort to chemical happiness 'til I got bummed-out because Sean flaked on plans to go out with me around half an hour beyond the last possible minute. Responded to my two reminder messages with an abrupt "Can't make it," no explanation given, no chance for me to question, his hangup chopping off the second syllable of a generic "later." I'd actually looked forward to seeing him. Must be a payback for something.

Whatever. I'd already gotten dressed, which is why I ended up here anyway, date or no date. Wouldn't want to waste a complete outfit, even if I'm basically bored with the scene at Lillith's. Wouldn't want to waste a dose of X, especially if it could make the old dive *interesting*.

I close my eyes and feel the touch of light to my eyelids, the caress of cigarette smoke to my cheeks. Ah, I could really get into a cigarette. Even better, a clove. I can tell this is good X, because I never crave cigarettes, don't even like to be near them. And Sean said the batch of X circulating now is bunk! *Damn*, was he wrong. I feel myself sifting into the wall, the back of my knees and shoulder blades turning to warm water.

Open eyes and there's a sea of phosphorescent splotches, glowing whitepainted faces, dark make-up around the eyes. Now the club is full of its regulars, dance floor packed with night's creatures, people lined up on either side of me. The room has come alive in no time, and I'm drenched in its electric energy, eager for something to happen. Ready to walk away from the wall and the chubby punk girl on my left who's sloshing beer with loud gulps. Ready for excitement, adventure like I used to have, instead of the ennui my life has become. Ready for some new kind of kick.

"Skin and Lye" by Malign starts up, Xavier's voice full of fury, voice growling and screeching over ominous background music. The crowd on the floor dances slowly, writhing, sending ripples of movement into the audience gathered around them, tendrils of smoke twisting around safety-pinned jackets and teased hair.

I breathe in smells of leather and hair spray and cigarette smoke, a long slow breath, their scent filling my nostrils, settling on the back of my tongue. I smack my lips. The X has hit me full-force, and I am on fire.

I see two figures standing out from the others, standing out from old friends of mine, fucks, whatever. Two figures draped in velvety black material, hooded cloaks framing their delicate features, fragile-boned faces. Strands of raven hair spill 'round the edges of their slate-colored skin.

I can't tell if they're male or female or both or neither, but they're pressed close together, leaning against each other, shoulder to shoulder. Siamese twins with the exact same build, except that one stands a couple of inches taller than the other.

Who are they? I've never seen them before, but they're too perfect to be real, too lucid to be a dream. Somebody *new* ! New, completely new and free of the "Oh, you'll have to meet so-and-so" shit that usually causes me to have numerous preconceptions.

Brow moist with sweat. My skin hot, alive. They're staring at me seductively, dusky eyes brazenly glowing, and I feel my blood rush. They're devouring me with their eyes.

I'm dying to speak with them, introduce myself, but I have no idea where to begin. Must be the drugs. They're beautiful, completely androgynous and alluring. How could I resist the opportunity to speak with a couple of people to whom it's obvious they can have anyone they want? It's been so long, so dreadfully long.

Dead Can Dance's "How Fortunate the Man with None" begins, and I feel Brendan Perry's smooth voice cover my limbs with a blanket of tingling sensations. The X is hitting me so hard, I'm on the verge of either exploding like a grenade or passing out. My eyelids flutter, the image of the duo blurry, the clusters of people in the room bleeding together into a smudge, like watercolors painted on a paper towel. I'm being reduced to the sway of the music.

"Hi." I hear a voice within earshot, and I open my eyes wide, focus. "I'm Byron."

I feel something twist inside my stomach. Now the erotic duo is directly in front of me, close enough to touch, the taller of the two extending a slender hand. *Byron.* So he's male. I place my palm within his, grasp it. Shudder at its warmth as he politely pulls it away.

"And I'm Gitane," a second voice adds, offers a hand of her own. My palm meets hers, rests against smooth skin. *Gitane.* A female. I examine her chest area as she retracts her hand, but none of her body shows through the material.

I study their faces, compare the similarities between their meticulously arched eyebrows, deep chocolate eyes, prominent cheekbones, well-formed noses, raspberry-stained lips. It's remarkable how closely they resemble one another, each a mirror image of the other's striking elegance.

It's impossible for me to speak, impossible for me to look away. The whole club has been shut out, and nothing but this sensual feast exists, my heart racing as I'm devoured by their ethereal presence and the refrain.

Byron and Gitane are statuesque, patiently await my response.

"How Fortunate the Man with None" crescendos, peaks with lavish strings and horns. Byron leans forward, centers his cool ivory face before mine, wraps his hand around my upper arm.

"With us," he says, face expressionless as he tightens his grip. "Now."

He positions himself between the punk girl and me, twists my arm like a slab of taffy as he scrapes me off the wall and slides behind me. Shoves my left hand up my spine, stops when my knuckles press between my collarbones. Steps forward, overtakes my balance, shoves me chest-first toward Gitane.

I stumble, feet sweeping the floor as he steps again, pushes me past Gitane, steps again, again. He weaves me through the mass of people standing around the dance floor, strands of their sticky hair brushing my forehead and cheeks, their sweat and perfumes stinging my eyes, dripping bitter taste between my lips as I try to cry for help. The weaving stops when we make it to a cluster of goths and cyberpunks blocking the doorway marked with a flickering "HEAD" sign in blue neon letters. There's a split-second pause; then he uses my upper torso to part the crowd, their shoulders and metal jacket adornments smashing against my ribs, shouts of "Asshole!" and "What the fuck?" following as he pushes me through the bathroom entrance.

The room is washed with dull yellow light. I feel my face squint in disgust, the stench of piss and lemon air freshener filling my nostrils as I'm led toward the urinals. Byron moves up to the left side of me and reduces his grip on my arm, frees it from its locked position. It drops, dangles. Gitane files in on my right, the two of them leading our dance across the slippery tiles, the floor slick with toilet water and spilled beer. We slide past an empty stall with its door open, a closed door, a closed door, an open-doored stall with a leatherman hunched forward taking a piss. Then we make it to the last stall, where a generic-looking guy with a brown buzz-cut is exiting. Gitane steps behind me, allows room for him to get around us. He does a double-take.

My feet slip as I'm shoved into the stall, but Gitane and Byron hold me up, prevent me from busting my ass on the floor. Byron slams the cubicle door shut, the sound of metal against metal echoing ominously. It fades, and muffled reverberations of Siouxsie and the Banshees' "Spellbound" remain.

Siouxsie's eerie voice still entrances me after all these years, voice rich with enchantment and disheartening splendor.

A flurry of hands unfasten my pants and tug them open, the air cool on my bare ass. Natural instinct overpowers drug euphoria, and I reach down to cover myself, suddenly aware what's happening.

"No!" Byron shoves me onto the toilet, my ass-cheeks slapping the porcelain seat.

"But I ... but I–" I hear myself speak, but my words are high-pitched and pleading, sound foreign.

"But you *what*?" He grabs the bottom seam of my shirt and rips it to the collar with a single flick of the wrist, tatters the velvet into two pieces.

"I'll use you as much as I want, day or night, for as long as I want." He tears the remainder of the shirt off me, tosses it onto the floor, whacks me across the ear. A lightning bolt of pain cracks into my temples.

Oh, my God, what have I gotten myself into? I look up at the two sets of eyes glaring at me and see a faint reflection of myself repeated across the four murky orbs, my pants wadded around the knees, private parts exposed, chest patterned with the fresh splotches of red and purple across it. I'm embarrassed at what I see, how I feel, vulnerable and afraid.

Byron leans forward and tenderly kisses me on the shoulder, his lips warm and smooth as liquid, hood tickling my jawline. "But you'll love it," he whispers against my neck, his voice deep and comforting.

I watch Gitane watch him lick a trail to my ear and flirtatiously flick the lobe, and I'm filled with a strange sensation of pleasure, a combination of submission and dominance and exhibitionism unlike anything I've experienced. Byron's hand moves up my thigh, and I'm scared, excited, my cock starting to rise.

Gitane unbuttons the neck of Byron's cloak and removes it from him, exposing the tight white skin underneath. She drapes it over the side of the stall and he moans into my ear, his hair tumbling down my back, his voice passionate as the sound of rustling velvet.

Gitane pulls at the neck of her own cloak and extracts it, exposing her small frame squeezed into black satin bustier. A boy who looks maybe 18 or 19 — must have borrowed the I.D. of an older brother or friend — opens the stall door halfway, tries to enter. The door bumps Gitane's back as she situates her cloak beside Byron's. She turns, notices his innocent face and laughs, her lips a violent red smile.

"Whoops! Guess we forgot to lock it," she says.

Boy takes a half-step back, blue eyes wide, disconcerted. Byron moves from me, pulls the door the rest of the way open. Grabs the boy by his shoulder, holds him in place.

"Well, hello," he says. "Watch."

Eyebrows raise in disbelief.

"Huh?"

Byron spreads my legs apart with his knees, pushes each to either wall of the stall. The metal partitions are cold. I flinch. Gitane pulls my head back by the hair above my neck, laughs again. My lips part and release a soft moan of embarrassment. She leans forward, positions hers around them and pulls back, strings of saliva snapping between us. They fall around my cockhead, cling to it as if it were a may-pole.

"I said *watch*."

Byron keeps one hand on the boy's shoulder, digs his fingertips into the flesh around the collarbone, extends his other arm to reach the half-hard bulge between my legs. He circles the head with index finger, smoothes the spit into a ring. Spreads it down my cock. Forms a fist around it, pushes down. Pulls up. Pushes down.

"He likes this very much, see?" He says, third person, detached. Sneers with the crinkles 'round his eyes. "See the way his whole body moves with the rhythm of my hand?"

The boy doesn't answer, also doesn't look away. Stands there in a stupor of fear and awe. He looks vaguely familiar to me, though I don't know why. Stares at me with iceblue eyes, looks down at my dick, now fully erect. The excitement in his face crackles, pops like baconfat.

Hand continues moving up and down my dick. I shut my eyes, moan.

Gitane scoops a breast out of her bustier, pushes two fingers between my lips, pries my mouth open, inserts nipple. I stroke it with my tongue, lap the saltysweet taste of her skin.

Open my eyes. She and Byron are violently kissing, lips pressed together, jaws in motion. Byron's eyes are also open. One of his hands still holds the boy in place, the other pumps my dick. He watches us, stops kissing her, smiles at me, takes his hand from my bulge. It bounces, rebounds from his touch. Throbs.

Slowly, delicately, he pushes away from me. Tugs on my bangs, forces my head upright. He unzips his tight pants and his cock falls out on its own, half-erect. Fingers run through my hair, Gitane's, Byron's. Pulls me closer. His dick is directly before me, its head large and light red.

"Come on," he says, his voice stern. "Suck it."

Split-second longer with cock before my face; then it disappears between my lips, into my mouth. Eyes close habitually. I take it all the way to the base, my nose buried in dark tuft of hair, his musky scent filling my nostrils.

"Yeah," he moans. "That's good."

And it is good. I love the way he feels in my mouth, the energy of his dick throbbing as he slides it against my tongue. Pulls himself out to the head. Pushes to the back of my throat.

I move my left hand between Gitane's silky thighs, nudge the strip of material covering her sex. Her clit is hard and slick. I rub my fingers against it, smear her wetness. Rub it harder, faster. Feel her thigh muscles tighten around my hand, her hips jerk.

I touch myself with my right hand, cock throbbing and burning. Thrust my forefinger deep into Gitane's wetness. Move my tongue against Byron's cock so slow it's barely moving.

Samples of bubbling water, hollow drumbeats, an angelic voice. Ambient dreamscapes seep into the stall, accelerate our sensual energy.

Byron shudders, starts pumping furiously. Almost too much for me to handle. Tears form in my eyes as his dickhead bangs against the back of my throat, balls slap my chin. My lips make sloppy smacking noises against the base of his cock, and a small retching sound escapes from the back of my throat. I desperately gasp for air, but I love it.

He loves it, too. "Oh, yeah," he says through clenched teeth. "Keep fuckin' blowing me. Suck me off, you little slut."

His deep voice intensifies my excitement. I stuff three fingers in Gitane, her inner lips hot and luscious. My dick drools, and I tighten my grip, pound in rhythm. Pound furiously.

I squeeze my tongue around his cock and look up, watch the muscles in his stomach tighten. Watch him groan as Gitane plays with his nipples. He thrusts his hips forward, greased cock rapidly gliding in and out of my mouth as he leans against the boy, cradles his arm around his neck.

The boy's eyes meet mine and a sharp rush of panic shoots through my chest. *Oh, my God. Those eyes. I know those eyes.* Reminders of that glossy blue, that soft face, that scraggly bleach-blond hair, the small silver hoop earring, swim from the depths of my memory, the inner recesses of my mind. *But it can't be, just can't be, they can't be.* My consciousness swirls.

I pull my hand from Gitane and long ribbons of wetness stretch down her slender legs, spill onto mine. Byron continues thrusting himself into my mouth with an increasing sense of urgency, groaning desperately, arm locked tight around the neck of the boy, standing solemnly, staring. *Those eyes. Those eyes.* Those eyes freeze my lips with a chill of horror, the edges of my teeth scraping Byron's skin as he gives himself a final shove in my mouth.

He pulls out and comes with an idle rush, sperm cascading from his cockhead and sticking onto my face and neck like ornaments, like quivering jewels. His discharge reeks of salt and soured milk. The small puddles collapse under their own weight and shimmy down my shoulder blades, my stomach, my shriveled cock, in thin pasty trails.

There's a trace of gummed-up whiteness in my eyelashes, but I don't move to wipe it away, don't move whatsoever. The boy's lips unfold in a soft gesture that could be shock or disgust or pity, and it's astounding how much I know him, remember him.

Byron examines his midsection, yawns, flicks a stray pearl off his pisshead toward me. It spatters into my right eye, crude and merciless.

An acidic stinging stifles my vision, makes me wince. I frantically knead my aching lids with the jointed edge of a fist, but slender fingers scramble around my wrist, pull my arm away. Within seconds, the fingers find their way to my face and calmly move back and forth on both eyelids, producing tears that wash the stinging away. The fingers then move to my forehead, my cheeks, and sweep off small lumpy bits, smooth my skin to dry stickiness.

I blink until the blurry orb I see transforms into the boy. It's the sandy-haired teenager who's comforting me, caring for me with his gentle touch, leaning forward into my muddled space, his azure eyes sparkling and curious.

He smells of soap. I realize he's moving towards me.

He presses his lips to mine and gives me a rough kiss, a kiss of inexperience, tongue darting around in my mouth, scraping against the rawness in my throat. The kiss is uncomfortable and long. His tastebuds feel like dry gravel as he pushes his tongue farther into me, wiggles it. It's as if he's trying to reach all the way to my heart, yearns to lick my soul.

I clumsily wrestle with him, attempt to bulldoze his tongue back to its home, when suddenly it hits me: I taste myself in his mouth. I twist my tongue around his, taste the sweet nectar of summertime at my grandparents, taste the excitement I felt sneaking out of the house to smoke pot with my best friend, taste the swarm of adrenaline I had when I lost my virginity. I taste the richness of memories, and I want to tumble into them, wallow in their splendor.

The boy breaks our embrace, backs away from me with a grimace, leaves me panting, my torso quivering. Gitane and Byron have clothed themselves, and he clings to them, glares at me with glittery eyes.

My stomach grumbles. I'm hungry for that taste I found, crave it the way a dieter does chocolate. I know I can't have it; I know the boy tore himself from me because of the bitterness he discovered back in my spongy cave of a mouth, a bitterness toward life and humanity that tastes like poison to a boy whose innocence remains unmarred, whose romantic ideals still seem plausible.

The frantic way he clutches Gitane and Byron, small arms sunk elbow-deep into their cloaks, tells me he's afraid my depravity will work its way into him like a virus. I'm sickened by the realization of what I am, this jaded monster I've become. But I wonder who Gitane and Byron are, why they've come to me, what they represent, what sort of lesson they're trying to teach.

Split-second and they are gone, stall deserted, door gaping wide, stained grey concrete wall replacing the line of vision where they were. I try to call after the boy, call my name, but it catches like a cinderblock in my throat. *His name, my name. He who I used to be.*

Tears blossom and flow like blood as I sit in this stall, frail and slump-shouldered, wishing I could return to the face that once was my cradle, my home.

Clint Catalyst is a Southern-fried Goth-damaged spoken word performer. After pursuing an extensive career in degeneracy, he has settled in Los Angeles, where he works as an art director/public nuisance. He has a BA With Distinction in English from Hendrix College and an MA in Writing from the University of San Francisco; in other words, he's deeply in debt to Uncle Sam. Clint's first book, *Cottonmouth Kisses*, is scheduled for release in April 2000 through Manic D Press.

The Last Words of Charlie Ballerina

by Thomas S. Roche

I knew the shit had hit the fan again when Petunia June and Little Mel Catharsis came stumbling into the Passion Flower all decked out in orange lace and sequins, respectively, carrying that pansy Frankie Ballerina all bloody and quivering between them.

Not that seeing Frank Ballerina bloody was a problem, or meant that anything at all was fucked up — in fact, it was often a sign that things were right. And if you're laughing at the pansy's name, don't. I've put Green Berets in headlocks for a whole lot less, and not because I like the guy.

Come to think of it, I shouldn't be calling Frank a pansy. I, of all people, should know better than to insult pansies so egregiously.

See, the score was this: Before Frankie's old man Charlie Ballerina checked out, he did the one thing that I never thought he would do. He gripped my strong hand in his weak one, pulled me down to his deathbed so he could whisper my ear. And said the words.

"Take care of Frankie."

Maybe I wouldn't have done it if old Charlie hadn't chosen that exact moment to issue his last breath. If the prick had lived another two seconds I would have had time to recover from the shock, the disgust, the revulsion. I would have had time to scream "Hell, no!" And maybe "Fuck off, you dago cocksucker!" for good measure.

But I hadn't. And who was I kidding? I couldn't tell Charlie B. to fuck off. And so the last words of Charlie Ballerina were those that would haunt me until the end of my goddamn life, or — preferably — until Frankie went the path his father had gone, which was going to be pretty goddamn soon if Frank kept insisting on bleeding on the floor of my club.

If I occasionally call Charlie an asshole and a scumbag and a rat-bastard, please don't think I have anything less than absolute respect for the guy. Because much as I grumble and bitch, I am not going to ignore a dying man's last request — not now, not then, not ever. And Charlie Ballerina was like a father to me.

Well, maybe more like a mother. Or an aunt. Or like a dirty, filthy, sleazy old cross-dressing uncle with a closet full of skin magazines.

"What the fuck happened?" I snapped at Little Mel.

"Don't you get cross with me, motherfucker!" Mel snapped back, her hip pointed threateningly, her arms crossed over her big tits. Her voice had more ice than the bag on Frankie's bleeding nose. She radiated feminine menace in that way that only a bisexual six-and-a-half-foot tall African-American ex-linebacker performance artist with enormous knockers and a baseball-bat dick can do. Which is to say, only Mel.

"I'm sorry," I said, putting up my hands, which were covered in Frankie's blood. Which wasn't nearly as satisfying as it sounds. "I didn't mean to be cross."

Mel growled and turned away. I shrugged.

"The prick was in Cassie's Back Door," said Petunia June. "Excuse my language. Started talking shit (excuse my language) about how he was going to take the Back Door over with your help, how you and he were going to rip all the Abba and Village People out of the juke box and put in some Frank Sinatra — real man's music, he said."

"Oh Jesus," I breathed, sinking into the chair behind the desk. "Jesus H. Motherfucker."

"Excuse your language!" said Petunia testily, ever the lady. "From what I heard, it wasn't pretty," she went on, sitting her fine, tight ass on the edge of my desk and lighting up a Virginia Slim. "The Mother Sharks were there — you know Cassie's been hiring them for protection."

"Oy vey," I groaned. As if in response, Frankie groaned, too, and shifted on the couch. He was starting to come around.

Mel had recovered from her funk. She knelt down and leaned over Frank, stroking his blood-caked hair. "Does the man with the big, ugly mouth need a blowjob?" Mel cooed, reaching down to grab Frank's crotch. Of course he was rock-hard — everyone's always figured Frank gets his rocks off by getting his ass kicked, since he does it so often.

"The Sharks busted him up but good," Petunia was saying. "Sam told me they broke his nose with a bottle of Jack and used a chain on his back, stomped his ribs pretty good. From what I heard, they would have castrated the pansy (excuse my language) if Sam and Dave hadn't dragged him away." She tossed her auburn hair and massaged her temples with the fingers of one hand. "The bad thing is, Highball Joe just told me he got a phone call from Cassie. She said the Sharks are coming over here at midnight to finish the job." She uttered a rueful laugh. "Might save everyone a lot of trouble if they do. Except they're gonna bust the place up once they're done with the pansy. Excuse my language." Petunia stretched, and the tight see-through orange lace dress she was wearing flashed a hint of her tiny white tits. She shifted against the edge of my desk and the dress inched up a bit, showing me the juicy bulge in front. Oh, what a pushover am I! A girl in a dress flashes a pair of 32As and a hard-on, talks about Frank Ballerina getting his nose broken, and immediately I'm rock-hard, even while an army of leather fags is on its way to bust up my joint.

"Sammy, Dave," I murmured, as if coming out of a haze. "Where the fuck were they while Frankie was getting his ass kicked?"

Frankie gave a loud moan. Mel got Frankie's cock out and took it smoothly down her throat, showing admirable skill. That's one thing I'll say for the pansy — he's hung like a horse.

"Mel!" I snapped. "Would you be careful with that? The pansy might have broken ribs or something!"

Mel let Frankie's cock slip out of her mouth. She held it there, jutting up hard and long, glistening with spittle and blood. Mel's lips were also slick with blood; I guess she'd kissed Frank on the lips before going down on him.

"You look here, Joey DiGiornio," said Mel. "I'll let the doctor do his magic, and you let Mel do hers. It's called *alternative medicine*."

Frankie moaned again, this time agony mixed with lush, rapturous pleasure as Mel gulped his prick again, working her own hard meat under the tight sequined dress.

"Sammy and Davie were outside, having a smoke," said Petunia, "when the shit went down. You know, that new no-smoking law."

"God damn it!" I growled angrily. "Fuckin' politicians! Health fascists!" Then, with my teeth gritted: "Go get them."

Petunia licked her lips. "Don't I get a kiss, first? You haven't seen me all day, sweet-ums."

"After I kick some dyke ass," I growled. "Go get Sam and Dave!"

Petunia just stared — not hurt, just shocked that I would talk like that to a lady.

"Look, baby, I'm sorry," I said, reaching for her with both hands. "I didn't mean it. I'm just a little pissed off right now. Of course I'll kiss you."

"Eat shit, you motherfucker," said Petunia, swirling out of my grasp and tugging her skirt down. "Excuse my language."

Sam and Dave stood in front of me sheepishly, staring at the ground. Their pinstriped slacks were rumpled and dirty, and there were spots of blood on Davie's lemon-yellow shirt. I guess they'd intervened when Frankie was in the thick of, uh, battle.

"I can't tell you how sorry we are, Boss," Sam was saying, not too convincingly. "You know how Frankie gets when he starts shooting his mouth off. I mean, it's like no one can shut him up."

"Yeah, and you figured it'd be better not to try, huh? Just let him get his ass kicked?"

Dave broke in. "Well. . . boss. . . it's not like he didn't–"

"*Don't even say it!*" I shrieked. Then, more calmly: "Look, I'm going to say it one more time, loud and clear 'cause with all that freakin' femme pussy you girls eat, I hear it's real easy to get your ears boxed by some babydyke's flappin' thighs, at least if you do it right. Izzat true?"

"Watch it, boss," growled Sammy threateningly, curling her lip in that way she has that always tells me when she's not kidding.

I grunted. "All right, well, then, listen careful." I leaned close and talked real loud, loud enough that Frankie would have been able to hear me if he hadn't been lost in a triple-X reverie. "Charlie Ballerina was like a fuckin' father to me. And on his fuckin' deathbed, he told me to take care of that *miserable piece of shit son of his!*" I could feel the veins in my temples standing out. "As distasteful as that may be to you, me, and everyone else who's ever met the guy, we're gonna fuckin' do it, understand?"

"Right, boss," said Dave, shifting uncomfortably.

Across the room, the half-conscious Frankie uttered a whimper, then a groan, then a thunderous "Oh, fuck yeah!" as he shot his load into Mel's open mouth. As Frank came, Mel drooled cum all over his belly and rubbed it over her face, lapping at it hungrily.

Mel always was a sloppy eater.

I continued on my tirade. "But that's just the start of the shitstorm tonight, you understand? Because now that Frank's insulted their taste in bad '70s dance tunes, the fuckin' Mother Sharks are on their way over to bust up the Passion Flower and finish their hack job on the pansy."

"Oh, Jesus," groaned Sammy, fumbling awkwardly for an unfiltered Black Lung. She felt in her pockets for her lighter.

"Well, gee," said Mel, smoothing the come over her lips. "Patient doing nicely, says Dr. Mel. Now I've got to go put my face on for my show at midnight."

"What the fuck are you talking about?" I blurted. "How are you going to do your show if the Mother Sharks are coming over here to burn down the fucking bar? You can't go on! The show's canceled!"

Mel's eyes were wide with surprise. She just stood there, hip pointed at me threateningly, her face glistening with semen and smeared lipstick and mascara, droplets of come running down her neck and dribbling to the floor. Only the world-famous Little Mel Catharsis could manage such extreme dignity in that kind of state.

"*Mister* DiGiornio," hissed Little Mel. "I understand that most of the girls you have performing in this second-rate sleaze joint are nothing more than hagged-out hairy-ass queens and scrawny 19-year-old trannies who like to shake their booty and get dollar bills shoved up their tight little pussy-asses. But I, Mr. DiGiornio, am an *artist*. My art is more important than a bar full of Mother Sharks or the *cojones* of the bleeding pansy who got us into this shit in the first place. My art is more important than a jukebox full of George Michael records or the Cole Porter boxed set, goddammit. The show will go on, motherfucker. So *don't fuck with me!*"

The three of us just stood there staring at Mel, amazed beyond belief.

"Tonight I am premiering *The Taste of Fuck*, remember?"

"Oh, shit. Baby, I forgot — look, there's no way–"

"Let's try again," Mel growled in that no-nonsense way she has. "Tonight I am premiering *The Taste of Fuck*, motherfucker, bikers or no bikers. Remember?"

"Oh, yeah. I remember now," I muttered after a full minute's silence.

"Besides," said Mel, turning on her heel. "That dyke professor up at the university sent a whole crowd of her students to see me tonight. There's gonna be like fifty of them. This is my first step toward tenure some day, Joey, once I finish my night classes and get that MFA, and some crowd of biker faggot sissies is *not* going to spoil it for me. And neither are you." The door slammed behind her.

I produced a death's-head Zippo and leaned over the desk, lighting Sammy's Black Lung. I took a little brown cigar out of the box on my desk and offered one to Dave. She took it, and I lit them both with the Zippo. I puffed thoughtfully.

On the couch, Frankie moaned, stroking his half-hard prick with his hand.

A light went on in my head.

"All right, boys," I said, my face twisting into a smile. "You heard the lady. The show must go on. The Mother Sharks are coming to do unspeakable things to our pansy friend Frankie Ballerina."

Sam and Dave stared.

"And we're going to give him to them."

"Huh?" they asked as one.

I shot a glance at the squirming, oblivious Frank, who was murmuring obscenities in a drunken slur. "Oh, baby," "yeah, baby," "grease it up a little, baby." What a putz.

I chuckled. "That's right," I told Sam and Dave. "We're going to solve this problem once and for all. We're going to give Frankie something to croon about. Pour me a drink, will you, Dave?"

OK, check out the scene. It goes down hard and fast, so pay attention. The Passion Flower, dark and crammed. Just like Mel painted it: tired old queens and hot little trannies floating like ghosts among the statues. Red velvet couches lining the walls, little round tables where the girls do table dances for ten bucks. For another twenty you get into the back room, with its velvet-lined cubicles with the curtains that stay open. Another fifty and you can close the curtain. Faceless, emotionless bridge and tunnel perverts: Guys with their souls on hold being led by the hand into the back room, desperate with fumbling hunger. And there inside it all, under cover of darkness: table after table after table of art students. Short-haired androgynes in little round glasses and Skinny Puppy T-shirts, modern-primitive tattoos on their necks and wrists, "Rammstein" scrawled across black leather jackets. Chicks in black turtlenecks with clunky tortoiseshell glasses — straight brown hair, short hair bleached blond, here and there a chopped-up blue or burgundy coif. Guys in tweed blazers and silk scarves carrying copies of *Faust* and *The Theater and Its Double*. Not my usual crowd. Holding court in the center of the art students: A woman with short grey hair and a pierced eyebrow that looked all inflamed. The kids all seem to have little spiral notebooks and fountain pens. I chuckle — they're going to have trouble writing things down fast enough to keep up with Little Mel Catharsis. They should have taken shorthand before tackling Performance Art 101.

It's one minute to midnight, and Sally Havana is finishing her show on Stage #2. Sally's this hot Cuban chick who used to be a Green Beret. She's the one I put in a headlock for laughing at Frankie's name. Wasn't even a laugh, really, just sort of a half-smirk. But that's another story. Anyway, Sally's got the tightest, cutest ass you ever saw — excepting Petunia, of course. I'm behind the bar, my hands in plain view but not too far from the pump-action 12-gauge just in case things go bad fast.

Burt, Killer Mike, and Pussy Face Joe are out of sight in the shadows, playing the part of three nervous suburb boys out for their first walk on the wild side, having a good time fooling around with Lulu and Samantha. They're acting drunk and horny. But I know the second shit goes down — if it does — they'll be stone cold sober and spitting fire.

Sam and Dave in the back room with Frankie. Ready for my signal.

Sally finishes up on #2, wriggling that pert little ass of hers as she slides behind the curtain. The club explodes with applause. The spotlight turns to Stage #1.

The stage has been covered in black plastic garbage bags duct-taped to the corners and layered three deep. In the middle of the stage there's an ominous-looking stainless-steel surgeon's table with a sheet over the "instruments." Next to it there's a 55-gallon oil drum with unsavory implements inside, out of view of the audience.

Just another night at the Passion Flower.

"And now," Highball Joe's voice came booming over the P.A., "Joey DiGiornio's Passion Flower is so very proud to present–"

A hush went over the crowd, especially the art students.

In the hush, I heard the roar of bikes outside.

Joe didn't miss a beat. "Our very own world-class performance artist! She's been vocalist for the punk band *Avast Ye Cocksuckers!* and first-string linebacker for the Barkertown Grizzlies! She's forever pushing the boundaries of art and life for your viewing pleasure! She'll turn you on, turn you off, she'll make you heave your Seven-and-Seven all over your date's lap! Ladies and Gentlemen, and all you people too, let's have a warm welcome for Little Mel Catharsis!"

Howls and screams and furious clapping. Mel took the stage, her stunning ebony frame clad in day-glo green rubber bra, panties and garter belt holding up hot-pink fishnet stockings. One of the art students put on his sunglasses.

The club was silent as Mel walked to the microphone. She gave Highball Joe the cue, and the music started — if you can call it music. A long, grating screech of electric-guitar feedback and nausea-inducing combination of sounds that can only be someone jumping up and down on top of a bass guitar and screaming "Mainline! Mainline!"

"I am a predator," Mel's voice boomed through the club as she whipped the sheet off the surgeon's table and produced a glimmering fistful of hypodermic needles. "I prey upon the flesh of the wicked. And none is more wicked than I! Aiiieeeeeee!"

With that bloodcurdling scream, Mel drove the first needle into her eyebrow, leaving the jutting, blood-slick point poking down near her eyeball.

"Ouch," she said matter-of-factly, her voice a seductive purr.

There were a few gasps and sick sounds from the audience. Several bridge and tunnel perverts ran for the men's room.

Mel drove more needles into her eyebrows as she moaned, "Oh, the pain is such succulent surrender! Can it be that the taste of blood is the taste of fuck? The taste of fuck? The taste of fuck fuck fuck fuck *fuck fuck FUCK FUCK FUCK FUCK!*" Mel continued on, screaming "fuck" louder each time until even the art students were covering their ears.

Then she reached back to her surgeon's table and produced a dozen eggs as the electronic wailing on the tape turned in to the sound of sobbing mixed with Mel screaming.

"THE TASTE OF FUCK! THE TASTE OF FUCK! OF FUCK! TASTE! OF FUCK!" Mel screamed louder and louder, smashing each egg violently on the top of her head so it splattered across the tables of the art students.

"Magnificent," I heard the dyke professor moan as Mel reached for more eggs. "Simply magnificent."

I guess that's when the art students decided to just *go with it.*

"THE TASTE OF FUCK! TASTE OF FUCK! OF FUCK FUCK FUCK FUCK FUCK!" Starting with egg #8, the eggshells were filled with stage blood.

I chuckled and puffed on my cigar. The evening had finally begun.

Mel was on her 16th needle and her fourth carton of eggs when the bikers busted through the front door. There were six of them, clad in head-to-toe leather — leather chaps, vests, and caps — and carrying lead pipes and baseball bats. One had a Colt .45 stuck into his belt. I recognized his face — he was Danny the Axe, number-two man for the Mother Sharks and eager to prove he was tough enough to be number one. I knew the bikers were here to do violence. But for now, all six bikers stood, staring gape-mouthed at the spectacle on the stage. Some of the art students were weeping openly.

"THE TASTE OF FUCK! THE TASTE OF FUCK!"

Mel lifted a watermelon over her head and smashed it on the floor, dancing around in the bright pink mass, kicking seeds and pulp into the audience as she screamed.

Danny the Axe tore his eyes off of Mel, with obvious difficulty. He yanked the pistol out of his belt and pointed it at me.

"We're here for your pansy brother," Danny screamed over the cacophony from the P.A. "He ratfucked our colors in Cassie's Back Door!"

"Man, that sounds serious!"

Danny growled. "Goddamn right it is, asswipe! We're gonna cut the bastard's balls off! You fuckin' try and stop us, we'll do a hack job on you, too, motherfucker!"

I nodded eagerly. "Oh, yeah, no problemo," I shouted. "Look, just get one thing straight! The guy's not my brother. And anyway you can have the little prick!"

"You motherfucker, you think you can fuck around with the Mother Sharks — huh?" Danny's eyes were wide and psychotic. But he was obviously fighting not to look at Mel, who was still screaming and smashing things and carrying on. "Pay attention, assholes!" he screamed at his men, who were enraptured by the weirdness onstage. "What did you say?"

"He's yours," I shouted. "I ain't protecting the little prick no more!"

"*THE TASTE OF FUCK! THE TASTE OF FUCK! FUCK! FUCK! FUCK! FUCK! FUCK!*" Fruit exploding everywhere.

"You're gonna give the little pansy up?" shouted Danny.

I shrugged. "Sure I will. Have him out here in a jiffy." I hit the button under the bar. On cue, Sammy and Dave came out of the back room, muscling their way through the churning crowd with a squirming and screaming Frankie Ballerina.

"No!" Frankie was screaming. "Those biker faggots'll fuckin' kill me!"

"Sorry, Frankie," I shouted. "I gotta give you up!"

"*THE TASTE OF FUCK! OF FUCK! FUCK!*"

The crowd was going wild. Horror and revulsion mixed with awe and rapture. People were standing up and screaming as Mel threw eggs into the audience. The front six rows were covered in what appeared to be gore, semen, and orange-yellow slime mixed with bits of flesh.

Art students were cheering wildly. A couple of the art chicks even stood up and whipped off their turtlenecks, swinging them over their heads as they screamed.

Mel produced a jack-o-lantern, lit an M-80 with a propane torch and stuck the M-80 into the pumpkin. The overripe fruit exploded, revealing that it was filled with turkey giblets and Karo syrup, which splattered over the audience, coating the nutty professor as she fell to her knees, wept, and wailed "Yes, yes, yes, yes, yes!"

"You're gonna get what's comin' to you," screamed Danny the Axe, reaching for his pants and yanking his button-fly open. He had his hard cock his hand in a second. "I'm gonna do you right here over the bar, motherfucker, and then — " With a wicked grin, Danny produced a shiny little stainless-steel cleaver.

Not really an axe, but close enough for outlaw bikers.

"No, no, no," wailed Frankie, trying to cross his legs.

"Yes, yes, yes," moaned the Professor, back in her seat and squirming, her hand having disappeared under the table.

"THE TASTE OF FUCK! OF FUCK!" screamed Mel, covered in undefined and undefinable goo. A spontaneous slam pit of art students had taken shape in front of the stage, with half-clad college girls and arty boys furiously pounding into each other. It looked like any second the fucking thing might become an orgy.

"THE TASTE OF FUCK!"

I had come around from behind the bar. This meant that I couldn't get to the shotgun if I needed it, but the .38 was still in the belt clip at my back. And I wanted to be able to shout into Danny's ear. "Only one thing," I screamed. "I give you the pansy, I gotta ask a favor of you. One hand washes the other, right?"

"Huh?" Danny had been distracted by the explosion of several stuffed animals filled with cornbread stuffing. The slam-dancing half-naked art students grabbed gooey fistfuls of stuffing and shoved them into their mouths like they were the Holy Communion, excuse my language. "The, uh, the Sharks don't give nobody no fuckin' favors, um. . . .Shit, what the fuck *is* that — hamburger?" He couldn't take his eyes off of Mel.

"It's cornbread stuffing," I shouted. "Give her a minute. She wanted to use live maggots, but as a club owner I gotta draw the line somewhere: No animal acts."

Danny paled.

"Look, Danny, I just want one small favor," I begged.

Stuffed animals were exploding everywhere ("There's the hamburger!" I interjected). An adorable little purple dinosaur burst and sprayed the audience with cow dung. As Mel screamed, the art students cheered. And Mel whipped out her cock.

And even in that furious whirlwind, the room suddenly went silent. For one frozen, fascinated, terrible second, everyone in the whole fucking club just fucking *stared*.

In that second, the silence was enough that we could hear Mel's satisfied, innocent, almost *childlike* giggle as she flashed her broad smile.

Then the next stuffed animal (a bunny rabbit) exploded, the noise of screaming and moaning resumed, the art students went back to their writhing.

Mel started pissing into the audience, swirling her prick in big circles and squiring fluorescent-yellow urine into the slam pit of graduate students.

Mel was a vitamin addict.

"Holy fuckin' shit," moaned Danny, his cock rock-hard in his hand. He was still jerking it furiously, with his breath coming short and his eyes fixed on Mel's long prick.

Now it was Mel's turn. Having emptied her bladder into the audience, Mel twirled like a ballerina, if you'll allow me the pun for an instant (Frankie was a shitty dancer), and violently stroked her cock to full erection. This brought a new series of screams from the audience. Mel began beating off at jackhammer pace.

"THE TASTE OF FUCK!"

Danny stared, gape-mouthed, and then his body shuddered and he let out a moan as he shot his load all over my Bella Noche wingtips. My eyes went wide. Danny looked down at the glistening tops of my shoes, obviously in shock. Like he couldn't believe he'd just shot on my shoes — especially not over a fuckin' *drag queen.*

"One favor!" I shouted at him over the din, gritting my teeth to keep from wringing his neck — those were $200 shoes, God damn it! I clapped Danny on the shoulder like me was my best friend. "Just one favor, Danny my man! Is that too much for one friend to ask another?"

"Uh — maybe — " mumbled Danny absently, seeming a little unsteady, even drunk, in his afterglow.

"I'm buyin' the Back Door," I shouted. In fact, I talked to Cassie just tonight and I want to keep you guys there as protection. We're closing the deal tomorrow. I'll have Mel performing there this weekend!"

"Wh — what?"

"THE TASTE OF FUCK!"

Mel screamed and moaned into the microphone as her huge cock began to spurt come out into the audience, coating the already filthy art students in steaming jizz. Almost all of them were naked by now, and the slam pit had descended into a furious, violent fuck-fest as Mel produced a rotary saw from the shadows behind the stage and dragged it up front, screaming as she started it up.

"THE TASTE OF FUCK! THE TASTE OF FUCK! FUCK! FUCK! FUCK!"

The professor sprawled on the corner of the stage as Mel brought the rotary saw down on her cock, neatly bisecting it with a sharp grinding sound as she screamed in agony. A spray of blood exploded into the audience, and then the torrent truly began, as Mel doused the furiously schtupping art students with red gore, still screaming in pain.

Every one of the bikers had crossed his legs when Mel brought down the saw. Danny's cock had gone limp, drizzling the remains of his thick load from the tip. He shoved it back into his pants and whipped out the .45 again, pointing it at me. My blood ran cold. Had I pushed it too far?

"You listen to me, motherfucker!" shouted Danny, so loudly that he seemed to drown out the rest of the din. "You try to buy the Back Door and you're a fuckin' dead man!" Then Danny turned and ran for the door, hand over his mouth. His cronies acted like they'd been given their reprieve from a death sentence. The second Danny turned, they turned, too. One of them didn't make it to the door before he puked over a whimpering, naked pair of art students who had drifted away from the slam pit and were coupling furiously on the red carpet. They didn't even notice.

Then, all at once, the feedback from the P.A. stopped.

"The taste of fuck," sighed Mel rapturously, and the curtain came down.

"No, no, no, no," the delirious Frankie was moaning.

"Yes," sobbed the professor, writhing and quivering in the mass of undefined goo at the edge of the stage. "Yes, yes, yes, yes, yes!"

There was a long moment of silence, broken only by the ringing in my ears and the wet sounds from the pile of art students.

"Well," boomed Highball Joe's cheerful voice. "That was ... *interesting.*"

The audience was a mass of weeping, cheering, writhing.

"Hey, dollface, do me a favor," I said to Petunia, who had slid up next to me during the performance. "Page that guy from the carpet cleaners, OK?"

"Page him yourself, motherfucker," said Petunia, sliding up closer to me. "Excuse my language."

"You still want that kiss, dollface?"

"How about I give one to you, asshole?" she sighed as she dropped to her knees in front of me and got my belt unfastened with one fluid movement. "Excuse my language."

See, she doesn't like people to know it, but little Petunia June was an art student once upon a time. In something called New Theater.

I guess this qualified.

It all worked out in the end. Cassie kept her protection, the bikers never fucked around with us again, and Frankie Ballerina finally learned his fuckin' lesson. I promised not to sell him to a rabid crowd of leather fags, and he agreed to behave himself. Which he did — most of the time. But that's another story.

Mel and that dyke professor ended up in bed together, even had a long-term love affair. Mel said the sex was so-so, but it was good for her career, and the Prof cooked a mean pot brownie. She even wrote a book published by some egghead press called *Scary Chicks With Power Tools* and included a lengthy section on Mel, with a four-page series of grainy black-and-white photos, Little Mel Catharsis slicing her massive schlong with a rotary saw with a spray of blood. A year or so later, there was an art installation at the Met that had the same scene in virtual reality, Mel in all her phallicidal charm.

Oh, and don't worry. Mel did have the operation eventually, but not with a fuckin' rotary saw. I mean, get serious! That was just her little invention, a dildo with a hydraulic system that would go from soft to hard and would even shoot goo when you worked the controls by clenching your butthole. Use stage blood in the hydraulic system and *voila!* The most realistic onstage rotary-saw penile bifurcation this side of my screaming nightmares.

Art students descended upon the Passion Flower like a plague of locusts, and I started up a twice-a-month open mike. Every other weekend became a frenzied orgy of artistic indulgence. They were lousy tippers, but I got a write-up in the local gay paper and that brought the big-spender closet cases in droves, so it worked out OK. Except for the nude show-tunes sing-a-long they talked me into, but that's another story.

The carpet cleaning cost six hundred dollars, but it was worth it. For the next three weeks, any time I wanted to inspire Petunia to new heights of sexual hunger, all I had to do was whisper "the taste of fuck" and she would purr with pleasure. Three weeks of sleazy sexual indulgence was the reward for true artistic transgression. It was a fair deal, as far as I'm concerned.

See? That's what I'm always trying to tell people. Art triumphs over muscle, brains over brutality, finesse over firepower. Sheer motherfucking weirdness over anything even remotely normal. Mel could tell you that one — be as outrageous as you can, and people will either turn and run screaming, or form a slam pit and start ass-fucking each other while you piss on 'em. Sure, Mel proved it to me in very real terms, but you know who really taught it to me to begin with? That sleazy old cross-dressing troll, Charlie fuckin' Ballerina. When he took in an orphan kid and refused to hide a goddamn thing from him but still let him make his own choices about life and sex and art. Like my real father was *ever* gonna do that.

"Don't try to keep up with the Joneses," Charlie told me one time, quoting some famous queen from NYC. "Bring those motherfuckers down to your level. And they'll fuckin' *thank* you for it." I don't think that's really the way the queen said it, but it was close enough for Charlie. And fuckin' close enough for me. Because the last words of Charlie Ballerina aren't really what he said to me on his deathbed, they're the words he said to me that sometimes I say when I'm standin' over his grave, thinking about the club he left me and the crazy fuckin' life.

"Don't ever let anyone tell you you're too weird," Charlie said to me one day as he sat in that big leather chair of his, dressed in hot pink panties and a horrifically clashing blue-green feather boa. "If they tell you that, then the *real* problem is that *you ain't weird enough.* 'Cause the day you're weird enough is the day those motherfuckers are *too shit-scared to talk to you!*"

Then he let out a fart, and that little pervert giggle of his.

And so, any way you slice it, *those* are the real last words of Charlie Ballerina. And you know what? The dirty old pervert still says 'em to me with love in his voice, every fuckin' day.

Thomas S. Roche is a journalist, spoken-word performer, and fiction writer. His books include the short story collections *Fragrant Sorrows* (The Orphanage, 1994) and *Dark Matter* (Rhinoceros Books, 1997).

"The law isn't justice. It's a very imperfect mechanism. If you press exactly the right buttons and are also lucky, justice may show up in the answer. A mechanism is all the law was ever intended to be."

— Raymond Chandler

"The paperback is very interesting but I find it will never replace the hardcover book — it makes a very poor doorstop."

— Alfred Hitchcock

"I have too great a soul to die like a criminal."

— John Wilkes Booth

About the Editor

Thomas S. Roche is a freelance journalist, fiction writer, spoken-word performer, and editor. In addition to the *Noirotica* series, he has co-edited two anthologies with Michael Rowe (*Sons of Darkness* and *Brothers of the Night*, both Cleis Press) and two with Nancy Kilpatrick (*In the Shadow of the Gargoyle* and *Graven Images*, both Ace Books). His own short stories have appeared in many anthologies, including the *Best American Erotica* series and the *Mammoth Book of Erotica* series. Some of his short stories were collected in *Fragrant Sorrows* (the Orphanage, 1994) and *Dark Matter* (Rhinoceros Books, 1997). To receive *Razorblade Valentines*, Roche's free e-mail newsletter about the *Noirotica* series and his other work, send e-mail to subscribe-thomasroche-announce@onelist.com. You can always find him by dialing www.thomasroche.com. You do know how to dial, don't you?

For a complete Black Books catalog:

• *phone (800) 818-8823*
  or fax (415) 431-0172.

• *visit our* **online** *catalog at*
  http://www.blackbooks.com.

• *send an email request to*
  catalog-Noir3@blackbooks.com.

• *mail a request to PO Box 31155,*
  San Francisco CA 94131-0155.

See the order form on the reverse for a partial offering.

ORDER FORM

Return to: Black Books, PO Box 31155-N3, San Francisco CA 94131-0155, or call (800) 818-8823 to order with a credit card, or fax (415) 431-0172 with credit card info. We accept checks, MOs, cash, Visa, MC, AmEx, and Discover.

Noirotica 3: Stolen Kisses, *edited by Thomas Roche*
The genre pioneered by Thomas Roche — erotic crime fiction. Contributors include Alison Tyler, Brian Hodge, Kate Bornstein, Michelle Tea, Michael Thomas Ford, M. Christian, Bill Brent, Maxim Jakubowski, Simon Sheppard, Lucy Taylor, Thomas Roche, and 14 others.

BLACK BOOKS

❑ *Please send me ____ copy[ies] of* **Noirotica 3.** *Enclosed is $19 ($16 + $3 s/h), or $20.36 if I am in California (includes sales tax), or $22 US if I am in Canada/Mexico, or $27 US elsewhere for each copy ordered. ISBN 1-892723-03-4.*

Best Bisexual Erotica, *edited by Bill Brent and Carol Queen*
Stories with a bi flavored tingle. Co-editors Carol Queen and Bill Brent have selected twenty-two stories for straight, gay, lesbian, bisexual, transgender, and fetish audiences -- in short, anyone literate with a libido. Contributors include the editors, Hanne Blank, Marilyn Jaye Lewis, Jill Nagle, 20 others.

❑ *Please send me ____ copy[ies] of* **Best Bisexual Erotica.** *Enclosed is $19 ($16 + $3 s/h), or $20.36 if I am in California (includes sales tax), or $22 US if I am in Canada/Mexico, or $27 US elsewhere for each copy ordered. ISBN 1-892723-01-8.*

Hot Off The Net: erotica and other sex writings from the Internet, *edited by Russ Kick*
Taboo subject matter. Brutal honesty and candidness. Experimental forms and styles. From personal confessions to the most outlandish fantasies, witness the future of erotic writing.

❑ *Please send me ____ copy[ies] of* **Hot Off The Net.** *Enclosed is $18 ($15 + $3 s/h), or $19.28 if I am in California (includes sales tax), or $21 US if I am in Canada/Mexico, or $24 US elsewhere for each copy ordered. ISBN 1-892723-00-X.*

The Black Book, *edited by Bill Brent*
The foremost directory of sexuality resources for all orientations, gender identities, and lifestyles in the U.S. and Canada. Over 2,500 listings.

❑ *Please send me ____ copy[ies] of* **The Black Book.** *Enclosed is $20 ($17 + $3 s/h), or $21.45 if I am in California (includes sales tax), or $24 US if I am in Canada/Mexico, or $28 US elsewhere for each copy ordered. ISBN 0-9637401-6-4.*

Black Sheets: *Our magazine of sex and popular culture. Kinky, queer, intelligent, irreverent.*

❑ *Please send me 4 issues of Black Sheets for $20, or $32 Can/Mex, or $36 elsewhere.*

❑ *Please send me a sample issue. Enclosed is $6 / $7 Can/Mex / $8 elsewhere.*

I am 21 years of age or older. _____

(signature required for magazine!)

_____
Name

_____
Address

_____
City   State   Zip

_____   _____
card number   expiration date

In case of a question about my order:

tel. number _____ email address: _____

I heard about *Noirotica 3* or got this copy at: _____.